Atlantis Land of Dreams

Edale Lane

Atlantis, Land of Dreams

by Edale Lane

Published by Past and Prologue Press

All rights reserved. No part of this book may be used or reproduced in any manner without written permission of the publisher, except for the purpose of reviews.

Cover art by Melodie Romeo

Edited by Duff McGhee

This book is a work of fiction and all names, characters, places, and incidents are fictional or used fictitiously. Any resemblance to actual people, places, or events is coincidental.

First Edition July 2024

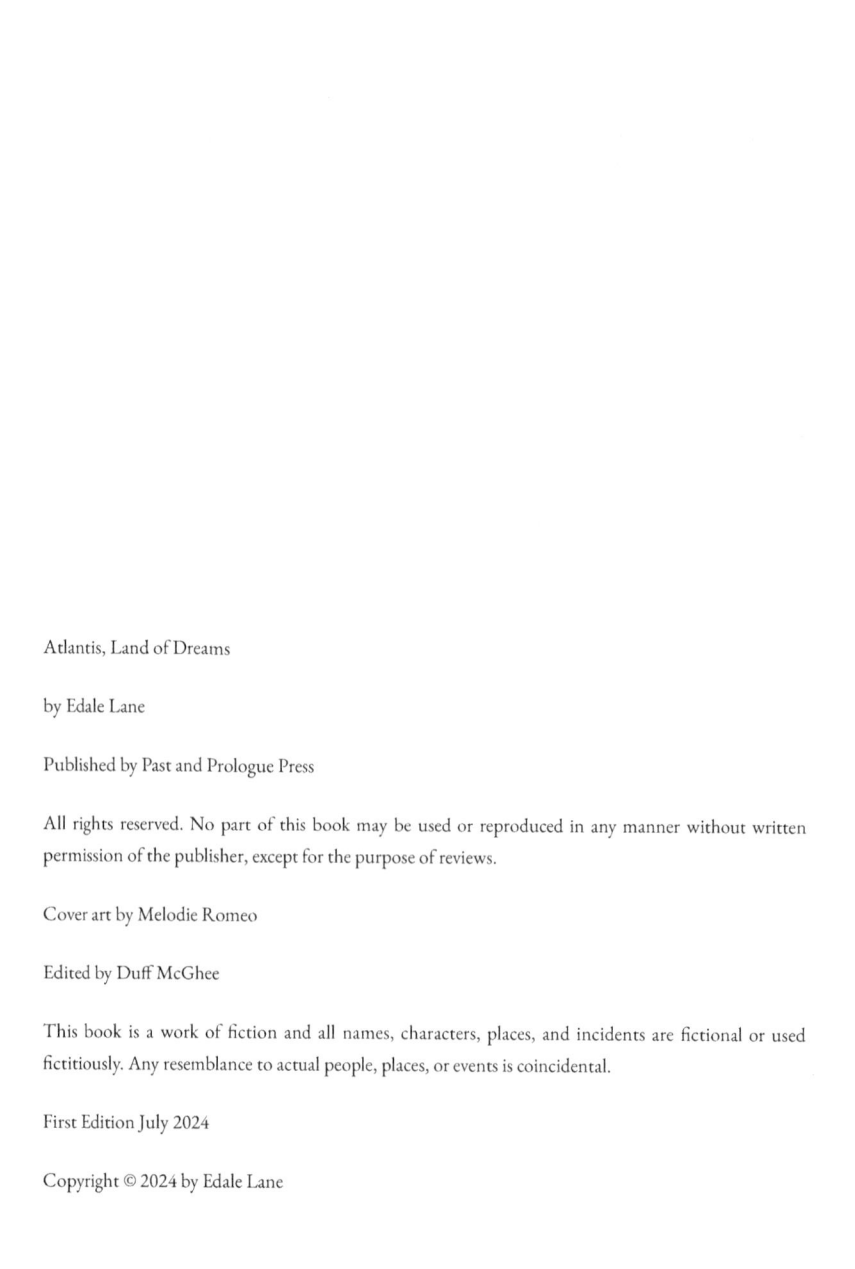

Copyright © 2024 by Edale Lane

To the piece of all of us that dares to believe.

CONTENTS

Acknowledgements	1
Foreward	2
Map of Atlantis	4
Part One: Paradise Shaken	7
1	8
2	15
3	23
4	31
5	37
6	48
7	56
8	62
9	69
10	75
11	80
12	87

13	94
14	101
15	109
16	115
17	124
18	132
19	139
20	148
21	155
22	161
Part Two: Paradise Fractured	169
23	170
24	177
25	184
26	191
27	199
28	207
29	214
30	221
31	228
32	236
33	244
34	251
35	260
36	268
37	275

38	283
39	291
40	298
41	305
Part Three: Paradise Erased	313
42	314
43	322
44	329
45	336
46	342
47	350
48	358
49	366
50	373
51	380
52	387
53	394
54	401
55	409
56	418
57	424
58	433
59	439
60	446
61	453
The Law	462

The Rules	464
Author Notes	466
Index	479
Sources	497
More Books By Edale Lane	498
About the Author	501

ACKNOWLEDGEMENTS

I wish to thank all the scholars and dreamers, both living and passed on, who came before me in presenting their representations of the world of Atlantis. Also, I could not have offered this story in so polished a form without the aid of my valuable editor, Duff McGhee, and my proofreader, Dione Benson. Thank you to my supportive partner Johanna White for sitting through countless documentary shows with me and serving as a trusted sounding board. I also wish to mention my grandchildren Mark, Asher, and Mila for keeping me young and dreaming.

FOREWARD

This book is a historical fantasy based on my interpretation of available documents, artifacts, geology, and other evidence pertaining to the ancient civilization known to us as Atlantis.

Hey, wait, you said "historical" fantasy. Isn't Atlantis completely fictional? I mean, in my history class they taught ...

You have every right to be skeptical, and, if you want to interpret this work as strictly a fantasy, you will be just as entertained. But, as a historian, I understand that our textbooks' interpretation isn't the only one. Documents get lost, destroyed, and rewritten. Wood rots, stones crumble, and artifacts are broken beyond recognition. We can't even provide a completely accurate understanding of societies for which we possess scores of relics. Remember Disney's *The Little Mermaid* and the know-it-all seagull, Scuttle? He taught Ariel that humans used a fork to comb their hair and all kinds of other wrong things.

Consider this. Anatomically modern humans, with the same brain capacity and speech capability as people today, have been running around Earth for at least the past two hundred thousand years. What's the likelihood our ancestors spent a hundred and ninety-five thousand of those years sitting around in primitive caves, hunting and gathering and then suddenly woke up one day and decided to build the pyramids? Or that having the same potential for ingenuity as you and I yet not figuring out if they put seeds in the ground, the desired crop would grow for a hundred and ninety-two thousand years? It's far more reasonable to believe advanced civilizations existed in the distant past for which we no longer have records.

The Younger Dryas was a geological era in our "recent" past full of cataclysmic events and upheavals that could have easily destroyed all traces of prediluvian civilizations, relegating their people and achievements to the realm of myth. Atlantis could well be one of them.

In the back of this book, you'll find research notes and references I consulted to arrive at my interpretation of this paradise and its destruction, along with a complete listing of The Laws and Rules. While some readers may believe Atlanteans came here from another planet, I have presented them as fully human. Although I cannot assert with certainty that these events actually took place or that they precisely depict the real Atlantis of antiquity, the explanations I present are plausible and credible. Science and archaeology can't prove this interpretation, nor can they disprove it. So, for everyone out there who ever hoped to dream there once existed an idyllic society—or could again someday—fasten your seatbelts, free your imagination, and let the adventure begin!

ATLANTIS

Terrible Ice

Gadlan

Kalpos Dakrun

Ruta I.

Opocalám Range

Anzar R.

Elapus

Evamont

Ampherium

Azaes Fire Mountains

Diaprep

Ormo Poseidona

Menosus

Autopolis

Atala

Ryzen

Skismengi Channel

Mestoria

Daya I.

"For many generations ... they obeyed the laws and loved the divine to which they were akin ... they reckoned that qualities of character were far more important than their present prosperity. So they bore the burden of their wealth and possessions lightly, and did not let their high standard of living intoxicate them or make them lose their self-control ...

But when the divine element in them became weakened ... and their human traits became predominant, they ceased to be able to carry their prosperity with moderation."

—— Plato, Timaeus and Critias

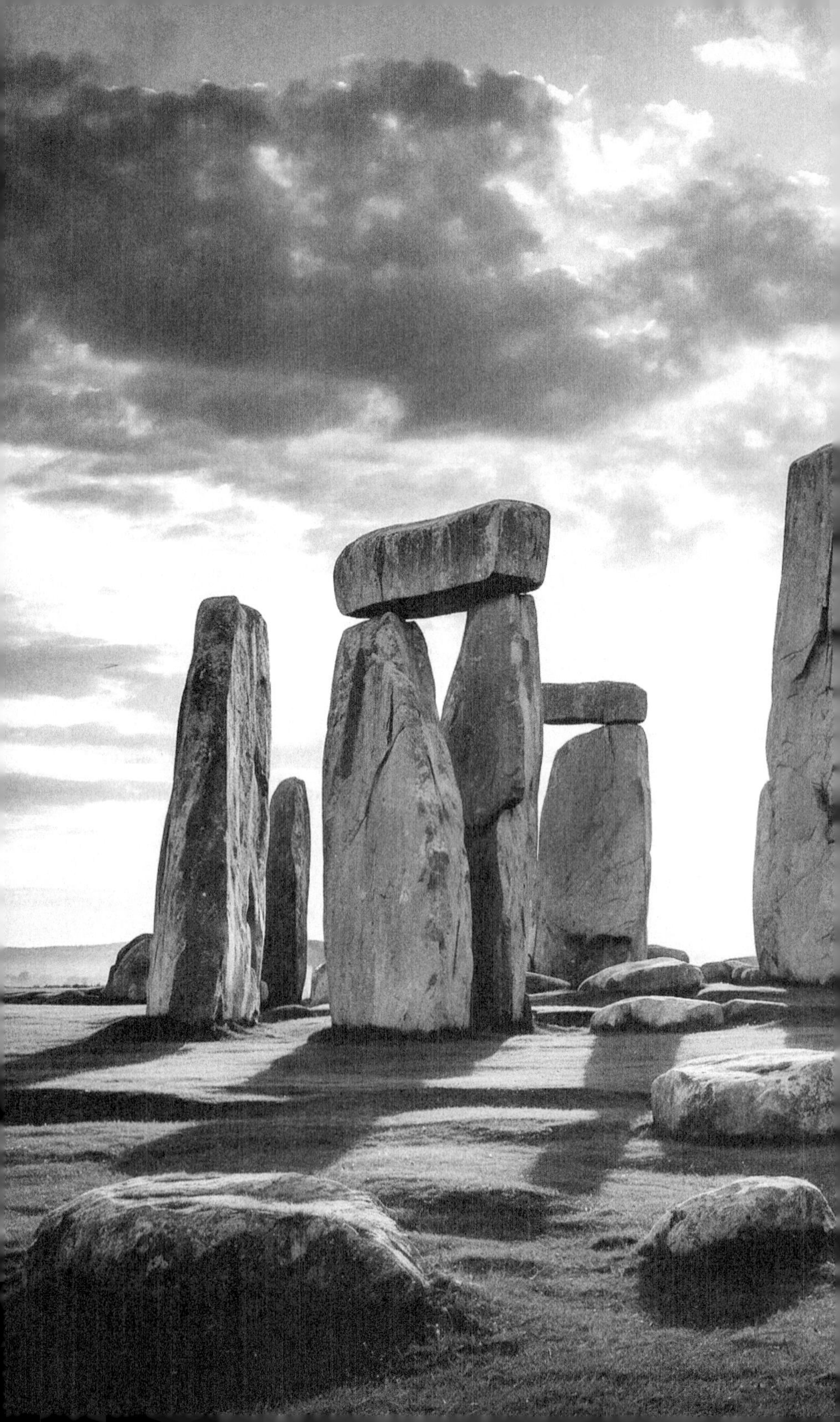

Part One
Paradise Shaken

I

In the year 1356 of the Third Age, near the village of Elyrna in the city-state of Evamont, Atlantis

Something wasn't right. Ariel sat cross-legged on top of the hill overlooking her family farm and sunk her fingers into the short, lush grass, appreciating the soft, living strands and the tendrils of energy they emitted. The sun rising behind her cast the plain in a wondrous, golden glow. She dug her nails and fingertips into the rich soil, reaching for a deeper connection to Gaia. With her spine properly aligned between the earth and the pastel sky, she closed her eyes and lifted her chin, inhaling a slow, deep breath.

Ariel listened. A gentle breeze rustled leaves in a nearby tree and a flock of geese winged overhead, producing impatient honks. Brushing discouragement aside, she focused on connecting to the spirit world and the Archangel Selaphiel, whom she beseeched to speed her prayer to the Creator. *Maybe music since she's the musician's muse.*

From a leather case that Ariel kept on a strap over her shoulder, she retrieved her ivory flute. She raised the blowing hole to her lips, positioned her fingers above their holes, and closed her eyes once more to concentrate on her music without distraction. She allowed her emotions to flow as she drew a harmonious melody from the instrument with the skill of one who had spent forty years perfecting her art.

Ratiki raised on his hind legs, peering curiously at Ariel with twitching whiskers and ears perked. The fat, spoiled raccoon crawled into her lap and curled into a contented ball. Her pet especially loved her music and didn't understand he was disrupting her meditation. It wasn't working, anyway.

She finished the modal tune before laying the instrument on the grass at her side and allowed herself a minute to pet Ratiki's soft, grizzled, gray-brown fur. He nestled under her palm and regarded her with a disappointed look. "I know you love it when I play the flute, Tiki, but I must find answers; and, to do that, I must ask the right questions."

Ariel shifted her gaze from his adorable, masked face to survey the fertile plain before her. Four houses made of mud bricks and wood erected on stone foundations and topped with orangey-red terracotta tiles stood in a group around a central plaza containing a well and water tower. One house belonged to Ariel, her mother, daughter, and Oma—her great-great-great-grandmother. The others were homes to her brother and his family, her uncle and his family, and four immigrant workers who shared in the profits from the expansive farm.

They were solid, well-crafted houses filled with comfortable furnishings, lovely décors, and all the modern conveniences. The cut, color, and shapes of the patio stones were pleasing to behold, as were the plants, shade trees, and spectacular views. Beyond the grouping of abodes spread more fields, then forests, and in the distance towered the majestic peaks of the Opocalám Range. Since the fall equinox had only recently passed, the rocky summits weren't yet covered in snow, but misty vapor encircled them as if cradled in the tender arms of a lover. Ariel couldn't see the waters of the impressive Lago Actoy because of the vast spread of trees, but she could estimate where the lake lay. A league to the south, she could make out the rooftops of Elyrna, the nearest village where a bathhouse, laundry, theater, and small temple were located. Every year she traveled to the Ring of Stones south of here for celestial celebrations and regularly visited Evamont, the capital of her city-state, though they weren't visible from her vantage point.

Down the hill behind her extended an enormous meadow spotted with shade trees where contented herds of deer, bison, cattle, horses, and elephants grazed—no doubt under the patient scrutiny of lions and foxes. Jaguars commanded the lands to the south with bears and wolves sticking to the highland forests. It was important to share the fertile lands with other species because the Creator valued them and intended for the creatures, plants, and features of the earth to work together for the benefit of all.

Ariel could still feel the vibrational essence of the herds, the geese, and her sweet, mischievous companion; her ability to communicate with nature was not currently in dispute. When had she lost her constant connection to the cosmos, to Universal Consciousness itself, and why hadn't she realized it until now?

As a child, manifesting was easy. She could think about wildflowers, and they would spring up all around her. Turning thoughts to things was a game she and Lysandra played for the sheer joy of it. As a youth, Ariel recalled the surge of energy when she perceived the power of creation flowing through her body like blood and fluid, crackling in the air like lightning in a storm. Conversing with archangels, ancestors, and the Infinite Creator had been as tangible as talking to her brother. Why was it such a struggle now? What had changed?

Fifty-two wasn't old. Oma Naunet was over three hundred. Sure, Ariel had raised two children to adulthood, but she was far from old. *If I raise my vibration, I'll feel it again. Surely, the fault lies with me, not the heavens. Let me retrieve my most joyful memory and embody the feeling of elated bliss.*

Rolling her shoulders, Ariel repositioned herself comfortably and stroked Ratiki for good measure before turning her palms skyward. The first thought to pop into her mind was of her and Lysandra. Those were always her most treasured memories, and a smile immediately blossomed on her lips. But, no. While conjuring powerful feelings of unspeakable joy, thoughts of Lysandra were always tinged with the pain of loss and longing, not what Ariel needed if she was to open her soul to the Oneness of all she sought. Knowing she would pull out a moment spent in Lysandra's arms when she lay down to sleep that night, Ariel tucked it neatly away, latching a door behind it, and chose the feeling of exuberant awe from when her son Mal'akhi was born.

It was a powerful vibration, one that thrust her into a sea of joy to make the ocean appear small. She was in her family home, her mother and the midwife at her side encouraging her, while her uncle, brother, and husband paced an outer room. "One more push," the midwife had instructed. Summoning all her strength, Ariel had pushed, and at once her labor pains subsided. She felt tremendous relief overtake her body as the baby emerged, but she couldn't see. She had stretched forward, desperate to discover if the baby was all right, if it was a boy or girl. After waiting so long, her arms ached to hold her child.

"It's a perfect little boy!" her mother had exclaimed. "Oh, Ariel, I'm so proud of you, so overjoyed for our family!"

The midwife wrapped her son in a soft blanket of llama wool that had been infused with blessings and handed him to her. The unspeakable joy of that moment had been irrevocably branded into Ariel's consciousness, a powerful blast of emotion for which there were no words. Still, she could replay the event in her mind and feel it all over again, as if it were happening for the first time. In her arms, she held a brand-new life, a whole little person who came from inside her, who was both a part of her and a separate being. It was the closest she had ever come to comprehending the fundamental Law of One. *We all came forth from the Creator even as Mal'akhi came from me. Everyone and everything is connected, born of Jjeevan Shakti, the life force, fashioned from the One who fills the heavens and the earth, unique expressions of a single Divine Energy. Speak to me again. Let me feel your presence surround me as I once did.*

As Ariel waited, basking in the glory of her joyful feelings, she felt a faint vibration, like a fly landing on the string of a lyre. The frequency touched her like a voice from a great distance, barely a hush, the flutter of butterfly wings. *Gather with the others, for you are chosen.* Before Ariel could reply or ask a question, the sensation lifted, and she once again sat on the grassy hill with a loyal raccoon nestled atop her feet between her knees.

Ariel let out a long sigh. "What did that mean, Tiki?" she asked, as if he would know. "Did I even receive a word, or was it only my imagination?"

At the sound of his name, Ratiki stirred, walked his hands up the front of her natural, undyed tunic, and sniffed her breath. *You are wise. You'll figure it out,* he conveyed to her through his compact electromagnetic signals. *Let's go have breakfast.*

With a laugh, Ariel ruffled the fur behind his head. "You don't worry about anything but food, little rascal. Maybe I could learn some wisdom from you, huh?"

Ratiki nodded, and leaped from her lap, dancing in a circle, urging, *Let's go! Let's go!*

Ariel pushed up and lifted her face and palms to the sky. "Thank you that my knees are strong and suffer no pain. Thank you that my days will be long upon the earth, and I will experience many wonders. Thank you for the wonders I've already seen, for the sun, moon, and stars, for my family and friends, for good food and fair weather, for the abundance that surrounds, hemming me in with beauty and plenty. I lack no good thing, for which I am ever grateful."

Upon completing her prayer, Ariel slipped her leather sandals back onto her bare feet and secured her flute in its case. Her stomach reminded her it was time to eat, anyway. She meandered down the hill with a fat raccoon waddling beside her, stopping occasionally when a smell caught his attention.

Ariel brushed her fingertips along the heads of wheat standing higher than her dark green sash belt, inspecting them with satisfaction. The grain was plump, the heads full, and the stalks were turning golden. They would soon be ready to harvest.

She and a bounding Ratiki passed the vegetable garden on the way to her house. Spotting a beautiful, ripe, ruby-red tomato, she reached out and plucked it from the vine. Next, a cucumber caught her eye, a clump of mature beans, full pea pods, a fat, purple eggplant, and fingers of zucchini. No, she'd have to come back with a basket.

"Look at what wonderful plants you are!" Ariel praised while radiating appreciation and love from her heart energy. "So productive for all these months." Her touch smoothed along the broad, healthy leaves and they seemed to smile at her. "You are the best vegetables I've ever grown! Nothing puny or unseemly in this garden. Good morning, bees!" She greeted the amber honeybees and striped bumblebees that rose from fresh blossoms to wave at her. "You are the most important members of our garden. Blessings on you, Bumbles. Blessings on you, Honeys," she proclaimed, motioning to each. "And no, you gorgeous butterflies—I won't forget you."

Ariel stopped to hold out her index finger. An orange, black, and white Monarch landed on it, its feathery feet tickling her skin. She smiled at the simple yet profoundly beautiful insect. "What does the world look like from your perspective, little one? No worries, hey?" It wiggled antennae at her, fanned its wings once, and took off. While Ariel possessed a talent to communicate with higher plants and animals, insects, small fish, crustaceans, and some other lower-functioning species didn't generate enough consciousness for her to tap into. She could appreciate them all the same.

Her gift also accounted for her farm's lack of fences and walls. Every spring, Ariel visited the wildlife in the area and warned them not to go into the garden or wheat fields lest they be killed and eaten by the men on the farm. Every few years, a squirrel, rabbit, or deer would call her bluff and end up in a pot of stew. The rest took a lesson from their mistakes and stayed clear.

She walked in the open front door with a big, juicy tomato in one hand and Ratiki riding her shoulder.

"You always know when the food is ready and arrive precisely in time to eat it," declared her mother with a sarcastic expression. Philomena slapped fists to her ample hips, a dusting of flour on her nose. "As usual, Oma and I do all the work while you wander around the fields greeting the day, and only the stars know what your straw-brained daughter is about."

Philomena, a vibrant woman of only eighty, still ran the household as she did when Ariel was a tot. She wore her long, black hair loose with a headband to secure it. Ariel favored the style, only her hair was medium-brown, and didn't sport her mother's light dusting of gray. While Philomena's disapproving eyes were a dark, oval cocoa, Ariel's were a deep-set blue-green, like the color of the shallow water surrounding an atoll.

"I'm right here, Grandmother—as if you didn't know," retorted the youthful Sheera as she sashayed into the main gathering room in a colorful, mid-calf toga cinched by a wide, golden band. She had her father's lighter hair, like a baked roll slathered with butter and honey. Like Ariel, she was taller than Philomena, but she had her grandmother's eyes and her father's lax sense of responsibility.

"If you wanted my help, all you had to do was ask," she said as she passed in front of her grandmother to pick up a smooth wooden plate. She began piling it with a round of unleavened bread, sliced fruit, and spoonfuls of yogurt.

"Sheera," Ariel growled in warning. "Show respect to your grandmother and gratitude for her preparing our food. You are not a child, but a grown woman."

"I know that," Sheera snapped, rounding on Ariel. "And I contribute as much as anyone to this family. I'm always here for planting and harvesting, and you aren't the only one who works in the garden. I made this dress," she declared, gesturing to herself in a way that caused her gold and orichalcum bracelets to jingle. "Mother, remember that dress I made for you?"

Ariel stepped forward and laid a calming hand on her daughter's shoulder. "I do. I'm pleased to wear it on special occasions and have received many compliments. I always tell people my talented daughter Sheera made it for me."

Sheera's shoulder slumped, and her gaze shifted from Ariel to Philomena. "I'm sorry, Grandmother. You are the best cook in Evamont, and I appreciate you for making breakfast. I was just up all night worrying."

"Whatever about?" Philomena pushed between mother and daughter to wrap a consoling arm around Sheera. Ariel took a plate and filled it with the delicious offerings. She knew about Sheera's concerns, her inability to choose between two lovers, both of whom were asking to marry her. There was something much more vital to be concerned about. The energies were growing weaker year by year. What would such a disaster mean for their future? Ariel needed to talk to Oma Naunet. There might be elders in the village who surpassed her in years, but few in wisdom.

2

Sheera and Philomena took their seats together, setting full plates in front of them. The room was spacious, with a dining table and benches, a matching buffet along an interior wall stacked with shelves holding more dishes, cups, and jars, and a comfortable seating area with pastel pillows and cushions to the side. Other walls displayed copious artwork of paintings, carvings, framed needlepoint panels, and sacred symbols. The wall behind the table featured a four-by-two-cubit mosaic of horses cantering through a meadow. A bright panel in the ceiling glowed overhead to aid the natural light filtering in through the windows.

"Taavi is so sweet," Sheera explained, "and he makes me laugh. He has such a cheery disposition and always makes me feel special and appreciated."

Philomena nodded, fully focused on her granddaughter as Ariel searched for Oma through the open back door. She spied her performing her morning movement exercises on the stone-paved patio. Ratiki stood on tiptoe and grabbed the hem of her tunic to remind her about his breakfast. Ariel smiled down at him and set a dish of fruit on the floor under the buffet. He expressed a quick thanks, and snatched up the first slice, nibbling while keeping a watchful eye out for anyone who may wish to steal his food.

Sheera continued in a frustrated fashion. "But Mahmoud!" She slapped the back of one hand to her forehead and fanned herself with the other. "He is so muscular and strong—a body Atlas would have envied—and with a fair face as well. He won the city-state games this past summer and all the young women swoon over him."

"You are an exceptionally attractive girl, Sheera," Ariel's mother praised, "and an artistic seamstress. Either man would be lucky to have you as a wife—as long as you treat him with respect."

"I know, Grandmother," she responded in a contrite tone. "I don't mean to be disrespectful; I just get so emotional. It must have to do with the cycles of the moon."

Ariel rolled her eyes and set her plate on the table. "I'm going out to greet Oma." Her mother nodded before returning her focus to Sheera.

"I'm walking to town shortly to meet with some friends," Philomena said. "Would you like to come along?"

The atmosphere shifted the moment Ariel stepped outside. The aroma of bread baking in the clay oven permeated the air, joined by a mingling of celery, basil, cilantro, mint, and the other potted herbs, extending their stems and leaves gloriously toward the morning sun that just crested the hill. Outdoor kitchens were preferred in central and southern Atlantis because of the warm climate and to discourage house fires. However, in the northern reaches of the island, where snow fell in winter, they were put inside for warmth. Cooking tops made of granite or marble inlaid with copper plates powered by the same crystals that ran the lights and fans were available, along with copper-lined, radiating ovens. While prevalent in city apartments, many people—especially in rural areas where dry, dead wood was plentiful, and nobody complained about a little smoke—preferred to cook with traditional fires and brick or clay ovens because they claimed the food tasted better. Also, the cooktops were slow to heat and remained hot after being turned off, thus creating a burn risk. Oma had always cooked with woodfires and charcoal and passed the tradition on to four generations.

Ariel watched her great-great-great-grandmother smoothly glide through her Ruh Mutaharika movements, pausing at each asana. At three-hundred-thirty-eight years of age, she *didn't* stand on her head; still, Naunet was an impressive woman. She was a couple of thumbs shorter than Philomena—only because of gravity. Her every joint functioned properly with each organ operating in perfect health. And though her hair, braided and wrapped in a bun, had turned snowy white, she stood with a straight back and had all her original teeth.

A robin caught Ariel's attention, and she glanced up to see it perch on the balcony railing above and to her left. The farmhouse's outdoor staircase leading to the bedrooms had been replaced several times throughout its hundreds of years of history, but the short, stone wall surrounding the broad patio was original. The branches of a peach tree extended over the two-cubit wall at one corner, far enough away from the sprawling, old, live oak in the yard to stay out of its shade. Clay pots of every size and description sprouted flowers, herbs, and berries across the top of the wall and on stands along the back bricks of the house.

Ariel was anxious to talk to Oma but didn't want to interrupt her morning routine, so she sat on a stool near the oven and watched. Naunet stood on one foot, her other raised to her knee, and let her arms flow upward until her palms pressed together above her head. After holding the pose and her breath for nine counts, the elder's arms breezed down while she transitioned to the other foot; then she repeated the motion. With both feet back on a smooth, slate tile, she lowered herself into a deep squat and circled her arms, gathering in the energies around her body. Next, Naunet sprang upward, throwing her arms open as if scattering autumn leaves, and a brilliant smile erupted across her lined face.

Dazzling particles of energy rained down on Ariel like the sprinkle of static electricity in a dry lightning storm, sending tingles across her skin. "You minx!" Ariel said with an amused expression. "You used to shower me with happy bubbles like that when I was a child."

"You look like you could use them again," the intuitive old woman answered.

Leaving the stool, Ariel stepped over and hugged Oma, pressing vibrations laced with worry to her chest. When she stepped back, she took her great-great-great-grandmother's hand. "Can we talk?"

Oma sighed. "I suppose my breakfast will have to wait."

"I'm sorry. Certainly, you should eat first. I apologize—"

"Enough of that, child." Oma shooed Ariel's apology away with the back of her hand. "Let's sit over here, away from your mother and daughter's endless chatter."

They moved to a bench at the far side of the patio, protected by the huge live oak, and sat together in the cool of the morning. A shadow drew Ariel's gaze upward for an instant. It was nothing—just a cargo sled transporting goods. They would fly over several times a day, traveling from one major city to another. Ice went south every morning. The markets couldn't open without ice to keep fish and meat cold, and people had to replace the blocks in their coolers a couple of times a week. Or it might be a shipment of precious metals from the mines of Gadlan or shellfish from Elapus, or perhaps wool. Ariel couldn't tell what products the air barge the size of an eight-man fishing boat carried. It was a silent vessel that left no sign of its passing in the sky. She knew the basics of how they worked with gyros and antigravity, like her family's personal sleigh, but Ariel wasn't interested in mechanics. She just knew to insert her thumb-sized, charged crystal into its slot and press her palm on the brass start plate. Her own body's electric current would then activate the processes to put the vehicle in motion. It was easy to steer up and down, side to side, and control the speed with a separate lever.

Will our mechanics stop functioning soon too?

Ariel returned her attention to Oma, comforted by the warm contact of their joined hands. "Something isn't right. Can't you feel it?"

She searched the wise sage's blue eyes for the answers she didn't possess. Oma nodded, the joy fading from her face. "Yes, Ariel. I've felt it for a long time, since before your mother was born."

Astonishment swept over Ariel. She angled her body toward Oma and gripped her hand tighter. "But how can that be? I only realized it today—or at least I only now acknowledged my suspicions as real."

"I hoped it was a temporary effect caused by the movement of one star or another, an atmospheric disturbance brought on by a weather system," Oma explained. "Nobody wants to talk about it; nobody *is* talking about it, but the energies our civilization—our people—have relied on for generations, from time immemorial, are waning, and have been my entire lifetime."

"But why? When did it start? What can we do to set things right?"

Oma's smile grew as she patted Ariel's hand and let her fingers slip away. "So many questions," she lovingly chided. "So many worries."

"Tell me, Oma. I need to understand. I thought something was wrong with me."

"No, my sweet girl," Oma assured her. "You are one of the few who still connect to the energies at all. There's nothing wrong with you, dear. It all started with the Conflagration." She leaned back against the stone wall and a bluebird landed near her, like it had come to hear the story. Ratiki padded out, picked up a twig, and curled beside Ariel's feet to play with it.

Ariel spared him a glance and returned her attention to Oma. "The great cataclysm that nearly ended the world."

"Yes. Thirteen-hundred and fifty-six years ago, just as a complete cycle of the zodiac was coming to an end, a great, glowing serpent streaked across the northern sky, dropping death and destruction in its wake."

"The comet," Ariel confirmed. She had learned this story in school. "Ice rocks and fragments from its tail, some the size of a house, struck the earth with such speed and fury they caused the ground to shake. The Azaes spit fire and smoke from their summits and the rays of the sun were covered up by dust and debris. Gigantic waves swamped the earth, and half our continent was lost. The comet's frigid blast flash-froze the lands and waters to the north, creating the Terrible Ice. Though Atlantis was spared being frozen, we were split into two islands—the big island of Ruta, and the smaller Daya in the south. Some people escaped to foreign lands while others hid underground. Sixty to seventy percent of the population perished, and the survivors had to start civilization over with nothing except their memorized knowledge."

Oma inclined her head in confirmation.

"But my lessons included no loss of abilities. The teachers said everything now is as it was before—even better."

The old woman tilted her head at Ariel with a contemplative expression. "Did you know that before the Conflagration, all Atlanteans could communicate telepathically with each other at a distance?"

Ariel leaned forward, her brow furrowing at Oma's revelation. Her lips parted, but no words dropped out.

"Everyone had the gifts of clairvoyance and nature speaking—like you with plants and animals," she continued. "Everyone was an air speaker with the ability to influence weather. There was no need for books or writing because people could merely tap into the Universal Consciousness whenever they wanted to extract information."

The intensity of emotion firing through Ariel's chakras went far beyond astonishment. Though she had never heard these things, her oma's words resonated as truthful to her.

"And instead of living for hundreds of years, our ancestors could live for thousands." Oma met her gaze. "In olden times, Atlanteans truly were human gods. I don't think anyone knows why it happened—whether they were being punished or if it was simply a natural occurrence, brought about by the movements of Sirius or the conclusion of the procession of constellations across the sky—but that cataclysmic event set in motion the weakening of the energies, or perhaps just of our ability to access them."

"How did you come by this knowledge?" Ariel asked. "You weren't born yet when it happened."

"No," she answered. "I haven't always been a farmer, you know."

"I know you lived in many places, enjoyed several careers, and had some interesting lovers." Ariel blushed and looked away. It seemed odd to think of someone so old and respected as once having been the life of the party.

"I once had a friend in Diaprep, a shipbuilder and adventurer named Noah. Now, this was three hundred years ago when I was younger than you are now." Oma pointed at Ariel and winked. "The man could dance, and he enjoyed his wine—finest shipbuilder in the world now, or at least last I heard." She raised a finger to her chin and glanced at the sky. "He'd be over four hundred if he's still alive. Anyway, one night after a solstice festival where he had become quite drunk, Noah invited me to climb a volcano with him, where he promised to show me a secret. I thought he meant something entirely different, but when we arrived at the appointed cave, we found an ancient man. He introduced me to his ancestor, Methuselah, who entertained me for hours with stories from before the Conflagration. You see, Noah's great-great-great-grandfather was one of the survivors. I believe his accounts and so should you."

"Everybody was a nature speaker? Telepathy?"

Oma nodded. "Now these gifts are rare and only present in individuals who truly and diligently seek after truth. Think about your mother, brother, children, and your lost husband. Did they possess special skills and talents?"

"They are all creative," Ariel pointed out. "Each is quite accomplished at something."

"But can they weave the energies? Can they interpret vibrations?"

Ariel's shoulders slumped, and she dropped her chin. She had never thought about it. Since she was a child, she had been a nature speaker—that's what her mother had said. But Ariel never thought of talking to and hearing nature speak as something extraordinary. It was just her. She was a farmer, after all. It made sense to ask the cows how they were feeling or to encourage the corn to grow tall with many ears.

When Ariel remained silent, Oma continued. "It wasn't long after the skies cleared, and the survivors emerged that they noticed the shift in the energies. Everything became more difficult, starting with recalling shared memories. So, the mothers and fathers set about creating a written language for us so ideas could be preserved. They began with symbology, where the icon represents an entire concept."

Ariel lifted her fingers to the gold ankh that hung from a chain around her neck. Lysandra gave it to her before she left, declaring her love was as undying as the symbol of eternal life. Ariel never took it off, even during the years she had spent married to Sheera's and Mal'akhi's father. The cool weight and shape of it resting over her heart chakra was a feeling she couldn't part with, even if Lysandra's path had diverged from hers.

"These are the symbols you see carved everywhere, especially on the oldest temples and buildings," Oma said. "But symbols alone were not sufficient, so they developed an entire language of logograms to represent words and word components. These were first carved into stone tablets and etched into metal plates, like the posting of The Law in every city, town, and village. But such tablets were big and cumbersome, so they developed paper from papyrus and used ink to write entire books filled with facts and ideas. A few hundred years ago, scholars condensed the logograms into a twenty-four-letter alphabet to create even more words—the reading and writing you were taught in school. They did this because it was the only way to pass the knowledge to the next generations. Did you know when I was a child I could commune with trees and animals like you do?"

"You could?" Ariel never knew.

"I don't talk about it because, by the time I reached a hundred, I had lost the ability. It was too sad to think about, so I put it away and moved on to other things. I pray your talent doesn't fade like mine did."

"But Oma, there must be something we can do," Ariel pleaded. She recalled the faint voice she supposed she had heard that morning. But it was nonsense. Why would she be chosen for anything, and for what? She didn't even know where she was supposed to go or who to meet.

Oma lowered her chin and shook her head. "I doubt there's anything we can do. If there was, don't you think the wisdom teachers would have figured it out by now? Do you know when I was a little girl it wasn't unusual to see five- and six-hundred-year-old folks operating a cart in the market? Now I'm the oldest person in Elyrna, a village of over two hundred. And when I was a child, a charged crystal could operate a home for a decade before it needed to be taken to the city recharging station. It isn't only our abilities that are fading; we could lose our technology too. Soon, Atlantis will be like Kemet and Kaptara—just another society of civilized yet ordinary humans."

3

Atala, capital city of Atlantis

"Explain your symptoms to me," Lysandra instructed her patient, who appeared to be in her seventies, not even middle-aged yet, but carrying about half a talent more weight than she should. She lay on a table-high treatment bed with an elegant, curved form topped by a plush cushion and tasseled pillows, making it ergonomically comfortable. Symbols such as palm fronds, ankhs, caduceus, coiled spirals, six-point stars, and three intersecting trinity rings had been carved into the legs and frame and painted. The confined stone chamber was one of eight on the second level of the structure, originally erected as a power pyramid. The eight rooms formed a box around a central atrium stretching from the first floor to the top where the enormous quartz crystal lay in an orichalcum cradle to absorb solar radiation.

While not a pyramid in the truest sense of the word, it was a step building in the general shape of a pyramid—a wide, square base, with each level indented and smaller until reaching the giant energy collection stone at the top. The first floor served as a gathering center and financial hub where business deals were made, and coins exchanged hands. The second story originally contained an indoor athletic center with sections for men and women to exercise in groups.

However, a few hundred years ago, it was redesigned to house healing rooms because of the amplified electromagnetic energy inherent in the structure. Above was the crystal recharging station where the half-million residents of the Atala city-state would bring their crystals to be re-powered.

The exterior walls were constructed of limestone blocks hewn with diamond-tipped laser cutters. Despite the pre-cataclysm debacle involving the misguided use of lasers as weapons, the first generation of Third-Age Atlanteans couldn't ban the technology completely. It was simply too convenient, too essential to give up. Who wanted to return to the time of shaping stones with a hammer and chisel? Lasers meant fewer workers cutting more blocks in a shorter time with less labor. So, the first Third Age Council of Rulers voted to restrict the use of lasers to cutting tools only, forbidding it as a weapon under penalty of death.

Lysandra, whose waist-length, brunette strands fell in a single braid down her back, stood on an intricately woven carpet padding the cedar-planked and volcanic tuff floors. The white linen chiton she wore created a striking contrast against her olive skin, and her generous breasts and rounded hips were accentuated by a broad-banded purple sash matching the ribbon in her hair. Her oval face was as smooth as polished marble and boasted a straight nose and full lips. The healer studied her patient with bold brown eyes framed by thick, long lashes.

"My joints ache," her patient moaned, "and my whole abdomen feels bloated. I lack energy and feel like staying in bed."

Lysandra touched the woman's elbows, shoulders, and knees, perceiving the unnatural heat and puffiness in her joints. "Have you been sick before?"

"Several times," she answered. "Each occasion worse than the one before."

Lysandra passed open palms slowly above her patient, checking for out-of-sync vibrations. It felt to her senses as if every life-particle in the woman's body cried out for help.

"Do you practice your Hatha each morning like we were taught as children?"

"I might miss a few days," she admitted. "Well, maybe more than a few, but I have so much to do. My husband expects me to perform miracles and I have my interests to pursue as well as satisfy his desires. There are only so many hours in a day."

"Yes, Fufi." Lysandra addressed her in a kind, gentle manner. "And how many of those hours do you wish to spend in pain? How many years do you wish to cut your life short?"

"Don't blame me for getting sick," Fufi huffed defensively. "I didn't do it on purpose, and I'm not the only one. Do you know how long I had to wait for my turn to see you? And there are seven other practitioners here today. Now, can you correct the problem, or do I need to make an appointment with one of them?"

Lysandra sighed. "I can reset your body's systems so they will work properly," she affirmed. "However, if you do not follow my prescription, this will happen again."

What is going on? Lysandra wondered. When she began practicing the healing arts decades ago, her patients had trickled in like drops of dew off the eaves in the early morning. She spent her days mending the broken bones of children who fell out of trees or elders who slipped on the stairs. Occasionally there was a difficult childbirth, and a midwife would send for her ... a laborer would sustain a serious injury, or a foolish overachiever would run his body into the ground working or playing too hard. While the increase in sicknesses had been slow and steady, it seemed to have soared over the past year. Lysandra had treated patients whose bodies grew unnatural tumors, whose hearts couldn't sustain a steady rhythm, who ran burning fevers, or whose bodies were covered in boils. She saw no reason for this constant stream of patients demanding to be healed, especially since Atlanteans so naturally healed themselves—or were supposed to.

On a small table near the treatment bed, Lysandra had arranged a variety of tools to aid in her process. She added a few pinches of lavender and vanilla powder to a shallow brass dish shaped like a hollowed-out turtle and lit the incense from a beeswax candle. Both were excellent scents for relaxation, calm, and pain relief. Beside the table stood a circular, concave bronze cymbal suspended in a frame. Lysandra struck it with a padded mallet three times while inhaling and exhaling deep breaths. The instrument was tuned to a frequency proven to aid the healing process, and its vibrations echoed through the chamber harmoniously. Next, she selected her sistrum, the one her wisdom teacher Quetzal had given her. She closed her eyes, focused on connecting to Archangel Raphael, and shook the brass instrument in a predetermined rhythm, repeating the words, "Ham, het, hum. Ham, het, hum."

When Lysandra's own body hummed with the frequencies she invoked, she laid the sistrum on the table beside the burning incense and picked up an ivory ankh, lifting it high over her head in both hands. She silently called upon Raphael, the deliverer of healing, a divine spirit who resided in the ether. Atlanteans of old had been in constant contact with the archangels and understood they weren't like humans, but spirit beings, void of shape or solid substance, who performed the roles the Creator designed for them. In the Third Age, it seemed the archangels were inaccessible to the masses. Now, only people trained in wisdom schools could tune to their vibrations.

Lysandra passed the ankh above her patient's prone form, seeking the source of her affliction. Fufi's whole body pulsed with irritation, every organ and tissue sending forth signals of distress. Laying the ankh on the woman's chest, Lysandra used her fingers to weave healing energies gathered from the surrounding air into a warm, comforting, energetic blanket which she spread over Fufi from head to toe. In her mind, she pictured each organ and tissue happy and working together as the Creator designed. "Thank you, thank you," she whispered reverently. She drew from her patient's flesh every unwholesome and useless particle, each tired and haggard wave, encouraging the healing energy blanket to take their places.

"How are you feeling, Fufi?" Lysandra asked.

"Much better!" The older woman sat up, seeming far more energetic than when she arrived. "That was powerful. I could feel tiny hands working inside my body to repair everything. It was so amazing!"

Biting back the impulse to tell the woman she could do this for herself in the comfort of her own home if she wanted to, Lysandra just smiled. "I'm glad to hear it."

And she was. In all of existence, no calling was more vital or fulfilling than that of a healer. Although it frustrated her, Lysandra remembered overhearing Master Raffi, the chief physician of Atala, say how average citizens couldn't communicate with their own bodies anymore. The fault may not lie with Fufi, but with something else. Still, the woman should take better care of herself.

"You must remember to include medicinal herbs in your diet and avoid overindulging, especially bread and rich foods," Lysandra advised. "Performing your daily exercises and meditation are crucial to your overall health. Think of your body as an energy crystal. If you don't recharge it regularly, it will run out of power and your lights won't turn on anymore."

"I'll pay more attention to taking care of myself," Fufi promised. She slid from the treatment bed and smoothed out her skirt. "Thank you, Lysandra. I hope it will be a decade or more before I need to come back."

"Take care of your trinity, Fufi—body, mind, and spirit—and I'll see you in two decades," Lysandra bade her with a smile. "Deal?"

The woman laughed and shook her head. "Deal."

Lysandra clamped the lid over the incense dish to snuff it out and prepare for her next patient of the day. There was a steady stream of them: a man with a bleeding hole in his side from a laser cutter accident, a young woman with a raging fever, an older man with a weak heart, and, yes, a child who fell from a tree and broke his arm. She applied her talents to each, and they all left happy and feeling better.

When it came to the healing center, status didn't matter—all people received treatment at no personal cost. The Fraternity of Physicians worked for the city-state government, as their service was considered an innate right of citizenship akin to water and air. But it wouldn't matter where their salary came from; no Atlanteans suffered poverty. The nation was so rich in resources, abundant foodstuffs, and assets amassed through trade that people fell into one of two categories—prosperous or exceedingly wealthy. No person lived in lack or went without comfort. If it wasn't for stories told by travelers from abroad or Atlanteans returning from voyages to the colonies, they wouldn't even know what the word "poor" meant.

By the end of the day, Lysandra was spent. Her process was physically, mentally, and spiritually draining, and she was ready to return to her apartment, eat, and go to sleep. She bade goodbye to her fellow healers and started down the stairs.

"Wait for me, Lysandra," called Master Raffi.

Lysandra laid her hand on the stair railing and waited for the chief physician to join her. The two-hundred-plus-year-old man waved and grinned as he trotted down the hallway in a red tunic and white stole with woven reed sandals on his feet. Wavy, gray hair bounced around his shoulders while a long, stately beard flopped against his chest.

"Let me walk out with you," he offered as he caught up to her. Together, they descended wide stone steps.

"Is it just me, or do we receive more patients every day?" Lysandra asked.

"It was a busy one," he concurred. "I spent most of it growing a man's leg back. It wasn't from a laser cutter this time," he added. "An ordinary axe, chopping wood." He shook his head. "Young people seem to have lost the ability to focus on their current task. He said he was thinking about other things while swinging the axe."

"At least yours was an honest accident," Lysandra said. "Most of mine had just gotten sick because they don't tend to their own bodies and energies like they forgot how or don't care. I don't know." She shook her head. "Impressive, though—growing a leg back. I wish I could have been there to watch you."

Raffi displayed a humble smile and shrugged narrow shoulders. "It was mostly Raphael's ether. I only directed it, and you would have been bored. Regrowing a limb is a tedious process."

They walked through the expansive main chamber of the energy tower with its lofty ceiling and fortifying columns. Every wall was an explosion of colorful art, each column decorated with painted symbols. Green plants sprang from clay pots, and a spraying fountain bubbled up from a natural spring in the center of the complex under the opening high above where the giant crystal soaked in sun rays. The marble floor tiles were laid out in pleasing geometric shapes of red, black, and white.

The old master stopped on top of one, a set of three intersecting rings. He glanced down at them, and voiced, "Ham, het, hum." The ideogram was a familiar one with multiple meanings, pointing back to the same concept. All Atlanteans understood the symbol which, like others, such as the spiraling vortex, chakana, and six-point star, were prominently displayed in temples and public buildings, in people's homes, and worn as jewelry to remind them of important principles.

This was the trinity sign, a reminder of the three states of being. Matter exists as either a solid, liquid, or gas, depending on its frequency. Likewise, humans exist as a trinity—body, mind, and spirit. It was also a sign of unity. The three rings formed more geometrical shapes within them in the forms of three Pisces, or fish shapes, and each of those broke down into two halves. Still, altogether, it was one figure—which was especially evident when displayed in three-dimensional, interlaced hoops of gold or silver. The symbol represents how everything in creation is connected.

"Ham, het, hum," Lysandra repeated. Still vivid in her mind from her wisdom school was the time when she had traveled outside her body to see marvelous wonders in the heavens and diverse parts of the earth. The transcendence had opened channels in her that aided her ability to stream healing energies from the cosmos into her patients' bodies, but the experience itself had taken her beyond all previous imaginings.

They continued past scores of others leaving work for the day or rushing in to make a last-minute financial transaction. "What are your plans for tonight?" Raffi asked.

"Resting," Lysandra replied with a weak laugh. They passed under the towering entry and strode between two colossal statues who guarded the doorway. To their right stood the figure of a bare-chested man wearing a kilt and a large, crescent-moon necklace, with one arm straight at his side and the other loosely held out, palm up in invitation. On the left was a stone woman in a sleeveless gown with one hand pressed over her heart and the other raised in the air in praise. Both were painted in realistic colors and had been there since before Lysandra was born.

They passed busy people on the three steps leading to the street, individuals self-involved in their concerns and affairs, whose eyes and ears no longer perceived the spirit world.

Raffi patted a bony hand on her shoulder and smiled. "I'll see you tomorrow then."

"Tomorrow."

Lysandra could barely put one foot in front of the other; they seemed as heavy as lead. The sun hung low in the sky to the west, reflecting off rooftops, bathing the fabulous city of dreams in an orangey-gold hue.

As her thoughts drifted, a cheery voice brought her back to the moment.

"Lysandra! How have you been? Let me look at you."

She glanced up into the square, ruddy face of her old mentor, Quetzal.

4

"Quetzal! Wonderful to see you," Lysandra exclaimed. A warm joy instantly flooded her soul to be in her teacher's presence. His amber eyes sparkled with cheer under bushy, red brows. Lysandra found it remarkable how at a hundred and twenty-four Quetzal's bright red beard only hinted gray at the corners of his mouth and his curly hair kept its fiery luster. Not only that, his broad shoulders and meaty frame appeared even more robust than thirty years ago when she began studying under him.

Lysandra wasted no time throwing her arms around his neck in a big hug, and he returned the embrace, kissing her cheeks. "You get more beautiful every time I see you," he praised.

"Oh, you charmer," she dismissed with a shy, but appreciative, smile. Stepping back, she laid her hands on his broad shoulders draped by a fir-green chlamys pinned around a white toga as a short cloak. "But what brings you to the city?" The central wisdom school he supervised lay at the foot of the Opocalám Range to the northwest of Atala.

"My brother Demetrios is performing in the comedy charades at the Amun-Re Theater tonight and I promised to come laugh and applaud for him. Won't you join me?" Quetzal draped an arm around Lysandra's shoulders and guided her away from the busy path of pedestrians. Most Atlanteans walked around the city, both for exercise and because there were few places to park a sleigh. Still, a fair scattering of the wheelless vehicles floated by at a cubit off the paving stones. Some were two-seaters, others four, shaped like old horse-drawn sleighs with running boards that set on the ground when they were parked. While most had folding canopy roofs to raise when it rained, tops were rolled down in the pleasant fall weather that afternoon.

"I'd love to, but I'm seriously drained of energy," she answered with regret. She truly loved the wise sage—not the way she loved Ariel, but like a father. Lysandra had a grandfather way up in Gadlan and her cousin Yaluk, who married Ariel's brother, but her parents, brother, and half-sister all perished in a shipwreck at sea. She wasn't close to her grandfather and never went to the farm to visit Yaluk because Ariel was there, and it would just be too hard. Lysandra had Raffi, her neighbor Helene, and Quetzal. They served as her family now.

"Then let me fix that." Quetzal winked. He slapped his thick hands together and rubbed his palms in a circular motion.

"You don't have to—"

"Physicians always make the worst patients," he quoted. "How often do you tell others to take care of their energy, to keep their vibration high, to take time to commune with nature or enjoy a hearty laugh? Hmm?" He pinned her with a knowing gaze from which Lysandra had no defense. Then he caught one hand behind her neck and pressed his other palm into the middle of her chest. A burst of radiant energy shot through her so potent it could have raised the dead. In an instant, her fatigue was gone, and she felt as fresh as a youth on a spring morning. It was exhilarating, and she had to wonder if this was what her patients experienced at her touch.

"By the gods, Quetzal!" she exclaimed, a little dizzy under the powerful wave he had administered to her. No one believed in the gods anymore, but the expression remained in common usage. The legend of Poseidon and his brothers Zeus and Hades dividing up the earth to rule it was a mere children's story in light of the knowledge Atlanteans now possessed, although it remained a popular one. The great sea god falling in love with a human, fathering a race of demigods, and naming the continent for his firstborn son was romantic. It provided outsiders with an explanation for their extraordinary powers, which are unheard of in the rest of the world. Feeling her old mentor's infusion of vitality consume her exhaustion and swallow it like it was pudding was enough to make her reconsider.

His bright, tawny eyes and wide grin gleamed at her, and the vigorous man crooked his arm for her to take. "Come, my dear. Let's grab a bite to eat at the Fatr Tári. They have the most excellent oysters. Then I'll ensure you get a good laugh before I see you safely home."

Lysandra twisted her mouth in consideration before giving in with a giddy giggle. "An offer I can no longer refuse—though I may have to forgo the wine if I'm still feeling intoxicated when we arrive." She took his arm as they walked toward the nearest bridge over the ringed canal.

Lysandra appreciated the beauty of the city where she had lived for the past twenty-five years. To her left lay an unobstructed view of Poseidon's temple atop a raised mound in the very center of the metropolis's layout. Its majestic pillars held The Law, engraved on sheets of orichalcum, where all could see them. Exquisite and commanding in its architecture and opulence, the temple served as the meeting hall for the Council of Rulers and was where all the ministry offices were located. Efrayim, the king of Atala, conducted business and held court in the impressive columned building dedicated to the legendary founding father. The king's palace was also located on the central island of the city, along with a grand library, a bathhouse, a gaming court, lush gardens, several high-ranking officials' houses, and the most expensive marketplace in the nation.

The power pyramid with the healing center had been built on the ring surrounding the innermost heart of Atala. It was important to keep the energy station close to the temple, but not so close an accident might destroy the cultural symbol of Atlantis or endanger its kings. This ring boasted more palaces, more bathhouses and laundries, a theater, a passenger ship port, the most exclusive inn, more marketplaces and eateries, a public water tower, the city guardians' headquarters, and the enormous elliptical circus racetrack and spectator stands.

As she walked with Quetzal over the arched bridge of mortared stones to the second ring encompassing the city center, Lysandra noticed the many pots of late-blooming flowers lining the waist-high safety walls. Barges and gondolas glided through the water beneath them—a flat stacked with crates and large clay jars guided by a man in a white kilt with a long pole; two ladies wearing flat-brimmed hats with high peaked crowns sat on cushions while a fellow in a blue tunic propelled them along with a pole from the stern. Both small crafts steered clear of the forty-cubit-long Phoenician ship moored to a dock.

"I've never eaten at Fatr Tári before," she commented, her skin still tingling from Quetzal's touch.

"You'll love it," he assured her. "Surely you've been to a charade comedy before," he added. "You can't just stay in your cubical wearing yourself out healing people all the time."

"More so lately than when I started my practice," she replied. "And, yes—I love the charades. Thank you for inviting me. I'm sure your brother will be fabulous."

They passed quaint villas with private courtyards, a busy market, loud with hagglers and vendors, the aromas of fresh bread and spicy herbs almost enough to smother that of the fish. "Isn't that where your apartment is?" Quetzal asked, pointing at a two-story building backing onto the outer edge of the ring-shaped strip of land.

"That's the one," she confirmed. "Second floor, facing north, with a little private balcony, and right next to a privy. Speaking of which." Lysandra nodded across the street to a public comfort station.

"So, now you're a clairvoyant as well as a gifted healer, I see," he laughed and led them across the rectangular cut paving stones, dodging a guy driving a donkey cart.

"No," she laughed with him. "Lucky guess."

Once seated in the grotto at Fatr Tári, a young golden-haired woman wearing a coral chiton with a white sash diagonally over one shoulder set water goblets in front of them. "Tonight, we are serving a choice of spinach salad with olives, cucumber, and tomatoes or creamy pepper oyster soup and barley bread, for starters. For the main course, there is a vegetarian option of oven-roasted artichoke with olive oil, capers, and garlic, and fresh carrots with dip. For a meat-based meal, we have dill-braised sea bass or pork sausage links with lentils. May I bring you beer or wine?"

A group of three musicians sat in a corner, softly playing a harp, a lyre, and a double auloi pipe, a reed instrument with an unmistakable sound. The grotto was lovely, each stone placed precisely according to its cut and hue, with a central fountain beset with ferns and lilies, and life-size statues of happy-looking men and women whom Lysandra supposed represented kings and queens from antiquity. A grand mosaic of ten kings chasing and fighting an enormous bull covered an entire wall. Now the Council of Rulers was composed of both kings and queens, but the ritual involving the bull hadn't been abandoned. Atlantean women took as much pride in their athletic prowess as the men did.

"I'd like the oyster soup with sea bass and a beer, please," Quetzal requested.

"And I'll have the salad, artichoke, and a small, white wine," Lysandra said.

"I'll be back with your bread and drinks shortly." The young woman spun around and sashayed through a door. Other patrons of varying ages occupied tables arranged in the intimate courtyard setting. With the fading evening light, bulbs hanging from brass chains emitted a soft glow, as did the white stones at the bottom of the fountain, beautifully illuminating the flowing water.

"This is so nice, Quetzal," she hummed, turning to face him. "You're right; I don't take enough time to enjoy myself. It's just that in the past few years, disease seems to be running rampant, and I don't understand why."

"Disease?" he questioned with a quirk of his burnished brows. Atlanteans were a tall race who came in a variety of skin, hair, and eye shades, yet men and women with Quetzal's coloring were rare. Besides the red hair, his skin was a pale pink, which she had treated for sunburn one summer. Deeper tanned skin and dark hair were more prevalent in central Ruta and Daya, but she couldn't say for sure about people in the far north. Perhaps they had fairer complexions.

He caught her gaze and spoke with the authority of his station. "Lysandra, my eager and brilliant student, surely you haven't forgotten the first foundation—the Law of One? There is no such thing as disease. There is only health and the absence of health, light and the absence of light, love and the absence of love. No darkness or poverty or evil like the superstitious children of other lands suppose—no two gods who battle in the skies, pulling the people back and forth like puppets. All creation, every filament and fiber, particle and wave, is derived from the same source, and it is good. The question to ask isn't, 'Where's the disease coming from?'—for there is no source of decay. You should ask, 'What is blocking the people's health?' The natural state of man is health, peace, prosperity, love, joy, compassion, wisdom, and clarity."

"Yes, Master Quetzal, I understand the principle. I misspoke, is all," Lysandra explained. "Then something of consequence is at play blocking the flow of health. I have noticed a falling away of people's dedication to The Law, to following its teachings and to practicing traditions we have held since at least the Second Age. But I'm getting patients whose hearts are filled with love, who follow The Law to the letter, who keep their bodies, minds, and spirits in proper alignment and still become ill. Last week, a member of the ministry called me to his home to treat his wife. She was only two hundred and eleven years old, yet she was withered and wrinkled like a raisin left too long in the sun. She died of age and decay when she should have had another hundred years. I don't know what to do."

The bright, young woman returned, setting two small barley loaves and their drinks on the table. "Your meals will be ready soon," she promised.

Quetzal took a long draught of his beer and let out a satisfied, "Ahhh." Setting down his cup, he leaned back in his chair and glanced around at the other diners, the wait staff, and the lovely ambiance of the grotto. "There is a matter I wish to discuss with you, Lysandra. But, first, we shall eat, drink, laugh, and be merry, for who knows when the stars will fall?"

5

Ryzen, on the northern coast of Daya, the southern island of Atlantis

Temen trudged through the afternoon shower on his way to the forum as the smell of steam evaporating off hot stones mingled with that of fresh-cut grass in his nostrils. The near-tropical climate was indeed preferable to the icy blasts encountered in the mountains of Ampherium or the winters of Gadlan, but it was not without its drawbacks. Some people wore wide-brimmed, conical straw hats to keep their heads dry as they bustled down the roadways while others took the shower in stride. The streets were more crowded than usual because a trading vessel from Kemet had arrived with a shipment of new cloth fibers called cotton. In mid-summer, when the commodity had first been introduced, people who tried it declared it was even lighter and better suited to the heat than linen, placing it in high demand.

Ryzen was the second largest city in Atlantis, after Atala, and this was the peak season for their citrus crops. Orchard growers from all over the area were in town with crates and barrels full to trade and sell, while daily air barges hauled shipments northward to the other city-states. The oranges, lemons, limes, and grapefruits could only grow on Daya where winters stayed free of frost, which could kill the trees. Papyrus, flax, hemp, orchids, and an abundance of fruits and vegetables that thrived in the heat were other important products. Temen was just happy that many people would come to hear him speak.

With his sandals splashing through a puddle and his sand-tinted tunic getting soaked through, Temen spotted Mandisa strolling along with Hashur, one of her two husbands. Inwardly, he balked at their arrangement, puzzled by why two men would want to share the same woman. Then again, they seemed quite affectionate with each other, too. *Mandisa*, he scoffed to himself in disapproval. Lykos had told him all he needed to know about the woman who held far too much sway on the island. Sure, she was influential and regularly celebrated for dissipating tropical storms and steering hurricanes away from their shores, but who knows if they would have hit or not even without the air speaker's interventions? *Lykos is more powerful than her.*

A handsome man of sixty years, Temen boasted a strong jaw and an aristocratic look. His light brown, full-bodied hair just brushed the tops of his muscled shoulders, but, unlike most men, he completely shaved his face. Rather than stand out because of a thin, splotchy beard that wasn't thick enough to grow in properly, he chose to distinguish his appearance with a smooth, youthful face.

He waved and jogged across the street as he neared Mandisa. "Hey, air speaker!" he called in jovial jest. "Can't you do a better job of controlling the weather?"

The short, full-figured woman near his age smiled at him with white teeth set against earthy, rich skin. Many narrow braids bound by colored beads adorned her black hair while orichalcum and turquoise jewelry stepped up the look of her everyday white tunic. The taller, younger Hashur erected himself protectively at her side, his blond hair appearing brown from the rain.

"Temen, good to see you this fine day!" she greeted. "It's a common misconception to say an air speaker controls the weather," she answered, wagging a finger with a painted nail at him playfully. "We can only influence the forces of the natural world. Not even the archangels themselves can control the seas or dictate to the wind. Besides, rain is our friend. Look around you," she said, extending an arm in an arc. "See how green and lush our land is? How productive our orchards and gardens are? 'Twould not be so without an abundance of rain."

"I hear you, Mandisa," Temen responded. "Are you and Hashur coming to the forum this afternoon?"

"Mandisa wishes to arrive at the docks in time to purchase some of the cotton cloth before it's all gone," Hashur replied in her stead. He brushed back one of her stray braids and settled a firm hand on her shoulder. "Then we are helping Agathon at the orchard."

Agathon was the third side of their odd triangle. There was nothing wrong with it, Temen recognized. He'd enjoyed two women at the same time for the exchanging of pleasures. He just couldn't imagine trying to maintain a long-term relationship with more than one person at a time. *Too much work.*

"I'm sorry we'll miss hearing you speak," Mandisa said, "but we have to pick the fruit when it's ripe."

"I will miss seeing you there." *Not*, he thought with his smile still in place. "Enjoy the rain."

The bathhouse and laundry were only one street over from the forum and Temen had plenty of time, so he stopped in to clean up before meeting Lykos. A tiny, brown person—who was clearly not a native Atlantean—met him with a towel at the entrance to the men's side of the public bath.

"Good afternoon, sir," he greeted, handing Temen the towel. "Would you like me to have your tunic cleaned and dried while you enjoy your bath?"

"Yes, thank you," Temen answered amiably. "Half a turn of the sand glass? I'm in a bit of a hurry."

"Yes, sir. I can have it ready for you by then."

When he reached the side of the pool, Temen loosened his leather belt, pulled the wet tunic off over his head, and passed it to the attendant. He was aware immigrants from Kush had agreed to indenture themselves as servants to the government of Ryzen for seven years in exchange for being granted permission to settle on Daya permanently. While under their contract, the immigrants would perform menial jobs, freeing Atlanteans to pursue their artistic and intellectual interests.

Before the Conflagration, no foreign-born people were allowed to move to Atlantis. As the chosen race of the gods, they had established colonies in both the east and west, helping to civilize the lesser humans, teaching them, guiding them, and establishing trade with them. It had all been very peacefully carried out—well, except for the incidents with Libya and Sindhu. After the great cataclysm, while Atlantis was trying to rise from the ashes of destruction, the Sindhi Colony declared independence and would have nothing more to do with their mother country. Then, about five hundred years ago, a major rebellion occurred in the Maghreb, resulting in many deaths. Since then, the bleeding-heart Council of Rulers decided that to improve relations with the developing world, they would allow a specific, predetermined number of immigrants to move to Atlantis and report back to their homelands that Atlanteans were wonderful, spiritual people who only desired to do good.

Temen socialized with half a dozen other men at the bathhouse, the weather and the harvest being the principal topics of conversation. Early afternoon was a slow time as most people came to bathe in the morning or late in the evening. Temen frequented the baths at various times almost every day because it was a great place to discover what was truly on the minds and hearts of the citizens. It was also a great place to sow ideas into other's minds.

When Temen had first journeyed to Ryzen, he had been between careers and searching for his life's purpose. Hearing a voice he believed to be the messenger Archangel Gabriel, he traveled from city to city seeking the man with a serpent staff he had seen in his vision. When he found the wizard Lykos, he knew he must become his student. Not only did Lykos fit the description from his vision, but he was an astronomer, an alchemist, and the headmaster of Daya's wisdom school. Since then, Temen had become a respected orator, a teller of parables, and a bit of a philosopher. Women—and a few men—flocked around him in admiration, each competing for his attention. His popularity and influence grew at the same time Queen Izevel's was on the decline.

Now, tutored in law and economics by Lykos, Temen had grown lofty aspirations. If a few factors moved in his favor, he could become king. According to the Articles of the Third Age, Atlantis is a confederation governed by an oligarchy of the kings and queens of each city-state. The people elect these positions, but the king—or queen—doesn't rule alone. A group of nine jurors are also elected to staggered terms of office who must approve any action of the ruler by a two-thirds majority. Then there are the various ministers in charge of their departments, but the important part is that if the jury passes a vote of no-confidence against the crown, a new general election will be held by the masses to either keep the current leader or replace him or her with a more popular candidate. Temen's goal was to become the most popular man in Ryzen, and thus pave his way to the throne.

☥ ⚛ ✞ ✡

Two hours later, the sun was out, and lines of men and women of all ages streamed into the forum, chattering excitedly as they mingled and selected snacks and drinks from the vendors outside. Distinct from the more intimate salons where like-minded people gathered to exchange ideas, the forum was constructed more like a temple with lofty columns and ample room for hundreds within the ornate hall. The polished marble floors gleamed, and voices echoed in the tall chamber. At one end of the rectangular building stood an elevated platform for speakers to use. Benches lined the walls, but the main floor remained open to accommodate wedding parties and other such affairs. Statues and bronze busts reminded the people of past rulers, while paintings celebrated the citrus crops and oceangoing ships. In the vestibule were private comfort stations, more seating, and a copy of The Law posted in large letters for all to read.

"You will be marvelous," Lykos encouraged Temen as he slapped a friendly hand on his shoulder. "You'll have them eating out of the palm of your hand."

"Now, don't forget to talk about the cotton," the older man instructed. "It's a hot topic that everyone is excited about."

Temen nodded, locking eyes with his mentor. Lykos didn't look like a wizard, and he didn't look eighty-two years old. His attire, consisting of a blue-gray, pleated, knee-length kilt, a decorative silvery cloth belt and apron, and a white linen shoulder shawl tied in front highlighted his impressive physique. A trim, black beard frosted with narrow smoky patches on either side of a jutting chin framed the cool, olive skin of his long face. He wore his sable hair cut short over his ears and at the base of his neck, displaying brushed nickel at his temples, while in front a longer swoop curled onto his forehead. Thin, arched brows stretched above penetrating eyes. He wore shimmering electrum wristbands and held an ebony staff topped with a golden serpent head.

"Thank you, my friend," Temen replied with a confident smile. "I won't forget the cotton." Having changed into a fresh white, sleeveless toga synched with a hand-width red and black woven belt, Temen strode through the crowd, shaking hands and greeting each citizen by name. Because he didn't actually care, he used mnemonic devices to remember them all. Pyrrhus had red hair, like a glowing pyre; Gashan, a homely woman with coarse hair, was Go And Shave Her Ass Now. Making these up amused him almost as much as conning the masses into believing he was the bearer of great wisdom and should be admired.

He took a cushioned armchair on the dais with Dareios, the slender, bald, esteemed minister of trade who was twice Temen's age, and Rhoxane, a younger, brunette beauty who inherited the bulk of the country's papyrus fields. She was considered nobility since her direct ancestor invented the method of producing paper from reeds and turned a worthless marshland into a fortune. Her latest acquisition was a personal shipping line. And since she and her husband had recently parted ways, Temen desired her. Well, let's not forget the goddess-worthy beauty. However, he would not let the tempting slit in her pastel blue chiton or its dangerously low neckline distract him for now … maybe later tonight.

Dareios stood and lifted a palm. The throng hushed and turned their attention to the front. There was standing room only in the forum, and the gathering spilled out into the vestibule. Temen sensed a tingle of electric energy shoot up his back from his heart to his brain, and his eyes gleamed with excitement.

"I am encouraged to see so many here today as we discuss the state of affairs in Ryzen. There is much to praise in our midst, and a few matters of concern. I have asked Temen to share the wisdom the divine energies have revealed to him. Temen?"

The people clapped their hands, and Temen stepped forward to address the crowd. "Ladies and gentlemen, I am honored to be here in the company of two such worthy individuals, our own esteemed Minister Dareios, and Lady Rhoxane." He motioned to them with a breeze of his hand and an admiring smile.

"Last week, I went into isolation to commune with the spirit world through fasting, prayer, and meditation. Refusing food and drink for three days, I was rewarded with a revelation, and I cannot rest until I share it with you, my friends—because that's who you are. Pyrrhus, Gashan," he called out, as he caught their eyes. "Apollos, Itzal. I could name you all if there was time; however, I must come to the point. We all know The Law. We live by The Law as Atlanteans have since time immemorial. But the wonderful thing about The Law is that it is a living entity."

Temen walked the platform using his arms, intonation, and animated facial expressions as he talked, his resonating voice reverberating off the chamber walls.

"We have three wisdom schools," he continued, "three great centers of learning where the brightest and best study to become spiritual masters. I admit, I was never fortunate enough to attend one of them, but my good friend Lykos has been the chief Master of the Daya Wisdom School for many decades."

Placing a finger to the side of his chin, Temen's voice took on a curious quality. "Did you know that there is more than one way to interpret the laws and rules, and that the wisdom schools do not even agree?"

Some in the crowd nodded, while a few murmured their surprise.

Pivoting to pace in the other direction, Temen pointed toward the vestibule wall where The Law was inscribed. "Take, for example, the rule, 'Do not eat or drink or do anything to excess lest your days be short upon the earth.' For millennia, debates have raged over what is meant by 'excess.' How much is in excess? One goblet of wine? Five? One pie? Six pies? What about two? Is two excess? And, if not, what about three? Where do we draw the line?"

Temen made a dramatic pause as if he were considering what the limit should be. "And then there's the rule, 'Pay laborers a fair wage agreed upon by the majority.' What is fair? Wages seem to fluctuate up and down based on the opinions of any ruling government. But I believe these ambiguities were purposefully included in The Rules so society could evolve, expand, and make necessary changes based on the current century while still remaining true to The Law."

"That makes sense," Dareios commented from behind him.

"So, what about the twelve fundamental laws? Are they not also open to interpretation?" Temen took a breath, stopped in the center of the dais, and clasped his hands behind his back, passing a contemplative gaze over the assembly. "Let us recite the Law of One together."

Temen led the people in reciting the first of the twelve laws. "The Lord our God is One with all and we are one with the Divine Power. All creatures and substances in the heavens and on earth spring from the same Source and are connected by invisible cords. Therefore, you are to love your neighbor as yourself because you and your neighbor are one."

As they concluded, the hall fell silent, and Temen picked up his sermon and his lively movements. "Some masters claim this law applies to all human beings who dwell on the earth, and there are a few who include higher-reasoning members of the animal kingdom as well. We understand the ether, which joins and makes up all forms of matter and energy in the universe, connects us to the ocean, the soil, mountains, and heavenly lights, but we do not say we must love them as we do ourselves, because they have no consciousness. There are masters—very wise and esteemed masters—who understand the word 'we' in the first line refers to Atlanteans, the favored offspring of the gods, that people native to this land are not only connected to the divine but are children of the creator, direct descendants of gods and angels. That is why we possess powers that lesser tribes do not. And the term, 'neighbor.' Who are our neighbors, if not the citizens of Ryzen, inhabitants of Daya, and native-born Atlanteans?"

After a brief pause to let his words sink in, Temen asked, "If all people of the world were created equal with the same access to the energies, why is it that only we are so long-lived? That only we have among us scores with special abilities? Why do our crops grow so much more abundantly, our brains conceive of higher mathematics, and our hands create such exquisite art? Why do our mines overflow with gold and precious gems and not so with the other peoples of the world, if we are all sons and daughters of the Creator?"

Shifting gears, Temen shrugged. "But I am not one to withhold generosity from those in need. The tenth law, the Law of Compassion, is not to be ignored. We are commanded—and indeed we are privileged—to help those less fortunate, to be generous and compassionate in all our dealings with others. To be a peaceful, loving society is at the core of who we are. How, then, ladies and gentlemen, do we handle the growing immigration problem?"

His question sparked some whispers, frowns, and head shakes as he hoped it would. "'What problem?' you may ask. 'Don't the indentured immigrants fill the jobs none of us want? Don't they clean the sewers, make mud bricks, and labor in the fields? Isn't that a good thing?' Conventional wisdom would have you believe so. After all, they don't even live that long and require few resources. Some even make good neighbors." Temen nodded in agreement with himself.

"So I supposed—until I received an unsettling revelation. While these foreign-born immigrants have been living among us, with their diseases and inherent limitations, they have intermarried with true Atlanteans, borne children of mixed blood. And, because of Queen Izevel's policy of accepting all these people from the Green Sea region and beyond, we have seen a rise in ailments among our own population. When a man once lived to five hundred, now we grow old and wither away at half that age. When a woman used to go her whole life without an ache or pain, she now must wait in line at the apothecary to receive treatments. The only thing that has changed, my friends, is this influx of non-native peoples. It is clear to see that this policy must be vetoed. It is one thing for trading vessels to dock at our harbors then sail away, and entirely different when they move here permanently, infecting our citizens with sicknesses and diluting our bloodlines."

A brawny man raised his hand and spoke out. "But I'm working on a deal to import cotton seeds and raise the crop on my land. Two families experienced in growing it are to move here from Kemet to help me get started."

"I understand the importance of the valuable new cloth and the plants that produce the fibers," Temen agreed, "which is why we should begin playing a stronger role in our colonies abroad. The way to best help and serve the less advanced societies around the world is through the colonial system. We will build schools to teach them math and engineering in exchange for the right to grow crops in their fields and cut timber from their forests.

"Listen, people; hear my warning. Our technology must be guarded at all costs. Suppose—despite all our efforts to vet immigrants—a group arrives for the sole purpose of stealing our crystals, or, worse yet, lasers? If these tools fell into the hands of primitive, violent men, the consequences could be disastrous. I understand the worthy ambition for your land to prosper by growing the new crop, but what if you controlled twice as much land in Kemet, Libya, Kush, or Halaf? What if the native people of those lands worked for you there? Then you could safely transport the cotton here by ship with no foreigners living and working on our soil."

"It sounds like we have been deceived," Rhoxane declared in an offended manner. She rose from the couch where she had been reclining and joined Temen at the front. "I thought having a queen we'd be in better hands than a king who needs his ego stroked and his fill of pleasures to keep him happy. But Izevel has made mistake after mistake. What can we do but petition our jurors to give her a vote of no confidence?"

At that, the hall erupted in heated debate, and, from the sounds of it, most people agreed with Temen. He turned an appreciative gaze to Rhoxane and smiled, exuding potent sexual energy. He picked up on her response, which was equally eager. His successful day was about to become a successful night.

Before he could escort Rhoxane out and back to her palace, Lykos appeared at his side, boring into him with his intense, dark eyes. "I believe we accomplished today's goal," he hummed into Temen's ear.

One of them, Temen thought, annoyed that the wizard had interrupted his flirtations with the lovely heiress. But he was powerful, as anyone in his vibrational vicinity could attest, and Temen needed him as a supporter and ally. "You were right, as usual," he replied with a smirk. "When I become king, just name the position you want, and it's yours."

"All in good time," Lykos affirmed. "I'm taking Minister Dareios and his wife out tonight, so we may deliberate how to persuade the other ministers. I believe you have a similar plan in mind for winning over Lady Rhoxane." His intuitive gaze passed between Temen and Rhoxane. Then he sparked a sprinkle of energy with the fingers of his right hand and tossed it in the woman's direction. With a sly smile, he added, "Enjoy your evening."

When Rhoxane took his arm and batted long lashes at him, Temen decided keeping Lykos on his team came with *many* benefits.

6

Atala, the same night

"Wow! They're performing at one of the best theaters in the city," Lysandra said in awe as Quetzal led her to the grand façade of the Sirius Amphitheater.

The limestone edifice extended the entire street length of the theater, primarily to keep out those who hadn't purchased tickets. It reached twenty-four cubits high, equivalent to a three-level house or a typical temple or library. Red, black, and white stones were inserted strategically to create harmonious geometrical patterns, and marble statues of famous actors, playwrights, and directors stood guard. Sturdy columns supported a portico to shade patrons who stood in line from the elements. That function wasn't necessary on the beautiful night, but the light panels glowing from its ceiling were. Although they had arrived plenty early, crowds had already gathered and slowly filed in.

The towering entry, wide enough to accommodate two lines of theatergoers, opened to the back of the stage platform. Bench seats carved into rock cliffs spread out in a perfect half-circle arc around the orchestra section. While some other amphitheaters, like the Clito, could seat upward of twenty-thousand spectators, the Sirius was designed for a more intimate audience of around six thousand. As with the larger venues, it was built without a roof. One job of the royal air speaker was to dissuade heavy rains from falling during performances, which generally ran after dinner time for up to four hours on workdays, and early to mid-afternoon on non-workdays. Glowing orbs along the stairstep rows of seats helped people find their places without interfering with them watching the performance. Naturally, the stage and orchestra areas were brightly illuminated.

"This is a good row." Quetzal pointed to a spot on the second tier of seats left of center where two could fit. The expected action was for the initial individuals to move toward the middle of the row, allowing for smoother seating from the aisles. This audience was mostly following etiquette.

"Oh, yes," Lysandra agreed. "We'll be able to see well from here."

They shuffled down the row to the first empty spaces and sat beside a giddy young couple who bounced with excitement.

"I saw this troop perform last month, and they were so funny," the woman enthused.

"My friend's brother is one of the cast," Lysandra replied.

"Bury a spoon!" she exclaimed, using a new colloquial expression the youngsters were all saying. "For real?"

"He has the role of Pleione," Quetzal informed her as he beamed with pride.

"Ladies and gentlemen!" shouted the announcer on stage. The chatter in the stands hushed to a whisper, and Lysandra turned her attention to the front. She still had her arm looped through her mentor's and for a brief second, she imagined she sat beside Ariel instead. It was silly after all this time but not a day in the past thirty years had passed in which she hadn't thought about her lost love at least once. She had trained herself to only dwell on happy memories or envision positive scenes of Ariel today, how she would be out enjoying herself visiting the elephant herd or maybe engaging in a family activity with her children. Lysandra hadn't talked to her, but she'd asked around. She was aware Ariel still lived and worked on the family farm back in Evamont and had married and had children, although she couldn't recall their ages.

It's almost harvest time, she thought.

The announcer continued. "I'm pleased to present to you the fabulous, the stellar, the legendary Pisces Players!"

Lysandra disentangled her arm from her companion's, joining the crowd in clapping and cheering for the actors. The announcer left the stage and two characters walked out. One was a woman dressed as Atlas, holding up the blue, brown, and green sphere of the earth on his shoulder. She wore a white kilt, a flesh-colored, sleeved tunic stuffed with padding to look like bulky muscles, and a false beard. Beside her was Quetzal's brother Demetrios in the role of Pleione, Atlas's first wife. With his face shaven smooth as a baby's bottom, an enormous, puffed-out blonde wig, and false breasts large enough for viewers on the top row to see, he wiggled his hips as he walked, displaying every feminine grace.

"Atlas, you sorry excuse for a husband!" she screeched in a sassy falsetto. "Put that world down and pay attention to me for a while!"

"But, buttercup," the actress protested in a voice straining to sound low, "I have a responsibility. Holding up the world is my job."

The Pleione character crossed her arms and spun toward the audience with her chin jutted up. "Well, you have no problem resting it on its cradle when dinner is served."

"Sure," Atlas answered in a reasonable tone. "I must keep up my strength in order to hold the world on my shoulders."

"And is that all you have to do? I swear, demigod or not, you are impossible to live with." Pleione pivoted toward him and gestured in his direction. "You track mud through the house like a pig, snore as loud as a bear, and pass wind like a hurricane. You never consider me or my feelings. I'll bet you don't even know what today is." As a perfectly outraged wife, Demetrios slapped fists onto padded hips and glared at the woman playing Atlas.

Atlas showed the audience a pitifully forlorn expression and shrugged his shoulders, one palm held out in innocence while he balanced the globe with his other.

"My birthday, you useless pile of muscles! You know nothing about women, and until you learn to appreciate me there'll be no more dinners—or after-dinner delights," she added to the audience with a hand to her mouth, "for you!" Spinning on a heel, Pleione stomped off the stage.

A bewildered Atlas looked to the spectators for help. "What should I do?" Interactively, people began shouting suggestions while others answered with hearty laughter. Lysandra cupped her hand to Quetzal's ear. "Demetrios makes a marvelous Pleione. He's so funny, and, by Triton, he looks like a real woman—a very well-endowed one, but still."

Quetzal smiled and nodded. "He's always loved the comedy charades and was born to play women's roles. He married the man who plays the priestess, and they make such an adorable couple."

Back on stage, Atlas reached a decision. "You're right, citizens of Atala." Setting the globe on a wood-framed cradle behind him on stage, he declared, "I must embark on a quest to discover the greatest mystery in all creation—what women want."

Applause and laughter followed the character as he strode in the direction of a new actor disguised as a woman who had appeared on the stage, reclining on a sofa. This one wore sexy, sheer lingerie, a copious amount of face and eye paint, and flashy, gold jewelry dangling from every appendage. A fountain of black hair flowed from a high tail.

"Hello, handsome," she called out in a seductive tone. "I hope you aren't in too big of a hurry. Why don't you bring that fabulous body of yours my way?"

Atlas stopped, assessed her, and turned to the audience. "There's a woman now! I'll ask her what women want." He strode over, looking pleased with himself.

The prostitute flipped her hair, batted impossible lashes at him, and pulled back a fold of light fabric, revealing more of her legs. Lysandra marveled at how smooth and womanly they appeared for a male actor, at least from where she sat.

"Good day, fair woman of Atala. I have need to ask your advice."

"You've come to the right place, you fabulous Titan," she answered enticingly. "I know everything about how to please a man."

"Yes, well," Atlas laughed, angling toward the audience. "Pleasing a man is easy. I need to know what pleases a woman."

She glided up from her couch, stepped to him, took his artificially-brawny arm in one hand, and lifted the other high, hoops jiggling and rings sparkling. "I find gold, orichalcum, diamonds, and rubies do quite nicely. Buy a girl beautiful things and she will do whatever you desire."

Atlas lifted a finger to his chin and displayed a thoughtful look. "Hmm. You could be right. I should buy Pleione fabulous gifts. Then she won't be cross with me."

"Forget about her," the harlot purred. "What about a trinket for me? I could pleasure you in ways you never dreamed." She ran her tongue around her lips for good measure.

But Atlas seemed unmoved by her charms. "Don't trouble yourself. I must be off to find a present for my wife."

Leaving a disappointed woman of the evening behind, Atlas strode to the other end of the stage where an actor stood wearing a modest, ankle-length, snowy toga and a white headscarf draped over luscious, long, red strands. No jewelry or cushioned sofa but a pedestal holding stone tablets with writing etched in them stood beside her. As with the other two, he had his face painted like a woman's and wore pads to assume a curvaceous figure. This was especially important for the play because Atlantean men and women wore basically the same clothing—tunics, togas, kilts, chitons, robes, and the like.

"Where are you going in such a hurry?" the priestess asked.

Atlas stopped and turned aside. "I am off to buy sparkly jewels for my wife so she will not be cross with me anymore."

"Is that Demetrius's spouse?" Lysandra asked. Quetzal nodded.

"Surely, you don't believe a new material possession is what she wants or needs."

With shoulders slumping, Atlas replied, "It's not? But the woman down the street said—"

"Atlas." The priestess put one hand on her hip and the other on the pedestal holding The Law tablets. "What does a prostitute know about things that please a wife? You should listen to me."

"All right. I'm listening."

"She wants to share her feelings with you. You must be romantic, shower her with attention and sentimental gestures," she explained, "not cold, impersonal stones. There is a garden behind my temple where you may select her favorite flowers. Take them to her and tell her you love her. Compose a poem expressing your deepest feelings. Then she cannot stay angry with you."

Looking at the crowd, Atlas said, "She makes sense too. Maybe I'll do both, just to be safe."

"Thank you, priestess," he said. "May you walk with the Creator in peace."

Atlas marched back to center stage where a bench had been set, complete with a bouquet of flowers, a white box wrapped with a red ribbon and bow, and a papyrus scroll and quill. The actress sat and picked up each item as her character mentioned it.

"I'm set now with a lovely new necklace and the most beautiful flowers from a sacred garden. All that's left for me to do is to write a love poem." Atlas picked up the scroll and quill, tapping the feather against his face as he tried to think. "My love is as strong as an ox and as viral as a bull. I would battle a troop of barbarians just to see your face."

"What are you doing?" asked a high-pitched voice. Another actor in the guise of a woman—this one a mother with two small children running in a circle around her yelling and squealing—lumbered by Atlas toting an enormous basket of laundry. The hair of her wig stuck out in disarray as if she had no time to comb it. She set the basket down and stretched, pressing a hand to her back like it ached. "Children! Be still!" They slowed and lowered their voices but did not be still.

"I'm composing a romantic love poem for my wife, so she won't be cross with me anymore."

"Ha!" the haggard mother laughed out sarcastically. "You call that a love poem? I've heard a parrot quote better verses. Look at you, with your strong back and bulging muscles." She propped a hand on her hip and motioned toward him with a wave of her other one. "I'll tell you the truth—your wife doesn't give a fig about your bad poetry. If you want back in her good graces, help her with the chores. When's the last time you shopped at the market, cooked a meal, or did the laundry? Do you sweep the floors, wash the dishes, or take out the trash?"

Atlas set down his scroll and quill and leaned his elbows on his knees, clasping his hands between them. With a look of embarrassment, he answered, "I don't know. I never thought about it."

"Exactly!" She pointed an accusatory finger at him and grabbed one rambunctious child with her other hand. "No wonder she's in a foul mood. If you don't want to end up getting kicked out the door, you need to pitch in and help. It's the best way to show a woman you care."

"You could very well be right," responded Atlas, as the mother picked up her basket and chased the skipping, giggling children off the stage. "I know what I'll do!"

With the gift box and flowers in hand, Atlas strolled to the end of the stage where Pleione was sweeping. With a gallant smile, he said, "Give me that broom, Pleione. You need your hands to collect the presents I have brought you."

"Presents?" She gave him a suspicious stare but passed him the broom handle and gathered the box and bouquet. She took a deep whiff of the flowers while Atlas began to sweep.

"I brought you flowers from the sacred garden as a symbol of my love for you, though you are more beautiful and fragrant than the rarest orchid." She set the flowers on a small, portable table the stagehands had set in place and opened the box.

"And I have brought you a jeweled, orichalcum necklace to demonstrate how valuable you are to me—more precious than the most expensive gem," he waxed eloquent. Pleione fastened the huge, flashy piece around her neck with a most satisfied expression.

"And I intend to help you with the chores some every day, because this is my home too, and you shouldn't have to do everything yourself." He continued to brush at the floor with an expectant look.

Pleione rushed into Atlas's arms, hugged, and kissed him, then stepped back, half facing the audience. "It looks like you learned a few things about women while you were gone. Maybe you'll get dinner after all."

Atlas beamed at her with a wide grin, then turned to the spectators with a hand to this mouth. "It looks like I'll get lucky tonight after all."

The crowd cheered and applauded. All the actors returned to the stage and took a bow.

"That was hilarious," Lysandra said to Quetzal, flushed from laughing so hard.

"Oh, they're just getting started," he assured her. "They do comical dances to music and poke fun at the king and ministers. There are a couple of other women who play men's roles, and you'll get to see them act too. Be careful that you don't lose your breath to an onset of the giggles."

"Too late for that!"

7

Lysandra laughed more as she recalled some of the funniest lines and scenes from the show with Quetzal while he walked her home. As usual, the wise sage was right—this was precisely what she needed. When they reached the archway into the courtyard of her building, his expression turned serious.

"Lysandra, I didn't come to Atala only to watch Demetrios perform." He took her hand and met her gaze.

Sensing his troubled emotions, she said, "Come upstairs with me and we can talk in private." He nodded and followed her into her cozy apartment. Lysandra touched her palm to a copper square on the wall just inside her door. Hanging orbs began to glow, casting the room in pale light. He closed the door behind them.

"I just charged my crystal last month," Lysandra lamented with a groan. "I must have gotten a poor-quality one and I might have to replace it. Let's sit over here so you can tell me what's wrong."

The variegated brick walls of her room followed no particular pattern, but the way Lysandra arranged it did. A cooking corner was situated beside the entryway, complete with a cooler box, cupboards, a preparation area, a water faucet and basin, and a cooktop boasting three round copper heating plates. Shelves above it held her dishes and cups. Off to the side, there was a humble table with a pair of chairs arranged beneath a window. Across the room stood a single bed and nightstand with a wardrobe along the wall by the foot. A comfortable lounging sofa rested beside the glass-paned balcony door, with a bookstand at one end. In the middle of the pine floor spread a beautifully woven, wool rug tying the two sides of the room together. The walls were awash with lush landscape canvases, animal portraits, still life, and imaginative uses of symbols in nontraditional paintings. In a corner, she had piled an easel, canvases, and a box of paints and brushes.

Lysandra steered Quetzal toward the table and chairs. "May I offer you a drink?" She raised the lid of the cooler, peering around the ice block at chilled selections.

"Water will be fine, thank you." Quetzal took a seat and glanced out the window at the view. Many lights were still on, as it was still too early for most to retire for the night.

Bringing two cups of water over, Lysandra slid into the other chair. "What's going on—really?"

"You are not the only one who has noticed changes occurring, and they aren't limited to Atala," he stated. "Average people can no longer heal themselves—this you have noticed. The crystals losing their charge after only a short while is another symptom. I haven't had a student embark on a spiritual journey outside their body in over a decade. Even masters are experiencing difficulty connecting with the energies and exercising our talents. Something is amiss, but I can't quite put my finger on it. Nothing like this has happened in my lifetime. Besides an influx of patients, what have you noticed?"

"Well." Lysandra had to think. She had been so busy lately she hadn't had time to ponder about much. "Using the energies drains me more than it did when I first started, but I thought it was natural. I've been exerting myself much more frequently and I'm not as young as I was."

"Psh!" Quetzal waved a hand. "Fifty-four, you're practically still a youth."

"Not anymore. That's something else I've observed; people aren't just getting sick—they're aging faster."

"What about your personal spiritual journey?" he pried. "I admit, it isn't as easy for me to connect, to weave patterns, to manifest my desired alignment.

What I could achieve ten years ago in half a turn of a standard sandglass now takes more than twice as long. I haven't sculpted in years. When I was younger, I couldn't go a week without generating some artistic creation. The energies would snap and crackle under my skin like ants in a stirred-up pile without an expressive outlet. When's the last time you painted?"

Lysandra glanced at her treasured tools shoved out of the way in a corner, dusty and neglected. Then she scanned her walls, trying to recall. She pointed to a watercolor impression of a regal elephant in a green meadow under a sunlit blue sky. "I painted Adira about ten years ago. I was worried I would forget her …" Lysandra's words trailed off and she sighed. "I used to love to paint. I still do; I just haven't been inspired lately."

"This is a little off-topic—and you may tell me if it's none of my business—but why don't you ever go home to visit?"

"This is my home now," she answered. He pinned her with a skeptical look and raised a brow. "What would be the point?"

"Are you still in love with her?"

Lysandra threw back her head, staring at a dim ceiling.

Quetzal's hand came to rest atop hers. She could sense the flow of compassion radiating through his touch to warm and console her. "It isn't good to be alone. I understand, when one lives for hundreds of years, our affections may ebb and flow like tides. We may grow in different directions, build up irreconcilable differences, or even decide we made a mistake. We cling to one another with passionate fervor, live together in peaceful comfort, or part ways and find someone new. You've done none of these things. Tell me you found another lover, another best friend to share your life with." He glanced around her solitary, one-room apartment. "Where is she or he?"

"You know the answers," she muttered. "There's been no one else. But like you said, I'm still young. Maybe in time, our paths will cross again—when she isn't married, and I have time to devote to her."

"That time may be sooner than you are prepared for," Quetzal stated.

Her eyes shot up to meet his in astonishment, and her heartbeat raced. "One crisis at a time, please."

"Lysandra, I spent weeks in Atala's library searching every tablet and scroll for something to explain what's happening and uncovered no clue. Afterward, I returned to the Central Wisdom School and conferred with the other masters. They, too, are concerned but can offer no answers."

Quetzal leaned back, trailing his hand away from hers, and peered at her curiously. "Have you heard a voice, felt an urging, a draw toward something or someone recently?"

"I always feel drawn to her, but I fear it has much more to do with my stubborn heart than any angel's call," Lysandra admitted.

"Three days ago, Thoth, the chief librarian of Atala and keeper of the Emerald Tablets, visited me on the sacred mountain, in the cave where you first learned to weave the energies," he said. Lysandra nodded. She would never forget the wonders she experienced there.

"He told me, after I explored the library on my quest for information, that he entered into a powerful meditation. Archangel Uriel spoke to him, saying those who are called should meet and receive instruction at the next full moon. I asked him, 'Who has been called?' He passed me a piece of parchment with nine names. Thoth said he wrote them down in a trance and only read them once he emerged from meditation."

Lysandra felt a stirring in her gut, a sensation of expectancy bordering on dread, as if she knew whose names he would reveal. Her mouth went suddenly dry, and she sipped her water.

Quetzal pulled a small papyrus square from the pouch on his belt and laid it on the table facing her. "Read them."

Her vibration wavered between distress and acceptance as she read the names. "Thoth, Quetzal, Noah, Ziusudra, Mandisa, Ptah, Ériu, Lysandra, Ariel." She looked up to catch his serious gaze. "But there are many people across Atlantis with the same names. This may not be—"

"Search your heart, Lysandra," he instructed and retrieved the list. "Have you not felt a tug? You said yourself, you are concerned because things are not as they should be."

"But I'm not important like you and Thoth," she replied in humility.

"You are a talented weaver of Jjeevan Shakti, who is in communion with Raphael daily."

"But Master Raffi is my superior," she argued. "Surely he would be called before me."

"Who can understand every mystery of the universe?" Quetzal asked. "I do not esteem myself so highly that I presume to be the greatest priest or wisdom teacher in all the world, yet my name is there. Tell me you've sensed no call from the spirit world, no desire to seek the truth."

Lysandra sighed and leaned back in her chair. "Who am I that Uriel would call me? Maybe I've felt unease and had disturbing dreams, but that doesn't mean I've been chosen for something special. You know I want to do whatever I can to discover what's happening; I just don't understand what help I'd be."

"We have amassed more wisdom than all the peoples of the earth," Quetzal explained, "and yet we on this mortal plain know so little. Who can fathom the Mind of God? In the books, I read that long ago Atlanteans enjoyed vastly more abilities than we do today, and they could easily flow in the stream of Universal Consciousness. They didn't need books to store knowledge or writing to send messages at a distance, for they could use their minds in marvelous ways we can scarcely imagine. But I know this: from our vantage point, we can only glimpse the connection between the nine whose names Thoth wrote during his rumination. I've never met a man named Ptah. There is a priestess called Ériu at the Northern Wisdom School, known for its emphasis on balance and acceptance, along with charity and generosity, but the chief of the school is Akna, and I've never met Ériu. The others I'm familiar with. Noah is a renowned shipbuilder and an exceedingly spiritual man. Ziusudra from Ampherium is the leading astronomer living today. Mandisa is an effectual air speaker and a very loving person."

"I don't see how Ariel and I—" Quetzal cut her off with a slice of his hand and used the interruption to take a sip of water.

"I know you—your heart, your dedication," he continued. "Though I only met Ariel once, the kindred spirit I sensed was so powerful. It was an instant connection like we had known each other since the dawn of time. Remember the significance of three, six, and nine?"

Lysandra nodded. "I remember everything you taught me. They are the fundamental building blocks of the universe. They can exist as energy without losing their identity. Not only are they fundamental to geometry and physics, but in esoteric philosophies as well. Three symbolizes our connection to the universe and creative expression, while six signifies inner strength and harmony. Nine indicates inner rebirth, letting go of what no longer serves us, and transforming into our better selves. But I don't see how that relates."

"The year is 1356. If you add thirteen, five, and six, you get twenty-four—which is divisible by three and six. The digits two plus four equal six. I don't know," he sighed. Leaning his elbows on the table, Quetzal pulled his fingers through his fiery red hair and dragged them down his beard. "Nine names were given. Thoth and I believe we have been called for some purpose. Therefore, we decided to contact the people on the list and plan to meet at the Ring of Stones on the plains of Evamont on the next full moon, which is in about two weeks. Will you go talk to Ariel and meet with us so we can try to figure this out?"

This was the request Lysandra had feared her mentor would lay before her. It dredged up feelings of guilt and loss she didn't wish to deal with. Yet her heart ached to see the love of her youth—the love of her life—again. *I can do this,* she told herself. *She will forgive me. If not, then she isn't the same Ariel Thoth is looking for.* A tingle in her belly, a nudge to her brain, and a flurry in her heart informed Lysandra that her Ariel was indeed the special talent whom any reasonable archangel would call to a vital gathering.

She moistened her lips, let out a breath, and nodded. "It won't be easy to get time off with this rush of patients to treat."

"I'll speak with Raffi in the morning before I leave town," Quetzal offered. "Trust me, Lysandra." He returned his big hand to hers and looked her straight in the eyes. "It will be all right. Regardless of being apart for thirty years, or whether you'll unite again in this lifetime, you and Ariel are still One."

Lysandra knew deep in her soul it was true.

8

Ariel's farm, two days later

Ariel loaded an empty basket, two tall clay pots with lids, several small jars, and a box in the back of the sleigh for her mother to take to Elyrna and fill at the market. Atlanteans didn't believe in being wasteful, regardless of their affluence. They understood the value of reusing and repurposing containers rather than piling them into unseemly mounds of rubble. Metals could be melted down and recast, clay pots and tiles crushed and used in brickmaking, and old cloth cut into rags for laborers to wipe their brows. Mostly, people took used containers to the marketplace to be refilled. Each of these was fashioned for beauty as well as functionality, as with everything in their society.

"Now, is there anything special you want from town?" Philomena asked. "I'd stay and help with the harvest, but you know I'd only be in the way."

Her mother must have made a goal of life to never touch a tool, muddy her feet, or engage in an activity that might sully her hands; however, she was a masterful cook and enjoyed making preserves and other essentials—skills at which Ariel never excelled. There was plenty to do, abundant time to accomplish it, and assigning each member of the family tasks they would enjoy was paramount. Mother could haggle with the most obstinate sellers in the market with much more ease and pleasure than laying a sickle to wheat or tying stalks into bundles, so why not let her do it?

"If you see a pretty scarf Yaluk would like, could you get it for her birthday?" Ariel asked as she secured the last slatted wooden crate in place. Their sleigh was a sleek walnut with red trim, silver railings and running boards, and padded leather seats. Because it was harvest time, no one expected rain, so the top remained curled down behind the back seat filled with containers. The front and back curved in a sleek, Apollonian design. A small compartment tucked beyond the foot pedals housed the vehicle's workings, which were efficiently small and simple—a few gyros and an antigravity bar, a steering and rudder device, and a braking system. All they had to do was insert a crystal into its slot and press the copper pad with their palm.

"And if you have time, you may want to get the crystal charged," Ariel added as she handed her mother into the sleigh.

"Good idea," she responded. "Yaluk's birthday already? If our family grows any larger, there won't be a week without a birthday or anniversary to celebrate." Philomena arranged herself comfortably in the driver's seat, then turned to Ariel, who tarried at her side. "What about you, sweetie? It's been a long time, and your children are both grown. You still aren't too old to have some more, you know?"

Ariel laughed. "You had your two and I've had mine. There are places I haven't seen yet, things I haven't experienced. I prefer to look forward rather than backward, and, no, I don't need a husband. I don't see you grabbing up a new one."

Philomena smirked and wiggled her brows. "Not yet," she clipped out with a humorous hint of promise. "But I have my eye on someone."

"You're incorrigible! Now, off to town with you," she laughed. "I've got to go help Aram and the rest of the crew. Tomorrow we'll all be helping the neighbors harvest wheat and rye, so we have to finish our fields today."

"Have a good time," her mother bade as the sleigh rose a cubit from the ground and silently floated down the road toward the village.

Ariel breezed back through the house, calling, "Sheera! Time to go cut grain."

"I'm coming!"

Ariel, dressed in an everyday tunic and sandals, with a headband around her flowing, brown tresses, snatched up a full waterskin on a cord and strode out onto the back patio just as her daughter trotted down the stairs in a rust kilt and matching midriff tie top. *She must have spent an hour on that elaborate braid and swirl thing,* Ariel thought of the styled honey hair her daughter wore.

"We're working in the field, not attending a dance," she commented.

"That's why I'm in my work clothes, Mother. Do you pay no attention to my wardrobe?" Sheera asked incredulously. To be honest, Ariel never noticed clothes—unless someone wasn't wearing any.

As they walked out the back toward the fields stretching across the valley, Ariel spotted her brother Aram with his family and her uncle Menandros with his wife and daughter. The four immigrants who lived and worked on the farmstead were just exiting their house when Ratiki scampered up onto the patio wall and made a flying leap for her shoulder. He stuck the landing only by digging his nails through her tunic into her skin.

"Ow!" Ariel yelped. "You must stop doing that," she scolded. "It hurts."

The raccoon rubbed his face against hers and tickled her with his whiskers. *I'm sorry,* he conveyed to her through the ether. *I never want to hurt Ariel. You are my human and I love you. But you should not have left me behind.*

She reached a hand to stroke his fur. *I wasn't leaving you behind. This will be a long, boring day for you, and you must stay out of the way, so you don't get hurt.* She caught his eyes in a serious exchange. *And no nibbling the grain on the sled. You may help yourself to stray kernels on the ground, and that's all.*

He nestled more snuggly around her shoulders and sniffed in her ear. *This isn't my first harvest, you know. I can behave.*

"Yes, you can," Ariel responded aloud with a smile.

"Yes, I can what? Pay attention to fashion?" Sheera laughed. "I should hope so! It's my career. Devorah—the top designer in Evamont with a chain of merchant stalls all across the city-state—loves my chitons and kilts. As soon as the harvest is over, she wants me to bring my samples for her to see. I'll be up all night tonight sewing!" She beamed with glorious glee. Just thinking about it flooded Ariel with a dismal dread.

"I'm happy for you, sweetie," she declared in all sincerity. "I'm truly glad you have found your artistic expression and can pursue it for your career."

"You love plants and animals and everything outdoors," Sheera confessed. "And I always help with the farm because I live here, but you need to start planning ahead," she said as they strolled through tall, sunny stalks with their grain heads gently dancing in the breeze. "I could be moving to Evamont soon and joining Devorah's staff."

"Then you'll be close to Mal'akhi," Ariel said. Her son was an athletic young man with noble aspirations and had joined the city guardians. Even though she knew he could handle himself, it was a dangerous job worthy of her concern. Then again, other people swore nothing was more dangerous than walking into a pride of lions and sitting down to chat with them about not eating the shepherd's sheep.

"Well, it depends on if I decide to marry Taavi or Mahmoud," Sheera considered. "Then my husband would have a say in whether we move." She shrugged.

"Hey!" Aram called and waved. "I thought you two would sleep all morning and miss getting this field cut."

"I had to see Mother off to town," Ariel replied. She loved her tall, lean, tawny brother, with his bright eyes and perpetual smile. He may not possess magical gifts or powers, but he had mastered the game of life and how to play it. The devoted family man understood the ultimate goal was simply to be happy. Of all the people she knew, Aram best mastered the art of being joyful in every activity, whether dancing at a solstice festival, chopping wood, cleaning fish, tending the fields, or changing an infant's swaddling cloths. *If you find something fun in everything you do, you'll never work a day in your life.* The principle was taught in primary schools, along with ways to do exactly that—singing, whistling, making a game of everyday chores. Some people were just better at applying it to their lives than others.

"Well, get your skinny butt over here, and let's do this thing," he grinned.

"Yeah, Aunt Ariel," agreed his youthful son Shemu'el, who resembled his father's look. "Did you remember to tell the crows to stay away?"

Hevel, her older, brawny, dark-complected nephew, flashed his brother a perturbed expression while he tossed a bushel bundle of stalks onto the sled hovering beside him. The airborne flatbed utility cart was of medium size, eight cubits long by three cubits wide, and had a low lip to keep things from sliding off the edges.

"Crows," he muttered. "Why is this family so accursedly cheerful all the time?" He took a powerful swipe at a patch of grain with a long-handled scythe. Its sharp Gadlan steel blade sliced through the stalks like butter and sent them tumbling to the ground. Ariel noticed her uncle, aunt, cousin, sister-in-law, and everyone else used laser cutters.

"Don't mind Hevel," Yaluk said in a sympathetic tone. With her olive skin, black hair, and brown eyes, it was hard for Ariel not to see Lysandra in her cousin Yaluk's features. They had all been close friends in their youth. Yaluk married Ariel's brother Aram; Lysandra was supposed to marry her. They would all live together on the farm and stay close forever.

"Don't mind Hevel," the young man grumbled. "That's the trouble with you—none of you mind Hevel. What I want counts for nothing. Stupid work! This is what we have immigrants for."

The four shorter men in white kilts standing nearby stopped and looked at Hevel with offended expressions.

"Son, you apologize," Aram commanded in a suddenly deep voice of authority. "We do not *have* immigrants. The government takes a portion of our crop for communal pantries and our tax allotments, and they pay our new friends to work here until they can become citizens. Where is this attitude coming from?"

Hevel heaved his scythe again, chopping a swathe of wheat as large as the sled.

"Honey, he's just angry and disappointed," Yaluk said, taking her son's side. "He worked so hard to get into the Central Wisdom School. This was the third year in a row he applied and got turned down. He has a bright mind and isn't happy on the farm."

"There are plenty of options besides a wisdom school," Sheera declared lightly—this from one who never wished to apply and would have run away the first chance she got.

"Sheera's right," Uncle Menandros seconded. "I went to trade school to become a goldsmith because, you know—playing with molten gold all day long. Who wouldn't like that? But after about forty years, shiny things didn't mean as much to me anymore, and I wanted to return to the fresh air of the countryside. This is where I met my second wife, Gamila here," he motioned to a woman half his age at forty-five. "We have Mara and I'm my own boss—can go fishing whenever I want. The point is, son, you'll get to do many things in your lifetime, and your interests and aspirations may change many times. Don't throw away your joy over a school. If the Universe has closed this avenue, it's only because there's a better one for you just around the bend."

"You sound like my father." Hevel scooped up an armful of wheat, wrapped a string around it, and tossed it on the sled with the others. "I wanted to go to wisdom school like Aunt Lysandra, move to Atala, and do important things."

"What could be more vital than providing food for people's tables?" Ariel asked. She passed a bundle of string to Sheera. "I'll cut and you wrap, all right?"

"That's our process," her daughter chirped.

Hevel quit complaining, and before long Aram had them all singing a cheery tune. It was a lovely fall morning, just as the air speaker promised. Ratiki didn't like Ariel twisting and swinging her arms, so he hopped down to dig about for dropped kernels, making sure not to stray too far from her feet. Gamila and Mara helped Sheera with bundling and stacking while Ariel and the men performed the heavier work. Like Oma Naunet, Ariel liked to keep her body fit and strong.

Upon completing a large section of the field, the crew took a break, and Ariel sat on the edge of a sled sipping from her water bag while Ratiki tried to unfasten her sandals. A bird passing overhead nudged her with its tidings. *Someone's coming down the road.* It flew on by and Ariel fixed a curious gaze on the road from the village. It could be her mother; Ariel thought she should have been back long ago.

Instead, a woman came into focus, sauntering the dirt path, and Ariel was seized by a feeling of familiarity—a sensation so powerful that it pulled her off the sled toward the visitor. She knew before she could even make out the woman's face. Lysandra's unmistakable aura struck Ariel with a jolt that nearly knocked her soul out of her body. *Lysandra!*

9

Ariel froze at the edge where the field met the road, her heart leaping into her throat. So many times she dreamed of this moment, though fewer as the years rolled by. *What do I say? How should I feel? Why is she here?*

Though thirty years older, Lysandra appeared even more beautiful than Ariel recalled, flawless and elegant in her flowing, mid-calf, sleeveless green and white gown tied by a simple braided cord. Unable to move or think or speak from sheer shock, Ariel's pulse raced, and she reminded herself to breathe. One thing was evident—Lysandra seemed as terrified as she was.

As she drew closer, Ratiki burst out of the tall amber waves and rushed in front of Ariel. He stopped, rose on his back legs, waved his hands at Lysandra, and sniffed the air with twitching whiskers. Ariel sent out soothing vibrations to tell him the stranger was a friend and no one to be alarmed about. *Is that what she is—a friend?* She had been ... and so much more.

By the time Lysandra reached her, Ariel's emotions twisted like a tornado, uprooting long-held assumptions, and spinning her mind in circles. She wondered if her physical form could hold it all without collapsing. Engulfed by the peculiar sensation, as if she were a fragile crystal, shattered by a powerful lightning strike, she could feel each shard raining down, scorching and cutting through the air, coming to rest on her skin. Still, she couldn't take her eyes off the woman she had loved more than life itself.

Lysandra's voice trembled as she stopped a mere half cubit away. "I'm so sorry," she whispered, her eyes brimming with regret. Ariel sensed the truth of her emotions and the conflict that raged there as well. Only a matter of vital urgency would bring her here like this.

"You're late," Ariel replied.

"You married," she rebounded with more intensity.

"Only because you left me." Ariel struggled to hold herself together. She was a grown woman, by Triton, not a love-sick schoolgirl.

"I didn't mean to." Lysandra sounded as disappointed as she had felt, and the sentiment glistened in expressive brown eyes that still mesmerized Ariel. "You knew Raphael's call was strong with me. Becoming a healer was my passion. To follow it meant I had to go away to wisdom school."

"But you were supposed to come back, Lysandra." Ariel could feel tears welling behind her eyes and permeating her voice. She would not allow them to fall. "The plan was you would come home during term break and tell me all about the wonders you learned and the marvels you experienced. Only you didn't. Did you forget about me?"

Ariel could sense her heart breaking all over again, and it took every ounce of discipline for her to maintain her composure. Ratiki must have also gleaned the intensity of the conversation, for he turned tail and lumbered back in amongst the grain stalks to escape.

"No, Ariel—never! Not a day has passed that I haven't ..." Lysandra stopped to swallow whatever pained sound was about to issue forth. Letting out a sigh, she asked, "Is there somewhere we could sit for a few minutes? I have important news, but this—what is unresolved between us—is vital too. I won't beset you with excuses, but I need to explain."

Sitting sounded good to Ariel as well. She motioned toward the square between the four houses where a bench rested near the well under an olive tree. "Over here." She led the way in silence, still in disbelief that Lysandra had finally come.

The bench wasn't very wide, so, through necessity, the two fit snuggly side by side. Fearing what might happen at this proximity, Ariel kept her gaze anywhere but on Lysandra's face. She could smell her, though—all citrusy and alluring.

"Wisdom school was nothing like the academy," she began. "We didn't follow a set schedule, and the training was intense. We went to a magnetically-aligned cave in the mountains to better connect with the energies. Quetzal taught our class how to transcend the limits of the third dimension, to open and raise harmonic frequencies. I learned to use Prana to access electrical energy in my and other people's bodies, to sense a patient's vibrations, to connect to the waves and particles in their flesh, bones, and blood, to align every aspect of their organs and systems with the one perfect health. But there was so much more, Ariel. I traveled outside myself to dance with the energies in the heavens. I could feel everything, everyone, the all of creation, experiencing the power of the Law of One. It was easy to forget who I was in the magnitude of it all, and I lost all track of time. It was like time didn't exist."

Lysandra peered around, trying to coax Ariel into looking at her. Giving in, Ariel met her gaze as her long-lost lover's hand came to rest over hers atop her thigh. It all sounded marvelously impressive, certainly more exciting than life on a farm.

"But I never forgot you, and I never stopped loving you," Lysandra professed. "If anything, learning to expand my heart doubled, even tripled what was already there, and I couldn't wait to share everything with you—to take you star-walking with me. But by the time I could return to Elyrna, you had already gotten married, had a child, and were pregnant with another."

"Lysandra, I waited four years," Ariel lamented. Reliving her heartache was like yanking her soul through a jagged sieve. "I thought, 'Maybe she doesn't get time off like at the academy,' but the courses were only supposed to last four years. Planting and harvest came and went with no word from you. When you didn't return at the end of the fourth year, what was I supposed to think? I figured you found a new life in Atala and didn't want to come back ... that you didn't want me anymore. So, yeah, I got married and had children because it's what people in their twenties do."

"I know," Lysandra agonized. "It took longer. Quetzal blamed some alignment of the stars for affecting the energies and it took us longer. I tried to connect with you through the ether, the way Atlanteans of old did, but I never received a return message." She sighed. "It was a long shot. I'm not a telepath. But Ariel." She brushed her thumb across Ariel's hand, glancing down at it and then back into her face. "Are you and he happy together?"

"We were for a while, I guess," Ariel confessed. "But he's dead now."

"Oh, Ariel!" Lysandra drew back in surprised grief. "I'm so sorry. I didn't know."

"Of course you didn't." Ariel let out a humorless laugh. "You don't even visit your own cousin. Yaluk decided you forgot her too." Upon seeing Lysandra's tears form, Ariel reached over and touched her arm. "Don't worry about it. It was ten years ago, so I'm done mourning the loss. Life goes on."

"What happened?"

Ariel lifted her gaze westward to the long ridge of blue-green mountains with their rocky peaks rising into clouds. "He ventured into the mountains alone on a vision quest, the way people do. He was supposed to be gone only three days, so he didn't carry provisions. But something must have happened—a puma, a bear, a fall into a crevice, a rockslide." Shifting her gaze from the ancient, majestic ridge, Ariel shook her head. "When he hadn't returned after five days, we sent for the Evamont Guardians, and they climbed the mountains searching for him. I dispatched hawks and eagles with whom I was friendly, and even their sharp eyes discovered no trace of the fate that befell him. Mal'akhi was young and impressionable and became infatuated with the guardians, revering them as tragic heroes who tried desperately to rescue his father. I suppose that's part of what led him to join their ranks. Sheera, my daughter, who was younger, was more devastated than I was, but she got through it. She's at the age now when finding her own husband is more important than air."

"And I wasn't here for you." Bitter regret permeated Lysandra's words.

"No, you weren't. Yaluk was, though. Our friendship has endured your absence." Ariel lifted Lysandra's chin with tender fingertips to meet her gaze. "Why didn't you ever come back?"

"I was afraid." Lysandra shook her chin loose and mopped at her eyes, unable to look at Ariel. "When I realized how long I'd been gone, what you must have thought and gone through, I was afraid to face you. I knew you had moved on, but I hadn't. And the longer I procrastinated, the harder it became, until the thought of seeing your pain and disappointment was overwhelming. I turned my focus to other things, to my work, my art, and my spiritual growth. I'd talk to you every day in my mind, remembering us the way we were before. Quetzal said I should come visit, but whenever I thought about boarding an air coach, this terror would rise up inside and it was just too hard. I know I broke your heart, but I broke mine too." Lysandra's voice wavered, and she looked away, wiping at a tear.

Ariel perceived the heavy truth of her confession. "But surely you haven't been alone all this time," she offered. "You've had other lovers, someone special to share your life with."

Lowering her face, Lysandra shook her head. "There was never anyone for me but you. I know I'm at fault, but my heart won't let go. All I can do is beg your forgiveness."

"Ah, sweetie." Ariel reached her arms around Lysandra and pulled her close, touched by her profound emotion and devotion. Ariel felt the gentle brush of her hair against her cheek, the warmth of her body, and the familiar vibrations resonating in her chest, which unleashed a powerful surge of love she had kept locked within all this time.

"I forgave you many, many years ago," Ariel professed. "Everyone understands that unforgiveness blocks the flow of the energies more stringently than any other frequency. I would have lost all my abilities, including any opportunity for happiness, if I did not forgive you with my total soul. I grieved so much more over losing you than I did when my husband of fifteen years went missing, which caused me to question what was wrong with me. But I let go of any blame, refused to allow bitterness a root, and declared it was just one of those things. I learned to be grateful to have had you in my life for a season and came to peace with the idea I'd never see you again."

Releasing her embrace, Ariel sat back and brushed a tear from Lysandra's cheek with her thumb. It felt so wonderful to touch her again, to bask in the aura of this amazing woman so pulsing with power and life-force energy with whom she had so many shared memories of love, laughter, and ecstasy. In this moment, she felt as if a missing piece of her spirit had returned, rendering her whole once more. But it was a piece she couldn't afford to plug back in place and then lose again.

As Lysandra trembled under her touch, struggling to form a response, Ariel asked the next logical question. "Why are you here now?"

Lysandra straightened, sucking in a rough breath, and faced her. Ariel waited patiently while she sniffed and steadied herself. Meeting her gaze, Lysandra exhaled, "Thank you. I should have known—and did—only fear got in the way. You are as lovely and amazing as you always were. Quetzal was right; you are the one Uriel has chosen."

Apprehension washed through Ariel as she recalled her concerns about the energies and the faint murmur of an angel's voice. "What do you mean?"

Lysandra's tears dried up as she shifted frequencies. "Have you noticed a disturbance in the ether? Maybe the animals are uneasy? Does the whisper on the breeze feel more like a lament than a song? Have you perceived a call, perhaps in a dream?"

Recognition quickened in Ariel. "It isn't just me."

"No," Lysandra confirmed, taking her hands. "It's everywhere."

10

"There you are!" declared Sheera as she marched up to where Ariel sat with Lysandra under the olive tree. With sweat pouring from her brow, she slapped a hand to her hip in annoyance. "We've started back to work." Though appearing impatient, Sheera spared a curious glance at Lysandra.

"This is your aunt's cousin Lysandra," Ariel introduced. "My daughter, Sheera."

While Lysandra cast a hopeful expression toward the young woman, Sheera's eyes narrowed, and she pursed her lips. "So, the mysterious Lysandra who abandoned her family has deigned to return after all this time." She crossed her arms over her chest and glared at her.

"Sheera," Ariel scolded. "Conduct yourself with respect and hospitality before our guest."

"You aren't the one who has to listen to Hevel moan and complain about being rejected for wisdom school," she retorted. "Though why he'd idealize an aunt he never met or wish to emulate her is beyond my comprehension."

"It isn't your place to judge," Ariel stated emphatically and fixed her with an authoritative stare. "Lysandra has brought me urgent news that we need to discuss with Oma." Taking Lysandra's elbow, Ariel stood, bringing her friend with her.

Sheera dropped her closed posture and assumed one of disbelieving dismay, waving a hand at Ariel. "This morning, you insisted that harvesting our entire crop today was more urgent than the tides! Now this virtual stranger shows up and you're all, 'Oh, I have to talk with her instead.'"

With forceful intent, Ariel issued her daughter a command. "Go back and help the others. Tell Uncle Aram something critical came up, and I'll be back as soon as possible. I am very disappointed with your poor attitude, but we'll discuss it later."

With a veil of embarrassment slowly forming over her features, Sheera nodded and turned to obey. She still had to throw another comment over her shoulder. "I'm telling Aunt Yaluk the mythical Lysandra has appeared at last."

"I'm sorry about that," Ariel told Lysandra with an exasperated sigh.

"Don't be. I deserve far worse than a little scorn from a young woman who lost her father and has to play comforter to my nephew," Lysandra responded. "She's right. I haven't met Hevel or Shemu'el, and Yaluk may have no desire to see me. I can't blame her, though it saddens me to learn my nephew has been turned down for wisdom school. They have stringent requirements for admission, but it's for a reason."

"I know." Ariel steered her toward her house. "Let's find Oma. I've already discussed the weakening of the energies with her, and I hope you bring new information to add."

They found Naunet sitting in the short grass on the little hill behind the farmstead, where Ariel often went for her morning meditations.

"What are you doing, Oma?" Ariel asked as they approached.

"Soaking up the sun, little one," she replied with radiance beaming from her wrinkled face. "Listening to the breeze. Remembering the time when I could commune with the animals. Lysandra, how nice to see you again."

Ariel smirked at Oma's dancing eyes and intuitive smile, hinting she held every secret in the world and enjoyed watching others guess at them.

"I am most blessed to see you again, Oma Naunet," Lysandra answered in respectful humility. She followed Ariel in sitting on the small mound beside the wise sage.

"I can see you are both troubled by more than your time apart—which hopefully has finally ended, for both your sakes," Oma said. "Now tell me, child. Why has Quetzal sent you?"

Lysandra seemed amazed, but Oma's awareness of the situation didn't surprise Ariel at all.

"Do you know Quetzal?" Lysandra asked in astonishment.

Oma shrugged. "When you've been around for over three hundred years, you find out who all the important players are. I suspect your wisdom master sent you, or you would not have come."

"You are truly wise, Naunet, just as I remember." The breeze caught Lysandra's loose strand that had escaped her long braid. Instinctively, Ariel reached over to smooth it back in place, only just stopping herself before doing so. She let her hand fall to the ground between them instead.

"Thoth, the chief librarian of Atala—"

"Yes, yes," Oma waved impatiently. "The keeper of the Emerald Tablets—we know who he is. Get on with it. When is the world going to end?"

Lysandra's mouth fell open and her eyes grew wide with dread. "No one mentioned the end of the world," she eked out.

"Oma, quit scaring Lysandra," Ariel chided. Then she turned back to Lysandra. "What did Thoth say?"

"Quetzal and I have both observed a slow, steady weakening of the energies we depend on for everything," she reported. "People are losing the ability to self-heal, and my practice is overrun by patients. And they are aging at an accelerated rate. Quetzal said his students lack natural abilities, and it is even difficult for him to commune with the spirit world. After searching the esoteric and historic texts, he could find no precedent for comparison. So, Thoth retreated into deep meditation and returned with a message and a list of names. He claimed Archangel Uriel, the principality of knowledge and wisdom, instructed him to call a meeting at the next full moon of nine individuals from across Atlantis."

Lysandra flicked Ariel a nervous glance and bit her lower lip. "It may sound crazy, but, Ariel, you and I are on the list." Ariel let out a heavy sigh.

"Ariel, why didn't you tell me you heard a call the other day?" Oma insisted in annoyance. "And after I shared with you all that Noah's great-great-great-grandfather had told us."

"Noah, the shipbuilder?" Lysandra questioned.

"Yes, yes, that Noah," Oma replied.

"His name is on the list too."

"I'm sorry, Oma," Ariel said. "I thought it was my imagination. Why would an angel call me? I don't have special knowledge. I haven't been to wisdom school and learned to be one with the cosmos. I'm just a farmer."

"Just a farmer, she says!" Oma groaned, throwing her hands in the air and shaking her head. "You are a powerful nature speaker, girl. The Creator is mother and father to all the earth, not only its people. If there is to be another great calamity, do you not think the Source of all love and compassion would wish to warn the beloved creatures, to save them as well, if possible? The Great Conflagration came upon our world suddenly, unexpectedly, and we all know how that turned out. Lysandra, is Ziusudra the astronomer on your list?"

"Yes," she replied in wonder.

Oma assumed a studious expression as she stared at a spot on the ground. "If there is a sign in the heavens, he would be the one to interpret it. And Noah, why of course Uriel would send for him. If we had been prepared thirteen hundred years ago, we could have saved so many more by getting them away on ships."

"But there was no warning before the Conflagration," Ariel pointed out. "Why warn us of impending danger now and not then? And there is no record of weakening abilities or waning energies before that disaster like what is happening now. In fact, you said people had more special powers in the Second Age."

"That part is still a mystery," Oma admitted. She shifted her gaze from one woman to the other, then aimed a bony finger at each. "You two must attend this meeting. It could be you each possess a piece of the puzzle, and only by putting your minds together will the truth come out."

"Less than two weeks," Ariel said. "At the Ring of Stones to the south of here, or—"

"Yes, that one," Lysandra confirmed. "It must be most centrally located or was chosen for another reason."

"It will only take a few hours from here by sleigh," Ariel considered. "I should travel the night before, so I may meditate and align my energies perfectly before the council convenes. It also gives me time to finish helping our neighbors with their grain harvests." She looked at her great-great-great-grandmother with compassion. "I'm sorry you lost your ability as a nature speaker, Oma. It must have left you feeling so empty."

"You have a kind heart, Ariel." The old woman patted her knee. "It happened long ago. Now I focus my attention on things I can still do, like enjoying playing with my family." Her warm smile touched Ariel's heart.

"Thank you, Oma. You're the best." Ariel leaned in and kissed her cheek, still troubled by evidence that might point to another looming cataclysm.

"You two need to go catch up and make plans for your meeting," Oma said as she pushed to her feet far more easily than Ariel could comprehend for a woman of her advanced age. "I'll go be ready to help your mother unload the sleigh when she returns from town."

II

Lysandra's nerves had at last calmed. All the worst scenarios her mind had conjured had now been put to rest. Ariel had forgiven her, and she was no longer married, yet there could be another someone special in her life. Despite everything wrong with the world, Lysandra breathed easier, knowing she was forgiven. However, that one detail didn't mean their relationship would pick up where it had left off—if it would at all. Lysandra realized she had messed everything up and, if they were to have a second chance, it would be up to her to make it right.

When she looked at Ariel, she still saw an abundantly free spirit, a remarkable talent, and long, toned legs that begged her to stroke them. She also saw a woman who had raised two children and experienced their whole lives in her self-inflicted absence. Did she still play the flute? Did she still dance at the festivals?

The sound of a distant trumpet pricked her ears, evoking a sense of wonder and a tingle of excitement. "Is that Adira?" She scrambled to her feet and glanced around. "Oh, Ariel! Take me to see the elephants!"

Suddenly, living in a crowded stone city far from the fertile plains with their magical beauty and abundant wildlife seemed foolish and absurd. Why did she ever wish to leave the home of her childhood? Having a nature speaker as a best friend was like being privy to another world. Ariel's talent emerged when they were in primary school, and she required very little guidance from the teachers to develop it to its fullest extent. Lysandra remembered how their peers had thought Ariel was odd because she would answer aloud when a bird or squirrel conveyed some emotion or idea to her.

She would never forget the day Ariel truly came into her power. A group of shepherds whose herds grazed near Elyrna became angry because a wild animal had attacked their goats, killing a nanny and two does. They armed themselves and set out to find and destroy the offending predators when a skinny, leggy twelve-year-old Ariel blocked their path. "What are you doing?" she demanded.

"Going to kill the beast that attacked our goats," the biggest man answered.

"Was it a wolf, jackal, lion, or bear? How will you determine the guilty party and be sure you have punished the right one?" They looked at her like she was crazy. "I will ask around to discover who killed your goats and why," she declared as if she were queen of the forest. "If the perpetrator has gone mad and cannot think reasonably, I will bring you its tail. But if there was another cause for its action, I will solve the problem and ensure the animal will not bother your herds again."

They had laughed at her, but Lysandra took her side and convinced them to let her try. They laid wagers on whether she would return alive. Lysandra, two years older, and taller than Ariel back then, went along to watch out for her friend—as if she could defend her from a tremendous brown bear. Ariel was never afraid. She began her investigation by asking the shade tree closest to where the attack occurred who did it. The tree told her it was a couple of juvenile wolves from up the mountain somewhere. Ariel tracked the culprits, asking of every animal she came upon until she found the two black wolves, whom she invited to sit down with her and explain themselves. They informed her that their parents had died months ago after the family had been dispelled from their pack over a leadership disagreement. That left them as immature pups with no adult to teach them to hunt. They set out to find the easiest prey so they wouldn't starve to death.

Then Ariel found a wolf pack willing to take the juveniles into their group and warned them that the shepherds were ready to kill any wolf taking a lamb or kid. The alpha male and female of the pack promised to keep the youngsters away from domestic herds. Ariel had stroked their heads, conveying love and appreciation to them, while Lysandra watched from a safe distance. It was the most remarkable thing she had ever witnessed. Lysandra fell in love with the young nature speaker that day and never desired to be with another, even though it meant waiting for Ariel to get older.

Ariel's serious expression mellowed, and a slow smile crept across her lips. "You always loved the elephants—especially Adira. I wouldn't be surprised if that was her calling for you. They have a marvelous sense of smell, you know."

Lysandra's heart flooded. "I know they are compassionate souls and so sweet and affectionate."

Ariel stood to join her. "Adira's the matriarch of her herd now. She'll be so happy to see you."

Walking across the meadow with Ariel made Lysandra feel like she was twenty again. Deer and bison grazed in the tall grass, undisturbed by their presence. A small herd of wild horses galloped by in the direction of a stream that Lysandra remembered being nearby. They had spent many an afternoon after school at that stream catching crawfish. Ariel was determined to communicate with them until one day she determined they just didn't have enough consciousness to connect with. Because of the years spent with Ariel and seeing the world from her unique perspective, Lysandra was still a semi-vegetarian. She wouldn't eat any meat from an animal with consciousness. Ariel had told her that ordinary fish and crustaceans had no self-awareness and she had never reached one's thoughts—if they even had thoughts. She assured Lysandra that chickens didn't mind people eating their eggs if they left them some to raise, and the goats and cows actually appreciated being milked. But knowing higher animals had feelings, Lysandra couldn't eat them—even if The Law didn't prohibit it.

As they neared the herd, a large female bounded toward them with her mighty, flapping ears perked and her trunk waving. A dozen others, most of whom were smaller, followed with curious expressions. Several were babies, filling Lysandra's soul with delight at their cuteness.

The big matriarch slowed to a lumbering walk only a few steps before crashing into the women. Towering over them, she lowered her head and explored Lysandra with her sensitive trunk. Even the healer, inexperienced in communicating with animals, could read the joyous expression Adira showed her.

"Adira says she is so glad to see you again," Ariel translated, "and what took you so long?"

"She remembers me!" Lysandra peered up at her amazing old friend and stroked the leathery skin of her trunk. The elephant's eyes danced with a glossy sheen as they gazed at her affectionately. "Adira, I'm sorry I've been gone for so long. I really missed you."

Standing at her side, Ariel pressed a hand to Adira's ribs behind her tall front legs, near where her heart beat its slow, powerful rhythm, and closed her eyes. Lysandra was torn between watching Ariel work her magic and gazing at Adira, recommitting her every nuance to memory.

"Of course she remembers you," Ariel responded. "Elephants are like people; they don't forget their friends."

"I painted a picture of you," Lysandra said as she petted and stroked Adira, reveling in the touch of her trunk and ears as she bestowed elephant hugs to her. A creature so huge and yet so gentle and loving still stirred a sense of awe in Lysandra. She felt the positive energy flowing between Adira and herself, the connection of oneness, that they both held the same life force and were sisters in this world—possibly the next.

"She says she missed you, that you are one of her favorite people, and she wants you to meet her family," Ariel said.

"I would love to meet your family," Lysandra answered with a broad smile.

Adira slid her trunk away from Lysandra's shoulder, took a step back, and made a deep, faint, rumbling sound. She flapped her ears and swung her trunk toward two females on her right. One of them stepped forward and extended her trunk. Lysandra held out an open palm for the new elephant to smell and touch her as she wished.

"These are her two sisters," Ariel introduced. "The brave one is Dalila and the shy one is Shesa." Shesa swished her tail and bobbed her head back and forth from a few cubits away while Dalila advanced a step to further greet Lysandra.

"I am so pleased to meet you both," Lysandra said, trusting Ariel would convey her meaning to the elephants.

Adira curled her trunk, opened her mouth, and turned toward a gathering of half a dozen or more smaller pachyderms. "Those over there," Ariel said, drawing Lysandra's gaze away from Dalila's attention, "are her children and grandchildren. I won't name them all at once, but she is very proud of her fine family."

"They are all splendid!" Lysandra praised. "And the little ones are so cute!"

While the adult females took their turns to greet Lysandra with curious looks and exploring trunks, two babies romped and played, clambering over a three- or four-year-old child who lay on the ground happily serving as their climbing mound. They snorted and squealed as they showed off their playful behavior.

"Dalila says that one," Ariel pointed, "the little boy is her baby. The older child and the other baby are Adira's grandchildren. That pesty one," she pointed to a standoffish male with his trunk around a sapling, tugging to rip it from the soil, "is Barak, Adira's youngest son. He's fourteen and soon will be kicked out of the herd to go join the bachelor group. Why is it that, regardless of the species, it's always the young males who cause the trouble?" she laughed.

"It's the male hormone their bodies produce," Lysandra answered in a medically professional tone. "Their youthful bodies can easily become overloaded with their new sex drive, which they haven't learned to control. This causes them to act out in undesirable or even aggressive ways."

Noticing the amused expression on Ariel's face, she added with a hint of embarrassment, "Which you already knew. It was a rhetorical question."

Ariel stepped around Adira to brush shoulders with Lysandra. "You carry around so much knowledge," she said in a tone of amusement tempered with admiration. "Some of it is bound to spill out."

They stayed with the elephants, laughing at the children at play and tactilely delighting in each other's touch for a while. Then Ariel checked the position of the sun. "I'd better go back and help with cutting sheaves before everyone is so upset with me they won't be able to sleep tonight. Goodbye, dear friends." She patted Adira's face and breathed into her trunk.

"I can help," Lysandra volunteered.

Ariel started for the farmhouses and field in the distance, and Lysandra fell in beside her. "You need to prepare a proper apology for your cousin Yaluk," Ariel dictated. She was right.

Visiting Adira and her family had launched Lysandra into a high vibration, but facing the stark consequences of her actions and inactions from years gone by gave her a sinking feeling. And then there was Ariel. *How can I convince her to give us another try? And would it even work? I can't leave Atala now, not until we solve the problem of what's causing people to grow sick and old. And she won't leave this paradise to live in a tiny city apartment. What would she do? Pull weeds and encourage flowers to grow? Somehow reason with rats and convince them to vacate the docks? Oh, Archangel Jegudiel, bestower of love and mercy, what am I to do? My arms ache to hold her, to regain the passion of our youth. The greatest desire of my heart is to be with Ariel.*

Ariel walked beside her in silence as Lysandra's inner battle raged. Whenever she decided to abandon her physician's station and move back here to live with Ariel, the powerful spirit of Raphael gave her heart a hard yank. *You would never be content to waste your gift here as a farmer. Would you limit your healing to cattle while your human brothers and sisters perish?* She didn't have any answers, only an overwhelming hunger to reunite with the woman she never stopped dreaming of.

When they reached the back patio of Ariel's house, they stopped, and Ariel pivoted to face Lysandra. "Upstairs, the second room on the right used to be Mal'akhi's. We use it as a guest room now and you are welcome to stay, have dinner with us, and spend the night. It will be a long trip back to Atala and you should stay—at least for tonight."

"What about your room?" Lysandra dared to ask. She would gladly humiliate herself if it meant having Ariel in her arms again, giving herself over to her, sparking pleasures in her as potently as she once had. Fixing her gaze on the most spectacular sea-green eyes the Creator ever fashioned, she lifted a hand to caress Ariel's face.

"You left me." Her voice dripped with a terrible sense of loss.

"I'm here now." Lysandra held her breath.

Ariel leaned her forehead to touch hers and laid her hands gently on her shoulders, pulsing them in tender touches. Her lips were so close, just a few thumbs away from hers. A quickening crackled through her veins and hope clamored to reach the surface.

"And after tonight?"

Lysandra released her breath. She didn't have a satisfactory answer.

"Lysandra, my love, I can't. I can't lose you again. If I go back with you, if I go forward with you, it has to be forever. Words cannot express how losing you made me feel, and I cannot—will not—go through it again. I understand the forces that keep us apart." Ariel's warm, moist lips touched her face like the brush of butterfly wings before she drew back to catch Lysandra's gaze. She trailed her fingertips from Ariel's cheek, the bud of hope falling into a deep ravine.

"I'll work with you," Ariel continued, "and the others to find the answers we need to unblock the flow of energies, to put everything right with the world again. But my feelings for you are too all-consuming to turn on and off like a light panel. I can't be with you if I can't be *with* you."

Lysandra licked her lips, which had gone dry, and nodded. "I know. I just want you in my life again. By the sun, moon, and stars, I'm still in love with you, Ariel. I must believe that somehow, somewhere, sometime, there's a solution for us too."

12

Ryzen, one week later

Temen, dressed in his best white tunic, with a crimson stole and a wide belt embroidered with an array of the most important symbols, sat beside Lykos in a position of honor near the front of the Ryzen Temple's assembly hall. The chamber, with its lofty rafters and ornate works of art, echoed with excited chatter from the crowd. The nine jurors—six men and three women—sat on the platform arranged to either side of the queen's seat, waiting for her entrance. Temen's speech, along with the general disapproval that had arisen organically from the populace, created enough of a clamor that the jurors called for a vote of no confidence. If six of the nine agree in this formal vote, all citizens present would be asked to cast their ballots to keep Queen Izevel or elect another nominee. Therefore, the massive complex overflowed its capacity as thousands had turned out. Lykos had assured Temen he would win.

Despite the wizard's promise, nerves twisted and churned in Temen's stomach. He smoothed a hand through his golden-brown locks, noticing his sapphire Poseidon ring. Temen didn't wear much jewelry because he didn't want to appear pretentious or grander than the common residents he sought to impress. He was one of them, only with more insightful ideas and charm. Yet he liked this ring and would often study the intricate engraving work and smooth, oval stone, admiring the craftsmanship that went into its creation. Atlanteans were known around the world not only for their advanced technology and "magical" powers but for their culture of creativity, their music and artistry, and the beauty they insisted upon in even the simplest household items.

It seemed like every man, woman, and child in the nation engaged in some sort of creative activity through which divine energy flowed—everyone except Temen. He had tried to take up woodworking as a child but was displeased with the imperfections of his carvings. Then, as a young adult, he'd attempted to learn to play the lyre, only he accidentally broke its strings and never picked it up again. Temen decided his expression of the divine creative spirit manifested through his talent for holding people's attention and attracting their favor. Since moving to Ryzen, he had accumulated more friends than most men did acquaintances in three hundred years. Society may not count it as art, but Temen took pride in his ability all the same.

"Here she comes," Lykos said with eagerness resonating in his voice. When the wizard's hand touched his shoulder, Temen's nerves settled to the smooth surface of a still lake, the fingers of anxiety evaporating one by one. In their place stood a stone wall of assurance, a bulwark of confidence.

The atmosphere shifted as Queen Izevel and her two male attendants entered, prompting everyone seated to rise in respect. The bulk of the crowd was already standing, but all hushed until one could hear the footsteps of a mouse, were it bold enough to enter the temple.

Temen had to admit she appeared regal in her purple gown highlighted in gold. She moved with an innate elegance that couldn't be taught, her chin held high, shoulders squared, and frosted blonde hair arranged in a twist atop her head, pinned into place with silver and emerald trinity rings. She looked exceptional for a middle-aged woman of a hundred and thirty-two.

Her younger, brawny attendants marched before her in white kilts and orichalcum regalia carrying a copy of The Law and a cubit-high, solid gold ankh. Each wore a black and white pleated head covering that fell to their bare shoulders. They silently took positions to the left and right of the ruler's crimson and gold seat of power, standing at attention while presenting their symbols of authority. When the queen lowered herself onto her throne, the jurors, ministers, and dignitaries also sat, leaving the rest of the crowded assembly to stand in their spots.

The eldest member of the jury moved to the edge of the platform where he could half face the audience and the officials on the dais. "Ladies and gentlemen, we gather for a most serious duty. Before we proceed, allow me to remind this gathering of the merits Queen Izevel has earned. Her bloodline can be traced back twenty generations to long before the Conflagration. In her family, six have served as kings or queens of Ryzen, three as rulers of Mestoria, and her ancestor Enesh was elected chief of the Council of Rulers who established the Third Age and began the rebuilding process after the great and terrible disaster. Izevel has herself made her mark as a civic leader by serving in various ministry departments, including finance, agriculture, and infrastructure, before being named Minister of Trade by her predecessor. She was duly elected and has maintained a spotless record of integrity as queen of Ryzen for the past twelve years. During such time, our city-state has remained at peace with our neighbors and trading partners abroad, has seen an increase in our citrus output, and has negotiated a favorable trade agreement with Kemet for the new textile resource, cotton. I will now turn over these proceedings to the minister of elections."

A man who appeared to be twice the queen's age pushed himself up and shuffled to the front. "May we hear a reading of the people's complaints?" His voice possessed more vigor than Temen had expected. Taking her cue, Rhoxane—whose provocative company Temen had very much been enjoying over the past week—climbed the stairs and read from a scroll. He tingled all over at the sound of her melodious voice striking blows against the queen. The list was quite extensive, tempting Temen's thoughts to wander into remembrances of gliding his hands, lips, and tongue over Rhoxane's fragrant skin, and the electric thrill of her touch on his. But this wasn't the time to get distracted by a female's attributes. He had to focus on winning the election.

Rhoxane concluded with the most heated issue—the influx of immigrants coupled with the surge of illnesses throughout the city-state's population. Then she gracefully descended the steps and took her seat on the other side of Lykos.

The minister of elections retook the stage. "You have all heard the queen's qualifications and the complaints against her. All who cast a vote of no confidence in her continued leadership raise your hands."

Despite murmurs and waving from the crowd, only the jurors' votes counted in this round. Temen saw seven raised hands—one more than was required to continue. His blood raced with excitement and his ego swelled. *I'm going to be king!* He bubbled inwardly like a child while maintaining an appearance of dignity.

"Seven," the minister pronounced. "The motion carries." Fully facing the assembly, he called in a robust voice, "Do I hear nominations for a replacement?"

A woman raised her hand and was recognized. "I nominate Trade Minister Dareios," she announced loudly, so all could hear. A few heads nodded, followed by hushed affirmations as members of the electorate quietly discussed him.

Then Lykos rose, his respected eminence recognized by all present. The hall fell quiet as he asserted, "I nominate the philosopher Temen to be our next king."

Hiding his pride, Temen ran a hand down his smooth face to his firm chin with a studious expression, as if he hadn't a clue he would be nominated. Nodding heads, smiles, and louder chatter swept through the hall in a wave of approval.

A juror who had voted to keep the queen leaped up and declared, "I propose we keep Queen Izevel. People always complain, but she has been an effective administrator and is open to considering your proposals."

Lykos glanced around, wiggling his serpent head staff as he moved in his seat. Soon boos erupted and citizens began shouting in angry tones.

"Order!" demanded the minister of elections. He stomped his foot. "We will have order!"

Lykos returned his innocent gaze to the platform, and the crowd quieted.

"We have three nominees for ruler of Ryzen," he proclaimed. "The current queen, Trade Minister Dareios, and Temen. Do these three consent to having their names placed on the ballots?"

"Aye," answered Temen and Dareios in unison. The queen nodded her head in a regal fashion.

"Very well. Return one week from today when ballots will be ready for you to mark the leader of your choice. As always, elections will be monitored to prevent extra votes from being cast. The doors will be open from sunup to sunset, after which the voting will be ended. Your nine duly-elected jurors will then count the votes together and announce the winner the next day. Transfer of power will take place at the observance of next month's full moon to give everyone time to prepare. Consider your votes carefully," he admonished. "This is a responsibility not to be taken lightly. This assembly is officially dismissed."

The hall erupted in conversations. Some attendees tried to wiggle through to leave while others were content to remain in place and discuss the candidates. Temen stood and Lykos shook his hand with a sly smile, starting a line of hundreds who passed by to shake the candidate's hand. Rhoxane slid in beside him, bolstering his mood even higher. Her whisper in his ear sent a tingle through his system to rival the one he experienced at the thought of becoming king.

"I'll use my influence to sway voters your way." She trailed delicate fingers across his shoulders and slipped into the mass of citizens.

Temen demonstrated his dedication to the residents of Ryzen by addressing each by name as he shook their hands, promising to meet their needs and fulfill their visions of government. Of course, he couldn't keep every promise; to believe it so was absurd. Still, it instilled a sense of security in the voter's minds, the illusion of Temen's concern for their welfare. Well, to be honest, he did want the people to be safe, prosperous, and happy. It was the best assurance he would remain king for decades rather than be tossed out after allowing the city-state to fall into ruin.

He truly had the people's best interests at heart, Temen told himself. How much work could be involved in being king, anyway? People would serve him his meals, provide entertainment, and he'd get to live in the royal palace—the second grandest in all of Atlantis. Most of the actual work would be done by the department ministers and the jurors. He would only have to make a few decisions, and he'd have Lykos to help with the heavy thinking.

With his spirit so light he could barely sense the floor under his feet, Temen smiled and greeted his voters while visions of power and luxury burst to life in his imagination. *And Rhoxane,* he mused as he considered the glamorous heiress half his age. *She could be an asset as a wife—if I want another one. Maybe an unencumbered bachelor's life would be preferable. Then I could enjoy many women ... and maybe the occasional man. I'll have to ask Lykos what he thinks.*

☥ ⚛ ✟ ✡

Hours later, Temen was finally able to exit the temple. If Lykos hadn't administered a dose of energy halfway through the ordeal, he might not have made it to the end. Still, he was extremely pleased with his reception and the number of voters who seemed to favor him over the queen and bald, old Dareios.

The sun hung low in the sky when he and Lykos descended the steps outside Ryzen Temple to the street. He hadn't seen Rhoxane for quite some time, but she was supposed to meet him for dinner. Waiting at the bottom of the steps was a trade delegation from Kaptara, a developing island nation in the Green Sea north of Kemet. He recognized them by their differing clothing and hairstyles.

"My lord," greeted a man who appeared to have seen fewer than forty winters. He bowed deeply, holding some sort of white linen wrap over his forearm, and his brown beard, trained to a point, looked strange to Temen. Though shorter than most Atlanteans, he was the tallest of his group.

"Allow me introduce," he said in broken Protelex, the common tongue of Atlantis. The man warranted his attention, though, as few foreigners bothered to learn their language, depending on translators instead.

"My name Hippolytos, from Kaptara. We see you maybe new king. Want to be good friends."

Hippolytos motioned to one of the others, who stepped forward with a bow to present Temen with a smooth wooden box. Whether from suspicion or just to act as a go-between, Lykos reached out, took the box, and opened it. Deciding it was safe, he passed it to Temen.

Temen peered inside to see the wool-lined box was filled to the brim with perfect white pearls. Hippolytos displayed a nervous, toothy smile while he waited for Temen's reaction.

He nodded, closed the box, and handed it back to Lykos. "Beautiful pearls, a very worthy gift indeed." He stepped among the Kaptarans and laid a friendly hand on Hippolytos's shoulder. "When I am king, we will negotiate only the best trade agreements between your kingdom and ours. Perhaps one day I'll visit your fair island and, when I do, I'll come to your house for dinner."

Hippolytos broke out in a wide, relieved grin as if he had just won a mountain of orichalcum. Temen fed off the men's admiration, pleased with their gift, and imagined many more to follow. He decided he would indeed enjoy being king.

13

Ryzen, the morning before the full moon

"Do you two wish to come along or not?" called Mandisa to her husbands, who trudged behind her with a trunk and two large bags.

"Well, if you didn't insist on packing so much, we wouldn't be falling behind," grumbled Agathon, the older of her two husbands. He was a scholar who had become discouraged by his teaching career at one of Ryzen's secondary academies and was on sabbatical, devoting all his energy to their citrus orchard. Though he lacked Hashur's brawny build, he sported the wild blue eyes, scruffy walnut beard, and flowing dark hair of a poet. His bronze coloring made a fitting mid-tone between Hashur's light complexion and Mandisa's deep brown.

"Why are you complaining?" Hashur asked as he balanced the trunk on one shoulder and hoisted a full travel bag with his other arm. "You only have one bag to carry."

"But it's heavy," he replied in irritation. "What'd you pack, stone tablets?"

"Don't be silly," Mandisa chided, with a glance over her shoulder. Her braids bounced merrily while her hips swung to the rhythm in her head. "Just a few comfort necessities. You two might be perfectly content to sleep on the ground beside the Ring of Stones, but I'll be on a cot in my tent with pillows and a soft blanket."

"Can't you just tell the ground and air to stay warm and dry so there's no need for all this luggage?" Agathon asked at the risk of sounding repetitive.

Mandisa flashed him a winning smile. "I predict two men will be very glad for the privacy of the tent after experiencing the full moon's energy in an open field."

Hashur and Agathon grinned at each other with a chuckle as they snaked their way through the busiest time of the morning. They passed massive columned edifices, quaint townhouse villas, and every imaginable structure in between. Mandisa slowed as they passed the market, her gaze roving over all the lovely merchandise.

"I thought we were in a hurry," Hashur said as he walked past her toward the city's northern gate. Agathon made use of the break to rest his bag on the pavement.

"We are," Mandisa mused. "But our air coach doesn't leave for another two turns of the sandglass."

"Two hours!" Hashur halted and turned a baffled expression toward her, easing the bulky trunk to the ground. "But you said—"

"Yes, yes, I know what I said," Mandisa answered impatiently. "I want the best seat, one by an eastern-facing window, and I wanted time to browse on the way. Why are you complaining? Whether we left when we did or an hour from now, the walk to the air dock is the same distance."

Mandisa admired a colorfully patterned bolt of linen, rubbing the fabric between her fingers. Then she brushed them to the pale blue of the chiton she'd just made from the new cotton. She had traded two bushels of oranges to a seamstress in her neighborhood who put out quality work. It was a fair trade, as it only took the woman one day to complete the dress. A smile lit her face as she delighted in the feel of her garment, silently offering praise and appreciation to Nature for producing the cotton, to the laborers in Kemet who had grown it, the merchants and seamen who brought it to their port, and the seamstress who cut, sewed, and dyed the cloth.

She noticed the warmth of the sun on her skin, just the perfect level for fall, unlike the discomfort—though necessary—of the summer heat. Realizing it would be cooler in Evamont, she had packed robes, wraps, and a pair of leather shoes, which she practically never wore except on winter's coldest days. Sandals were so much easier.

A whiff of fragrance caught her attention, and Mandisa wandered to the perfume cart.

"We just got this one in," the merchant, a young woman who must have just completed secondary school, said, waving a beautifully painted glass vial in her direction.

Taking it, Mandisa examined the scene of ocean breakers crashing against a rocky cliff with a solitary tree leaning its boughs toward the waves. In the sky blazed a setting ball of sun spreading yellow, orange, pink, and red streaks across the water. All that detail, and the bottle was no larger than the palm of her hand. Mandisa sniffed at the small, round opening on top, finding it carried a pleasing aroma as well.

She handed it back to the girl, who smiled expectantly while she replaced the cork. "What do you think?"

"Very nice," Mandisa cooed. "Who painted the bottle and who created the fragrance?"

"My father is a chemist," she said. "He mixes all our fragrances. My mother and I are both artists, but *I* painted this one," she relayed with pride.

"She'll take it," Agathon said. He laid two silver coins bearing the image of Clito on the face side on her cart's tabletop. "Is this enough?"

"Well," she hedged with a grimace.

Hashur stepped forward and added another silver coin. "There. Never let it be said our wife doesn't get the very best."

Mandisa had never been one for haggling. She reasoned the craftsmen and merchants needed to earn a living like she did, and, since there was plenty to go around, what was the point? Still, she had friends whose favorite game was bargaining with sellers at the market. Many of the merchants seemed to enjoy the interaction as well. Mandisa figured she had enough of striking compromises when dealing with the weather.

"Thank you," the young merchant woman said as she gathered the coins. "You will not be disappointed." She wrapped the precious bottle of perfume in a wool cloth to protect it and tied it with a string, then handed it to Mandisa. "Have a joyful day."

"Without a doubt," Mandisa answered. "Blessings on you and your family."

The men resumed their burdens to carry as they strolled into the food portion of the market. Mandisa gravitated that way, her husbands following with more interest lighting their faces. "Agathon, Hashur, why don't you both select some rations for our journey? You know what I like. I'll meet you outside the gate at the air dock," she said. "There's something I need to check on before we board the coach for our flight."

"Sure, sweetie," Agathon said.

"We'll pick only the freshest and best, honey," Hashur vowed.

Carrying only her personal shoulder bag, with her new bottle of perfume safely tucked inside, Mandisa strode through the open gate in the city's stone walls. It was quieter out here, though some citizens were on their way to the five-league-long bridge that connected Daya to Ruta. Since she was heading to the Skismengi Channel, she fell in with the others along the main road.

A glance to her left at the massive air dock and the lack of people lined up to board the passenger coach assured her she had plenty of time to take her water readings. The flying vehicle worked on the same electromagnetic principles and antigravity technology as the cargo sleds, only it was shaped like an oversized, long sleigh with walls, windows, and a roof. With a tin frame and painted balsa wood coverings, the inside was pleasantly decorated and held seating for up to forty passengers on comfortable cushioned benches. Each row of seats had a glass windowpane for people to enjoy the view as they traveled. The operator sat at the controls in the bow while people's bags were stored in the rear.

Safety ordinances prohibited air coaches from flying over incorporated cities and towns, which is why the dock was outside the walls of Ryzen. Mandisa and her husbands didn't have to pay to fly in the coach, as they were run by the government to facilitate transportation, encourage interaction between residents of the ten city-states, and promote tourism. Many inhabitants of Daya benefited by taking excursions to northern climes during the tropical summer months and receiving visitors and their coins during the winters. In addition to incurring no expense, traveling by air coach was safer than taking a small, personal sleigh on a long trip. If the coach accidentally collided with a bird in midair, it would suffer no ill effects, whereas a small vehicle ran the risk of crashing, killing all inside, as had happened before.

Once past the colossal air dock and its several parked coaches, it was only a short walk to the monumental bridge. Known as the longest bridge in the world, it had taken decades to complete, even with the use of laser cutters and a tremendous labor force. In the past, Ruta and Daya were not separate islands but one cohesive continent. The first government of the Third Age recognized the importance of reuniting them and made the construction a priority. It spanned the Skismengi Channel at its narrowest point and determined where the new city of Ryzen was built since its predecessor now lay in ruins four hundred cubits below the ocean's surface.

Upon smelling the salt air and feeling the breeze from the protected strip of sea, Mandisa departed from the road and traversed sandy soil populated by wild-rye dune grass, sand crabs, beach hoppers, and gray and white sandpipers that strutted about, nabbing morsels with their long, narrow beaks.

When she arrived at the shore, Mandisa slipped off her sandals and waded into the calm water, avoiding stepping on a starfish. Due to its protected nature, this stretch of beach experienced gentle tides, with hardly any waves breaking along the sand. She lifted her palms and her face to the sun and gave thanks. The atmosphere here was heavy with sorrow, a grave reminder of the violent upheaval that had shattered the continent not so long ago.

The air speaker closed her eyes and took several slow, deep breaths, listening to the sounds of the water, feeling its liquid energy around her ankles. She dug her toes into the sand, sensing individual grains and the body of sand as a whole.

"Thank you for the ocean, the cradle of life, for its bounty, the fish and seaweed to sustain our bodies, the artery that connects us to other lands while blessing us with distance from any who may wish us harm. Even here in this narrow channel, the earth breathes as the tides flow in and out. The sun, the air, the water, the fish, and me; we are all one. Thank you. Thank you. Thank you."

Lowering her hands, Mandisa swayed, lulling herself into a trance, and reached out with her senses to the water, the air, and the sand. In her mind's eye, she could see the tiniest particle, the most minute wave. The blood and fluids of her body attuned to the pulse of nature around her. She radiated the vibrations of questions and opened her heart and mind to receive answers.

Today she wasn't asking for rain or sun or for storm systems to alter their paths; she beseeched the elements to speak to her, to impress upon her any distress or changes in their energies. In return, she assured the spirits of air, water, earth, and fire that she desired to intercede on Gaia's behalf to find a solution to any problem that may exist. Opening all her chakras, Mandisa listened with her inner ears, tuned to frequencies few humans could hear. Even when evoking the name of Sekhmet, Mother of Power and of the Sun, the response she received was faint, as if coming from a distant star rather than the liquid that lapped at her legs. The message seemed odd to her, and she wondered if it was relevant at all. Perhaps when she gathered with the other wise ones and heard what they had to report, it would make more sense.

With gratitude to the elements, she splashed back to the beach, slipped on her sandals, and walked to the air dock, pondering the signs and portents, puzzling over the possibilities. As she neared, she overheard Hashur and Agathon talking with the porter who was loading their luggage.

"How can the two of you share a woman without killing each other?" he asked, only partly in jest.

"We love her," Agathon answered as if their arrangement was the norm, "and each other. We say I'm the brain, Hashur is the muscle, and Mandisa is the heart. Doesn't it require at least three legs to balance a stool?"

"Besides," Hashur added with a grin and a wink to Agathon. "Have you ever been under the sheets with an air speaker?"

"Can't say as I have," the porter replied as he loaded their last bag. "Mandisa is the only one I'm aware of who practices on Daya. I've never even met another one."

Hashur draped an arm around his older, slimmer husband. "Imagine doing it outdoors under a full moon during a dry lightning storm with the most beautiful woman the Creator ever put on this earth. She has more energy than a thousand—"

Agathon's elbow jab into Hashur's ribs stopped his colorful story short, and he looked up to see Mandisa staring at him, arms crossed, and brows raised. "Go on," she prodded. "Don't let me stop you. I have more energy than a thousand what?"

His pale face went beet red. "Greetings, honey." He swallowed and gave her a sheepish grin.

Rushing to his rescue, Agathon said, "This fine gentleman loaded all our things on the air coach, and we selected the very best culinary delights to eat on the flight." He held up a bag, which Mandisa had to admit smelled scrumptious.

She laughed, rolled her eyes, and squeezed between them, taking each's arm. "Let's go get my spot by the window before they're all taken."

"I hope this trip will deliver results," Hashur said in a skeptical tone. "I'm missing my team's push toss game for this."

"That's where I know you from!" exclaimed the porter, who apparently was still listening to them. Mandisa was accustomed to it. People found them a novelty when they didn't think twice about a man with two wives. "You're a fabulous player; with the Ryzen Bulls, right?"

Looking back at the man with a smile, Hashur nodded. "That's me."

"I never miss a match." The man beamed at them and waved. "Blessings to you all and enjoy your flight."

Mandisa had to admit she felt privileged to have both a learned academic and Apollonian athlete for husbands. "You fellows are pretty terrific lovers yourselves," she purred to them just before stepping onto the coach.

14

At the Ring of Stones, the night before the full moon

Ariel lay with Lysandra on the smooth ground of the meadow, under a double layer of woolen blankets, staring up at the canopy of stars. The dark rift ripping through the Milky Way seemed more pronounced than usual in the clear, black sky, despite the light from the rising Harvest Moon in the east. Ratiki lay curled in a ball between their knees, unconcerned about stars or omens or looming catastrophes. Laughter and sounds of passion drifted through the air from a tent some fifty cubits away, spurring a longing in Ariel's body to recover lost bliss with Lysandra. Even if she wanted to, far weightier matters troubled her mind.

"Are you sure you wouldn't rather sleep in the tent with Quetzal?" Ariel asked.

"No." Lysandra's voice was sweeter than the loveliest music, and just being near her reawakened Ariel's youth. She tingled all over, as if tiny spirits danced across her skin, bidding her to join them. "I'd rather be with you. Besides, Quetzal's tent is full, with his brother, Thoth, Thoth's daughter, and their dog. It's nice for me to be out here under the heavens. With all the lights in Atala, I never get a view like this."

Satisfied, Ariel let the matter rest. "But you left your body, danced among them," she breathed in awe. "What was it like?"

"Otherworldly," Lysandra said. "Strange and yet somehow familiar. How would it feel for you to connect with every plant and animal at the same time?"

"Confusing," Ariel admitted. "Overwhelming, too much information, like standing in a crowd where everyone is talking at once and you can't hear yourself think."

"But if you stay with it," Lysandra suggested, "and allow the waves of consciousness to wash over you, you learn to ride them, to single out vibrations to explore, and to meld with them all at once. It was so incredible that, for a time, part of me didn't want to come back. I felt warm, safe, and loved, a part of everything that ever was or ever will be. Then I missed earthly things, friends, you, us... the smell of flowers, the texture of wood, the taste of your lips. If I had realized—"

"Enough regret," Ariel said, cutting her off. "Everything happens for a reason, and there is a season for everything under the sun. If I plant corn or tomatoes in the fall, they will die in winter before producing their crops, and if I sow spinach or cabbages in the spring, the summer heat will scorch them and cause them to wither. It's enough to know you didn't forget me."

"Never," chimed Lysandra's rapid reply. "Look!" She pointed up and Ariel saw it at once. "A shooting star. I wonder what causes them to stream across the night sky?"

"I wonder if it will crash into someone else's world and cause a great calamity like what happened here, or worse," Ariel wondered as dark shadows formed in her core. "Are there people like us out there on other worlds?"

"I can't say if they are like us or not," Lysandra answered with consideration. "I heard voices and sensed other presences in the cosmos, but, because I couldn't see them, I don't know if they are like us or not. Perhaps they were spirit beings or the souls of humans who passed on. I searched for my parents."

Ariel moved her hand over the short grass under the blanket until it found Lysandra's hand. She recalled the grief Lysandra endured when they received word her family's ship had sunk at sea, how stricken she was that she had been denied the chance to tell them goodbye. This happened while they were together, shortly before Lysandra left for wisdom school. Even though she hadn't been close with her much older half-sister, losing her too meant she would never have the opportunity. Ariel sent heart energy through her touch to soothe and comfort Lysandra as she recalled the anguish she had experienced.

Lysandra took hold of the offered hand and laced their fingers together. "I didn't see them, but I sensed their presence. I felt loved and appreciated, and ..." She squeezed Ariel's hand before relaxing her fingers. "I felt like they were proud of me."

"Oh, sweetie, they are," Ariel avowed. "How could they not be? You are the most amazing woman." Rolling on her side and leaning over, she brushed a kiss to Lysandra's cheek. "And I must let you sleep now so we can be ready for tomorrow."

As Ariel rolled back to her spot a safe cubit away, Lysandra confessed, "I'm not sure I can sleep. There's too much to think about."

"Clear your mind," Ariel said. "Listen to the hum of the insects. Close your eyes, focus your attention on their song, and let them lull you to sleep."

"I'll try," Lysandra responded, still loosely holding her hand. "Thank you for letting me lie beside you, for being my friend again."

"Sweetie, you were never not my friend. Now, crickets, frogs, katydids, and sleep."

Long after Lysandra had drifted into the steady, shallow cadence of breath that accompanies slumber, Ariel gazed up at the stars, exploring the Universe for answers.

☥ ☬ ✞ ✡

After breaking their fast and the arrival of the last group, Ariel and the other eight called individuals entered the sacred Ring of Stones while their families, friends, and attendants gathered and waited outside the monolithic structure. The pillars were arranged to align perfectly with the astrological equinoxes and solstices. The grass was still pressed down from the fall equinox festival that had been held here less than a week ago. Ariel was glad to see the merrymakers cleaned up after themselves, although she was certain they had help from birds, mice, and other small animals. A wreath still hung over an opening left behind by Alban Elfed feast-goers who celebrated the second harvest and the second day of equal light and dark of the year. The astrological calendar moved into Libra, the sign of balance, and people offered prayers before shorter, colder days ahead. Because of the timing of this meeting and its grave nature, Ariel didn't attend the Alban Elfed commemoration.

The observatory, with its magnetically-charged pillars, stood in a meadow on a vast plain about halfway between the city of Evamont and the Azaes Fire Mountains. This was imperative so that neither the Opocaláms to the west nor the volcanoes in the east blocked the rising or setting of the sun on the four key days of the year. Abundant wildlife shared the plain—including a troop of monkeys watching them in curiosity from a broad monkey pod tree a hundred cubits away—with pastures, forests, and small villages. Though not near the large Azubu River, smaller tributaries cut through the land, some meandering toward the wide stream, while others wound their way to the ocean.

Unlike Lysandra, Ariel didn't know any of the wise and important men and women of Atlantis, so she stayed close to her friend and tried not to attract attention. A mature man who appeared older than Quetzal stepped forward with a staff in one hand and a cubit-high bone ankh in the other.

"That's Thoth," Lysandra whispered.

The librarian who had the vision, Ariel recalled as she studied him. He stood out from the others, dressed in a unique white robe with a cowl neck and three-quarter-length sleeves, adorned with gold wrist bracers embellished with turquoise and ruby stones. A teal and cream Nemeš headdress with dangling lappets framed a long beak nose, sharp eagle eyes, and a clean-shaven face.

He lifted the ankh and staff with strong, sinewy arms that belied his age and proclaimed in a resonant tenor voice, "Let us give thanks."

Thoth led the assembly in an exercise in gratitude, which was vital if they were to receive any word from the archangels, spirits, energies, or the Creator.

Everyone understood the significance of the Second Law, the Law of Gratitude. *In all things, give thanks, thereby creating more to be thankful for. Appreciate creation, offer praises, and speak blessings always.* Since Ariel was a tot, Oma had taught her to observe the Law of Gratitude daily and in all things. Sometimes, that proved easier said than done.

Ariel cleared her mind of questions and conjectures long enough to focus her energy on being thankful. It didn't matter what one was thankful for or to whom they expressed appreciation; it was the frequency of the emotion that lifted the practitioner to the correct wavelength required to receive a message from the higher beings. She was grateful to have reconnected with Lysandra and whatever it would mean going forward.

After reciting a litany of appreciation and raising their joint vibrations from doubt and fear into hopeful expectancy, Thoth brought the exercise to a close. Then he asked Lysandra to lead them in the 137 movements of the Ruh Mutaharika, the "moving spirit" exercise and breathing practice. Atlanteans had practiced the ancient ritual of centering one's breath, body, and mind for as long as memory or records existed, dating to the First Age. While it had been tweaked over the millennia and observed in different styles and variations depending on locale, the fundamental purpose, motions, and poses remained the same. It was taught in primary schools, and most people, including Ariel's oma, performed the exercise each day as part of their morning routine.

As the group took their final bow in unison, a sense of calm settled over Ariel, and she perceived peaceful vibrations projecting from all around. After a moment of silence, Thoth opened the dialogue.

"Ladies and gentlemen, it is not I who has summoned you all here, but Archangel Uriel, the master of knowledge and wisdom. He has already spoken to each of you, alerting you to the truth that something is wrong with our situation. Before we discuss what that might be, I invite each of you to give a report of what you have witnessed and experienced that has led you to accept Uriel's call. Quetzal, will you begin?"

Leaning on his staff, Thoth lowered himself to sit on the ground, and the others—except for Quetzal—followed his lead, including Ariel. She supposed this meeting could last all day.

Lysandra's wisdom teacher presented quite a contrast to the librarian, with his wild, red hair and beard and brawny musculature. Ariel supposed as a young man he may have competed in javelin and discus throwing, surely winning the stone toss.

"Thank you, my friend," he said with a nod to Thoth. "I am Quetzal, a master of the Central Wisdom School who has been privileged to experience many wonderful things in this life. I have taught students for nearly a hundred years, one of them sitting with us today." He smiled at Lysandra, and Ariel's heart glowed with love and pride.

"Like most of you, I'm concerned that Atlanteans' special gifts, talents, and abilities were somehow disrupted by the Great Conflagration thirteen hundred and fifty-six years ago. Psychic and vibrational abilities that were common to everyone suddenly became rare. The wisdom schools were initiated in the first years following the catastrophe to pass on the knowledge of masters to students who showed aptitude in one of several fields—clairvoyance, healing, air-speaking, nature-speaking, channeling, telepathy, astral projection, levitation, precognition, and others. At first, we were flooded with talented students, but as the centuries progressed, the numbers dwindled. So, we started accepting students without abilities who possessed a strong desire to learn esoteric principles. Our screening process is thorough, and only young men and women with the greatest potential are seated in the classes. Yet, in the past two decades, I've come across none who could manifest a single power, travel outside their bodies, or even receive a word from the spirit world. This decline troubles me greatly."

Ariel could sense his honest concern and watched with empathy as he swept a hand in her direction. "What will happen when Lysandra's generation grows old and leaves our descendants without healers? Ariel and Mandisa are the youngest talents I'm aware of with their gifts." He faced another woman, one with golden-red hair and a face full of freckles. "I only briefly met Ériu this morning and am not acquainted with her gifts, but these women are all in their forties and fifties—not old, but where are the younger generations of talents?" He shook his head and sat down.

Thoth motioned to the old man on the other side of Quetzal. He bore a large frame, and his snowy gray beard flowed past his belt. Quetzal reached out to assist him, and Ariel couldn't help but notice that he seemed to be the eldest of the group.

He frowned, narrowing bushy, caterpillar brows, and wiggled a finger in one ear. His brown, wool tunic and worn sandals informed Ariel he wasn't concerned with his appearance, while his tan skin, weathered like an ancient papyrus scroll, proclaimed his love of the outdoors. "I'm Noah, and I haven't a clue why I'm here. I was minding my own business, meditating my salutation to the day like I always do, counting my blessings, praising my Creator, when out of the blue this voice says, 'You have been called. Rise up and meet at the Ring of Stones on the next full moon.' Naturally, I assumed it was because of the wine I'd drunk the night before. But after the same thing happened three mornings in a row, I replied, saying, 'Why me?' The angel—or whoever—said my special gifts and talents would be needed soon and I should prepare.

"Understand," Noah said, propping one hand on his hip and lifting the other to his chest, "that I have no special abilities at all. I can't even predict the weather, let alone influence it. And I'm not a leader. It's everything I can do to keep my family in line—a task at which I don't always succeed. Nevertheless, a higher being called me, so I have come." With that, Noah sat back down.

"You're the shipbuilder who is friendly with my oma," Ariel said as she gazed at him with affection.

"I am a shipbuilder," he answered warily. "Who's your oma?"

"Naunet. You took her to see an ancestor—Methuselah," she excitedly recalled.

"Methuselah!" exclaimed another man Ariel didn't know. She assumed he might be Ziusudra since most of the others had been introduced. "Then he must have shared first-hand knowledge from before the comet disaster. I'll be wanting to talk to you." Noah nodded in response.

"Ériu, my dear," Thoth motioned to the woman with the strawberry-blonde tresses. "You speak next."

"Blessings to my brothers and sisters gathered here," she said in a cheerful, lilting voice. She didn't stand like the others. "I'm a teacher at the Northern Wisdom School—though not the chief master," she specified. "My emphasis is in harmony and balance, both in nature and within our spiritual and physical persons. Our school is located on high cliffs overlooking the eastern ocean on the border of Gadlan and Elapus. Umm ..." She bit her lip and displayed a tentative grin. "I don't have any extraordinary talents, but I love trees and sea creatures."

She peered at the sky as if words might fall into her mouth while tapping her leg like a drum. It was evident to Ariel that Ériu was the youngest of their group and feeling nervous. "I head up several projects. One is a collection of seeds, and another is a study of the languages of other civilizations from around the world." Her face brightened, and she pointed at Thoth excitedly. "We have a library!"

Thoth and Quetzal exchanged a look, making Ariel curious about what they were thinking. Then Thoth asked, "And you heard or felt a call?"

"Yes, but, like Noah, I presumed I was mistaken. I mean, why would Uriel call me? I'm not even wise." She shrugged. "But, when I received a message from the master of the Central Wisdom School saying I was supposed to be here, I came. Really, everyone—I don't know how I can contribute, but I'll work hard and do whatever you all need me to. I want to help."

This theme of members of their circle feeling too unimportant stretched far beyond Ariel. The last thing Ériu said caught her attention: *I want to help.* Maybe it was just that simple. Maybe these nine were here because they cared enough to say yes with no specifics to go on, no plan or direction—just a willing spirit and compassionate heart.

Thoth nodded and passed his gaze to the next person in the ring. "Ariel?"

15

At Lysandra's nudge, Ariel stood up and looked around at the others, most older, and all more learned than she was. "I'm Ariel, a farmer, and I've been blessed with the ability to communicate with plants and animals. It seems to me like something anyone should be able to do. No one taught me, although my great-great-great-grandmother had the same gift when she was younger. Anyway, I don't know why I was called to join you esteemed masters. I've felt the energies weakening for some time now, which has hindered my meditations. When I was inquiring of the spirits what was wrong, I received an impression I was supposed to come and meet with somebody about something. Then Lysandra came and told me about Thoth's message and my oma said we should come."

Not knowing what else to say, Ariel returned to her spot on the ground.

"Ariel, have you talked to any animals or trees about your unease?" Thoth asked.

"I—" *Damn! Why didn't I think of that?* "No, sir. The thought didn't occur to me. Honestly, I assumed the problem lay with me rather than the ether."

He nodded in understanding. "And Ériu, how many languages do you speak?"

"I'm familiar with twelve from lands to the east and two from the peoples to the west," she answered, "but am only fluent in eight."

"Fluent in eight languages?" Noah exclaimed with a look of astonishment.

"I know it isn't many," she answered as though embarrassed. "Our study group has compiled the basics of twenty languages; I just haven't had time to master them all yet, and I'm unsure of a few pronunciations."

"And she says she has no abilities," scoffed Quetzal with a laugh. "Lysandra, please share with the group."

Lysandra remained seated, and Ariel shot her a perturbed expression. *She made me get up!*

"I'm a physician and graduate of Quetzal's wisdom school. I've been practicing for about twenty-five years and have noticed an increase in disease and chronic ailments, gradual at first, but, in the last few years, at an alarming rate. People are aging faster and dying of natural causes younger. It is as if they are losing the ability to self-heal and regulate their own bodies. Some patients seem unconcerned with even trying to uphold good health for themselves, preferring to have a physician do it for them. While my connection with the power of Raphael is still strong, I've run across blocks in other areas of my life and meditations. I exhaust my energy by performing the simplest procedures."

She paused to glance at Ariel and then Quetzal. "I haven't mentioned this before, but in case it bears relevance ..." She swallowed and stared blankly at a spot in the middle of the circle. "I have treated children whom I believe were the victims of violence."

"Violence against children?" Ériu exclaimed in disbelief. "But the twelfth rule states we are to love and nurture our children, brothers and sisters, husbands and wives, and those who have none. Who would ever harm a child?"

The darker-skinned woman, whom Ariel had yet to be introduced to, let out a bitter, scoffing laugh. "Some teachers in Ryzen pervert the meaning of The Law, while other citizens ignore it altogether."

"In Diaprep as well," Noah grumbled. "Not that there's been an outbreak of crime, but the city guardians have had to break up fistfights among men who persist in their anger rather than observe the sensible ninth rule."

Do not let the sun set on your anger, but make peace with your Creator, yourself, and your neighbor before you lie down to sleep. All are One. The words of the long-memorized and respected rule formed in Ariel's mind automatically. The Laws and Rules had been given to them by their ancestors for society's benefit and that of the individual. They were not harsh or demanding, but common sense.

"Why would anyone be so foolish as to bear a grudge?" Lysandra asked in bewilderment. "Everyone knows such emotions block the flow of good health and a long life. And yet, I suspect that is why some of my patients suffer. Others, however, are kind, loving souls who follow the sacred teachings and still fall ill or ache with pain." She glanced around at the circle, her gaze landing on Quetzal. "That's all I have to share."

"Thank you," Thoth said with a nod. "We will discuss all these matters, but first let's hear from Mandisa."

"Creator's blessings to you all." Mandisa, with her dusky skin and array of black braids, stood, extending open palms toward the assembly. She was an attractive woman, appearing to be younger than Ariel's mother, with lively eyes, an abundance of curves, and dressed in bright colors. "I'm an air speaker from Ryzen with forty years of experience, which may not sound like much. Still, the elements consider my suggestions, and we work well together. I've noticed a couple of things that have changed since I began my discourse with the weather. First, there's been a rise in air disturbances and an influx of storm systems for me to deal with. I realize this is typical being near the tropics but, for the past twenty years, severe storms, with unprecedented wind speed and surge height, have increased from a couple a season to nearly ten times that. And they are getting more difficult to dissipate or push off to the south, thus sparing our coasts from damage. I hardly have time to devote to our orchard or my own spiritual growth because of tending to ions and wind currents and excessive amounts of rainfall. Secondly, the ocean is getting warmer. It isn't noticeable to average citizens—about three units in forty years. I've kept readings and checked again just before leaving Ryzen yesterday morning. Master Thoth, I don't have access to ancient records; however, I'm aware of the great cold spell that followed on the heels of the Conflagration. It would seem natural that water temperatures would warm to their pre-disaster level, so I'm not sure if this indicates a problem or not. Ariel, have you discussed it with the sea creatures?"

Ariel peered around at Mandisa. "No. I wasn't aware this was an issue. Most marine animals are not long-lived enough to notice so gradual a change, but, now that you mention it, I will seek out some older whales and inquire with them. Whales are fully cognizant mammals with a complex vocabulary, and they remember." Mandisa nodded at her, then returned her gaze to Thoth. "I can't tell you what's causing the disturbances or why severe weather is on the rise. I can tell you it's becoming increasingly difficult for me to meet people's expectations, though whether the fault lies with the weakening of my abilities or the elements is something I hope you can tell me."

Thoth nodded and Mandisa sat down. "Ptah." The librarian motioned to a muscular man who appeared to be older than Ariel yet younger than Quetzal. As he pushed up and stretched to his full height, he resembled a copper mountain, if mountains wore natural off-white kilts with red and yellow trim and sashes. Dark brown hair framed his smooth, square jaw while a broad nose dominated his serious face.

"I am Ptah, architect and mathematician from Autopolis. I have designed and overseen the construction of many of the more modern structures in central and southern Atlantis and written treatises on numbers and sacred geometry, yet I don't know why I have been called here. A week ago, I was preparing to start my day with meditation and exercise, when I thought I heard a faint voice call my name. Like Noah and several others, I assumed I had imagined it. I know nothing of signs or portents and have never possessed special abilities that have grown weaker. But if the archangels desire a new temple, I can design and construct the best."

With that, the brawny fellow sat and resumed his silence. "Thank you, Ptah," Thoth acknowledged. "I am certain Uriel has a plan for you in all this. Ziusudra?"

A man of at least two hundred used his staff fitted with a silver chakana—an equal-armed cross with a hole in the center—to pull up with. The elder's slight frame belied his noble bearing, while his white toga and dark blue stole billowed around him like a flag in the wind. His bark-brown and gray hair was cut short behind a high forehead while a neat mustache and chin beard of the same hue adorned a pointed chin. A gold crescent moon pendant dangled below a long, thin, warm-ivory neck with a bulbous laryngeal prominence.

"I am Ziusudra, astronomer of Ampherium." His voice was as smooth and genteel as his appearance. "It would appear I have been studying the stars since before all of you, save Noah, were born. I have made some observations but need access to more ancient star charts than I currently have. Thoth, do you have charge over any such records?"

"I might," he answered. "If you show me what you have, I can tell you."

Ziusudra nodded and continued. "As you know, the great sky serpent—the deadly comet—brought destruction in its wake thirteen hundred and fifty-six years ago, taking with it half our continent and blotting out the sun for years. A flash freeze—far more devastating than what befell our country—gripped the lands and waters to the north and created the Terrible Ice. Astronomers should have seen signs, and should have known the comet approached, yet somehow their vision was obscured, or their calculations were flawed. No one was prepared for what befell the earth. Thank the Creator it was not a direct strike, or none would have survived. We also understand an entire procession of the zodiac cycle took place between the first great cataclysm of antiquity and the Conflagration. Clearly, another cycle hasn't ended so quickly. Our sphere is currently a half sequence through Leo, but I'm most concerned with Sirius, which is on an approach to pass nearer our sun."

He let out a sigh, passing a gaze around the ring, and absently fingered the pendant on his chest. "If I had older star charts, I would compare them to what is in our skies now, to test a theory. The problem we face is either a weakening of the cosmic energies that have bathed our people in power for millennia or something blocking those energies from reaching us. Is it Sirius's activities? Perhaps. There are a few other possibilities as well. Ptah, as a mathematician, you understand how the heavenly bodies move in ellipses, rotating around their midpoint, and that our solar system is one of many in the cosmos. But what if the whole of everything also moves and shifts positions? What if our planet, perhaps our entire system, is gradually spinning into an emptier portion of space?"

"Nothing is empty," Quetzal observed. "The ether is teeming with waves of energy we cannot see, yet we witness their effects."

"True," Ziusudra agreed. "But consider the ocean, how some parts thrive with plants and creatures while in other places they are fewer and farther between. Likewise, look to the skies. Are the stars uniformly spread out, or do they gather in clusters? Earth could be passing through a thin place in space where the energies themselves are less dense and, therefore, harder for humans to connect with."

While Ariel's brain worked on processing this theory, the astronomer proposed another.

"Or, what if when the fallout from the comet struck the earth causing the upheaval, earthquakes, volcanic eruptions, giant waves, and sudden cold, one of the larger pieces—or a combination of small ones—knocked the earth off its previous angle of alignment? We all comprehend how vital proper alignment is to our well-being; think about what it must be for the globe. Even a slight change of a degree or two could block the flow of energies we have been accustomed to. But without direct access to Universal Consciousness or ancient star charts from well before the Conflagration, I can't make that determination. Unfortunately, if any of these theories are true, there is little or nothing we can do about the situation other than adapt and wait."

When Ziusudra sat, the council remained so still and quiet that Ariel could hear nothing except her own heartbeat. She swallowed, digesting the information the astronomer presented. One thing needled at her and, without realizing it, she shared the thought aloud.

"If there is nothing we can do, then why would Archangel Uriel call us here?"

"Why indeed?" Thoth seconded with raised brows.

16

The nine individuals, vastly different in backgrounds and abilities, looked questioningly from one to another. Lysandra wondered what Ariel was thinking. *Why couldn't I have been a telepath?* Despite being unable to read Ariel's thoughts, Lysandra could feel the same sense of unease radiating from her as from everyone else.

"May I offer a suggestion?" Quetzal asked. Thoth nodded. "Lysandra, did you bring any herbs with you, the kind used to enhance visions?"

"I did, just in case," she answered, anticipating what his suggestion would be.

"I propose we take a break to consider the information we have thus far. Ziusudra, you could consult with Thoth about finding ancient star charts, and any others of you who wish to discuss among yourselves, may do so. We should meet back here after dark, under the power of the full moon, and inhale the vapors of Lysandra's blend to enhance our communication with the energies and voices of the spirit world. We will pray and seek guidance from angels and ancestors and from the Creator. When we all come back to ourselves, we will share our impressions."

"It is a wise course of action," Thoth approved. "All in favor?"

All around the circle nodded, lifted a hand, or voiced their consent. As the meeting moved into recess, various members broke off to talk with each other—Ptah went with Noah, Thoth with Ziusudra, and Quetzal with Ériu—leaving Mandisa with Lysandra and Ariel. That wasn't a problem; Lysandra wished to get to know the intriguing air speaker better, as this was the first time they had met. With a longing glance at Ariel, she thought, *I'll have time alone with you before we're done.*

"So, you can converse with animals." Mandisa struck up a conversation with Ariel as the three of them wandered toward the monkeypod tree. The shorter woman smiled with admiring eyes at the two of them. Lysandra wished to hold Ariel's hand, to establish and maintain at least that contact with her. Maybe if she channeled the full force of her love through her touch, Ariel would understand that she never intended to leave her and how much she wanted her now. But this wasn't the time.

A bushy, fat raccoon bounded after them, probably bored by humans sitting around conversing in a language he couldn't comprehend.

"And you talk to the rain and wind," Ariel responded with friendly curiosity. "There's an air speaker in Evamont who works with the farmers on the plains, especially at planting and harvest time. We need rain after planting and a dry spell at harvest. Karpos. He does good work."

"I know him," Mandisa replied. "He's a good fellow. And Lysandra, you're a healer and attended Quetzal's school. Tell me—does he truly know as much as it seems?"

"He is the wisest man I know," Lysandra answered honestly.

"I've never taken a drug in my life," Ariel said, stopping far enough from the tree they could hear the monkeys' chatter without being close enough for one to drop on them. "What does it do? Is it safe?"

"Perfectly safe the way I administer it," she stated. "I mix the herbs in little clay pots and light them to create a type of incense that dulls the noisy thinking side of our brains and enhances the imaginative, intuitive side. You should never take it when you're going to be driving a sleigh or using a laser cutter, but, in this setting, all will be well. You may inhale as much or as little of the smoke as feels right to you and push it aside when you've had enough."

"We used an enhancement that way my first year at wisdom school to help us leave our bodies and experience our true energetic forms," Mandisa said. "No ill-effects I can recall, but it made one student in our group sick to his stomach."

"So, you said the oceans are getting warmer," Ariel mentioned to Mandisa, changing the subject. Instead of listening to her reply, Ariel turned around and faced the monkeys with an annoyed expression. One pointed at them and curled its lip while Lysandra could swear two others laughed at them. Some youngsters swung from branch to branch as if chasing each other while a mother carefully groomed her baby, eating the insects she pulled off it.

The raccoon reared up on his back legs, narrowed his eyes, and chattered something toward them. Quieting him, Ariel lifted a hand and appeared to shove some air at the monkeys. The offensive ones responded by shaking their heads and covering their eyes before scampering off to the other side of the massive shade tree.

"What was that about?" Lysandra asked.

"I apologize," Ariel said and brushed back a strand of hair. "Let's go in the other direction." She pivoted, but Ratiki had to administer one last scold to the offenders before jogging to the front of the line. They strolled back toward the Ring of Stones, their path winding along the outer edge, leading them to the designated sleeping areas.

"Those monkeys were making fun of us, saying we were silly girls who came too late and missed the festival," Ariel explained. "I informed them we were here for much more important matters, and they should have better things to do than gossip about humans they don't even know."

"We saw how they reacted," Mandisa said in amazement. "They seemed to be ashamed of their poor behavior. I didn't realize animals had such complex thoughts and emotions."

"Oh, you should meet the elephants," Lysandra answered, drawing a smile and warm laugh from Ariel.

"The higher-level animals are sophisticated indeed," Ariel explained. "Just don't waste your time trying to reason with a dodo." They all laughed. "But, seriously, animals have brains and hearts, don't you Ratiki?" At his name, he turned his masked face up at Ariel, curiosity gleaming from his eyes. "They produce electromagnetic fields just like people do, and, while they don't have the same organs, trees emit vibrational signals as well. The weather, on the other hand ..." Ariel shook her head. "I don't see how you do it."

"While not possessing human-like qualities as the animals do, air, water, earth, and fire produce their own electromagnetic currents," Mandisa responded. "Though they lack consciousness, even rocks emit vibrations. What do you think it was like before the Conflagration when everybody exercised these abilities and dozens more?"

"I wouldn't have a job," Lysandra noted with a hint of humor. "But I'd gladly give up my calling if it meant everyone could heal themselves, mend their own broken bones with a thought, and live a thousand years." Her words sounded suddenly poignant in Lysandra's ears as her heart absorbed their impact.

"I feel like playing my flute," Ariel said with another swift change of topic. She knelt beside their bedrolls and dug through her bag to find it. The raccoon helped with the search, retrieving a ball that he began to bat around and chase across the ground.

"Do you mind if I join you with my drum?" Mandisa asked.

"Not at all. Here we are." Ariel took out her flute and blew warm air into its hole while Mandisa moved off to the tent where the noises had come from the night before.

"Do you still paint?" Ariel asked.

Regret plucked Lysandra's soul. "I did for a long time; I want to. I don't know why I haven't lately. Maybe because my practice is so busy."

"Lysandra." Ariel stepped near to her and caught her gaze with kind, fathomless eyes. "I don't want you to be lonely. I want you to be happy."

"You make me happy," she replied without thinking. "Just seeing you, being near you, even in these trying circumstances, makes me happy."

A misty longing consumed Ariel's countenance, and she flicked away her gaze. Hearing footsteps, Lysandra glanced over her shoulder. Two men, one athletic and young, the other studious and older, followed Mandisa.

"Please allow me to introduce my husbands. Agathon," she said, motioning to the slender, dark-haired, older man who held a lyre. He gave them a polite bow. "And Hashur." She indicated the broad-shouldered, sandy-haired younger man with a charismatic grin.

"Pleased to meet you," Lysandra said. "I'm Lysandra and this is my friend, Ariel."

"A trio then," Ariel agreed pleasantly. "Music is the gateway to the heavens, the perfect way to achieve the proper mood." Returning her gaze to Lysandra, she added, "You're welcome to join us and listen if you like."

"We would love to," Hashur replied. "Wouldn't we, Lysandra?"

It was all Lysandra could do to refrain from breaking out in tears of joy. She delighted in Ariel's music and had missed it so much. Sure, she had attended concerts and recitals by musicians whose technical performances might have been more perfect, but the tone and emotion Ariel infused into her playing were beyond compare. Anticipation of the dulcet sounds filled Lysandra with joy, and fond memories nearly drowned her.

"Yes, we would," she replied.

As the three merged their sounds, making melodies and harmonies, both familiar and improvised on the spot, others soon gathered around to absorb the uplifting frequencies and become lost in the purity of the moment. Ziusudra joined them on his pipes, which encouraged Lysandra to take out her sistrum and shake it in tempo to Mandisa's drumming.

Lysandra never thought of herself as a musician and she had in the past only ever used her instrument in healing rituals, but Selaphiel's lure pulled her in. Once she lost herself to the tune and beat, Lysandra felt the spirits move within and through her in a new and intimate way. Because of the collective nature of the art, it stirred her differently than painting did. She felt much more in charge of her creations with paint and brushes in hand; this was what she imagined channeling to be like. They became the vessels the song flowed through, and it was glorious.

After a while, the energies waned, the musicians ceased to play, and everyone went their way, finally leaving Lysandra alone with Ariel. "That was intense and magical," she said reverently.

"It was especially nice co-creating with you and the others," Ariel said as she lay down on her blanket. The sky above them remained clear, with a scattering of clouds. "When did you learn an instrument?"

"At wisdom school," Lysandra answered, gathering her knees in her arms as she sat beside Ariel. She lay her head on them, turning her face to the woman she loved, still tingling from head to toe. "I only learned to use the sistrum as it applies to my craft, though. Musical frequencies aid the healing energies."

"They do," Ariel agreed, "which may have something to do with why I remain in good health."

"Well, combined with proper nutrition, movement exercises, and observing The Law."

Ariel glanced over at her. "I suppose you're returning to Atala tomorrow."

"It depends on what happens tonight," she answered honestly. "We may all receive assignments. Ariel, I want you to know—"

"Please don't," Ariel interrupted, turning her gaze back to the sky. "I can't afford to have my heart broken again, Lysandra, and we both need to focus on the predicament at hand."

Lysandra let it drop. Ariel was right. The current situation demanded their full attention and was of far more consequence than their relationship. "I'll get us something to eat and drink and then prepare the herbs for tonight," she said.

⚲ ⚛ ☥ ✡

As the sun bobbed low in the western sky, Lysandra mixed dried herbs, crushed mushrooms, and peyote in a large bowl. Then she spooned portions out into nine small, clay incense jars equipped with holes near the bottom for airflow. She distributed them to the council members when they filed into the Ring of Stones as the full moon rose in the east. They all sat in a tight circle in the middle of the observatory, silently preparing themselves for the spiritual journey. When the sun's light was completely gone and the big, bright harvest moon ruled the starry sky, Thoth raised his palms and spoke.

"Spirits of our ancestors, angelic energies, and great Creator, hear us. We are the faithful, those who answer your call. We trust you to answer ours and show us the truths of what lies before us. Thank you, divine beings, for your mercy and compassion, for your unfailing love. Lead us in the paths you deem best. Give our eyes visions and our lips prophecies that we might fulfill our purpose in the world you created."

Taking a fire stick, Thoth struck it to flame, lit his incense, and passed the box to Quetzal on his right. Each person lit their herbs assuming an aligned posture with their palms resting on their thighs, knees, or at their sides facing upward in a receiving pose. Lysandra closed her eyes and inhaled the pungent smoke. Soon she felt light, as if she floated above the ground, above her body, only vaguely aware of anyone else's presence. She focused her attention on one thought: *what is wrong with the world?* Planets and stars went spinning and whirling around her, and visions from the past, the present, the future, and faraway galaxies flashed behind her closed eyelids. Colors and sounds, both cheery and frantic with horror, blasted through her awareness, but nothing seemed to make sense.

Lysandra saw her parents, brother, and half-sister waving to her from their ship, sinking from the onslaught of a rogue wave in a storm at sea. She viewed foreign lands where she had never traveled, some with seas of sand and others covered in lush vines, both with colossal stone pyramids. Last, she witnessed a lush landscape of short, verdant grass with a ring of stones erected on a plain. Women in long robes gathered there to honor nature at a solstice celebration; they all seemed to look like Ériu. When she opened her eyes, her Ring of Stones topped by a great full moon came into focus. It had been an interesting ride; unfortunately, she had no clue what it meant.

Lysandra absorbed the moon energy, thankful for the sensation that danced along her skin, and, presently, the others emerged from their visions.

As they gave their reports, several mentioned pyramids in foreign lands and Noah also received an image of people on board a ship in a storm, although he didn't know if they were Lysandra's family or not. Ériu said she saw fair-skinned men wearing wool kilts of many colors, dissimilar to those popular in Atlantis.

"I had trees and animals calling out to me from around the world," Ariel relayed, "some of species I've never seen before. They were all afraid, and I wanted to comfort them, only they couldn't hear me. It was sad and distressing."

When all had given testimony, Thoth rose, leaning on his staff, his bald head gleaming in the moonlight's brilliance. "This is what we must do," he declared with authority. "Each of you use your gifts, your connections, your sources, to inquire and gather more information. Ziusudra, come with me to the library in Atala to search the oldest records for what you need. Ptah, assist Ziusudra with his calculations so his theories might be tested. Ériu, prepare a list of your languages, who speaks them, where these people live, and have it sent to me by messenger. Then continue to study the ones you have assembled. Noah, ask captains of trading vessels about news from our colonies and if anyone else is concerned about unusual occurrences. Mandisa, set up your climate studies and pay special attention to weather anomalies. Lysandra, prepare me a copy of your patient records, citing specific ailments, their reoccurrences, and check for patterns. Ariel, travel from one end of Atlantis to the other, inquiring of the trees and animals about how they are feeling, and what they have seen and heard. Quetzal will assist me in research and meditation as we seek the answers we need. Let's plan to meet back here on the plain at the Winter Solstice. I will speak to the Evamont ministry, asking them to move their celebration to the city this winter and explain why we need this spiritually significant location for our deliberation. Is this satisfactory with all?"

Everybody agreed, and the assembly was dismissed. No one spoke as they drifted out of the observatory to rejoin their parties in the camp, probably still woozy or floaty from their visioning. After visiting the portable privy that someone set up, Lysandra went to her spot and crawled under the blankets, trying to make sense of what she'd seen and heard. Ariel soon joined her.

"That was a strange experience," Ariel said. "I saw smaller, hairless elephants with modest tusks and ears, great, black apes as large as a human, and tall, buff-colored, bouncy creatures with feet like skids, powerful tails, and ears sticking up from cute faces. I don't know any of their names, and yet they all cried out for me to help them. I'm glad the harvest is in, because it looks like I'll be traveling for the next few months."

"You're the lucky one," Lysandra replied. "I'll be stuck at home, and, when I'm not treating patients, I'll be compiling the records Thoth requested. But this I vow," she declared, catching Ariel's gaze. "I will make time to paint. If nothing else, this retreat has stirred my creativity, and I can't wait to put brush to canvas again."

With desire crawling under her skin once more, Lysandra asked, "When you get to Atala, will you come see me?"

Ariel released a sigh and took her hand under the blankets. "I could do that. I'd enjoy seeing you work, although I'm not sure if it's allowed."

"If the patient doesn't object," Lysandra said as hope leaped in her chest.

"I'll want to see Thoth's library, too. I've only been to Atala once," she admitted. "Many years ago, at King Efrayim's coronation. My husband wanted to go, and we took the children. I thought about you. I wondered where you were, what you were doing, who you were with, but I didn't go looking for you."

"Why would you?" Lysandra asked. "You had a husband and a family."

"Yeah," Ariel replied softly. She squeezed Lysandra's hand before letting it go.

Instantly, Lysandra wished it back, her warm touch both tender and strong, the connection that time and heartache had failed to sever. They would get through this challenge, and then Lysandra could concentrate on reconciling with Ariel. *I could move my practice to Evamont,* she considered. *By sleigh, I could travel back and forth to the farm. We could make it work for both of us.*

With hopeful feelings lifting her soul like a dove on the breeze, Lysandra drifted off to sleep.

17

Ariel's farm, the next day

Ariel parked the sleigh in front of their farmhouse after dropping Lysandra off at the air dock in Elyrna. It wasn't a city, but the village had a large enough population to run an air dock. A dozen or more commuters took a coach daily to and from the capital of Evamont for their jobs. Spending two days with Lysandra had been bittersweet for Ariel, drawing powerful emotions to the surface that she would have to press down and lock away again. *She still wants you,* a voice from within taunted. *Maybe for a night,* her better sense replied. *She is the one who left and stayed away for thirty years—not me.*

Though Ariel used the facts in her inner argument, she fully understood the circumstances and the truth that Lysandra never intended to hurt her or even end their relationship. It was still hard for Ariel to fathom the notion her former lover had never held to another. *Too many thoughts; too many emotions,* she decided, shaking her head as she climbed out of the sleigh with her bag. *I have an important mission ahead.*

"There you are!" Sheera declared in an accusatory tone as she marched out to meet her. Ariel's able-bodied daughter snatched the travel bag out of her hands and turned toward their front door. "I'll carry this for you, and then I need your advice."

Ratiki hopped to the ground and scampered over to the olive tree, checking for fallen fruit.

"Thank you, dear," Ariel responded, dreading what crazy caper her daughter was up to now. "Anything I can do to help." Sheera never took her advice. Why did she still bother to ask?

Her daughter took her bag in, set it in the front room, hopped on the sofa, and patted the teal and white blanket lying over the cream cushion. Ariel joined her, trying to direct her full attention to Sheera.

"Everyone else is processing grain from the harvest while I'm doing the wash. Well, not at the moment as I hung the linens to dry, but I'm in charge of the meal, just so you don't accuse me of being lazy," Sheera stated with a pointed expression.

"So, I plan to invite both Taavi and Mahmoud over for dinner—separately, of course; not at the same time—for you and Grandmother to meet. Then tell me which one you think I should choose to marry." The young woman beamed excitedly, quite pleased with her plan.

Ariel smiled and stroked her daughter's arm. "You'll have to rely heavily on your grandmother because I must go out of town. But you should pull Oma in on it. She's wise, and nothing escapes her notice. She will know if either young man is hiding something."

"You're leaving again?" Sheera huffed. "But you just got back. I suppose I could plan the dinners for when you return from this trip."

"Sweetie, I have to be gone a long time," Ariel explained. "Maybe months."

"What? But you can't go, not now," Sheera protested. "Can't you just meet them both first, then go do whatever? And why suddenly all this traveling? Is it for nature speaking?"

"Yes, dear, it's for nature speaking. I've been asked to tour the whole country from top to bottom and survey all the flocks, herds, forests, and species for an important national project. It's quite an honor to be chosen and I can't postpone it."

"Well, bury a spoon," she pouted in obvious disappointment.

Ariel rubbed her shoulders, giving her an affectionate hug. There was no point troubling her daughter with suspicions of doom and gloom when they had no actual evidence yet. And if some cataclysmic end of the world was coming, all the more reason Sheera should enjoy her youth and dream over marriage prospects rather than lock herself away to quiver in terror.

"What does that even mean?" Ariel asked of the young people's novel expression.

"I don't know," Sheera answered. "It's just what you say when something's extreme—good or bad, I suppose." She lay her head against Ariel's for a moment, settling her emotions. "How did you know Dada was the right one for you?" Sitting up straight, she sought Ariel's face for an answer.

Staring out the window, Ariel fingered her chin and lips, while composing a proper response. "I had gone through a difficult breakup not long before I met your father and had been feeling rather underappreciated. He was handsome, charming, and quite fascinated by my unique abilities. He made me feel special ... wanted. And he wasn't intimidated by a strong woman. Everyone liked him and he was no stranger to farm work. We both wanted children and a simple life, so it just worked out. When he asked me to marry him, I didn't accept immediately. I meditated and inquired of the angels if this was the best course of action. Despite our dreams and goals being cut short, I'm grateful every day I said yes. I can't imagine the world without you and Mal'akhi in it. Having you is worth it all."

"Ah, that's sweet," she cooed with a shy smile. "But did you love him?"

Ariel met her daughter's gaze. "Yes, I loved him. I remember he was so excited as he prepared to head up into the mountains for his vision quest. It thrilled my heart that he was finally seeking spiritual growth, that he was raising his expectations. When he was packing, he bubbled with enthusiasm, talking up a storm about what he hoped to accomplish, how he knew he was ready, and that everything was about to change."

A misty feeling snaked through Ariel as she recalled the last time she'd seen her husband. "He said, 'Maybe I'll come home with a gift too.' I think I loved him that day most of all. He was a simple man and a good father who neither ignored me nor suffocated me with attention. He loved to go into Elyrna every weekend to debate with others at the salons, and, once a month, he'd fly to Evamont to attend the forum." She laughed. "He was obsessed with keeping apprised of news and gossip, what was happening in foreign lands, all that stuff. How were we to know he'd die in the mountains without even leaving a body behind for us to bury? I took comfort in the knowledge he had gone in search of the spirit world and—while not as either of us intended—he found it."

Sheera rearranged a strand of Ariel's hair, gliding her fingers through her silky, medium-brown strands. "You have always been a wonderful mother—loving and strong, demanding at times, but also extraordinarily forgiving. Tell me—the lover you broke up with, or who broke up with you, before you met Dada; was it Lysandra?"

Ariel tilted her head at Sheera as astonishment overtook her. "I don't give your intuitive side enough credit. You so often behave like a typical young woman that I forget you are still my daughter."

"It makes sense why she never came to visit, if that was the case," Sheera reasoned. "Otherwise, she was just being a snooty bitch who thought she was too good for the rest of us. I didn't get that vibe from her the other day. So, she was avoiding you all this time. I suppose her visit and your meeting yesterday have something to do with this national nature survey assignment, and it must be important."

"You, my amazing daughter, are correct on all counts," Ariel affirmed with pride in traits Sheera kept secret most of the time.

Sheera stretched up from the sofa and smoothed out her colorfully patterned skirt. "Then it will be up to me to keep Grandmother in check while you're away."

Ariel stood with her. "It's a good idea to bring Taavi and Mahmoud each to dinner to meet the family. Remember," Ariel charged, resting a hand on her daughter's shoulder. "Ours is a long life. You can have all that your heart desires, just not all at once. Choose the suitor who feels right to you for this time in your life, the one you fit with, the one who makes you happy, with no consideration for what others may think or say. They don't count; only you and him. Decades down the road, who knows?"

"Yeah," Sheera said with a sigh. "You never know what's around the bend."

Brushing a kiss to her daughter's cheek, Ariel made a request. "Look out for Ratiki while I'm gone?"

Sheera let out a huff. "That pesky rascal? Do you know he got into my best roll of linen, scratched around, and made a nest in it?"

"Please?" Ariel flashed her a desperate expression.

"Well," Sheera muttered, before her face lit with warm affection. "He is adorable and makes everybody laugh. I'll be sure he doesn't starve or get eaten while you're gone."

"That's my girl," Ariel beamed. "And I'm proud of the woman you've become."

Ariel found Oma at the winnowing house with her mother, Aram, Yaluk, their sons Shemu'el and Hevel, Uncle Menandros, Gamila, and their daughter Mara, all hefting sheets filled with grain heads into the air for the breeze to blow away the chaff. "I'm here to help," she announced, receiving a grunt from her uncle, a glare from Gamila, and an inquisitive look from Oma.

"So lovely you could join us," Aram greeted cheerily, without a hint of sarcasm. The space was hard on her eyes and throat as millions of tiny particles hung in the air despite the aid of a gentle wind. "How was your meeting at the Ring of Stones?"

"Interesting," she replied.

"Hulla and the fellows could use your help next door threshing," Menandros grumbled. "First she runs off to visit that fancy woman from the capital while we cut the sheaves, and then she conveniently has to attend a meeting to get out of threshing and winnowing."

"Hush, you coot!" Oma reprimanded. "Ariel is about important business. Has she ever missed harvest labor before?"

"There was one year," Gamila began, then at Oma's glare, held her tongue.

"They don't need help threshing, stupid brother of mine," Philomena declared indignantly. "The big stone wheel runs on crystal power. All they do is feed sheaves in, pull empty stalks out, and sweep the kernels into wheelbarrows to bring over to us. I need someone to help me fill sacks, stitch them closed, and stack them on the sled. You just want my fingers to be frazzled to the bone while you pump a sheet in the air."

"No, I don't." Menandros twisted his features at her and shook his head. "I just didn't think you needed help. After all, you're so good at everything."

"Ha!" Philomena exclaimed.

"I'll help you, Mother."

"And so will I," Oma said. "My arms are tired of flapping up and down."

Ariel accompanied Oma to sit with her mother and they each picked up a cloth bag. Using wide, hand-held grain scoops, they shoveled kernels from the threshing floor into the bags while Philomena stitched her full one closed.

"Tell me about the meeting," Oma whispered, leaning in with a spark of intense interest in her aging eyes.

"What meeting?" Philomena asked. "I thought you were off with Lysandra reconnecting the past couple of days."

"It was kind of both. Oma, I met your old friend, Noah," she said with a sly smile and a wink her mother didn't see.

"Well, stars above!" Oma laughed. "How is the old fool?"

"Still building ships," she answered. "He has a younger wife and three sons, with wives of their own."

"I wonder if that makes his second or third wife," Oma mused. "You live to pass four hundred years, and you'll go through a few."

"You didn't," Philomena mentioned. "You had the same husband for a hundred and six years and didn't remarry after he died."

"Baa," she scoffed, waving a hand in the air. "One husband was enough. I then became a free spirit—go where I want, do what I want. I've earned that privilege. Besides, I have you all to keep me company. Now, about the meeting."

Ariel glanced around at the others, who were busy tossing wheat and chatting about some upcoming event in the village. With her bag filled, Ariel passed it to her mother. "No definitive causes or solutions, but an astronomer named Ziusudra has some theories. Thoth is leading the inquiry and has given me an assignment. Mother, I'm sorry to push Sheera off on you, but she wants to invite her suitors to dinner and ask your opinion of them. I have to go on a cross-country tour to speak with all the animals and trees."

Philomena smiled. "I'd love to host Sheera and her suitors. I presume she'll want to cook, though, to show them what she can prepare." She paused to nibble on a nail. "That's all right. I'll help her and make sure it comes out tasty. I know she can put together a stunning outfit to wear, but cook? Now, what's this about interrogating animals?"

Ariel laughed. "Not interrogate, just ask what they've noticed that seems out of order. The giant tortoises and whales will be most helpful, as they live the longest and may carry stories from their ancestors. One of my most important interviews will be with the Oldest Tree, a sequoia in the forests of Ampherium."

"Dear," her mother addressed with the first tinge of concern, "what is this all about?"

Ariel exchanged a look with Oma. "Everyone asked to attend the meeting has noticed some changes—mostly minor ones—and we're trying to decide what's causing them. You shouldn't worry." *Yet*, she thought.

"Well, if any weddings get planned, we'll be sure to schedule them for after you get back," Philomena said. "Mine included." Her face lit with a playful, rosy glow, and she batted her lashes at Ariel and Oma.

"Really?" Ariel buzzed with excitement. "The fellow you were telling me about?"

"Eadric." Her mother nodded and tied off her last stitch. "I'm not too old to enjoy myself, and, unlike Naunet, I like to wake up to the same man every morning."

"You make me sound like a hussy," Oma mumbled offendedly. She squared her shoulders, jutted up her chin, and passed Philomena another filled bag. The suggestion was so absurd that it made Ariel laugh.

"I love you both!" she declared, kissing both women's cheeks. "No weddings until I return."

"And when might that be?" Philomena asked, quirking her brow in suspicion.

Ariel's enthusiasm shrank. "I'm not sure, but I'll likely be back near Winter Solstice—not *for* Winter Solstice, as we have another meeting planned on that day, but around then."

Philomena's eyes widened. "So long? Goodness gracious. What is it the young people say these days? Bury a spoon!"

Hearing her mother use the latest colloquialism sent Ariel into another wave of laughter, and Oma joined her.

Ariel would help her family today, but tomorrow she'd be off on her adventure, or so she thought of it. *Let me plan the most efficient route,* she strategized while stuffing bags with grain. *I'll start at the southern tip and work my way north. I'll travel light and carry plenty of coins so I can purchase what I need along the way. And I'll take a scroll and quill to write everything down on.* Surely, I'll learn something of significance, and it won't be wasted effort; even if not, I'm finally making time to visit all the places I've never been before. I'll swim with dolphins, climb the highest mountains, and see the Terrible Ice.

Just thinking about it sent a shiver down her back. Few people ventured to the northern peninsula to see it, but those who had returned with frightening tales of its enormous, looming presence like a wall marking the end of the earth beyond which nothing could survive. *What is beyond the ice—just more ice?* Maybe she'd find out.

18

Atala, later the same day

Lysandra opened her apartment door as her neighbor Helene, from two doors down, approached through the second-floor breezeway. "Oh, good, you're back," the shorter, younger woman greeted with a dimpled smile. A halo of tight brunette curls reminiscent of a mohair goat framed her round face. "How was your conference?"

"Informative," she answered, not wishing to share details. Though no one specifically required them to keep their discussion a secret, Lysandra deemed it shouldn't turn into rumor.

"Here, let me help you," her eager friend offered, and lifted Lysandra's travel bag.

"Thank you." Lysandra held her door wide, inviting Helene inside. Once inside, she opened a window to freshen the small space. "Is Timoleon back yet?" she asked.

"Not for another week," she sighed and set the bag on the kitchen table. "He loves the adventure of traveling and makes good money as first mate, but he's gone so much it's almost like we aren't married at all." Then she grinned, with a hint of color rising in her cheeks. "But when he is home, he sure lets me know it!"

Lysandra laughed. "It's like the best of both worlds," she said. "Half of the time you get to do what you want, and the other half you enjoy married life."

"I suppose," Helene agreed. "I'm just so glad I have a friend close by, so I don't get lonely. Hey, there's a concert at Paradise Hall tonight and I was thinking about going. The Canary Quartet from Elapus is playing and I've heard they're terrific. My boss gave me two tickets, which I suppose were to make up for me almost getting injured when a riot broke out a few days ago."

While the invitation to the concert was nice, Lysandra's mind shot to attention at the word "riot."

"Helene, come sit over here and tell me about it," Lysandra requested, showing her to the little sofa by the balcony door.

"Oh, they're playing some classic favorites, like *Poseidon and Clito—*"

"No, not the quartet—the riot." She sat on the cushion, and her friend followed.

Lysandra had been tired from her trip, the physical and emotional stress, and her mind had darted like a hummingbird all day between daydreaming about getting back together with Ariel and the possibility of a coming apocalypse. She needed something else to think about, and, really, a riot in Atala? Unheard of!

"Crazy, right?" She fluffed her hair with a smoothly manicured hand and flashed Lysandra a bewildered expression. She was still in her official blue chiton with a white sash bearing the Atala government symbol of a crossed crook and flail. "I mean, we sometimes have people grumble about paying their taxes, but mostly everyone is fine with it. I mean, they don't have to pay for water, sewer, transportation, or medical services, and there are price caps for rent and other important things, so nobody gets overcharged."

Helene took a breath and rested her hands on her lap. "So, anyway, I was standing at my booth smiling at citizens as they came in, when this angry man—must have been twice my size—pushed his way to the front of the line, actually cut in front of an elderly lady!" she exclaimed in horror.

"Was something wrong with him?" The very idea of a big man pushing in front of an elderly woman was mortifying, not to mention illegal.

"I'll say!" Helene asserted. "He banged his fist on the counter, waving a piece of parchment in my face, and yelled, 'This is robbery! I refuse to pay!' Everyone in the tax office stared at him like he had two heads. I backed up, holding my hands out to show him I wasn't a threat—I mean, can you imagine anyone thinking *I* was a threat?"

As far as Atlantean women went, Helene was indeed on the small side. Lysandra, engaged in her story, shook her head. "Definitely not a threat."

"Right? So Tepoz—he's my supervisor, the assistant to the tax minister—came over and tried to calm the guy down. Then he took a swing at Tepoz—with his fist! Tepoz ducked, and the man whacked the side of the counter, hurling it into me."

"Oh gods, Helene—are you injured? Let me take a look." Lysandra gently laid her hands on Helene's arm and shoulder, seeking what needed her attention.

"I'm all right," she answered shyly. "Tepoz sent me to the back room to lie down with an ice pack and self-heal. It was only a few bruises. It took three city guardians to haul the angry man away. They called for a priest because he had to be crazy, right? Nobody acts that way."

"They didn't use to," Lysandra said, recalling the little boy she had treated with the swollen lip, black eye, and arm twisted out of joint. *Noah mentioned men breaking out into a fight as well. Could this blatant disregard for the law, or inability to control emotions, have anything to do with the other problems we're experiencing? If Atlanteans lose our close connection to the divine energies, we could end up as depraved as other races of humans. Please, Archangel Michael, protect me. Don't let that ever happen to me!*

"So ..." Helene perked up, a bright grin beaming across her youthful face. "I have two tickets to the concert." She pulled them out of the pouch on her belt and waved them at Lysandra.

Returning a soft smile, Lysandra consented. She knew the professional quartet would never live up to Ariel and her pickup group improvising beside the

Ring of Stones, but she enjoyed music, and it would be nice to do something fun with her neighbor.

"Thank you, Helene. I'd love to go with you. I just need to run over to the bathhouse and freshen up. What time do you want to leave?"

"At dusk?"

That gave Lysandra two turns of the sandglass to get ready—plenty of time. "I'll meet you in front of our building."

Helene gave her a friendly hug and hopped up. "I'll see you then," she chirped and dashed out. Lysandra's gaze was drawn to her easel, canvases, and paints tucked away in their corner. "And I'll be visiting you soon, too," she promised.

☦ ⚛ ✢ ✡

*R*yzen, a few days after the full moon

"Be careful with that," Temen directed to two young men in white kilts who were packing an exquisite vase, hand-painted with grandly attired musicians holding a lyre, harp, flute, and drum, encircling its bulbous lower third. "It was a gift from a generous, admiring patron."

Rhoxane breezed across the main room of Temen's modest villa, with the thinnest of fabrics veiling pink undergarments, and pointed at a painting of three scantily clad, muscular men engaged in a game of jump the bull, with a very well-endowed bull taking center stage. "Tell me you don't plan to hang *this* on the palace wall," she remarked in disgust.

"Why not?" Temen asked, puzzled by her objection. "As one of the ten kings of Atlantis, I'll get to take part in the fabled bullfight."

"Do you even know what it represents?" Lykos inquired in a most disagreeable tone that confounded the king-elect even further.

"Of course I know what it means," Temen snapped in offense. "Man exercising his domination over the animal kingdom, or something about fertility." Lykos probably lectured him on this subject years ago, but Temen couldn't keep all the stories straight. Besides, he had more important things to think about.

Three weeks from today, he'd be standing before all the important people of Ryzen, along with foreign dignitaries, to be crowned ruler. King Temen. His chest puffed up with pride at the thought.

"On the surface, men associate the bull with fertility, true enough," Lykos replied from his seat at the table across the room. He had a scroll, quill, and ink, scribbling words on papyrus. He was always writing something. *I don't like his patronizing tone. After all, I'm the one who's going to be king, not him.*

"But the bull also symbolizes the human ego, which must be sacrificed in order for us to become one with the Universal Consciousness," the wizard continued. "We must die to self to be raised to eternal life, Temen, a very important concept. It doesn't matter if you believe it or not; when you speak with the other kings in the council, you must know these things."

Temen frowned. "Oh, yeah, the other kings and the Council of Rulers," he muttered.

"Don't worry," Lykos directed, with more cheer in his voice. "We've almost two months to have you ready before the assembly meets in Atala. I guarantee they'll be impressed with you. Now, we have more important matters to decide, such as who you will appoint as your chief ministers. It would be wise to keep some of the current officeholders for several reasons."

"Yes, yes," Temen replied impatiently. "You there!" He pointed to the young man with the black hair and beard. "Pack the painting and do not damage it. Rhoxane, dear, you should bring artwork you appreciate to the palace as well. I'm not demanding everything be what I alone prefer."

She planted a kiss on his cheek and flashed provocatively dangerous eyes at him. "Oh, don't worry; I will."

Lykos had the audacity to groan. "Look, *advisor*." Temen rounded on the old wizard and stomped across the plank floor to stand over him. "I know what I'm doing. I'm allowed to bring with me whomever I wish to stay in the palace, and, at the moment," he flashed a playful grin over his shoulder at the woman eying him lustily, "it's Rhoxane. And why not? Simply because we aren't married? Do you think the people will talk and grumble? That they won't approve?"

Suddenly, Temen was pricked with a dreadful fear. The citizens ousted Queen Izevel because they didn't like what she was doing. They could do the same to him.

"That's it, isn't it!" His eyes widened in understanding. "You're afraid the voters won't approve of their king keeping a mistress. But Rhoxane is beautiful, rich, and from an important family—a historically prominent bloodline. If she was to conceive a child, it would need a proper father."

Temen spun around and strode back to Rhoxane. He never planned to marry her ... well, maybe; he just hadn't decided yet. Besides, it had been easy enough for him to get out of his first marriage.

"Rhoxane, what have I been thinking? I've been far too caught up with politics and persuading the minds of the masses and forgot about what matters most—us."

He took her hands and dropped to his knees, gazing up at her with his best expression of devotion. "I realize we haven't been seeing each other long, but, in these past few weeks, my affection for you has grown exceedingly. I can think of no other woman who would make a better queen. Please, my love, forgive my oafish attempts at courtship and agree to be both my wife and queen."

An expression of immense satisfaction spread across her face. When she glanced over his shoulder, he swung his head around to see Lykos nod his approval—as if he or Rhoxane required it. A second's anger flashed through him before it evaporated into glorious anticipation. When the glamorous woman lowered her seductive gaze to his, he felt himself harden with desire.

"Yes, Temen," she replied in a husky tone. "I would love nothing more than to be your wife and queen."

With a buoyancy that could launch an air coach without the aid of antigravity, he leaped to his feet, wrapped her in his arms, and kissed her deeply.

"Sire, about these ministers," Lykos reminded him.

"You select them," Temen commanded. "Rhoxane and I have a wedding to plan."

It seemed Lykos never smiled, but when Temen glimpsed him as he passed, escorting Rhoxane to his bedroom, he was certain the old wizard wore a satisfied expression. "Capital idea of yours, Master Lykos," Temen whispered in shameless revelry. "I think the people will be pleased."

19

The Mestorian Rainforest, a week after the full moon

Gentle droplets filtered through the canopy of mangroves to the patch of earth Ariel occupied. The brackish water of the estuary spread out before her with the thick gnarl of arching prop roots forming a woody net at her back. More of the specially adapted tropical trees lined the opposite side of the peaceful inlet that was home to a plethora of species. A brown pelican perched on a root runner that stretched over the surface, its keen gaze scanning for a tasty morsel while a great blue heron stalked the shallow waters on stilt-like legs.

Ariel locked eyes with an armored alligator twice as long as she was tall, lazing in the water with its head—covered in sunbathing babies—resting on the sandy ground. While the crocodilian line was ancient, this individual claimed to be fifty years old, around Ariel's age. With a few deep breaths, she achieved the vibrational signal produced by the alligator and sent her a soothing frequency of friendship. The reptile introduced herself as Ixquic, which means "Mother of Heroes."

Not wishing to get into a long discourse on her many children and how heroic they must all be, Ariel got straight to the point and asked about any noticeable changes in the ecosystem. Ixquic hadn't noticed anything, but the blue heron spoke to her through the ether.

"Frogs." He imprinted not the word, but the image of a frog into Ariel's consciousness. The scene the heron transmitted was one of thousands of frogs, then hundreds, and finally a few dozen. Then, not wishing to tempt the alligator, he spread his glorious, wide wings and took to the air, crossing the bayou to land on the other side.

The pelican plunged its bill into the water, bringing it out with a gular pouch full of small fish. *Plenty of mullet*, the bird relayed and flapped its wings.

Thanking the animals for speaking with her, Ariel climbed up onto the knobby roots of the nearest mangrove until she could reach its trunk. She rubbed her palms together while clearing her mind and then pressed one to the tree's trunk. Closing her eyes, she sent feelings of appreciation and respect from her heart, through her shoulder, arm, and hand, pressing the energy into the tree. Then she waited, her eyes closed and her heart chakra open. Mangroves were not long-lived trees, and this one was likely no older than the alligator. Still, trees often noticed things animals didn't.

Plants were harder to interpret because they didn't communicate through thoughts, images, mannerisms, and body language the way animals did, but through secreted chemicals and vibrational frequencies alone. Ariel could only count on instinct and aid from the spirit world to interpret the language of trees. The sensations she received from the mangrove involved anxiety over the weather and something she supposed meant "hot root syndrome." That fit with Mandisa's report on warming water temperatures and more extreme storms. The electromagnetic atmospheric activity and the warmer water were stressing the tree. But was that all?

Ariel climbed back out of the thicket of rainforest to the deafening cry of howler monkeys. They must have never met a nature speaker before because, when she asked them to be quiet, they rushed out of the trees to stare at her and began conversing with each other about this freakish human who impressed her thoughts into their brains. Not wanting to waste time on the monkeys—or, heavens forbid, get them excited enough to start howling again—Ariel kept going.

Just before leaving the forest, a sleek, black jaguar lumbered down the trunk of an enormous kapok tree and stepped in front of her, twisting her tail and licking her lips. Ariel calmly sat on the wide knee of the kapok, radiating confidence and friendship toward the gorgeous feline. She opened her palms to the big cat, letting her know she was neither prey nor predator. The jaguar turned and paced a few steps back, eying her curiously, then settled down in a patch of soft ferns to groom herself.

"You are so beautiful," Ariel praised with complete candor, "unmatched the perfection of your grace and strength. Tell me; does anything feel wrong to you?"

The cat stopped licking and caught Ariel's gaze. *You feel it too?* she asked. *You don't look like an old one.*

"I'm not," she replied, inputting the meaning of her words into the feline's awareness.

My grandmother told me what her grandmother told her going back many generations, the jaguar relayed in curiosity. *In the time before, humans and jaguars could converse, but, in the time after, the ability was lost. How can you then converse with me?*

"There are a few of us who are still blessed with the gift," Ariel explained. "What do you feel?"

My grandmother says the air is lighter than it used to be. You will return it to normal?

"I don't know if I can," Ariel admitted, "but I'll try."

I will help you if I can. You know where to find me. She rose and stretched with a big yawn sporting long, sharp teeth.

"What is your name?"

Moonshadow, she answered with a deep, panting mew before disappearing into the thicket.

Ariel walked back to the city of Mestoria, where she had spent the night, heading for the river docks. Palm trees lined the thoroughfare, and people driving sleighs had their roofs up to keep out the rain. However, the shower did nothing to interfere with commerce at the marketplace, where every stall had a canvas top. Shoppers wore wide-brimmed, conical straw hats or carried umbrellas as they bustled about the streets. Few men wore tunics, as almost all were in kilts alone, and many of the women dressed in short kilts and midriff-revealing breast wraps. If they wore any shoes at all, they were thong sandals. Ariel had never seen so informal a society before. Yet, between the heat and moisture, their attire made sense.

Buildings and houses had pointed, triangular rooftops with water-collecting gutters channeling the flow off into large barrels, and a towering step pyramid dominated the skyline, topped by its huge, energy-gathering crystal.

"Ice blocks!" shouted a vendor from the market. "Get your ice blocks here—straight from Gadlan!"

Passing the market, Ariel walked along the cypress planks of the river docks where fishers brought in their day's hauls. She headed for the harbor hut at the end of a pier and stepped under the thatched roof to escape the rain.

"Look, I told you already," came the irritated growl of the tanned man stacking boxes. He turned around, presumably for more scolding, then dropped his bearded jaw in surprise. "Oh, I'm sorry. I thought you were somebody else. We're going to be closing soon," he said. "What can I do for you?"

"I need to rent a small boat," Ariel replied.

"Now?" The man gave her a skeptical look. "It's raining and will be dark before long. Most tourists rent boats in the morning, so they'll have all day to explore the river and bayous."

His advice made sense, and she had plenty of time. Ariel felt more anxious than normal, wishing to find her answers as quickly as possible, as though the weight of the world hung in the balance. She knew she could find giant tortoises and dolphins when she went to Menosus and wished to consult with anteaters and sloths here. *Macaws live a long time and they're easy to talk to. Better in the daytime.*

"Very well," she replied. "I'll return in the morning. Hey, who has the best food around here?"

He grinned. "My grandmother! She runs an eatery called the Puckered Pineapple and they serve the best local cuisine, authentic Mestorian dishes with just the right mix of spicy and sweet. Tell her Bobo sent you and you'll be treated right. See you in the morning?"

"Sounds like a plan."

Ariel enjoyed her meal and returned to the inn after dark, and, though it had stopped raining, the humidity remained high. She changed into a dry tunic and climbed into the hammock provided for sleeping. The inn—with its open window walls that could be pulled down and secured during storms but stayed up for abundant airflow the rest of the time—was quite different from those she was accustomed to. She suspected spiders, ants, and scorpions—as well as alligators and jaguars—could just wander in while she slept. She closed her eyes under a thin sheet of mosquito netting and listened to the song of the tree frogs.

Frogs, the blue heron said ... fewer frogs than there once were. Frogs eat mosquitos while larger animals like herons and snakes eat frogs. He would notice if there were not as many around, but what does that mean? Maybe they moved to a different part of the island with fewer predators. Frogs have very basic brains and don't seem to think at all, but instinct could have directed them to move. Or did the bird mean something else? I didn't notice an overabundance of snakes, lizards, large birds, or baby alligators, not enough to eat all the frogs. In time, she drifted off to sleep.

☥ ⛥ ☩ ✡

The next day, Ariel rented her boat and paddled up and down the Swazi River to the songs of birds and insects. This time, pinpricks of sunlight penetrated spots in the canopy like tiny streams of lasers while the lazy flow of the stream moved her along. Wild orchids and exotic blooms in a full array of colors burst out of the foliage and along tree branches wrapped in vines, lending fragrance to the stuffy air. A thirty-two-year-old sloth took its slow and exacting time to express that she had no complaints to submit while a fifteen-year-old scarlet macaw registered a long list with her, starting with the howler monkeys.

By the end of the day, though filled with wonder and amazement at the plant and animal life of the rainforest, Ariel was no closer to uncovering what was causing the energies to lose their power. The next day, she took a shuttle coach to Ryzen and walked several leagues from the air dock to Mandisa's citrus orchard.

Though still bordering on tropical and rife with humidity, Ryzen's landscape was far less of a jungle and more of a lush, temperate region that seldom saw a frost. Broadleaf vegetation sprang up along the road with a mix of nonconifer evergreens and deciduous trees lining one side, while a rolling meadow of tall grasses and solitary shade trees spread to the other. A herd of gazelles munched away, with a few keeping watch for jackals or lions who may lurk on the plain. The wild landscape changed abruptly when rows and rows of short trees came into view, as far as Ariel could see in all directions. Workers were harvesting from hovering sleds, filling crates with orange and yellow fruit.

With the smell of citrus renewing her energy, Ariel followed the path to a layout resembling her farmhouse with a few variations. The main abode had a southern orientation, with a covered veranda supported by white columns in front facing the well. The brick structure was two levels high, featuring a modestly-sloped roof and an upper-level terrace topping the small part of its "L" construction. Rather than cream or white, the exterior walls were a pleasing shade of rosy-pink, and dark walnut beams formed a tasteful contrast. Flowers and green leafy plants exploded all around, and outdoor seating had been arranged with comfort in mind. To one side was a covered post shed where a sleigh and several sleds were parked and a structure resembling a warehouse flanked the other side of the compound.

Hashur smiled and waved at her as he exited the open doorway. "Welcome, Ariel!" He greeted her with a hug and kiss on the cheek. "You should have sent word when you were arriving, and one of us could have picked you up at the air dock."

"Thank you, Hashur, but it was a pleasant walk which gave me time to enjoy the scenery, not to mention talk to a woodpecker."

"Mandisa is out in the grove supervising the last of the crop being gathered," he said, "and Agathon is in town, probably browsing a library or bookstore. Excuse me for a moment; Mandisa wanted me to call for her as soon as you arrived."

The strapping man, whose personality reminded her of her brother Aram, stepped over to the well and lifted a horn with a cord tied to it from one of four posts supporting a shallow pyramid-shaped covering. He pressed it to his lips and blew. While not as obnoxious as the howler monkeys, Ariel was certain anyone for leagues around could hear it. Come to think of it, she should have one on her farm for just such a purpose.

"Come, sit in the shade, and let me get you a drink while we wait," Hashur invited. "I'm a little sweaty from stacking crates in the warehouse, and hopefully my odor isn't offensive. Would you like orange water or lemon water, and ice or no?"

Ariel followed him into the shade of the veranda and sat on the cushioned sofa he directed her to. "Iced lemon water sounds very refreshing. You are so kind even your odor wouldn't know how to be offensive."

He chuckled and poured their drinks into tall cups of blown glass, decorated with painted etchings of pink flamingos and cattails. Her first sip really hit the spot.

"She'll be here soon," he said, settling into a wicker armchair set at an angle to her.

"Whose land?" Ariel asked.

"Mandisa inherited it from her grandparents. No one else wanted the work and responsibility of so large a grove. Now, don't go thinking Agathon and I are gold diggers who seduced her for her property," Hashur added playfully. "We both brought abundance to this union as well, but I enjoy the peace and quiet of the countryside, and the work keeps me in shape for my athletic pursuits."

"Welcome!"

They turned to see Mandisa slide in on a sled stacked with orange crates, her sandal-clad feet dangling from the side. This time, the stylish woman wore an everyday work tunic and had gathered her array of braids back with a yellow headband. She parked the sled at the edge of the veranda and joined them with a smile and a light sheen of perspiration on her face.

Hashur hopped up and greeted her with a quick kiss. "I'll take these to the barn."

Ariel stood to meet her hostess, who pulled her into a light embrace, also kissing her cheek. "I don't want to get you sweaty," she offered in humble apology.

"No worries," Ariel replied. "I'm honored to receive such a warm welcome at your home."

"Certainly! You are like family, and you must stay here while you're in Ryzen," Mandisa invited. She settled onto the sofa and patted the spot beside her for Ariel. They had only met for the first time at the Ring of Stones, but Ariel sensed a connection to the gifted woman as well.

"That is most kind of you."

"You may want to steer clear of the city, though," Mandisa said as she smoothed her tunic over her ample curves. "It's like a henhouse at feeding time right now, what with the new king about to be installed and all."

"Izevel is no longer queen?" Ariel asked.

"There were protests and a new election was held, but I don't waste my energy on politics," Mandisa asserted. "Why should I be preoccupied with a new king when we are all gods?"

"Or used to be," Ariel bemoaned. She ran her fingers through her hair in frustration.

"Ariel, don't despair. We are still who we have always been—children of the Creator," Mandisa counseled. "The loss of abilities or waning of energetic forces doesn't change the fact that we are divine spiritual beings exploring the world in human bodies. Even if our years on earth are cut in half or more, we know we'll live forever. I have touched the field, mingled with the souls of our ancestors, and felt the power that creates worlds flow through my physical body. Even if we become like average humans, we are still extraordinary. As long as we value love and use our imaginations for good, the Creator still lives in us, and we in the Creator. As above, so below."

"As within, so without." Ariel completed the familiar concept stated in the Law of Reflection and represented by the symbol of intersecting triangles pointing up and down—otherwise known as the six-point star. "I do not doubt our divine origins or our spiritual immortality. It's just that things on earth are changing, and change can be unsettling, even if we don't allow it to produce fear in our hearts."

"Yes, change can be hard," Mandisa agreed. "I don't want to lose my gift as an air speaker any more than you wish to lose the ability to converse with plants and animals. Maybe we can find a way to stabilize whatever is happening before it goes that far. Now, tell me what you have learned thus far, and I'll share the bits I've interpreted."

20

Atala, a week later

Lysandra stood on her tiny balcony, with just enough room to set her easel and not knock it over, to capture the best light for her painting. With her prepared pallet in one hand and a superior-quality brush made from the sable hairs of a Gadlan weasel in the other, she applied the paint to the canvas. She didn't have to wrestle with her ethics because the company that made the brushes kept the weasels on a farm and sheared them like sheep each summer, so no animals were harmed to make them. "But," she had once wondered, "do the weasels like living on the farm or are they being held against their will?" She had planned to get Ariel to ask them one day, although she only half wished to learn the answer. They were excellent brushes.

She dabbed and stroked the pigments on the canvas, mixing colors to achieve the desired hue, and the more she painted, the more inspired she became. Letting go of her conscious plan, Lysandra allowed the energies that surrounded and filled her to guide her hand, transforming her simple landscape into something else.

Consumed by the passion of creating, she propped a new canvas on the easel and filled it with shapes and colors without planning or looking at any subject.

It almost felt like she was in a trance—light, ethereal, her imagination galloping like a wild horse. She lost track of time and the sun set without her realizing it. When the flurry of inspired painting fell away and she came back to her normal way of being, three completed works leaned against the wall and one rested on the easel in front of her.

The knock sounded at her door again. Again? How long had she left someone knocking without answering them? Mortified at a breach of hospitality, Lysandra set down her brushes and pallet and rushed to the door. Expecting to see Helene or possibly Quetzal, her breath caught in her throat at the sight of Ariel standing here. For a second instance that evening, she felt as though trapped in a temporal vortex, disoriented and elated at once.

Ariel smiled at her. "You've been painting."

"Uh, yes. How do you know?" It was a lame response, but Lysandra had been caught completely off guard.

"Because you have a little—" Ariel's finger brushed Lysandra's cheek, sending a tingle of pleasure racing through her system.

"Oh, right." She hid her desire behind an embarrassed smile and absently rubbed the spot, which only smeared more paint on it. Lysandra stepped back, opening the door wide. "Won't you come in? I'm sorry, I wasn't expecting you."

"I felt it was only fair to return the favor," Ariel quipped as she strode into the small apartment, giving it an assessing glance.

Well, that was warranted, after the way she had shown up at Ariel's farm unannounced.

"Is this Adira?" she asked, peering at the elephant's image. "You mentioned painting her."

"Yes," Lysandra confirmed, as she glided to Ariel's side. "I had to do it from memory, but—"

"It's quite good," she commented. "You always were a brilliant artist. And I see I interrupted your painting tonight."

As Ariel strolled past her toward the open balcony door, a glint of gold flashed from the neckline of her rust-colored tunic. *Is that the ankh I gave her? Could she have kept it all this time?* Lysandra dared not ask lest the answer be no.

"I haven't even had a chance to look at them yet," she said instead, rushing to get ahead of Ariel. The attempt failed.

Ariel studied the piece on the easel with a tilt of her head. "What do you mean you haven't looked at them yet? You didn't paint them blindfolded, did you?"

"Not exactly." Lysandra joined Ariel in viewing the most recently finished work. "I was in some sort of artist haze, just letting the creative energies flow, you know? Not planned, just ..."

"I know what you mean," Ariel answered, as if she didn't think Lysandra was crazy at all. "That happens to me sometimes when I'm playing my flute and just let the music take me where it may. Is this a constellation?"

Lysandra scrutinized her work of tiny white dots on a background of darkest blue. "Maybe."

"This looks like Leo," Ariel said, pointing to a group of stars, "and this one could be Aquarius."

"But Leo and Aquarius don't appear next to each other in the sky." Lysandra was puzzled by what her own painting depicted. "We are currently in the age of Leo, so that part makes sense."

"I don't know. You painted it." Ariel stepped onto the balcony to look at the other pieces, and Lysandra turned on the outside light and joined her. "A ship at sea." Ariel crouched beside it.

"I thought it might have had something to do with my parents' shipwreck, especially since I reached out to them at the Ring of Stones, but I'm not sure."

"Lysandra, you're a talented artist, but this doesn't look like any ship I've ever seen," Ariel commented. "Where are the oars or the sails? It looks more like a giant floating barn than a ship. And, look—there are more of them in the distance."

"I don't know," she answered in bewilderment. "I told you I was in a haze."

"All the more reason we should interpret your prophetic paintings correctly," Ariel declared and moved on to the first one she had painted.

As soon as Lysandra's gaze fell on it, she shrank in humiliation, a knot of anxiety twisting in her gut. "Maybe I wasn't under any spiritual influence for that one."

Ariel's blue-green eyes caught hers with a sarcastic expression. "Do you think?"

Honestly, Lysandra didn't remember painting Ariel and herself holding hands, and, inspecting the background, the location didn't seem familiar to her at all. The idea of confessing to Ariel that she had also painted this piece under the influence of the energies terrified Lysandra. She wouldn't believe her and would think it was a manipulative ploy to get them back together.

"You can't deny me hope," she answered, trying to force a laugh. "Come in and let me prepare a meal for us."

Ariel's brows furrowed, and a seriousness fell over her expression. Then she returned her gaze to the painting. "When and where is this supposed to be?"

"I—um—I told you; it's just a dream."

Stretching to her full height, Ariel observed, "You are a poor liar; always have been. This is your impression of some future event when you and I travel to a foreign place. I don't recall this landscape, though I must give you credit for making me appear more attractive on canvas than I am in person."

"But you *are* beautiful," she blurted out, immediately wishing to rein in her words. Lysandra retreated into the apartment and paced to the kitchen. "I have a variety of fruits, nuts, and vegetables, and can heat some bread. Or I have shrimp and cornmeal to make those fried cakes you used to like."

She felt Ariel's presence a breath from her ear before she spoke. "You don't have to be afraid of what I'll think or say or do, Lysandra. You should know how I feel about you; I just can't go through losing you again. That doesn't mean we can't work together as friends to help solve the problems Atlantis faces. No beef?"

Lysandra spun around with a horrified expression. "Certainly not! You have friends who are cows. I would never—"

"Just because I don't—"

"Many people avoid meat in their diets," Lysandra asserted. "Fish has health benefits, but the rest is unnecessary to maintain physical wellbeing. Besides, I can't unknow what you've shown me about the animal kingdom."

Ariel presented her with a warm, amorous smile of appreciation and brushed a hand across her shoulder. "I will love whatever you throw together. Just make what you were planning to have for yourself."

Her electric fingers trailed away, and Ariel returned to inspecting her dwelling. Lysandra laid some fruit and salad fixings out on a cutting board and turned on a small oven to warm bread left from yesterday. "When did you arrive in the city?"

"Last night," Ariel replied. "I spent most of today at Thoth's library researching old treatises on natural history and writings from a time when nearly everyone could commune with nature as only a few can today. Ziusudra had mentioned a first great cataclysm that occurred long millennia in the past that we never learned about in school, so I tried to access information about it."

"Any luck?"

Ariel pivoted and strolled back in her direction. "The references are all very vague, just that terrible earthquakes shook the world, land masses shifted, climate changed, the first Atlantean civilization was destroyed, and the survivors had to start over. We know considerably more about the Conflagration, as it was much more recent. There was an interesting story dating from shortly before the Conflagration about a lush garden in the center of the continent where a vast number of species cohabitated. All the people there could converse with all the animals, and they lived in great peace and prosperity."

Lysandra turned from her chopping to look at Ariel in wonder. "It sounds marvelous. What happened to it?"

"The story didn't say, but I'm guessing the Conflagration happened, the great and awful comet represented by a devouring serpent image in the sky. It had to have altered the earth or the energies somehow. It was only afterward people began dying younger and losing their abilities."

"Yes, but it wasn't instant," Lysandra said as she piled fruit and greens into bowls. "Maybe something new happened afterward, just a few hundred years ago, that has affected the changes. What do the animals and trees say?"

"I haven't found any old enough to recall, although Moonshadow—the most gorgeous black jaguar I've ever met—thought I was an 'old one' since she didn't know nature speakers still existed."

Lysandra laughed and pulled the bread from the oven. "You are far from being an old one, dear."

"I always believed my connection to the energies would grow with age," Ariel said with regret as she sat in a chair at the table. "Instead, they've weakened. Oma lost her connection to nature years ago. I hope that doesn't happen to me. Having this gift makes me feel like part of the One. I don't know how Oma keeps her faith."

Lysandra set the bowls, bread, and two cups of wine on the table and joined Ariel. "You are more than your special ability, Ariel—so much more. Don't forget it."

She responded with a weak nod and began eating.

Lysandra shared her research and Helene's story about the out-of-control man at the tax office while they ate. They talked about Yaluk and how she neither held a grudge nor welcomed Lysandra back with open arms—a kind of unemotional acceptance of her absence in their lives. "But I will do better," she vowed. "You know, either of you could have come to see me, too."

"I did."

At Ariel's revelation, Lysandra stared at her, setting down her utensils, her mouth open in astonishment. "When?"

"The first time, you had been in wisdom school for about a year and a half without coming home or sending word," Ariel relayed. "I flew down to Atala and took a sleigh out to the school. They told me you were up in a cave in the mountains and couldn't be reached, so I left you a letter."

"I never got it." She hadn't. Did the secretary or attendant, or whoever, lose it, or just forget to give it to her? "Ariel, I swear—"

"I came again about two years later, only this time they said your class was on a field trip to Menosus to swim with dolphins."

"Yes," Lysandra recalled. "Something I'm certain you've done. It was ... indescribable."

Ariel nodded. "They are remarkable creatures, and in so close a frequency to the Creator. We can learn much from them. I left you a letter that time as well."

Lysandra felt sick inside. "What can I say? I never knew you came, and I never got your messages." Propping an elbow on the table, she rested her head in her hand, unable to look at Ariel. "Ariel, I'm so—"

A hand closed over hers, with comfort radiating from it. "I wasn't going to mention it, but you brought it up. The time for sorry is past. We need to be raising our vibrations, not lowering them with past regrets. Would you like me to stop by early in the morning to perform our Ruh Mutaharika together? Then I'll be leaving Atala. I wanted to watch you work, but maybe another time."

"I'd honestly like you to stay with me instead of at an inn, but—" Glancing at her single bed, Lysandra yearned for the opportunity to make up for lost time and show Ariel the intensity of her love. She knew deep down that it was an impossible dream—for now, anyway.

"Yes, please come," Lysandra concluded. "I'll have tea ready at first light."

Ariel stood and, with a bittersweet smile, said, "You have a lovely apartment. Thank you for the delicious dinner, and I'll see you in the morning."

Before Lysandra could see her to the door, Ariel was gone.

The healer wasn't certain which was more difficult, mending her patients' misfunctioning bodies or warding off the momentum of regret building inside her. *It serves no purpose. What's done is done. You didn't know she came to see you. You got so caught up in fresh knowledge and novel experiences that you lost track of time. It's nobody's fault; it just happened. The important thing is that you move forward correctly. Don't make the same mistakes or even new ones.*

"I have to get it right this time," she voiced to her empty room.

21

Ariel had prepared herself emotionally to see Lysandra again that morning. The look on her face when she'd told her she came looking for her was almost more than she could bear. If she hadn't left when she did, she might have given in and shared that small bed with her former lover. Although she still loved Lysandra, Ariel had to protect her own heart first.

Lysandra welcomed her in, and they made small talk over morning tea and biscuits. It felt so natural to share the simple ritual, like returning to the home one grew up in. Even though they had each evolved and experienced vastly different lives, Ariel noticed how easily they fit back together, as if they had only parted ways last week.

With the balcony door open, a gentle breeze caressed their skin as they performed their meditative exercise movements in the center of the room. Soon, Ariel noticed their breathing had fallen into sync, while their forms and stances flowed in such harmony it was as if they rode a current in the same vessel. Sinking deeper into the moment, she sensed their two frequencies flux into one, Lysandra's emotions and thoughts melding with her own in a most intimate union.

By the final bow of the sequence, the attraction between them had become so powerful that Ariel wasn't sure what had just occurred. Without a word, she pivoted and enveloped Lysandra in her arms, relishing the feel of her, inhaling her intoxicating scent, perceiving that even their heartbeats danced in unison. She wanted to kiss her, to join her body to her love even as their souls had just joined, yet she was reminded of how high the stakes were, and how devastating it had been to lose her the first time.

"I don't have to live in Atala," Lysandra murmured into her ear. "Evamont needs physicians too." She had wrapped her arms around Ariel and hugged her with equal fervor.

"I have many stops to make," Ariel breathed against Lysandra's neck. "The dolphins, the Oldest Tree." She swallowed, her common sense wrestling with her passions. "I'll see you again on the Winter Solstice at the Ring of Stones. We'll see how you feel then."

"I know how I'll feel."

"I don't yet." They loosened their embrace and Ariel took a step back, smoothing her hands down Lysandra's arms to take her hands. They gazed at each other for an extended moment, radiating love, hope, and apprehension. "You breezing back into my life after so long has done more to shake me than shifting stars and waning energies, because you mean more to me than any of it. I need time to process it all, and the fate of the world must take priority over my singular desires. Be safe, my precious one, and I'll do the same."

It was like escaping the pull of an immense electrolyzed magnet to wrench herself away from Lysandra. The shared experience of the morning was so intense that Ariel could barely accept it as real.

"No matter what happens, just remember I love you, now and always," Lysandra professed after her as Ariel retreated to the exit.

"I'll always love you too," she hurriedly added and closed the door behind her.

☥ ⚛ ✟ ✡

Offshore of the Menosus Islands; three days later

The waters of the Ormo Poseidona off the southern shore of Menosus weren't as warm this time of year as they were in summer, but not too cold for Ariel to go for a swim. As she paddled farther from the beach, she radiated signals into the sea, calling for dolphins. A passing manta ray caught her attention as it gracefully glided by, and she offered it a friendly greeting.

It wasn't long before a pod of five dolphins encircled her, chirping a cheerful greeting. The youngest flipped his nose in the water, squirting her playfully while his mother made a slow approach and kissed Ariel on the lips. It was easy to sense their jubilant vibrations, and each one had to come in close for a pat. An especially affectionate male brushed her side as she floated in the gentle waves, then flipped over on his back, presenting his belly for her to rub.

Ariel was happy to stroke his smooth skin, reveling in touching each member of the group. Dolphins were fully cognizant creatures with advanced brains, memory, reasoning, and emotional development. They were friendly, easy to talk to, and didn't know how to lie. In her experience, dolphins, more than any other member of nature, maintained constant contact with source energy and, while they didn't engage in religious rituals, were highly spiritual beings. Ariel often envied their freedom and simplicity of lifestyle.

"I am happy to meet you too," she replied, conveying her words in energy patterns they could comprehend. Ariel wouldn't be surprised to learn they could understand human speech as well, but now was not the time to test the theory.

They exchanged pleasantries and Ariel watched the young one show off his jumping skills, rewarding him with a belly rub like she had given his older brother. Their mother chattered on about an orca who had lost his mind and was killing dolphins in the waters farther north. She seemed uncharacteristically ill at ease over the matter, which Ariel could understand. Although she had heard of the occasional orca feeding on other members of the whale family, she knew their typical meals were fish or sea lions, depending on where their territories were, and which pods they belonged to. Hearing the story brought to mind the recent instances where men had behaved violently toward others.

Anyone—human or whale—who was in proper alignment with source energy would never do such a thing.

"What else different have you noticed?" she asked of the group. She laid her hand on the head of the lead female while the others chattered and splashed. The mother of the group relayed their responses to Ariel.

Different? How do you mean different?

"Things that don't seem right. Changes in the sea and its creatures. Does the water feel warmer than it used to?"

Maybe; I don't know. I'm only twenty years old. We've traveled a few places, but mostly stay close to these islands. There are lots of fish and, if we stay out of the channel where the ships go, nobody bothers us.

Tell her about the giant shark! The little one was filled with nervous excitement.

"What giant shark?"

You know we have to be wary of sharks because they'll eat our kind, but they usually steer clear of a pod. Not long ago, a huge shark prowled after us for days. We finally had to coordinate an attack on it to drive it away, but I don't think that's what you are asking us.

"No." Ariel sighed yet kept her affectionate contact with the dolphins. Underneath them, she noticed a shadow and glanced down, supposing it might be another ray. Instead, an old green sea turtle, with a heart-shaped shell at least three cubits long, glided beneath them. Ariel reached out to it with vibrations through the water. With a flip of its back feet, it veered upward to meet them with a curious expression on its adorable face.

"Greetings, fine turtle. Won't you join us?" Ariel invited.

The mother dolphin extended her welcome as well. Her sister and niece remained in the circle and the big and little males played about. *The nature speaker is asking about changes in the ocean,* she told the turtle.

He poked his head above the surface, scrutinizing Ariel with wise, old eyes. *You must mean the reef.*

"What reef?" Ariel inquired. "What about it?"

The big turtle bobbed in the water, keeping his place with careful movements of his front flipper-feet. His vibrations, though not as human-like as the dolphins, were still easy for Ariel to interpret.

To the southeast of the last island, there has always been a thriving colony of coral, a reef system supporting a vast community of sea creatures. I can recall sixty rotations of the earth, more perhaps, I forget. In the past decades, the reef has been in decline, and just weeks ago, when I swam by, more than half of it was dead. Dead coral, white and sad, skeletons and encrusted bodies on the sea bottom. So sad.

Ariel felt the impact of the turtle's grief like a punch to the gut. Thousands of species depended on coral reefs, whether directly or indirectly. But what would kill it? Warmer water?

"Do you know why? What is hurting the coral?"

The turtle offered her a despairing gaze. *I don't know. I know the sharks who once lived near the reef have moved on in search of new waters to hunt in. One took off a bit of my back flipper!* He rolled to the side and waved it for her to see.

"I'm very sorry about that," Ariel empathized, understanding the sharks had to eat too. "If you stay near these islands, you should be safe. Sharks avoid humans."

But the nets or ships might get me.

Not near the smallest island, the mother dolphin excitedly explained. *Hardly any people live there, and they are friendly. The ships all go around the bigger islands. I'll show you.*

How kind! The sea turtle oozed with appreciation.

We'll give you a ride back to shore, offered one of the other females to Ariel, her voice carrying the promise of safety and support. Ariel clasped the sleek dorsal fin of each, feeling the smoothness and power beneath her touch, and they merrily towed her back to the beach. The boys, not to be left out, jumped and splashed behind them all the way.

Ariel mulled over the additional information while her heart delighted in her visit with the marine animals and her toes dug into the sand. She pulled her dry tunic over her wet undergarments and slipped on her sandals before heading back to the vacation resort she was staying at. Then it was off to the port to inquire of the fishermen there.

Menosus was a group of three smaller islands off the mainland of Ruta, administered by Queen Meresankh, and served as a primary travel destination. In winter, residents of Gadlan or the mountain region of Ampherium came to get away from snow, while in the summer citizens from all over enjoyed the beaches, lighthouse, and entertainment venues. Aside from tourism, Menosus also had a thriving fishing and seafood industry. The attitude was almost as laid back as Mestoria had been, only without the jungle. Here palm trees, flowering shrubs, and music ruled, the sounds of instruments and singers accompanying Ariel wherever she went. It truly was a great place to raise one's vibration.

Several days later, before leaving for her next destination, Ariel spent a lazy afternoon sitting on the dock across the channel from the famed lighthouse. She hadn't found a giant whale, which was disappointing. A passing stork told her it was the wrong time of year for them to be passing on a migration.

The cylindrical tower of limestone and granite stretched fifty-six cubits above the main shipping channel to and from Atala and was painted white with red and black stripes. At its pinnacle shone a bright, rotating light amplified by a shell of polished orichalcum that could be seen for many leagues in even the most impenetrable storm. And though storms were rare—thanks to practitioners like Mandisa—they still posed potential danger to people at sea.

Pondering the significance of "Poseidon's Eye," as the lighthouse was called, Ariel entertained the idea this was the function of their new association—to point the way to safety. And even though she didn't yet perceive the true nature of the danger, nor could guess the path to safety, her inner being etched the impression into her awareness. *You are a beacon in the dark.* Closing her eyes, she gave thanks for answers she had yet to receive.

22

Immortal Glade, in the forests of Ampherium, two weeks later

As the earth rotated nearer to the winter solstice, a chill grasped the highland valley of Immortal Glade, home to the giant sequoias. Ariel had purchased a long, green, woolen cloak and wrapped herself in it as she stood at the base of the Oldest Tree. She rubbed her palms together as she took deep breaths, her exhales puffing steam into the frosty air.

Sequoias were a living example of how community connection provided strength and sustainability. Though their roots were relatively shallow, they stretched out and intertwined with the roots of their neighbors, forming an underground web of stability, hugging each other in a tight embrace.

Besides being the oldest living thing in Atlantis, she was also the biggest by far. The trees towered above the musty forest floor from massive trunks that made Ariel feel like an insect by comparison. Upon reaching a meditative state, she placed her palm on the tree and let the vibrations flow.

The colossal Sequoia had been an adult before the Conflagration and recalled the entire incident with horror. Half of her forest had been lost to earthquakes and landslides, enormous boulders plowing paths down the mountainside crushing her brothers and sisters, parents and children. Of those who survived the initial phase of the disaster, half again—primarily the oldest and youngest—starved to death from lack of sunlight for the several years that followed. She and the other survivors had entered a dormant state and had been robust enough to wait it out and rebound when the sun returned.

Ariel was impressed by the depth of feeling emanating from the Oldest Tree, and she reciprocated with compassion. It was always easier for her to listen to trees than to relay her thoughts to them, but she tried to ask the vital question.

"How is the world different since then? What has changed?"

She impressed on Ariel something about the positions of the stars in the heavens being slightly altered, then projected an idea she could fully comprehend. *The earth has always teamed with energy—pulses, signals we use to carry our messages from one to another. We draw sustenance from them as well as the physical elements in the soil. When I emerged from my hibernation, they seemed less vital. Every cycle they grow dimmer, like a star drifting away from the earth. We can still see its light, but not as brightly as when it was near.*

That impression resonated with Ariel mightily. Not only the energies in the air but those in the ground had waned as well. The problem wasn't limited to humans; the whole earth had been affected. Ziusudra's theories rang in her mind, and she hoped he found something meaningful in the ancient star charts.

Ariel thanked the tree, imbuing it with vibrations of appreciation and unity. After all, everything was One. She and the tree shared a symbiotic relationship and had both been formed from the same source materials; they merely experienced life in diverse ways. The tree wasn't superior because of its size, and she wasn't superior due to having hands and feet. In Ariel's eyes, they were of equal worth.

☥ ☬ ✛ ✡

Gadlan city-state, two weeks before the Winter Solstice

"I'm taking you to meet my husband, Céthur," Ériu said as she pressed her palm to the start plate in her sleigh. "He's a miner and superior forger."

Ariel granted her a curious look as she strapped on her safety belt. "He doesn't live out here with you at the school?"

Ériu laughed. "Céthur stay cooped up at a school? No, he's a rugged outdoorsman who isn't happy without an axe or hammer in his hand."

"How do you make such a relationship work?" Ariel was truly curious. They hovered over the stone-paved street, moving slowly until they cleared the wisdom school grounds. Then Ériu hit vertical, and they were soaring above the treetops, heading toward the distant row of snow-capped mountains.

"We *love* each other," Ériu chirped, as though it was obvious.

Ariel had woken a black bear from hibernation in Ampherium, gathered the stories of manatees in Kalpus Dakrun, the Bay of Sorrows in Elapus, and conversed with eagles in the Azaes Fire Mountains. The bear had no complaints, the manatees were happy they could enjoy moving as far north as Elapus because of the warming water, and the eagles informed her the rabbit and rat populations were so extensive that hunting wasn't even a challenge. When she had asked them about energetic vibrational changes, they acted as if they didn't know what she was referring to and replied, *Isn't this how the world has always been?*

Thrilled to have seen every landscape of the continent and interacted with hundreds of species, Ariel was still disturbed that she hadn't uncovered the answers the team needed. She persisted in her meditations each day, even when failing to connect with the energies. Sometimes, for a fleeting moment, she would feel a radiant sense of unity with everything around her like she had in her youth, appreciating its wonder, and yet was constantly aware that one day soon it could be gone.

"We both return home to our villa by the river in the little village of Leontiri every weekend and holiday," Ériu continued. "Our child is grown now and doesn't need or want our constant supervision. It works because we each get to pursue our interests and still share quality time together regularly. We vowed years ago to never bring work home with us and have stuck to it. What about you?"

"I live on our family farm with my daughter, mother, great-great-great-grandmother, and a host of other relatives," she answered, still pondering Ériu's unusual arrangement. "My son is a city guardian in Evamont, so we get to visit often, and my husband died years ago."

"I'm sorry to hear it," Ériu responded. "And no one since? You said it was years ago."

Ériu flashed her a look of concern. "It's complicated," was all Ariel said before changing the subject. "So, a seed collection. Are plants a passion of yours?"

"I love everything green," she replied with a wide grin. "And learning, of course. I have catalogued over two-hundred thousand seeds!" she exclaimed. "I have them divided into categories and cross-referenced."

"And you keep samples of each at your school?"

"Indeed," Ériu nodded. "Extras of the ones the wizards and alchemists often ask for in making their potions. Did you know we have a telekinetic? He can levitate and move objects with his mind. I don't have any special abilities," she exhaled in disappointment.

"I think being fluent in over eight languages is a special ability," Ariel said.

"Well, I've been really working on number nine. Oh look, we're here." Ériu lowered the sleigh in front of a group of timber-framed buildings and the opening of a colossal mine. Smoke poured from chimneys—an unfamiliar sight on the plains of Evamont—and several thumbs of snow covered the ground and roofs. As if she read Ariel's mind, Ériu added, "It's not that they don't have crystals out here—they use them for lights and other things—they just insist a wood fire is warmer and cozier."

A brawny man with a frizzy, brownish beard and rosy cheeks lumbered from the mouth of the mine, fully enveloped in wool clothing. Ariel pulled her cloak tighter and curled her toes as she followed Ériu out of the warmth of the enclosed sleigh. The unlikely pair shared a kiss and Ériu looped her arm through his, bringing him to meet Ariel.

"This is my incredibly handsome husband, Céthur. Céthur, my new friend, Ariel. She's here to see the Terrible Ice."

He extended a hand, and they shook, exchanging friendly vibrations. "Pleased to meet you, Ariel," he declared in a booming baritone.

"Pleased to meet you as well." Glancing around, Ariel noticed the camp bustled with activity, from men and women guiding ore carts to cats and dogs chasing each other through the snow.

A woman nearly as stout as Céthur stuck her head full of curly hair out a doorway and shouted, "Stew's on!"

"Would you like a bite and a pint?" Céthur invited.

"Don't let him challenge you to a drinking game," Ériu warned with a playful laugh. "No one holds his drink like my husband. He'll take you for as many Poseidon gold pieces as he can."

Ariel laughed, even as a shiver ran through her.

"Come inside where it's warm, my fair women," Céthur directed. "Ariel, you'll need some proper boots and a wool cap and scarf if you're aiming to venture to the north shore."

The interior of the building, Ariel supposed to be a tavern, bore plank walls with minimal decorations. The stout woman with an apron wrapped over her toga slapped mugs of beer on a table. "Well, come on, then!" she commanded before swaggering to the stove to dish up the stew.

"Where can I buy them?" Ariel asked as the three sat at the heavy oak table.

"Nah!" he said, waving a hand at her. "I'll loan you what you need. No use purchasing Gadlan attire you'll never wear again. So, you wish to see the Terrible Ice, do you now?"

"She's a nature speaker," Ériu supplied. "She also wants to talk to northern seabirds."

"A nature speaker, eh?" He leaned back in his chair and squinted at her with a dubious expression.

"Yes," Ariel answered. "Do you go deep into the earth in this mine of yours?"

"Aye," he answered.

"Have you noticed any changes over the decades, if I might ask?"

A wiry, ancient-looking fellow with a cottony beard, sitting at the neighboring table, inserted himself into their conversation. "Now I'm not an air speaker by any means, but I've known this mountain for nearly three hundred years."

Ariel swiveled in her chair to regard him.

"I can tell you the energy in that mine isn't what it once was, and that's a fact."

"I believe you," Ariel responded. "Thanks."

"Oh, it still produces gold like it always has," Céthur declared. "So, I'm not sure what old Barak is talking about."

"I was working that mine before you were a twinkle in your great-grandfather's eye," Barak snapped. "There's been changes in that there mountain."

No doubt, Ariel thought.

⚲ ☖ ✞ ✡

Ariel didn't ask what was in the stew; she just ate it and thanked everyone for their hospitality. Then Céthur flew her to the farthest northern point of Atlantis. Nobody lived up there, just snow, ice, rocks, and a few puffins, hardy walruses, and sea lions. Ériu's husband stayed with the sleigh while Ariel carefully made her way over frozen ground in the watertight leather boots he loaned her, a thick wool cap snug on her head.

She stopped just a cubit from the edge, peering down at the violent waves crashing against sharp shards of jagged pillars below. Through holes in the meandering mist, she spied something mammoth and white looming in the distance. Ariel knew from her geography class at the academy that the Terrible Ice was thirty leagues from the tip of Gadlan, and yet it towered over the troubled swells as clearly as she could view the Opocalám Mountains from her farm. Céthur had told her the ice wall was two leagues high, and she had scoffed at the absurdity. Only now, when faced with the monstrousness of the frozen fortress, did she believe him.

Ariel blinked and adjusted her cap. Maybe it was a trick of the clouds, a reflection off the water. She couldn't have fathomed the feeling of awe and terror seeing the formidable feature would evoke in her had she not looked upon it with her own eyes. She just stood there staring in disbelief while a stiff wind whipped at her cloak and stung her cheeks.

Presently, an enormous white albatross glided in on charcoal wings twice as long as her arm span. She sent him a friendly greeting, and he landed a few cubits away, standing as high as her chest. Ariel had never met an albatross before but knew they could travel great distances, even around the world.

After exchanging pleasantries, Ariel asked the albatross, "Have you flown over the Terrible Ice?"

Oh, yes, he answered. *Many times.*

"Tell me, what's it like on the other side? It is just leagues of ice covering the top of the earth?"

Oh, no, he answered, becoming animated with joyous elation. *My grandmother said it used to be, but now the terrible cone of ice is gone. There's just water behind the wall—lots and lots of water—like the ocean!* he proclaimed and flapped his wings with excitement.

Panic gripped Ariel's heart like an eagle's talons, and her eyes shot wide in horror. Water like an ocean was bottled up behind the Terrible Ice? And when the precarious wall could hold it no more? "Deluge," she uttered in stupefied dread.

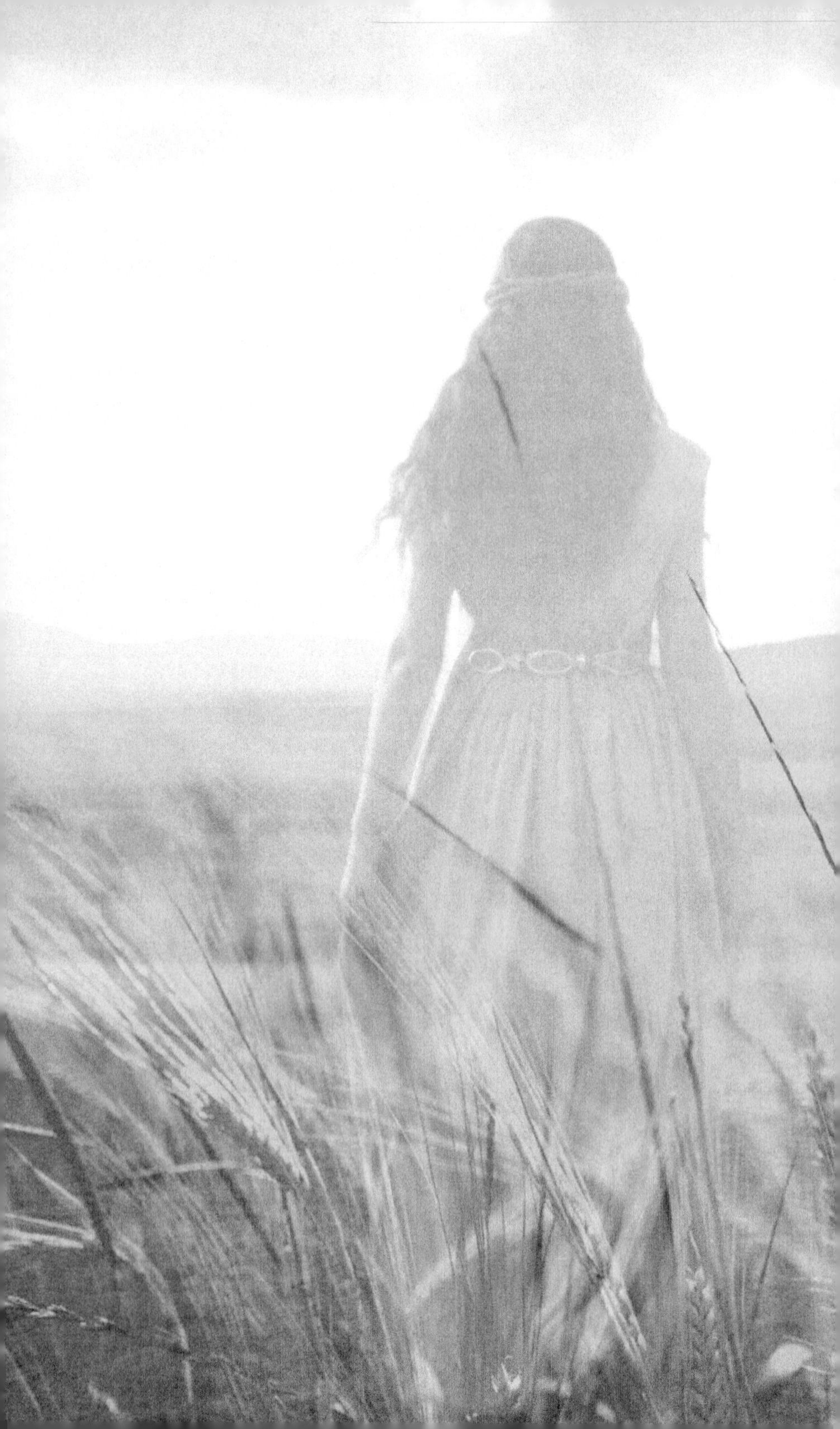

Part Two
Paradise Fractured

23

Atala, ten days before the Winter Solstice

Temen had been enjoying mingling with the kings and queens of Atlantis as an equal. It filled him with a special sense of pride every time he was addressed as "King Temen." People waited on him, opened doors for him, and showed him every preferential courtesy, just as he had always dreamed. The feast that opened the council session had been scrumptious, and musicians, dancers, and performers of every kind had provided entertainment in the grand Temple of Poseidon. He had been thrilled to join the others in the ritual bullfight, and he hadn't forgotten Lykos's lesson, so he could converse intelligently with his peers about its significance.

He had, however, been terrified when the male aurochs was released into the temple's main hall, as it was enormous with sharp horns and powerful hooves. Then, just as he was about to flee in terror, he was overtaken by a wave of confident courage. After all, he couldn't run and hide when a couple of much older women faced the bull unafraid. Besides, Atala's leading physician, some skinny, ancient-looking fellow called Raffi, was on standby to repair any injuries the beast might cause. They had to jump or vault over the aurochs, or at least make a valiant attempt, since it was his first try, and Temen had not shied away.

He found it surprisingly exhilarating. Next, they each took sharpened staffs of cedar, cypress, pine, or some kind of softwood, and speared the sacrificial bull with them. Each ruler had to lodge their weapon into the bull's flesh, thus no one of them killed him but all of them together. The horns were set on display and the meat roasted for another feast for the kings, queens, attendants, and families to partake of, while some unfortunate souls had to clean the temple hall.

Temen had enjoyed recounting his valor over the dangerous animal to Lykos and Rhoxane at the feast, though Lykos didn't appear as enamored as Temen thought he should have been. The kings and queens had faced the peril, not Lykos, who only watched the proceedings from afar. They had brought two others with them, a lady-in-waiting to attend to Temen's new bride and a personal assistant for him. They were all given rooms in the audacious palace where King Efrayim lived.

Yes, those first few days had indeed been exciting, and right on the heels of his wedding ceremony and coronation. Now the tedium of reports from the ministers and requests from departments had become a dull chore. Not wishing to raise a point that might prolong the proceedings, Temen simply voted with the majority whenever a motion was made. His primary goal in this conference was to make friends with the other kings and queens and gain their good favor. Toward that goal, he took turns socializing with various ones—today's being their host King Efrayim, King Kleitos of Evamont, and Queen Meresankh of Menosus.

"Then my son—who clearly knew more than his old man—" Kleitos expounded in some tale of misadventure, "said, 'Look, Dada, no hands!' right before his horse galloped under the low-hanging branch of a live oak and swatted him right into a mud puddle with a squishy thump."

Temen laughed because everyone else did, though he didn't understand how the story was supposed to be funny. The three were enjoying a noontime meal at a round, stone table in the courtyard near a chiminea positioned to warm them in the cooler winter air. If the sun had been shining, they wouldn't even need it to be comfortable. *Air speakers,* he grumbled to himself. *They're all charlatans.*

Kleitos, an olive-skinned man around Temen's age, drained his goblet of wine, dribbling some down his smooth-shaven chin. He caught it with a cloth before it could drop on the sharp, white tunic he wore with a blue stole draped over one shoulder. Temen found him to be open and friendly, even though the disheveled brown curls bouncing at his shoulders and dangling gold earrings were hardly regal.

"Good gods, Kleitos," Meresankh cried through her bubbling laughter. "I presume he wasn't injured."

Meresankh's melodious tones drew Temen's attention to the older woman, who was supposed to be a hundred and twelve, though she didn't look a day over seventy. Downy brunette strands swept up from her heart-shaped, sandy-tan face into a chic updo. Her exotic eyes with their long lashes pulled his gaze from her slender figure, fitted precisely by her two-tone aqua and white chiton, the colorful, flowered scarf draped around her near-bare shoulders, and the pearl and shell necklace dangling at her delectable throat. *Too old for my taste and no match for Rhoxane, but I can still appreciate beauty when I see it,* he told himself.

"Only his pride," Kleitos assured them with a grin. "I must say, Efrayim, your cooks do a fabulous job. I'm thoroughly enjoying my meal; however," he wiggled his brows and tapped his empty goblet, "I could do with more wine."

Efrayim lifted a hand and his chin, scanning the courtyard for an attendant.

Now Efrayim looked like a king—an appearance Temen intended to imitate. The man at least thirty years his elder was tall and still sported a muscular build. He carried himself with a stately bearing and kept his salt and pepper hair and beard neatly cut. He had the typical rose-beige skin coloring of those from central Atlantis, and his formal white toga, mid-calf in length, was bound with a black belt. A red stole, imprinted with various spiritual symbols in gold, added a touch of elegance, as did the orichalcum and silver entwined laurel he wore.

The other kings and queens chatted around similar tables in the picturesque courtyard. Temen had noticed that the paving tiles were laid out in patterns representing the various symbols Lykos had taught him. Yes, he'd probably learned them as a child in school, but who can remember all that? Painted pots contained winter-blooming cacti and cold-hearty flowers his first wife had called tricolor violas.

"Your palace, temple, this patio," Temen expounded as he gestured smoothly with an outstretched palm, "along with your entire city is so luxurious and refined." He could appreciate beauty too.

"I cannot take credit for that, my friend," Efrayim responded in humility.

The attendant appeared and topped off all their goblets from his wine bottle. "Will there be anything else?"

Temen was pleasantly full after his meal, although he wouldn't mind a small bite of something sweet. "Do you have any plakous," he asked, trying to sound regal and sophisticated as he requested the sweet and savory dessert.

"Yes. How many?"

"I'll have one too," Kleitos boomed out in cheer. "Make it four, my fine fellow—one for each, but no more. We wouldn't wish to become gluttons," he added with a wink at Temen.

"No," Temen concurred. "We kings uphold The Law and Rules; we don't break them."

"King Temen," Meresankh addressed with concern in her tone once the attendant was gone. "We have received disturbing reports regarding a change in immigration policies in Ryzen. Could you enlighten us on the situation there?"

"Indeed, fair queen." Temen squared his shoulders and took a sip from his wine while deciding how to best describe the issue. "My predecessor came under fire because her immigration policy was too lax. Although I fully appreciate the vital role those who arrive on our shores from foreign lands provide, we must be vigilant, lest unenlightened civilizations acquire our technology and use it for destructive purposes. Additionally, the immigrants to Ryzen brought with them foul ailments that forced our citizens to seek cures from physicians at a much greater rate than ever in our city-state's past. My first duty as king was to enact a temporary ban on immigrants until our ministers and jurors can devise a better policy."

Meresankh nodded thoughtfully. "We have seen an increase in illnesses in the past few years as well."

"And so have we," Kleitos seconded. For the first time during their lunch, he wasn't smiling.

"I shall add the issue of mounting illnesses to our agenda," Efrayim stated with serious gravity.

A few years ago, Efrayim had been elected chief of the Council of Rulers by the others serving that year and he would hold the office for another decade unless a special vote of no confidence was called. Lykos had explained the position was primarily ceremonial—that he held no more power than the other kings—with the chief serving as a moderator or facilitator for their annual council sessions. Still, all the others looked up to Efrayim and valued his opinion the most. "Make an ally of Efrayim," Lykos had instructed him. "It is how you will get what you wish from the council."

Temen watched eagerly as the attendant set plates of the cheese and honey pastry in front of them, anticipating the delightful combination of sweet flavor and crispy texture on his tongue, and all thoughts of politics and policy vanished.

☥ ☬ ✢ ✡

Atala, later that night

When Ariel swept into Lysandra's apartment, she kicked the door shut and gathered her in a possessive embrace. With driving need, she closed her mouth over Lysandra's lush lips and drank. If they were all about to die, this was how she wanted to go out.

Twirling her around, Ariel pressed Lysandra's back to the closed door, deepening the kiss, delirious with untamed desire. Her heart and breath raced while ravenous hands took possession of her lover's alluring body.

She moaned with pleasure as Lysandra responded in like fashion, tugging her tighter and sliding a thigh between her legs. She wore a light, flowy, knee-length gown that compelled Ariel to picture the soft, luscious curves that waited for her beneath it. Burrowing her face into Lysandra's neck, she trailed her tongue and lips over skin that tasted of frankincense and saffron, a mix of woody citrus and spicy honey. A light remnant of paint odor clung to her hair, bringing Ariel a burst of joy.

Neither spoke an intelligible word, but Lysandra's whimpers and sighs expressed all Ariel needed to hear. She caught the hem of Lysandra's gown and pushed it up, gliding her hands along her thighs and abdomen as she raised the garment and dropped it to the floor. Meeting Lysandra's gaze, perceiving the heated passion that flashed from her dark eyes, Ariel dove into another kiss. Her core tightened as Lysandra's hands busied themselves tugging off Ariel's tunic—which unfortunately required her to briefly break contact.

Ariel sensed a flood of heart vibrations radiating from her lover as Lysandra closed her arms around her once more, leaning against the door for support. A lightheaded euphoria flowed through Ariel, and she thought about the bed only a few cubits away. In her initial urgency, she hadn't taken the normal, progressive path or even planned for when her knees would lose their strength. But this was far from the first time she and Lysandra had made love, and who knew when the Terrible Ice would break?

It all came back to her, every shared touch and zealous kiss, every laugh and tender moment. The years fell away in the blink of an eye, and she felt at home, right where she belonged—where she had always belonged. The debate was over; there'd be no more waiting, no more fear of loss. Whatever the future held or however long or short-lived it would be, she intended to spend it with the woman she loved.

When Lysandra quivered in her arms, Ariel pulled her along to the bed as if they were escaping a bridge about to collapse. Their first time was hot and hard, branded by driving necessity, as if she would burst into flames if she wasn't touching Lysandra. As the urgency waned, Ariel took her time on the second round, visiting familiar, favorite places and relishing the tender pleasures she savored at Lysandra's caresses.

Lying together while catching their breaths, the musky scents of sweat and sex infusing the air in the cozy room, Lysandra asked, "What made you change your mind?"

Ariel traced a loving fingertip across Lysandra's collarbone as a lump formed in her throat. Not only did she love Lysandra more than life, but she also recognized, deep in her inner being, that this was her soulmate, the person she wished more than anything to spend the next hundred years loving.

Raising on an elbow to gaze into her captivating face, eyes so astute and brimming with purity, lips still puffy from being pressed to hers, and a flush of heat glowing under her dusky complexion, her response was bittersweet, almost to the point of tears. "We're out of time."

24

Lysandra peered up at Ariel, her satisfied bliss sliding into confusion. She had dreamed of this moment, longed for it for what had seemed endless ages. When Ariel rushed through her door and into her arms, she thanked all the divinities for answering her prayers. No words were needed to reaffirm the profound emotions she held for Ariel or the everlasting bond they shared. She delighted in reacquainting herself with details of Ariel's body—the scar on her knee, her second toe longer than her big toe and the cute way her baby toes curled in, the little mole on her right breast, the dark blue vein in her left. Both of her breasts were fuller than Lysandra recalled, but Ariel had nursed two children, and they retained the perfect balance of firm and kneadable. Her lover had maintained her physical strength, if not increased it, and showed no signs of weakening stamina.

The triumph of their union pushed Lysandra over every edge—physical, spiritual, and emotional—sending her trinity of beingness dancing in jubilation. Everything felt right with the world again, and Lysandra experienced a profound sense of belonging in Ariel's embrace. But now, she detected a stringent level of unease in her partner and resignation in her singular eyes.

"What do you mean?" she murmured as a thread of dread twisted through her nerves.

"I know why Noah was called to the meeting at the Ring of Stones," she revealed.

Lysandra rolled on her side to face Ariel and cupped her cheek with one hand. "Tell me."

"Have you ever seen the Terrible Ice?"

"Once," she answered. "Quetzal took his students by ship to show us the power of nature and for us to experience being small by comparison. It was so endlessly vast and as tall as the highest mountains."

"Did he tell you what was behind it?" Ariel asked.

"Ice," Lysandra answered matter-of-factly. Everyone knew this. She let her fingers trail away from Ariel's face to slip through her silky strands.

"It's melted." Ariel let her words hover until Lysandra's widening eyes revealed her comprehension.

"You mean—"

"Atlantis is in its direct path and will be inundated with floodwaters like the continent has never known. We can't wait for the solstice, Lysandra; I need to go see Thoth tomorrow," Ariel dictated. "I know the Council of Kings is meeting and people need to know. We must start preparations immediately."

"But how can you know when it will break?" Lysandra loved her beautiful country, its people and culture, The Law and Rules, and the connection she felt to everything and everyone. Where would they go? What would they do? Was her whole life about to change?

"I can't," Ariel admitted. "It could be tomorrow or in a hundred years, though sooner is more likely than later."

"What does the melted ice have to do with the weakening of the energies, though?" Lysandra was assailed with more questions than she ever had as a student, questions that carried far graver consequences.

Ariel turned her face into Lysandra's hand and kissed her palm. "I'm not sure the two have anything to do with each other. But whether there's a common cause, the threat of imminent annihilation takes precedence over waning energies."

"We'll go to the library first thing in the morning," Lysandra proposed. "How did you find out? You didn't climb the ice wall, did you?"

Ariel shook her head and lay back on the pillow in what appeared to be exhaustion. "The albatross who flew over it told me. Stupid bird thought it was wonderful news."

"Now wait." Lysandra moved her hand to encircle Ariel's midriff, taking comfort in the feel of her body so close to hers. "You didn't see this for yourself?"

"I saw it through the bird's memory," Ariel explained. "After he first told me, I tapped into his consciousness and replayed what he had seen; I didn't just take his word for it. A vast ocean, like the Atlantic, as far as the east is from the west."

Ariel wove her fingers through Lysandra's, caressing her palm with her thumb in gentle circles. "That was four days ago," Ariel said. "I went straight home from Gadlan to visit my family—couldn't tell them, but I just had to see them. Then I spent a night in Evamont and stayed with Mal'akhi before getting passage here. I've barely eaten or slept since—" Releasing Lysandra's hand, she caught her behind her neck and pulled her closer, meeting her lips with an affirming kiss.

"I love you, Lysandra—always have. I just had to be with you tonight. Maybe I'm overreacting, and it could be decades before a crack forms. I'm not a mathematician or one who studies the physical features of the Earth, but I'll bet Mandisa could speak to the ice and get a pretty good idea of how long we have. Out there at the top of the world, such an undeniable intuition struck me such that I couldn't ignore."

"Thoth will know what to do," Lysandra assured her. "Lie in my arms and rest, my love. If the flood comes tonight, at least we'll journey to the afterlife together."

Lysandra cradled Ariel, who snuggled into her embrace with her head on her shoulder. In soothing tones, Lysandra crooned a lullaby her mother used to sing to her as a child, hoping it would ease Ariel into sleep. When she sensed that slumber had overtaken her lover, Lysandra stared at a dark ceiling, allowing the overwhelming events and revelations of the night to follow thought trails and emotional roads until she fit them all into their proper compartments. It proved almost too much to process. Sometime before dawn, she followed Ariel into dreams.

☥ ☿ ✝ ✡

When a ray of sunlight streaming through the window awakened Ariel, she felt much better than she had in days, maybe years. The feel and scent that were expressly Lysandra lay beneath her, teasing a smile to her lips and heart. She took a deep breath and slowly let it out to center herself before waking her lover with a kiss.

"I need to meditate before we talk to Thoth," she said. "Today, more than ever, I must be in proper alignment. Pray the spirits speak to me."

Lysandra's sleepy eyes opened to hers, and she covered a yawn. "We'll need to get dressed, I suppose."

Ariel laughed at her, tempted to begin their day with a more intimate exercise. "Where is your comfort room?"

"First door on the right," she said. "I'll throw on clothes—if you insist—and put together something to eat. May I join you in the Ruh Mutaharika?"

"I would like that very much."

Ariel picked up her undergarments and tunic from the floor and put them on along with her sandals before slipping out to use the privy. The water system worked on gravity. City water towers and rooftop cisterns collected rainwater which flowed down through pipes into homes and buildings with underground sewer systems that drained into distant cesspools or the ocean. Private elimination stations were equipped with water tanks above the bowl that washed the waste into the sewers when flushed. It was a very efficient process and, to make sure there were no problems, city-state infrastructure planners had installed canals and aqueducts in regions receiving less rainfall and pumping stations that could be operated if gravity ever needed a boost.

When Ariel returned, Lysandra had dressed and put on water to heat for tea. She took her turn at the privy while Ariel cracked some eggs into a bowl.

They exchanged stories of what each had been doing in the intervening time since Ariel's first visit over breakfast, then focused on their morning practice to prepare themselves for the day.

Because Lysandra was expected at the healing center in the pyramid, they set out for the library early. Ariel rapped at the locked door, and, when nobody answered, Lysandra crossed the street to Thoth's house. She returned with three people in tow. Thoth was draped in a gray cloak around his robes to ward off the morning chill.

"Ariel," he greeted with a modest bow. She was certain from his expression he wasn't happy to have been rousted so early.

"Master Thoth, I don't mean to trouble you, but what I learned can't wait another week," Ariel explained as he unlocked the building.

"This is my daughter, Isis," he introduced, "and her husband, Osiris."

"I'm honored to meet you," Ariel said.

She presumed Thoth's wife must be many years younger than him because Isis appeared quite youthful to be the old man's daughter. She had his coloring and intelligent brown eyes with her straight, black hair cut above the shoulders of her cream chiton's tan stole.

Osiris was a slim young man with a curious braided chinstrap beard and short walnut hair combed back from his cool, dusky face. He wore a teal kilt with a black apron and a golden cape draped over his bare shoulders.

Ariel didn't want to appear rude and would love to get to know the couple when she had more time; however, a sense of urgency compelled her to skip pleasant conversation and race to her point.

"Isis shows great aptitude for healing," Lysandra said. "I believe with the proper instruction she could become a master physician."

Although Ariel was anxious to tell Thoth what she'd discovered, she was still overcome with awe at the interior of Atlantis' foremost library. The columned granite and basalt construction was as impressive as any temple and shelves of books stretched so high in the main room that ladders and interior balconies had been built to access them. Lower stacks of tablets and scrolls formed rows at one end of the hall, while tables surrounded by comfortable seating provided space to view the volumes.

"High words of praise coming from you, Lysandra," Isis responded in humble appreciation.

"Tell me, my child," Thoth instructed as they settled in the first seats they came to. "What troubles you so that you must drive me from my breakfast table?"

Ariel related the story to him, along with the other reports she had gathered on her travels. "We must hasten to save as many lives as we can," Ariel pleaded.

"I understand your alarm," Thoth said in measured reserve, "but 'tis just over a week until our fellowship convenes at the Ring of Stones. Others will have news to share as well, and Ziusudra is convinced the problem lies in the stars."

"But Thoth, with all due respect," Ariel argued, "if the Terrible Ice should fracture before then—"

"My dear Ariel," he interrupted, patting his aged hand on hers. "I can sense your great compassion, the most worthy and divine of qualities. Things concerning the earth happen slowly. Surely the ice wall will not shatter in a week. If that were the case, it would already be cracked. Our sea patrols and fishermen would have reported such a noticeable event if it had already occurred."

"The Conflagration descended suddenly, altering the whole earth in the course of a day," Osiris mentioned.

"But that disaster fell from the heavens," Thoth reminded him with a motion of his hand. His golden wristband flashed as a stream of light from a tall window reflected off it.

"I could get my Major Arcana deck to help us discern the meaning of this information," Isis suggested. Intuitive practitioners had been consulting tarot cards for guidance since before the Conflagration; however, because so much information had been lost, no one living was aware of their origin nor how long they had been around.

"We will consult every source of knowledge in due time, my dear," Thoth said. "Today is your test for admittance to the Central Wisdom School for the courses beginning in the new year. You should focus on that. You show aptitude for several gifts and require guidance to discover and develop those that best suit you. The world will not flood today."

Though Ariel still had some reservations, the powerful aura exuded by the sage master and the unwavering certainty in his words helped ease her anxieties, if only momentarily.

"Ariel, it was good to bring this information to my attention, but we need to add it to the rest our members will bring to the Ring of Stones," he said, catching her gaze with his keen eyes. "I now have something new to research. We have scarce texts on ice ages, but I will dig in to see what I can discover. In the meantime, you might enjoy conversing with Osiris, who is also a farmer, as well as a student of the mysteries. You two may find you have much in common." He pushed up with a laugh. "I forgot my staff."

"I'll get it for you, Dada," Isis offered as she sprang to her feet.

"No, precious." He smiled and lifted a hand to her shoulder. "You get ready for your entrance test, and Lysandra, I'm sure Raffi is looking for you. Ariel, you're welcome to stay as long as you like."

"Thank you, Master Thoth," she responded and passed her gaze to Lysandra.

"Will you be here when I get back?" Lysandra asked in a voice packed with hope.

Ariel nodded. "I'll work with Osiris today, if you're agreeable," she added, glancing at the younger man, who affirmed his consent with an amiable nod.

"Then I'll see you at dinnertime."

A spark leaped in Ariel's sacral chakra as Lysandra smiled at her on her way out. Perhaps the world wouldn't end today.

25

The Ring of Stones on the Winter Solstice

Ariel tried to be patient as the fellowship of gifted and elders went through their morning exercises together. She comprehended the significance of beginning the day with gratitude, prayers, and meditation, performing their physical movements as well to get the air and blood flowing properly through their bodies; yet she felt like a chariot race driver trying to hold back a full team of powerful steeds who chomped at their bits.

At last, the group took their seats in a tight circle in the center of the observatory. She positioned herself close beside Lysandra to draw energetic support from her, as well as a pleasing physical touch.

"Now," Thoth directed, drawing the members' attention, "we will hear from each of you what you have learned."

The scholarly man's formal attire, bald head, and clean-shaven face set him apart, but it was his meek authority that truly commanded attention. Their fellowship had no designated leader, yet all present presumed Thoth to hold that position.

"I know this sounds crazy," Noah spoke up with a skeptical expression, "but I'm convinced Archangel Uriel spoke to me in a dream, commanding me to build a gigantic boat unlike any I've constructed in the past. It was so real because he gave me exact measurements and specifics which I wrote down as soon as I awoke. Naturally, I presumed I could have been wrong because the ship design made no sense."

"You aren't crazy," Ariel blurted out, unable to keep quiet any longer. "And we'll need more than one vessel."

"You were in my dream," Noah said as he blinked at her and scratched his chin between tufts of his long, gray beard. "You were calling animals to board the ship, and you, Ériu, were loading on crates of seeds. Thoth brought scrolls and tablets, and Lysandra carried medicines and herbs. As I recall, you were all in my dream. Why do we need giant ships?"

"Because there's going to be a tremendous flood," Ariel declared with conviction. "The Terrible Ice will crack from the pressure of a thousand waterfalls and an ocean's worth of water will inundate Atlantis and all parts of the world touched by our ocean."

Everyone began chattering in alarm at once and Thoth struck his staff to the earth, sending a wave of vibrations through them all. They hushed, and he spoke. "Ariel gained this report from an albatross, not the brightest of Source's creatures. She has brought this matter to my attention, and, while it sounds incredible, Mandisa's records of rising water temperatures and changes in weather patterns support the theory that the ice above the great wall has been melting, though we cannot judge from here to what extent. Is it only melted in summer, freezing back in the winter? Has only the top cubit or two returned to seawater while beneath over a league deep of ice remains frozen?"

"We should send an expedition at once to see for ourselves if this danger exists, and estimate how much time we have to prepare," Quetzal suggested.

"I could help," Mandisa offered. "The ice could tell me if a breach is imminent."

"But what does melting ice have to do with the weakening of our connection to Source energy?" Ptah asked.

"They are two separate issues that I believe are both being caused by cosmic events," Ziusudra asserted, lifting a bony finger that matched the elder's thin build. "If we can plan our excursion to the Terrible Ice for tomorrow, I wish to explain my findings."

The group settled down, and Ariel felt some ease now that people were taking her claims seriously and preparing for the next phase of action. *Quetzal is right,* she thought. *We need to examine the sight ourselves to determine the extent of the threat.*

"Very well," Thoth consented. "First, let's conclude our discussion of the melting glaciers. Quetzal, do you volunteer to lead an exploratory crew to the Terrible Ice tomorrow?"

"I do," he confirmed with a decisive nod.

"I'll go," old Noah volunteered. "If I'm supposed to build these improbable floating monstrosities, I want to see why."

"And I should go," Mandisa seconded.

"I'm going where Ariel goes," Lysandra declared. "Besides, if anyone gets frostbite or slips on the ice, I'll be there to heal them on the spot."

"My husband knows someone with an airship who could take us," Ériu offered. "And he loves an adventure."

"It's decided then," Thoth confirmed. "Ziusudra, Ptah, and I will stay behind while you young people and Noah brave the frozen elements. I now turn the meeting over to Ziusudra."

"I first wish to thank Quetzal and Thoth for assisting me in researching the archives and Ptah for providing precise calculations," the renowned astronomer acknowledged. "While there is always a margin for error, I believe I have discovered the cause of the problems we've been experiencing."

When he fingered the sickle moon pendant at his throat, Ariel was reminded of the gold ankh dangling from a chain lying over her heart. She found it interesting that a man wore the symbol that many women had adopted as a goddess sign of feminine empowerment. However, Ariel had learned in school that men possess feminine energy and women possess masculine energy and that both are important to balance. Masculine energy centers on reason, while feminine energy aligns with intuition. So, really, the symbols had nothing to do with gender.

The crescent moon was a reminder of cycles—the ebb and flow of the tides, the waning and waxing of the moon, birth and death, and the seasons of planting and harvest, therefore, fertility. The schools taught about short rotations, like day and night, and extremely long sequences, such as the astrological precession of the equinox, which took over twenty-six thousand years to complete.

Satisfied and excited about tomorrow's mission, Ariel leaned her shoulder against Lysandra's, listening to Ziusudra's discoveries.

"Deep in the lower archives, in a section I hadn't visited before, we discovered an ancient star chart rolled up and tucked away as if hidden on purpose," Ziusudra said. "This would have been done long before Thoth was born, and he was only aware of the post-Conflagration constellation maps on display on the main level. I can only guess why the leaders who emerged immediately following the catastrophe believed they should bury the truth and keep it from us, yet I still beg forgiveness from our ancestors. Long have I faulted them for not being watchful of the skies, for failing to predict the path and timing of the sky-serpent comet, when in fact they were not to blame."

Curiosity swept Ariel into the story. Lysandra's fingertips found hers beneath their arms and she discretely joined them. It didn't matter if the others knew about their rekindled love; in fact, Ariel would be happy to shout it from a mountain, only this wasn't the time.

"During the Second Age, and likely all those preceding it," he explained, "there was another planet between Gugulanna, our closest planet, and the giant planet Enlil, called Phaëton. While there's no notation as to the cause, this planet was unexpectedly ripped apart in a violent cataclysm that destroyed it. Enlil's powerful gravity pulled some fragments toward it, but the sun's gravity is greater. Our earth lay in a path directly between Phaëton and the sun and was close enough that any debris headed this way would have struck our planet before a warning could be issued.

"Ancient accounts claim this demolished planet had water like ours, and that ice and wreckage from its obliteration formed the comet that the survivors of the Conflagration witnessed streaking through the northern skies. As pieces broke off and fell to earth, they shook the planet, causing earthquakes, volcanic eruptions, and leaving devastation in its wake. Other chunks of Phaëton must have hit the sun, causing even more disruptions. Accounts tell of intense balls of heat and radiation lighting forests aflame in parts of the world, thus giving the disaster its epitaph of the Great Conflagration. People near the seashore escaped in boats while others took cover underground, but the majority perished."

Ariel recalled the testimony of the Oldest Tree, and her heart was rent with deep compassion for all those who died in the calamity.

"Much of what I've relayed thus far isn't different from what you already know, except for the next part. When comparing the pre-Conflagration star maps with today's, it's obvious that our vantage point has shifted by approximately seven degrees. This event disrupted earth even more than we knew, explaining the sudden freezing in the far north and the creation of the Terrible Ice. Gaia was slammed so violently that the seas sloshed like water in a shaken bowl, with waves as high as mountains. The earth's crust cracked and broke in places, causing landmasses to rise and sink, and, when the waters calmed, former coastlines had been swallowed up.

"But the vibrations from the exploding planet, the change in the earth's tilt, the solar flares, and our realignment with the stars could have all adversely affected our connection to the energies, or even the strength with which they reach us. Then we found one more anomaly."

Ziusudra unrolled a star chart showing all the constellations in their formation around the earth's skies. "This upheaval occurred over only a few days—weeks at most—causing drastic changes, driving many species into extinction, just as our planet moved into the Age of Leo, a fire sign, at the completion of a twenty-six-thousand-year cycle. While I can't prove it, I believe our whole solar system, our quadrant of space, has shifted into a less energetic part of the field. There is nothing we can do to repair the damage or to regain the easy, common connections our ancestors had to energetic powers.

"Did you know this Ring of Stones once produced enough electromagnetic energy that it was used as a teleport station? The energies have already dissipated much and will, unfortunately, continue to do so. Have you been told why obelisks are being erected across Atlantis?"

"We were told they are needles pointing to the cosmos as reminders we are children of the Creator and children of The Law," Mandisa responded."

Ptah shook his head. "I've worked on their construction. They are to boost the flow of energy between pyramids and in cities with high-energy consumption."

Ariel wondered why people weren't being told the truth. Was it because the kings believed they could solve the problems or simply to prevent people from panicking?

Ziusudra nodded and continued. "Our power-collecting pyramids may function for another hundred years, but will eventually fail, so we need to invent new technologies. As for our human-divine conduit, I believe individuals who discipline themselves, adhere to The Law, and seek communion with angels, spirits, and the Creator will still be able to experience fellowship, but the time of widespread self-healing, spirit walking, teleporting our thoughts or physical bodies is behind us."

It was as though every set of shoulders in the circle slumped, and every head bowed in sorrow. His prediction was one nobody wished to hear.

"So, the problems we are seeing with people lashing out in anger, hurting each other, the decrease in health and longevity, will just continue to get worse?" Noah asked, his voice choked with disillusionment.

Ariel could sense the despair and hopelessness among her peers and her heart was weighed down as if by an anchor. Lysandra squeezed her hand, laid her head on her shoulder, and wiped at a tear.

"There is always room for hope," Thoth encouraged. "Just because a thing will not be as easy for most people doesn't mean it can't be done. Teach your sons and daughters the way; guide them into the light and they, too, can enjoy the wonders you all have lived. The Law is eternal; it doesn't change. Manifestation might not be instant anymore, or even easy, but the laws still work. We might not be as constantly aware of frequencies, but they are still there, all around us, in everything. Sowing and reaping, cause and effect, the cycles, the laws of harmony, balance, reflection, and attraction are still in force."

Thoth picked up a stray pinecone and dropped it. "See? Gravity still functions, the cycles continue to turn, and everything is still energy. Do not despair but give thanks! Without challenges, we can't grow. We are still children of God, heirs to eternal life. No comets or floods or any other tribulations can change that. Even if the sun, moon, stars, and earth were to disappear from the heavens, we would still be part of the One. It is Law and cannot be altered."

The wise librarian's words resounded as truth in Ariel's ears. Still, it would require quite an adjustment. And what of those individuals who, without a strong call, would abandon the teachings of The Law? Would they become violent and depraved like the uncivilized tribes she had heard about?

"There is hope for our descendants," Ziusudra added, "so we must preserve our wisdom, hiding it, if necessary, until that time. If the calculations Ptah and I made are correct, in fewer than twelve thousand years, when the earth enters the Age of Aquarius, we should be returning to a more energetic portion of space, where the ether is thicker, and the energies will once again be vibrant and easy to connect with. Eleven thousand and seven hundred years is not so long a time for humanity to learn and wait. The Creator will surely send teachers and prophets, wise enlightened ones, to guide the way for any who would listen. It will be apparent who they are by the way they show compassion. Those who seek the truth will find it. Those who do not will doom themselves to hells of their own making. Yet, even then, once their physical bodies die, they will return to the light. All is not lost."

26

The northernmost tip of Atlantis, the next day

Ariel wondered if she should have purchased the cold weather clothing when Ériu's husband Céthur handed them back to her in the station of the Northern Outpost air dock. He had brought extras for the other members of her party to the cabin flanking the boarding platform. Outside, snowflakes drifted from a cloudy sky, landing on their sleighs and the excursion air coach they would ride to view the ice.

"Are you sure this thing will fly?" Noah grumbled as he narrowed his brows on a rickety-looking, ten-seater air coach and crossed hairy arms over his muscular chest. Its size fell between that of a personal sleigh and a traditional transportation coach, with a few dents and a bent running board. At least the coats of bright yellow and red paint looked new.

"It'll fly with me manning the controls," boasted Barak, the fellow with the snowy beard whom Ariel had met on her previous visit. Where Noah was tall and robust, Barak was shorter and smaller boned, though they appeared to be about the same age. Barak pulled a wool cap over his ring of white hair and a bald crown. "I built this here craft myself back before I took to mining."

"Wasn't that about three hundred years ago?" Ariel inquired, while she secured the brown, ankle-length woolen robe with a corded belt.

Barak cackled, displaying a missing tooth.

"I've never worn boots like these," Mandisa commented as she pulled them on. "I must say, they don't feel bad."

"Thank you, Céthur," Lysandra said as she wrapped a dark blue cloak over the long-sleeve tunic their host had provided. "You are most generous and accommodating to our little expedition."

"Nonsense!" he dismissed with a friendly expression. "I haven't been up there to see the ice in over two decades. This'll be a treat."

"Do we have everything we need to take?" Quetzal asked, passing a glance around at the team. Bound up in borrowed winter wear, Ariel, Lysandra, Mandisa, Noah, and Ériu, stood in a semicircle with Céthur and Barak, all facing the mission's leader.

"I have a pen and parchment to take notes," Ériu responded.

"And I've a pick-axe, steel-tipped spear, plenty of rope, and there are snowshoes in the coach if anyone wishes to take a walk on the glacier," Céthur stated.

"I have a bag of emergency medicinal supplies," Lysandra said. She lifted it and slipped the strap around her neck and shoulder.

"What else do we need?" asked Mandisa.

"Did you put a freshly charged power crystal in this beat-up tin tube?" Noah asked, directing his query at Barak.

The old miner screwed his face, scrunched his brows, poked out his lips, and glared at Noah. "Of course I inserted a fresh crystal, you ninny! Do you think a turnip cart tipped over and spilled me out yesterday?"

Noah smirked and rubbed a leathery hand to the back of his neck. "Well, I suppose you don't wish to crash any more than we do."

"In that case, let's load up and move out. I'm anxious to discover what's truly beyond the Terrible Ice," Quetzal said.

Barak stepped on board first. "Ain't nothing but a frozen wasteland. Southlanders," he muttered and shook his head.

It didn't take the party long to fly the thirty leagues to reach the towering ice cliffs, and then they began their ascent. Peering out the window, Ariel spotted the outline of a massive blue whale gliding beneath the surface, probably scooping up krill. She hoped she'd get a chance to talk to it when they were done.

They continued to push higher and higher, thanks to the craft's antigravity system. Everyone remained conspicuously quiet. Ariel's stomach felt uneasy as she had never flown so high before, and it was likely most of the others hadn't either. Because the vessel's operating system made no sound, the eerie silence only amplified the sense of dread Ariel felt in the coach. All she could see through the window were puffs of cloud.

"Just sit tight," Barak said to his tense passengers. "I'll know when we're high enough, cloud or not."

Lysandra's hand gripped Ariel's, and they exchanged a nervous glance. "It's all right," Ariel said in comfort. Sensing Lysandra's unease, Ariel calmed her own anxiety and focused on radiating confidence to settle her lover's. However, when the coach jerked and sputtered, she determined there could be something to worry about after all.

"What's wrong with this bucket of bolts?" Noah demanded as they bumped the edge of the Terrible Ice, sending a spray of frosty bits in their wake.

"I thought you said you put a new crystal in before we left," Céthur added in an accusatory manner. "It sounds like the power is trying to go out."

"I did!" Barak exclaimed. "It shouldn't be doing this."

Quetzal opened his window, allowing a wintry blast to whip snowflakes inside. "I know these run quiet, but," he began. Then the coach's assent stopped.

"Do something!" Noah shouted.

Céthur scurried to the front to help Barak with the controls. "What do I need to do?"

"Pry open that panel down there," Barak directed with a confused scowl. "I'll see if there's another fresh crystal in the box under my seat."

A violent shimmy ran through the length of the vessel, and then Ariel's stomach slammed into her throat as gravity took over. Someone screamed; it could have even been her. Lysandra grabbed her arm with one hand and the side of the plummeting air coach with the other. Quetzal snatched Céthur's pickaxe from the seat, grabbing it firmly in both powerful hands, and sank it into the side of the ice wall through his open window. It dug in, slamming Quetzal's muscled body into the roof of the coach, but he held on.

The other men acted in quick succession. With a swift strike, Noah drove the claw end of his hammer through the glass into the glacier, securing a second anchor. Abandoning his attempt at repairs, Céthur jabbed the pointed tip of the spear through the nearest pane and into the ice. Mandisa had moved to the center of the coach and, with her face and palms lifted upward, called upon the air. Ariel noticed when the updraft pushed against the craft's floor to help keep them from falling any further.

The vehicle seemed to stabilize, allowing Ariel the luxury to breathe again. Her eyes met Lysandra's. "Are you all right?" She nodded and grabbed Ariel in a tight embrace.

"Found it!" Barak cried. He pulled out the old crystal and inserted a new one in its place. The antigravity came back online, and the men tugged their tools out of the icy wall. With three windows busted, cold air whipped around the inside, but Ariel was too busy giving thanks to notice.

"You said the other crystal was good," Quetzal commented in irritation.

"It was," Barak insisted. "Do you want to continue or turn back?"

"We're almost there," Ariel declared. "We have to see what's behind the ice."

"Take us up," Noah demanded, "and be quick about it before we have another power failure. I didn't pass four centuries just to crash at the base of the Terrible Ice."

Ériu rushed into her husband's arms. "I wasn't ready to lose you," she gushed. "We're both much too young to die. Quick thinking, you fellows, to catch the ice like that."

"Good thing Quetzal is the size of a mountain and about as stubborn," Noah replied.

Moments later, Barak landed the air coach on the rim of the ice wall and removed the power crystal to prevent any extra energy from draining out of it.

"What happened back there?" Céthur asked with a disgruntled huff.

"I swear, that was a fully charged crystal," Barak rounded on him in defense. "It should have lasted weeks, if not longer."

"It's the distance from the Gadlan power pyramid," Quetzal answered in realization. "You said it's been twenty years since the last time you flew to the Terrible Ice?"

"Yeah, but ..." Barak began, then plopped back into the driver's seat and scratched his beard. "It worked fine before."

"Ptah said they've been erecting obelisks to boost the power between pyramids," Lysandra mentioned. "That means the crystals' energy doesn't extend as far a distance as it used to."

"Let's complete this survey and get back down to sea level before that one runs out," Noah suggested.

"Mandisa, will you come out with me on the ice?" Ariel asked.

"Certainly."

Céthur passed them each a pair of snowshoes which they strapped around their boots. Then he opened the coach's door on the side away from the ice cliff's steep drop-off. While chilly, the air outside was no colder than the ambient temperature inside the compromised coach, though pockets of fog drifted in front of them like sheets hanging on a line to dry.

"I'm coming with you," Quetzal stated as Ariel took a cautious step from the coach onto the ice.

"Wait!" She was sure everyone heard the crack under her foot as her weight came down on the surface. With her hands pressed against the doorframe, Ariel lifted her foot back onto the running board. As she stared ahead, she sensed energy flowing from Mandisa behind her, and the veil of fog parted. A ray of sunshine burst through the dissipating vapor and sparkled on the gently rocking crests of waves. The wall of Terrible Ice extended about ten cubits from the abyss to the melted waters that lay before them, just enough for their air coach to rest on.

"Great Poseidon!" Céthur exclaimed.

"We must know how deep it is," Quetzal directed as he squeezed into the doorway with Ariel.

"You're too heavy to leave the coach," she exclaimed, pointing to the crack she had made. "In fact, I suggest we engage the antigravity."

"Not yet," Barak called from somewhere inside. "The air coach will float if it must. We need all our power to ensure we don't crash during our trip back to the coast."

"Let me go," offered Mandisa. "I mastered the basics of walking on water, so if the ice breaks under me, I won't sink. I need to connect to these waters anyway, to learn how far and deep the thaw has gone."

Ariel and Quetzal moved back out of the way and allowed Mandisa to pass. Ariel sensed Lysandra brush up behind her.

"She'll be fine," Lysandra assured her. "I've seen air speakers walk on water before."

Ariel leaned into her as they both watched.

Mandisa took two steps, just enough to reach the edge of the melt, kneeled, and rested one hand on the ice and the other on the water. While Ariel suspected Mandisa weighed more than she did, the ice didn't crack for her.

The air speaker inhaled deeply and closed her eyes, focusing all her attention on the water energies. Ariel pushed a good luck vibration her way while fighting off a tingle of nerves. Between almost crashing and then seeing the melted ice for herself, her anxiety level was higher than she could recall since Mal'akhi fell off the roof as a youngster and she rushed him to the healer in Evamont.

It seemed like an eternity. Noah paced the coach, sighing about how long it would take to build the humongous ship from his dream. "Three hundred cubits long," he expounded. "Can you believe it? And fifty cubits wide, thirty tall, and three levels. No oars or sails, just sealed up with pitch to prevent leaks." He rubbed the back of his neck and shook his head.

"What is she doing?" Ériu asked. "Why is it taking so long?" She clung to her husband, who enfolded her in his secure arms.

"She's doing fine," Quetzal said in a confident tone. "Mandisa knows her business. Ariel, it isn't that I doubted you," he began, pivoting in her direction.

"I'm not offended, Quetzal. We need to have facts and measurements we could only gather by being here. I honestly hoped to discover I had been wrong."

A creak sounded, and the coach pitched about ten degrees toward the rear starboard side.

"Everybody hold still," Céthur commanded. He released Ériu and held his arms out in a steadying motion.

"It feels like the back quarter is sinking," Noah speculated. "We need to hurry and take off."

"For now, everyone slowly shift your weight to the port side," Barak instructed. "I'll go ahead and insert the crystal but won't turn the power on until I have to."

"Mandisa?" Quetzal called to her. "We need to go."

She didn't respond, only continued her communication for at least thirty more heartbeats. Then she rose and walked back to the coach. Céthur closed the door and Barak powered up the transport.

"Mandisa, can you ask the wind to help push us home?" Barak asked. "Seeing how you're on such friendly terms and all. I'd hate for this crystal to go belly up before we make it to land."

She nodded and returned to her meditation while everyone took their seats and strapped in.

Ariel draped an arm around Lysandra's shoulders and pulled her close. Lysandra reached around her waist, taking hold of her other hand. "That was close," she whispered. "I was scared for a minute."

Letting out a laugh in relief, Ariel admitted, "So was I—for a minute. But between Quetzal's magic and Mandisa's gift, I doubt we were ever in real danger."

"It isn't magic," Lysandra explained. "He has an amazing way of weaving energies, almost like having multiple gifts, as I suppose was common before the Conflagration. In my opinion, his faith and wisdom are without peer."

"I should hope so," Ariel responded, "what with him being your teacher and all."

When Mandisa finished beseeching the wind, she sat in the middle seat, and everyone except Barak's attention focused on her. She rolled her neck with a sigh, then passed a serious glance around the battered coach, meeting each individual's gaze.

"There's good news and bad news."

"May as well start with the good news," Ériu proposed optimistically.

Mandisa nodded. "We have some time to prepare."

"Then Ariel was right," Lysandra pronounced. "The ice will break and flood Atlantis."

"Yes." Silent grief permeated their midst. Mandisa continued. "The thaw descends more than a league into the ice and continues to melt deeper every day. By the time it reaches sea level, the ice wall can no longer hold it back."

"How long?" Quetzal asked.

"Four and a half, maybe five years—if nothing speeds things up. If no ship crashes into the ice wall to weaken it; if no added solar radiation attacks it; if all factors remain the same, we have between four and five years to get as many people, animals, and items of cultural significance to safety as possible. The volume of water behind the Terrible Ice will do more than flood Atlantis; it will inundate the entire Atlantic world, including the Green Sea and the lands it touches. With the projected rise in sea levels, coastal cities are at risk of being submerged indefinitely."

A long silence followed her announcement, and then Quetzal spoke. "This is why we were called to the Ring of Stone. This is what Archangel Uriel sought to bring to our attention. We have been warned, given a chance to save everyone and everything we can. Let us rejoice and be grateful. Let our hearts be filled with praise! Our ancestors received no warning ahead of their destruction, but, with all our frailties, we have been found worthy. Thank you, divine Creator, the Compassionate One of the Universe. You have called us out of Atlantis to be a part of the rest of the world. Guide us on our journey."

27

The Atala Library, the next day

Lysandra sat with her comrades at a conference table in a downstairs room in Thoth's library, with panel lights gleaming brighter than those in her tiny apartment. Their expedition party had rushed back to Atala to meet with Thoth, Ptah, and Ziusudra, who had stayed behind to double-check sources and calculations. The room was conspicuously lacking in opulence, with only one wall painting and a map of Old Atlantis adorning windowless block walls.

"There is no doubt," Quetzal stated, his red hair and beard disheveled from lack of time for a bath and proper grooming. Lysandra wished for a bath herself, but time had been of the essence. At least she sat beside Quetzal in a clean white chiton, which made her feel more like herself. Ariel was on her other side, with Mandisa next to her. The others were seated across from them with a reflective Thoth at the head of the table.

"Four or five years, you say?" Thoth repeated.

"That's what the vibrations in the ice and thaw water indicated," Mandisa verified. "Barring any further disruptions."

"We have to bring this before the Council of Rulers," Ariel stressed in concern. "If we start relocating citizens to the colonies now in an orderly fashion, all can be saved."

"Many won't believe the warnings," Ptah pointed out. He rubbed his square jaw, then let his rough, coppery fist fall to the table. "They will refuse to leave their homes. Most of you spend your days surrounded by spiritually-minded peers while I spend my time with developers, city planners, and construction workers, many of whom have left the teachings of The Law as far behind them as the rest of us have the myths of Poseidon, Zeus, and Hades."

"I understand the prevailing mindset," Lysandra concurred. "It's becoming increasingly difficult for me to persuade my patients that if they would only follow best practices of nutrition, movement, and breathing along with the wisdom outlined in The Law, they wouldn't get sick to begin with."

"We cannot change the axis of the earth," Ziusudra remarked, "or alter the movements of the stars. As it becomes more difficult for people to connect with the energies and to perceive and interpret universal frequencies, more will give up trying. But we all here are proof it can still be done. People will believe our report and heed our warnings, or they won't. Each person is responsible for his or her own decisions."

Thoth nodded. "We must inform the Council of Rulers. However, if they choose not to act, we will move forward with our agenda, convincing as many as we can to join us."

"It wouldn't be proper for us to all just barge into their session," Ériu said.

"I will take Ziusudra," Thoth stated, "for he is well-respected by the kings and queens, and Mandisa because she spoke to the ice. We three will serve as witnesses and wise counselors and report back to you what they say. In the meantime, continue the discussion here."

When Thoth left with Ziusudra and Mandisa to bring their report before Atlantis's rulers, the others looked to Quetzal to take charge. He leaned back in his seat and smiled. Lysandra felt the tingle of his invisible touch and recognized he was soothing everyone with psychic projections.

"Noah, your role is obvious," the wisdom master began.

"Yeah," he grumbled, "build this monstrous ship."

"No."

Noah started at Quetzal's response, his brows shooting up in disbelief. "But my dream—"

"We'll need more than one," Ariel supplied. "We'll need to convey at least a mated pair of every species of animal—more of domestic animals we use for eggs, meat, and milk—plus all of us and our families, neighbors, and others who agree to come. Even at the size you quoted, we'll need more than one ship."

"At least four," Quetzal specified. "We don't know how bad the devastation will be in other parts of the world, and to ensure our bloodlines and our culture survives—and yes, Ariel, our plant and animal species too—we'll need to send ships both to the east and west. Five or six arks would be preferable, but I realize each of these will take a long time to construct. We will get you as many workers as you need to complete the project on time."

Noah's eyes bulged, and he exhaled a breath while rubbing the back of his neck with a thick hand. "Ariel," he addressed, turning his attention to her. "It's not a problem when I build a normal boat, but for this?" He sighed, leaned back in his chair, and shook his head. "This will take entire forests. Will you talk to the trees, find volunteers? I can't just wipe out a forest like that. It would amount to genocide."

"I'll come with you when we're done here," she agreed. "I'll explain the situation and find trees who are willing." She moved her hand under the table to Lysandra's and took it, lacing their fingers together. Lysandra met Ariel's gaze and assured her with a nod that she could do it.

"But there's something I don't understand," Noah said. "How will we also store enough food for all the animals for who knows how long, and what's to keep the carnivores from eating the rest? Sure, Ariel could soothe them and explain their precarious situation, but they still have to eat. And are we supposed to find three or four other nature speakers for the other arks?"

"We can ask other nature speakers to assist," Ariel answered. "I'm not the only one. But about the uncertainty of how long we'll need to feed them ..."

As she trailed off, an idea popped into Lysandra's mind. "I know! Remember how I made the dream-walking incense to assist our search for answers at the fall equinox?" The others nodded with curious expressions. "I can create a similar potion that will put all the animals to sleep. That will slow their metabolisms while keeping them still and calm. The physicians on each ship can administer it and, together with a nature speaker, they can manage them all. We could wake one group at a time so they could drink, eat a little, and move around to sustain their bodies, then put them back to sleep again."

"Bears and reptiles do it every winter," Ariel added enthusiastically. "Lysandra, you're brilliant!"

Ariel's proclamation thrilled and embarrassed her at once, and Lysandra felt warmth rise in her cheeks.

"It *is* a brilliant plan," Quetzal seconded. "Ériu, we need to do the same with your seeds. Each ark must carry a full supply of seeds for every grass, grain, fruit, and vegetable, every flower, shrub, and tree. We don't want to leave any species out because they are all valuable."

"We can't forget bees." Ériu lifted a hand to emphasize her point. "I don't think just bringing along two of each kind will do."

"Hives stored safely in boxes on each ship are more practical," Ariel agreed. "Noah, you and I need to map out the details of creating suitable quarters for the different kinds of animals."

He nodded his agreement, and Quetzal moved on. "Ériu, the report you sent about the languages your team is studying and where each is spoken is of great importance. Once we decide where we hope to end up, you can teach us the language spoken there. We should arrive prepared and ready to communicate with the indigenous people."

"Of course," Ériu affirmed with an eager expression that made her freckles seem to dance.

"I'm uncertain of my role," Ptah said with a discouraged frown.

Lysandra had another idea. It seemed like she had overflowed with them since getting back together with Ariel. The first night they'd spent in each other's arms was a dream come true, and all those since had been just as magical. She grasped the concept that being in a high-vibration state was the key to accessing her creative abilities, and nothing so powerfully raised vibrations as being in love.

"Our colonies," Lysandra replied. "If you and a building crew went ahead of the migrating people to establish infrastructure, it could convince citizens to go. I know Ziusudra said the crystals may only operate for another hundred years or so, but, if you erected pyramids and obelisks to generate and transfer the sun's power to the giant mother crystals, then at least migrating Atlanteans would have the technology they're accustomed to. And if you can use antigravity and laser cutters for the stones, you could complete pyramids in time for their arrival."

"There could be other important building projects as well," Noah added. "You could make the pyramids watertight to protect the locals from rising flood waters, or even underground safety retreats. I'm not meaning you do everything yourself, but I'm sure you have peers you can trust to work with. Source knows I'm going to need a boatload of help, if you'll pardon the pun."

"These are all excellent ideas." Quetzal's amber eyes sparkled at them with his praise. "We will need to coordinate with Atlanteans who are presently living in Kemet, Libya, Pelasgoí, and Maanu, the continent to the west. I doubt the Sindhu former colony would welcome us, but Kush might. I've been to the Mayeb Peninsula once. The people are wary of strangers, but their land is flat and in danger of flooding. If I had help with the language, I might convince them to relocate temporarily to a mountainous region."

"Let's see what Thoth and the others report from their meeting with the Council," Ptah suggested. "Then we can plan who should go where. With the rulers' support, all this preparation will go much smoother."

"We should have food and drink prepared for when they return," Lysandra suggested. "Ariel and I could go to the market and pick up some things."

"Capital idea," Quetzal agreed with a knowing grin. His cheeky tease materialized in her mind. *Don't get so distracted you forget to come back.* She smirked at him and rolled her eyes as she stood.

Leaving Ériu and the men behind, Lysandra climbed the stairs to the main level, with Ariel right behind her. Her self-reflection shifted from inspiration to brooding. Once out of earshot of the others—though she had no clue what distance Quetzal's perception roamed—Lysandra turned to Ariel, whispering with insecurity in her tone.

"Everyone brings unique skills necessary for this rescue mission to succeed, except for me." She stopped and leaned her bum against a tabletop. "I mean, there are hundreds more physicians who could concoct a sleeping agent where there are only a handful of other nature speakers and air speakers who still have command over their gifts. There are other wisdom journeymen and additional masters, besides Thoth and Quetzal, whose abilities exceed mine. And even though Ériu may not have earned her master's status, she has the vital seed bank and can converse in many languages. I feel honored, but inadequate."

Her gaze met Ariel's in a moment of doubt. Despite her uplifting emotions of love and bliss and discounting the flow of ideas she had produced, doubt still wedged its way into her consciousness, threatening to drag her down with cruel observations.

"Did Quetzal make a mistake? What if I wasn't truly called, and the paintings, the dreams, were just tricks of my imagination?"

Ariel gripped her hands and brushed a tingling kiss to her lips. Compelling radiance shone from her face. "You were meant to be here. First, imagination always precedes manifestation. Only that which is imagined can enter the physical reality. Second, do you honestly think Thoth misread the intentions of the archangel who gave him the names?" She made an adorable "tisking" sound as her eyes twinkled playfully.

"There are two vital points you must believe," Ariel stated more seriously. "As above, so below; as within, so without. It doesn't matter what you can do, Lysandra; it only matters who you are. Your caring soul, your willing spirit, your connection to the energies, your selfless wish to help others, to heal them, to make the world a better place. You do that every day just by breathing and radiating love into the air."

"But—" Lysandra dropped her chin, admitting the truth to herself. "Not all my desires have been selfless. My most fervent hope and prayer has been to have you back in my life."

Ariel pressed her lips to Lysandra's forehead and brought her arms around her, making her feel loved and wanted, making her feel worthy of her attention if nothing else.

"Which brings me to my second point." Ariel slid two fingers under her chin, lifting her face to meet her gaze. "You asked, Source answered. But would you have ever reached out to me, come to see me, and ask me to come back to you if necessity hadn't pressed you into doing so?"

Lysandra had to think about that. "Maybe one day." She sighed. "Probably not."

"Sweetie, a day hasn't gone by that I didn't think of you," Ariel confessed as she cupped her cheek in a vibrant caress. "Sometimes with pain and regret, but often with fond memories and dreams of a future together someday. But I wouldn't have gone looking for you again because I thought you had moved on and forgotten about me. I've spent the past few months first wrestling with the anguish of your return and the loss of so many years we could have had together, and then expressing profuse gratitude to all the heavenly beings for bringing you back to me. You just can't put forth so strong a desire into the Universe and then not expect to receive your answer. We are all divine beings, though, as humans, subject to failure sometimes. And even if you can't see how special you are, I can confirm you were called, if for no other reason than because I need you to be with me."

Her kiss carried with it the conviction of her words, the assurance of her emotions, and the promise that, whatever their future held, they would face it together.

"Thank you," Lysandra murmured when she could speak again. "We might have lost our ability to communicate telepathically, but we can still send and receive vibrations like your trees do. I never stopped thinking of you, either. Every time you felt happy for no reason or sensed a friendly presence when you were alone or gained a second wind when you were tired, that was me thinking about you, sending love to you from far away."

Ariel's lips closed over hers, taking her mouth with passion, the fullness of her lover's desire encompassing her like a heavy cloak, hemming her in with a protective nature. The bond they had once shared had returned with power, and Lysandra drank it in like a potent wine.

"I suppose we should get food from the market," she offered reluctantly. With her confidence renewed and Ariel in her arms, she could hardly consider anything except kissing her again, and all she envisioned to follow.

"Yes," Ariel uttered against her lips. She pulled back, a curious, mischievous expression crossing her face. "And I want to walk by the Temple of Poseidon. Maybe we'll get to see the kings and queens from a distance."

Lysandra gaped at her. "The market in the inner ring is the most expensive anywhere."

Ariel laughed. "I didn't say we had to shop there. Let's just go have a look at the proceedings and then stop by a more reasonable marketplace."

"Alright then. To the temple we go." Lysandra's heart felt light again, inconceivably blissful, with every speck of doubt brushed away as she strolled beside the woman she loved through the city of dreams.

28

Temen, looking regal in his new ankle-length white toga, sat on one of the ten thrones arranged in a circle in the Council of Ruler's meeting room at Poseidon's Temple. He chose a purple sash and drape so it wouldn't be the same color as King Efrayim's. His sash sported a row of golden chakanas making him appear spiritual. Somewhere in his bored mind, Lykos's lessons about the equal-armed cross with the hole in the middle rattled around and he could hear the old wizard's gruff voice.

"This is one of the most important symbols, so pay attention!" *Blah, blah.* "The perpendicular arms of the cross represent the intersection of the spiritual and physical plains. See how the hole rests in the midpoint? It is through this eye we connect to the metaphysical realm, where our true power comes from. See the three steps of blocks in the figure? They stand for the celestial world of the stars, the physical world on Earth, and the afterlife and spiritual reality. Geometrically, by connecting points and drawing arcs, many other symbols reside within the chakana."

Temen had turned a palm-sized icon of gold over in his hands and poked his finger through the hole. "I don't feel anything in here," he had grumbled to his teacher. "It's just a hunk of metal." He held it up and peered through the ocular.

Lykos had snatched it away from him. "Of course you don't feel anything, you simpleton! This is a symbol, understand? The actual opening to the spirit world lies in your third eye, a tiny, specialized gland in your brain that receives and transmits universal light."

Temen had scowled at him, citing he had only two eyes, but this had all been long before Temen rose in prominence and was elected king. He wished to stay on Lykos's good side because he had witnessed him do frightening things using energies he pulled from thin air. And when he allowed himself to admit it, Temen realized he would never have been elected without the wizard's help. But Lykos didn't talk down to him anymore—mostly. They had a partnership that benefited them both.

"Now let's hear from Energy Minister Korinna," Efrayim said, recognizing a woman in an endless roster of men and women who droned on about what was right and wrong with their arena of authority, and they all required more funds to make improvements.

These meetings had been going on for three weeks now, and every day after the exciting kick-off had been the same dull routine. First, a priest led them in prayers of thanks, which could go on until Temen thought his skull would burst. It reminded him of life with his ex-wife. Then a guru of some sort took them through their morning movements and poses. This was supposed to get them properly aligned for the day, but Temen thought it would make much better sense to get up and stretch halfway through the morning when he was in danger of nodding off amid the tiring proceedings.

Despite how unenthused he was by the topics of discussion, Temen had fooled everyone into believing he was engaged and concerned, enlightened and bold. He presented a man of action who wasn't afraid to jump the bull or dispute a finance officer's findings. Lykos's tip had been right. Temen gained status with the others when he had pointed out that the finance officer had been skimming a considerable amount from his department's budget, which was entirely uncalled for. The man already made a comfortable living; why get greedy?

While the blonde woman, far too frumpy to warrant his attention, droned on about crystals and power stations, three people strode into their chamber unannounced. One spoke with authority in an elderly-sounding tenor voice. "I can tell you what's wrong with the system."

The interruption grabbed Temen's attention, and he stared up at the intruders. *Mandisa,* he grumbled to himself while displaying an amiable outward expression.

"Ziusudra!" Efrayim rose and bowed to the honored astronomer, and all the other kings and queens followed his lead. Temen jumped from his seat with haste to show the elders their proper respect. "Thoth, what a pleasant surprise," the moderator welcomed. "You have news about the energy crystals?"

"We have news about a great many things," Thoth said, and the three visitors bowed to the rulers. Thoth and Ziusudra carried their walking staffs and were dressed in proper conservative attire, while Mandisa, in her brightly-colored garments and straw sandals, appeared like she was off to visit the beaches of Menosus. She had rearranged her black braids since the last time he had seen her, but she bore the same smirky superior attitude he had always sensed in her.

"We apologize for appearing without invitation, my lords and ladies, but we bring news of the most urgent matter," Ziusudra gushed in a respectful tone. What were these two learned men doing with the likes of that imposter, Mandisa? *Air speakers,* he grumbled to himself in disapproval.

"If it's about why crystals are failing all over the continent, I'd like to hear it," Energy Minister Korinna said with a hopeful expression. She eagerly yielded the floor to the trio.

They proceeded to talk on and on about the alignment of the stars, the angle of the earth, the great comet, and the twenty-six-thousand-year cycle, all of which might as well have been in a foreign language. Still, Temen had honed his acting skills and passed himself off as being intellectually intrigued by their theories and evidence.

"So, you are suggesting, to compensate for all these cosmic events we should increase the height of our pyramids, the size of the quartz mother crystals, and erect more obelisks to act as power boosters," Temen summarized, displaying a thoughtful countenance.

"Under normal circumstances, that could stretch our technology another hundred years," Thoth answered, "except—"

"Except we need to be developing new technology, an alternative power source for the future," King Kleitos interjected.

"No." Ziusudra passed a bleak stare over the assembly. "Within five years, this entire continent, what remains of it, will be underwater. A great flood is coming, and we must prepare."

The hall erupted in heated discourse, everyone yelling at once.

"What do you mean, flood?"

"Leave Atlantis? Preposterous!"

"Where's your proof?"

"Where will we go?"

"Order!" Efrayim shouted and stomped his foot. "We are the kings and queens of Atlantis; we do not panic."

The rulers quieted and returned to their seats, though everyone was shaken by the report.

"Who saw the melted waters behind the Terrible Ice?" Efrayim asked in a calm tone of reason.

"Quetzal, Noah, Ériu, Ariel, Lysandra, and myself, along with the men who guided us," Mandisa testified. "I connected to the energies of the ice and water to determine the rate of thawing and integrity of the ice wall."

"I recognize Quetzal's name," said Queen Meresankh, "but none of the others."

"We answered Archangel Uriel's call," Thoth stated. "We set out to find the answers to the problems we face. Ziusudra is our most renowned astronomer; his calculations are without question."

"I agree," Temen answered in a measured tone of contemplation. "However, I know Mandisa. She is an air speaker of Ryzen, an honorable and well-intentioned woman. Even if she and the others saw melted ice in one spot above the glacial wall, that doesn't mean it is all melting. We recognize air speaking is the most unreliable of the gifts. How many times has one attempted to dissipate a storm, warm or cool the air, and have the opposite effect manifest? Even they admit they are powerless to control the weather." A few heads nodded as the others whispered to each other.

"Tell me, Thoth, Ziusudra," King Masuda of Gadlan charged. "Have you other proof than this air speaker's word?"

Temen didn't know the big blond king well, but he liked him. He bore a rugged man's appearance, from his bushy yellow beard to his hairy barrel chest. He might have worn more jewelry than modesty would accept, but most of the gold and gem mines were in his city-state, and it was only right that he supported them with his patronage. Masuda was a practical man, an athlete before turning to a life of service, and the only king younger than himself. Here was someone as skeptical as he was about Mandisa's findings.

"There is other evidence," Thoth stated. "Rising sea temperatures, erratic weather patterns, a dying coral reef off Daya Island. The fact is whether it does so tomorrow or in a hundred years, the ice wall will break and the ocean's worth of water that's been trapped behind it will inundate Atlantis with the greatest flood of our history."

"You hear that?" asked King Tecuani of Ampherium, catching the other ruler's attention. "It could be a hundred years from now. There's no need to be hasty."

"Easy for you to say," Meresankh retorted, her exotic eyes wide with alarm. "Your city-state lies in the mountains and highlands of Opocalám. It would be easy for your people to take refuge, while my city-state is a group of islands barely above sea level now."

The tall, thin King Tecuani, who rather resembled a weathered clothesline post, crossed his arms over his skinny chest and glowered at her. A silver and emerald headband held back thinning hair that dangled to his shoulders. Temen supposed he used a dye potion to keep it black, considering he was almost two hundred years old.

"That is not why I suggest we take more time to investigate these claims," Tecuani insisted. "I wish your people to be safe as much as mine, but I also do not want to trigger a panic."

"I know Mandisa too," Meresankh proclaimed, "and, while nobody is perfect, she seldom makes a mistake."

The kings and queens discussed and debated the issue until the heated emotions and snapping voices gave Temen a headache. That was the problem with an oligarchy, intellectual and spiritual or otherwise. If one man ruled over all of Atlantis, the matter would have been resolved in minutes. He would make a decision, set a course of action, and that would be it. Instead, eight other people's opinions, philosophies, and life experiences had to come into play. Everyone wanted to put their city-state's considerations first, and suddenly they were all experts. Boring as it was, their session had been flowing along quite smoothly until Mandisa and crew showed up to throw a stick in the works.

"I can see it is going to take some time to sort this flood prediction out satisfactorily," Efrayim concluded as he drew their focus back to him. "I move that, after our lunch break, we commission a team to further investigate the melting of the Terrible Ice. If more experts agree the danger is indeed rapidly approaching, we can consider a campaign to encourage citizens to emigrate to our colonies for starters. I do not want any Atlanteans to be in peril, nor do I wish to frighten them into committing rash acts. We know violence has been on the rise and Ziusudra's explanations make sense. We must keep the economy going and allow people to enjoy their lives for now. If we determine the danger is as near as Mandisa predicts, then we can act in the background to ensure safe transportation to the colonies for our population. Can you imagine the mayhem if they learn another cataclysm is upon us? And what if we are wrong and nothing happens?"

The king of Atala turned to Mandisa and her two respected sidekicks. "We deeply appreciate you bringing this threat to our attention, as well as suggestions on how to approach the energy crisis. Please send any further developments you discover to my office in writing. We must all work together to ensure our civilization survives."

Taking that as their cue, the three left the chamber. Temen was hardily relieved when they were dismissed to lunch.

He shook Efrayim's hand in a firm grip. "You handled that brilliantly, friend. Ziusudra and the others brought troubling reports, but they should have scheduled an audience rather than interrupt our meeting uninvited. Still, being an accomplished diplomat, you soothed each ruler's concerns without offending our guests."

"Thank you, Temen," he answered in a pleased manner. "Years of practice prepared me for being elected moderator, and I strive to let all voices be heard. We should never slight learned men, or air speakers for that matter. They perform valuable services to our nation, but they can get carried away with their 'words from the Universe' and prophecies of doom. Still, we must take this threat seriously. Our ancestors didn't—and look what happened to them."

After sweet-talking Efrayim, Temen's next goal was to have lunch with King Masuda of Gadlan to cultivate a stronger friendship with the man. *He could be another valuable ally.*

He caught up with Masuda as they exited the front of the temple. "Greetings, Masuda," he smiled, falling in beside the giant of a man as they descended the steps. "You made some valid points in the discussion today. Do you mind if I join you for lunch?"

"Not at all," he replied. "I'm meeting King Ahau at the oyster bar down the street."

Temen flashed him a winning smile, thinking, *If you're going to wear a long beard like that, the least you could do is comb it once in a while.*

An astonished voice cut through the midday bustle. "Temen?"

He glanced up and across the street, past a couple of sleighs, a horse-drawn chariot, and a dozen pedestrians. "Temen—it *is* you!" the woman shouted in disbelief, causing a scene.

For a second, his feet froze in place, and the fear of all the gods descended upon him in a whirlwind. His heart pounded in his chest and his eyes rounded to twice their normal size. *Where is Lykos? I need Lykos!*

From behind, he felt the bolstering confidence of his wizard's magic settle the terror and return his dignity. He cocked his head at Ariel in curiosity, and answered, "I'm sorry; have we met before?"

29

Ariel stared at Temen with her mouth agape, as if nobody else was on the street.

"What's wrong, Ariel?" Lysandra asked. "You look like you've seen a ghost."

Trembling with shock and disbelief, she pointed and answered loudly enough for all to hear. "That's Temen, my dead husband—at least that's what he led us to believe ten years ago."

"You must be mistaken." A man in a black and silver kilt with a teal cloak draped around bare, muscular shoulders appeared at Temen's side. She presumed by his serpent-headed staff he was a wizard. She recognized his vibrations when they struck her, and she warded them away.

"This is King Temen of Ryzen, and he is happily married to the Lady Rhoxane," announced the smooth-talking fellow with his neat chin beard and penetrating eyes.

"It's all right, Lykos," Temen said as he struck a regal stance, one arm protectively outstretched before the wizard. "This poor, bereaved woman merely has me confused with someone else. Let us leave her to grieve her loss while we dine together. We have weighty matters to attend to this afternoon."

"Wait!" Ariel yelled as he and his companions turned their backs on her. "You abandoned your children! How could you do that?" They kept walking, ignoring her. Anger flashed through Ariel like a raging bull, and she started to run after them. Lysandra's hand caught her arm.

Ariel spun and shook loose. "Let me go! That man—"

"Is the king of Ryzen," Lysandra cut her off. "Did you love him so much that you would chase after him now?"

"No," she declared, "and at the moment I want to pummel him until he can't get up. He's supposed to be dead. My daughter cried and cried. We had a funeral."

Ariel sensed the fire in her veins flaring through her whole body, threatening to consume her with wrath. She physically trembled with its force. Suddenly, she couldn't catch her breath, felt light-headed, and her knees buckled. Lysandra wrapped an arm around her and guided her to a nearby bench surrounded by dwarf evergreens.

"Breathe," Lysandra instructed. Ariel obeyed while she tried to orient herself. She was never shaken this way, never got so angry. Never. It must have been the shock—no, the betrayal. "Are you certain it was him?" Lysandra's voice was gentle, timid even. "It's been ten years."

"It's him!" She didn't mean to snap out the words. Ariel turned her face into Lysandra's neck, comforted by her nearness. "I'm sorry. I didn't mean to frighten you. It's just ... unbelievable."

"You said you were married for fifteen years? Sweetie, how well did you know him?"

"Obviously not as well as I thought I did." While still feeling shaky, Ariel sensed her fury subsiding. "He seemed like a normal guy. He was charming and thoughtful, and so good with the children. But he couldn't have loved any of us, not and take off like that."

She lifted probing eyes, brimming with disillusionment, to the compassion revealed in Lysandra's sweet gaze. "He left his children to believe he was dead. Who does that? What kind of imposter did I marry? And why would he have wanted me to begin with? Most baffling of all, how did he get to be elected king of Ryzen? I thought he was a good friend, a devoted husband and father, but I never mistook him for being bright."

"I don't know," Lysandra empathized as she rubbed her hand across Ariel's back.

"What's this, now?" Mandisa asked. "Ariel, are you all right?"

She peered up, raising a hand to shade her eyes from the sun. Mandisa, Thoth, and Ziusudra stood around them with expressions of concern.

"Temen, the new king of Ryzen, is her missing husband," Lysandra said. "It was quite a shock to see how well he was doing for a dead man."

"Well, bury a spoon!" Mandisa exclaimed.

Hearing the expression everyone used, without having a clue what it meant, made Ariel laugh. She shook her head and knuckled away a tear she hadn't previously realized stained her cheek. "My daughter says that."

"Should we do something?" Thoth asked. "Go after him and exchange harsh words?"

"No." Ariel didn't want to have anything further to do with the deceiver. "He has a new wife now, a new life, and it doesn't include or concern me. I need to forgive him and go back to living as if he was dead. I'm just not sure what to tell Mother, Sheera, and Mal'akhi."

"We're sorry," Lysandra said. "We were going to pick up food for everyone at the market and I wanted to show Ariel Poseidon's Temple, not knowing such drama would ensue."

"Here, child." Ziusudra reached a bony hand to her, and Ariel allowed him to help her to her feet. "Temen talks a good game but has no understanding. He could never have risen to power so quickly on his own."

"He has a wizard with him," Ariel said. "Lykos."

"Yes," Mandisa answered with a grave nod. "He was the headmaster of the Southern Wisdom School for decades until he went on sabbatical a couple of years ago. He's maintained his association with the school, but now I see what he's truly been up to. I don't understand why a brilliant energy master like Lykos would look twice at someone like Temen—no offense."

"None taken," Ariel replied as they crossed over the bridge to the second ring where the library was located. "I'm the one who feels like an idiot now."

"Don't," commanded Thoth. "An accomplished charlatan can fool even the wisest sage under the right circumstances."

She nodded but still felt stupid and ashamed. "Thank you for being such supportive friends. I'm blessed to be in your company."

"I don't think Temen believed us about the ice wall breaking," Mandisa said.

"I'm not sure any of them did."

"They don't want to believe it," Ziusudra clarified. "It is unfortunate, but understandable."

"They'll believe when the waters come," Thoth said. "But we'll discuss what the rulers said after we purchase the food for our midday meal. We launch our plan today."

✝ ☖ ✣ ✡

It was hard for Ariel to focus on mapping out a strategy with thoughts of Temen being alive and the king of Ryzen running on a loop in her brain, but she tried. Having Lysandra at her side helped. Maybe her soulmate hadn't been there to deal with her husband's loss the first time, but she was here now, lending unwavering support and a quiet strength for her to draw from.

This is what was always lacking between me and Temen, she recalled. *A vital spiritual connection. I thought it was because he didn't have a special energetic talent like she and I shared; now I realize it was because he was a fraud.*

"Phase one," Thoth said, drawing her attention away from her personal troubles. "Preparation. I agree with the rulers that we don't wish to cause panic. Word will get out and people will be curious, but there are always rumors of one sort or another. Let's not broadcast prophecies of doom, please."

"I agree," Quetzal said. "Noah should begin construction on the arks right away. The folks of Diaprep are accustomed to seeing him build ships, and no one will think anything of it."

"I can help him secure a larger workforce than usual," Ptah said. "You mentioned me taking on projects in the colonies?"

"Yes," Quetzal confirmed. "Where have you traveled and were well received?"

"I've been to Kemet," he said. "The locals revere our colonists there and have already erected some impressive monuments. I was called to the Giza Plateau to make some structural improvements to a colossal tribute to Leo they fashioned attempting to appease the constellation after the Great Conflagration."

"I've seen a representation of it," Thoth said. "The Great Sphinx is aligned perfectly with Leo in the sky on the night of the Spring Equinox. Is it an ideal location?"

"Giza is along the Nile River, about sixty leagues from its delta on the Green Sea," Ptah reported. "The ground is solid in places around the plateau and many people farm the rich soil near the river. We started our colony there around a thousand years ago when it was all lush and green, flowing with milk and honey. The Conflagration didn't devastate the land of Kemet the same way it did here, but it triggered a climate change in the region, which has been slowly turning to desert ever since."

Thoth nodded. "It sounds like an ideal place to build a power pyramid. Ériu, your husband is a miner?"

"Yes," she answered, bright eyes eager to contribute.

"Ask if he can locate and extract a sizable, suitable quartz stone from the mines to serve as a mother crystal. You'll need to store it in secret so we can transport it to Giza when Ptah's pyramid is ready to receive it."

"We must save the chronicles and wisdom books," Thoth said. "Ptah, I'll go with you to Giza to inspect the site. Arid conditions would be perfect for preserving papyrus manuscripts. Ideally, I want to establish several libraries in different locations, just to be sure knowledge doesn't perish."

"I met a starling once who fancied himself an explorer," Ariel said. "He boasted of a vast, high mountain range east of the Sindhu valley with a small tribe of humans who were nature speakers. He said he conversed with them like he did with me. High mountains should be safe from flood waters."

"I've heard of the Kirāt," Thoth responded thoughtfully. "If I am not mistaken, some of our ancestors who escaped the Conflagration settled among them in the highlands."

"Kirāt, you say?" Quetzal asked. "When I was young, I had an astral visitor from far away during my meditation. She might have said she was Kirāti. If so, they are a spiritual people with whom we could be compatible."

"I can't live on the rooftop of the world," Noah protested. "And, yes, Methuselah mentioned them to me once or twice. Sounds like a safe place for your library, though."

"In southwest Maanu, I've heard about cities in the clouds," Mandisa said. "They say there's a great lake in the Copper Mountains that provides for the people. If these mountains are as high as tales make out, they should provide a safe refuge."

"Let us divide into groups," Ziusudra proposed. "Some will work here while we send a delegation to Giza, Kirāt, and the Mayeb. Ériu, do you have languages for these regions?"

"Indeed. Many people speak the Kemetic dialect used in Giza," Ériu said matter-of-factly. "I'm not entirely sure the eastern language I know is the common tongue of Kirāt, but I speak Sindhi as fluently as Protelex. I'm also well-versed in the Xi language in the narrow region of Maanu, but I can't go everywhere at once to translate."

"I can speak Kemetic," Thoth said. "Quetzal, how fast can you learn Xi?"

"With Ériu's tutelage aided by deep meditation, perhaps a week," he replied in an optimistic tone.

"You're talking about going to desert and mountainous regions," Ariel pointed out in concern. "While we'll be transporting llamas, goats, bears, and eagles that thrive in high altitudes, we have no desert creatures, and most of our flora and fauna aren't adapted to survive on mountain tops."

"Don't worry, Ariel," Thoth said with a smile. "They can stay on the arks until the seas have subsided enough for them to emerge in a biome that suits their species. Now, Ériu, teach Quetzal the language and then you travel with Ziusudra to the eastern mountains of Kirāt. Lysandra, if you and Mandisa will accompany Quetzal to Maanu in the west and connect with our colonists there, then Ptah and Ariel can accompany me to Giza. Ariel, that will allow you to evaluate the climate change occurring in the region. Noah needs to get started building the giant ships. Can we all be ready to depart a week from tomorrow?"

Ariel exchanged a glance with Lysandra. Just as they were rekindling their lost love, Thoth's directive to separate them and send them to opposite sides of the world came as a devastating blow. Yet she understood the magnitude of their mission. Her feelings were only a gnat compared to the survival of their civilization.

As if she was thinking the same thing, Lysandra asked, "How long will we be gone? My medical practice—"

"Don't worry, Lysandra," Quetzal said, patting her hand with an understanding smile. "We only need to talk to the locals and inform them of what is about to happen. Then we'll search for the best place to send citizens. We'll be back by spring, and there are other physicians to treat the people of Atala. You, my dear, are more special than you realize."

She nodded in resignation.

With a deep frown, Noah inquired, "And what if the Council of Rulers doesn't choose to act? What if they refuse to start a relocation project and declare us to be reactionist fools?"

Ziusudra answered, "Don't worry about the politicians, Noah. Just do what must be done."

30

That night, Ariel found solace in Lysandra's embrace, knowing it would be their last for a while.

"Tell me what you'll be doing," Lysandra entreated. She brushed back Ariel's hair and sprinkled kisses along her shoulder and neck that were sure to reach her ear soon. The tender sensations sent a shiver of pleasure through Ariel.

"I must go home for a few days," she explained. "I'll stop by Evamont to visit my son, and the farm for Mother and Sheera. Then I have to go to Diaprep for Noah to find a forest willing to sacrifice all its trees for the arks—maybe more than one forest. Oma might like to come; she used to be friends with Noah in the wild days of her youth. We're to board a trading vessel out of Atala bound for Kemet a week from tomorrow. It's exciting because I've never traveled abroad, but it'll be a long time to endure being apart from you."

Lysandra chuckled. "Like thirty years wasn't a long time." She took Ariel's earlobe between her teeth, nipping it gently before teasing it with her tongue.

Ariel elbowed her and smirked. "An hour is too long to not be holding you." She flipped around to face Lysandra in bed. They had already dispensed with clothes, so those were no longer a barrier, to Ariel's delight. "And what about your plans?"

"Quetzal arranged for my leave time with Raffi and I'm to start the language classes with him and Ériu tomorrow. I've never tried learning another language, so I don't know how hard it will be. Anyway, Mandisa has to go home to check on her orchard and her husbands, but we plan to tutor her on the ship. Our transport leaves out of Autopolis a week from tomorrow. Quetzal says the weather will be warmer than here, that they don't have a winter season at all, but to bring a warm cloak in case we journey up into the mountains."

Lysandra stopped her itinerary long enough to indulge in a generous kiss. "How are you feeling after, you know, seeing *him* today?"

Ariel stroked Lysandra's smooth skin beneath the linen sheet, immersed in the pleasure it brought her, hoping her fingertips gave more than they received. "It was quite a shock at first and I ripped through a line of emotions, felt like a fool, but now ..." She took a deep breath, let it out slowly, and took Lysandra's mouth in a seductive kiss. "I don't care. He could have just asked for a divorce like a normal person. I'm abiding by the ninth rule and will not let the sun set on my anger. Temen is out of my life, and you are back in it. I count that as a major victory, one I'm ready to celebrate."

She sensed Lysandra's relief wash over her even as her talented healer's hands did the same. Desire ripped at Ariel's core, igniting a fire in her blood. She slid a leg between her lover's thighs and drew her closer with a hand behind her neck.

"What about you?" Ariel asked between kisses. "Traveling the ocean by ship?"

Lysandra clung to her, burrowing her face under her hair and breathing into her throat. "I'm more worried about your passage than mine. They were sailing east and never made it to the Pillars of Hercules before the storm hit. Mandisa will be on our ship, but my family didn't have an air speaker, and neither will you."

"We have been called, the nine of us, my love. Archangel Michael will protect us." Ariel's voice was raw and husky, heavily affected by Lysandra's mouth passionately laying claim to her neck. Another swell of pleasure broke through her when her lover's fingers closed in on a sensitive spot, but she needed to add one more thing before losing the ability to form words. "I can always call on a whale to save me."

☥ ☗ ✚ ✡

Evamont, the next day

"Mal'akhi!" Ariel cried out as she jogged past men and women, carts and sleighs, down the paved streets, waving to her son. Although a light mist sprinkled from a cloudy winter sky, her forest green woolen wrap protected her from the mild elements.

He pivoted, blue eyes rounding, and stared in horror as his mother chased after him with a beaming smile. A rosy red flushed his fair cheeks, bordered by wavy fawn hair and the fuzz of a soft beard and mustache.

"Mother," Mal'akhi grumbled between gritted teeth. "What are you doing? I'm on patrol with my squad."

Ariel came to a halt before the group of three men and a woman dressed in City Guardian garb. The uniform consisted of Evamont-blue kilts, padded vests topped with diagonally crossing white leather armor, and matching blue waist capes affixed by silver-plated wesekhs. Each carried a steel-tipped spear and bore the guardian emblem of an eye within a triangle inside a circle.

"I know, but can't a woman invite her son and his co-workers to lunch?" Ariel grinned brightly and hugged Mal'akhi, who gave up his protest and hugged her back. They kissed each other's cheeks, and Ariel gave thanks that, while Mal'akhi favored his father's appearance, on the inside he was every bit her son.

"Yes, but not while we're on duty," he replied, his expression turning serious. "How long are you in the city?"

"Not long," Ariel said. She fell in line between her son and a darkish fellow, while the woman and a stout guardian with a bushy black beard closed ranks behind them. "I would be pleased to meet your friends, though. Perhaps we could stop at that refreshment stand over there and have a quick chocolate?"

Mal'akhi glanced over his shoulder at the older, stout man, who responded with a sharp nod. "We can do that."

Ariel leaned in and whispered, "Are they your friends? Are they a trustworthy lot?"

"Yes, Mother," he replied in a hushed, suspicious tone. "We've been together all year."

"Here we are," Ariel called and led the way to the vendor. "A round for our guardians in blue and myself, please," she ordered with a smile. She handed him the proper arrangement of coins.

The vendor gave each a ceramic mug of the steamy chocolate, and they gathered around a small outdoor table covered by a broad umbrella. "So, what brings you to the city?" Mal'akhi asked.

"You, precious. I have to go on another long trip in a few days."

"Again?" Mal'akhi's frown resembled a small child's pout. "You can tell us what's going on."

Ariel appreciated the thick, flavorful beverage before setting her mug on the table. She smiled and patted his arm. "I've won free passage to visit our colony in Kemet," she sang out. "I'll get to meet new species of animals and see the big stone lion you might have heard about. It will be quite the adventure."

"That sounds terrific!" cheered the dark-complected guard, who appeared to be near her son's age. "May I come with you?"

They all laughed, but Mal'akhi met her gaze with a skeptical look. "You will enjoy meeting the new animals," he said.

"It's a long way," commented the older guard. "I hope you don't get seasick."

Ariel hadn't thought of that. *If only Lysandra was coming with us.*

"Mal'akhi, there's something I need to tell you before you find out another way," she uttered gravely. There was no easy way to do it, and she really didn't want to, but now that Temen was king of Ryzen, word would get out. He may even travel to Evamont on state business. She didn't want Mal'akhi to be blindsided the way she had been.

He swallowed his chocolate and set down his mug, cocking his head inquisitively at her. "What?"

"Help, guardians!" shouted a woman running from across the street. She gripped a scarf over her head and splashed through a puddle, dodging a grumpy old man who shook his cane at her.

"What's the rush?" he scolded.

The team leader leaped to his feet. "What's the matter, miss?"

Mal'akhi and the other two followed the older man's lead and stood as well, spears at the ready.

"There's been an accident," she shrieked, trembling and oscillating between looking at them and over her shoulder. "At least it started that way."

"Show us," commanded the black-bearded leader.

Ariel downed the rest of her chocolate and followed closely in the squad's wake.

"Two sleighs collided at a corner, knocking over a vendor's cart," the frantic woman explained. "I don't think anyone was hurt, but the drivers began to argue, then punches were thrown, and—oh gods—I've never seen such a fight!"

Breaking into a run, the four guardians, Ariel, and the witness arrived on the scene too late. A crowd had gathered to watch—some yelling, some crying, and some simply staring in shock. Breaking through the throng, Ariel couldn't believe her eyes. In a grim scene, a young fellow loomed above the motionless body of an elderly man, clutching a metal running board covered in blood. With his shaggy, damp hair matted against his forehead and his face twisted in fury, he panted for air.

"What have you done?" the crew captain bellowed in disbelief. Ariel squeezed past to kneel beside the man on the ground while Mal'akhi snatched the bent skid from the angry man's grasp.

The perpetrator pushed the wet hair out of his bitter eyes and pointed at the elder, lying curled in a ball at his feet. "He was supposed to stop at the corner," he snapped. "He didn't stop—ran right into my sleigh. Look at the damage he caused!"

When Mal'akhi's team members tried to fasten restraints around the violent man's wrists, he spat vile curses and punched them. It took all four guardians to subdue him.

Blood mingled with little trickles of rainwater swirled through the cracks between the paving stones and raced toward the drain. Ariel laid her hand on his cut and bruised forehead. "Sir, can you hear me?" He didn't respond.

"Make way!" a man's deep voice boomed out. "I'm a healer. Let me through!"

A man twice Ariel's age crouched opposite her over the victim and went to work. He closed his eyes, vocalized a chant, and passed his hands back and forth a few thumbs above the bleeding victim's body.

"Is he—" Ariel held her breath, peering hopefully at the physician.

"Hush!" he barked.

As her soul compelled her to help, Ariel closed her eyes and focused her energy on this man's well-being. Vibrations flowed from her heart, through her arms, and out the palms of her hands as she aimed them toward the wounded man. While she was no healer—not like Lysandra—Ariel understood how frequencies worked and the powerful Law of Compassion.

Presently, the physician relaxed his arms and exhaled a weary breath. "The injuries to his brain were too severe. His skull was broken before we arrived, and, while I could sustain his heartbeat and breathing, it wasn't enough. We can heal many things; traumatic brain death isn't one of them."

Ariel said a silent prayer to follow the stranger on his journey into the afterlife, and felt a peace settle over her as if he was saying, "Thank you, but everything is all right now."

"I sensed your energies assisting me," he said, looking at Ariel. "Are you a student of the healing arts?"

"No, a nature speaker."

He nodded. Another squad of guardians arrived, and Ariel backed out of their way while they collected the deceased's body. Mal'akhi's leader said, "We've got this criminal under control now. Go spend a few minutes with your mother."

He thanked him, took Ariel by the arm, and led her away. As they walked, she commented, "Things like this never used to happen."

"Violent arguments and breaking of the statute rules have been on the rise the past several years."

"What will happen to the man who killed him?" Just saying the words felt like ashes in Ariel's mouth. Murder in Atlantis was unheard of. This is how the barbarians behave. Didn't that young man understand The Law and Rules, culminating in the sixteenth rule: *Do to others what you wish to be done to you, for we are all One?*

"He broke the first rule: do not commit murder," Mal'akhi pronounced. "We'll hold him until his trial before King Kleitos and the jurors. Only a majority decision of the Council of Rulers can impose a death penalty, and I can't recall one ever being issued. Typically, the judgment is for the guilty party to pay recompense to the person who was wronged, but he can't bring the man back to life. Therefore, he might be sold into slavery abroad or banished from Atlantis forever, forfeiting his life in a sense. Thankfully, it isn't up to me."

Returning to the hot chocolate vendor, they found their table cleared; at least the rain stopped. Her handsome son, who stood a couple of thumbs taller than Ariel, turned to her with an intuitive gaze and took her hands in his. "What did you come here to tell me, Mother?"

She let out a resolute sigh and bolstered her courage. "It's about your father."

31

Atala, that evening

After exchanging pleasantries with the other rulers, Temen returned to his palace guest quarters to freshen up and change clothes before going to dinner and the theater with his beautiful new wife. They had continued the discussion of Mandisa's impending disaster, and, thankfully, none of them noticed or cared about the spectacle Ariel had caused yesterday. He supposed an apocalyptic prophecy took precedence over a case of mistaken identity.

"There you are, Temen!" Rhoxane marched to meet him at the door with irritation in her mannerisms. "Why didn't you tell me about that crazy woman from yesterday? I had to hear it in the palace baths. If some hussy is trying to steal you from me, I intend to teach her a lesson."

He held up his hands in surrender. "My sweetness, nobody is trying to steal me from you, and she would fail miserably if she tried." Presenting her with an adoring smile, he explained, "I didn't want to bother you with such nonsense. I know how easily your feathers can get ruffled. You're the only woman for me."

Temen drew her into a firm embrace and kissed her. "Rhoxane, darling, you smell divine. It will only take me a few minutes to be ready to go out. I want to show you an evening you'll not soon forget."

"Well," she purred, running a finger down his chest with a seductive smile, "if you're certain it was nothing."

"I'm certain she's long gone and will give us no more trouble. Poor woman's husband died, and I must resemble him. I don't think she was trying to extort us for money or any such sordid affair. Let us enjoy our evening and not speak of it again." He sealed his request with a kiss and slipped into the bedroom to change.

Temen had always been attracted to people with energetic gifts because he desired the power to use them himself. Somehow, he believed if he was close enough to such a talent and spent enough time with him or her, he'd pick up on how it was done. After being turned down by the Northern Wisdom School, Temen had married a spunky air speaker with that goal in mind. However, their relationship had been more thunder and lightning and less sunny skies, so they divorced. The failed marriage may have something to do with his dislike of air speakers.

Hoping to try again, Temen moved from Elapus to the Evamont village of Elyrna. On his second day in town, he witnessed something he'd never forget. A small child was playing near a narrow well when he fell in. All those around—including Temen—rushed to help rescue the little boy. The stone mouth of the well was too narrow for an adult to fit inside, so Temen had lowered the bucket down from its rope and the child's mother cried for him to put his foot in it and grab hold of the rope to be pulled up. They could hear his frantic cries and he said his foot was caught on something. They knew at least his head was above the water, but nobody could go down to get him.

Then this tall, lean woman with medium brown hair and a monkey on her shoulder ran up to them. He recalled she wasn't a remarkable beauty except for her compelling eyes. She said to get her a length of rope and she would retrieve the trapped child. While someone fetched the rope, the woman talked to the monkey, instructing it to climb down the well, tie the cord around the child, wiggle his foot free, and they would pull them both out.

Temen had scoffed. Monkeys are good climbers, but they can't tie knots, and how could it even understand what she said? To his amazement, the clinging little primate chattered back to the woman, bared his teeth in a wide grin, and hugged her before descending into the deep hole with one end of the rope. A few minutes later, he helped the child's father pull him and the extraordinary monkey out safe and sound. Temen witnessed how everyone in the village honored the nature speaker, saved her prime merchandise at the market, and offered her preferential seats. *I want people to respect me like that,* he determined. When he learned she was sad over being abandoned by her former lover, Temen engaged the one skill he had—charm—and started courting her.

Two children and fifteen years later, Temen had become bored with life on a rural farm. Sure, he went into the village and the city to debate in the salons and forums, practicing his rhetoric and pontification, but he was no closer to discovering the secret of how to use the energies. When he would ask, Ariel would effervesce about gratitude, tapping into the spirit of The Law, and meditating. She could make flowers pop out of the grass; he wanted to make precious gems pop out of rocks.

Many men and women, when seeking a closer relationship with universal forces, would embark on a spiritual vision quest—a time away from other people and distractions to focus their attention inward and upward. Inspired by the success Ariel's brother achieved on his vision quest, Temen set off to climb a mountain to be nearer the ancestors, angels, and Creator. For three days, nothing happened. He became so discouraged that he was ready to give up when he heard the voice calling to him with promises of a powerful destiny he alone could fulfill. All he had to do was find the wise sage to instruct him and assist him in his rise to the authority he was meant to have.

It wasn't like Temen had never loved or cared for his family; of course he had. But they had served their purpose in his life, and it was time for him to move on. Could he have gone home and said goodbye first? Perhaps. But that would have been hard. He would have needed to explain, and what if his son, who was on the verge of puberty, had wanted to come with him? He hadn't been afraid to face them; no, that wasn't it at all. There simply was no time to waste. Atlantis was a big country, and he had to find a specific wizard, and, oh, what knowledge and power Lykos commanded! His old life didn't matter anymore. Temen was fulfilling his calling as king of Ryzen, and maybe one day, king over all Atlantis.

With perfume combed into his hair and wearing a fresh, warmer wardrobe appropriate for the winter evening, Temen returned to the main room to find Lykos seated beside Rhoxane on the crimson sofa cushion engaged in quiet conversation. He frowned.

"Lykos," he addressed. "Rhoxane and I are about to enjoy a meal and entertainment. Was there something you needed?"

Rhoxane scooted away from Lykos, and he rose to face Temen. "I don't mean to interrupt your plans, but I need to know the council's decision regarding the impending flood."

Temen scowled. "They'll still be debating it next year," he groaned. "A survey team was sent to the Terrible Ice, and they've called for another astronomer to verify Ziusudra's calculations. I wouldn't worry about anything Mandisa says. She's odd and unreliable at her station."

"On the contrary," Lykos declared. "She and the others are correct." He clasped his hands behind his back and began a slow promenade around the room.

Stunned, Temen dropped onto the sofa beside Rhoxane, who seemed to be taking the revelation in stride. "What? Are you sure?" This was not the news Temen wished to receive. What good was it for him to become king if they were all about to die?

"Positive. I arrived at the same conclusion about ten years ago," he expounded. "If Thoth and Ziusudra didn't figure it out soon, I would have had to bring the ominous report to the council myself. This way is much better. If the calculations are off, let them assume the blame."

"But—" A quiver ran through Temen and a little nausea with it. "Why didn't you tell me sooner?"

"Everything in its season, Temen. You don't plant tomatoes in Capricorn." When Temen stared at him with a blank look, Lykos huffed out, "It wasn't time yet. Now it is."

"Time for what? To plan our escape?"

Rhoxane took his hand and leaned into his shoulder. "Time for you to step up and lead, to be a hero to the people," she proposed. "The thought of facing this situation without your strategic expertise would have me trembling with fright. As it is, I know I'm safe in your hands."

"But what can we do?" Temen begged. "We can't change the stars or stop the melting." His mind raced as he tried to hold down a growing dread, and he gripped Rhoxane's hand tighter to keep his own from shaking. Then a thought popped from his mouth. "We could construct a great wall in front of the Terrible Ice to hold back the water when the ice breaks."

Lykos pursed his lips and stroked his beard. "I don't think even Atlanteans could succeed in so massive an effort, even if we quarried every stone on the continent. We need to think about where to relocate the citizens of Ryzen. It will need to be somewhere we're familiar with, somewhere safe." The wizard resumed his stroll across the floor with occasional glances at the ceiling.

"I met with some merchants from Kaptara," Temen suggested optimistically. "They were very deferential toward me."

"Kaptara is but one island in the Green Sea," Rhoxane noted. "I doubt it's big enough for all of us."

"Kemet is quite large," Temen said. "And we have a colony in good standing there."

"Yes, but ..." Lykos hesitated. "What about Pelasgoí? It's a sparsely populated peninsula connected to an entire continent many times larger than Atlantis. They have some mountains, a good wine country, and an established fishing culture. Hundreds of small islands depend on the support of the mainland."

"Didn't our colony in Pelasgoí declare their independence a few hundred years ago?" Temen inquired, unsure of the date.

"A hundred and twenty-four, to be exact," Lykos supplied. "Ungrateful half-breeds. The Atlantean colonists intermarried with the inferior races, producing a polluted population. We were forced to remove our technology and clear out our library there lest they use our knowledge against us."

"I don't think they would be very welcoming," Temen replied with a confused frown. "Maybe Kush."

Lykos halted his march and sat on the low table across from Temen and Rhoxane. "We are Atlanteans, not cavemen, and you are a king, not an indentured servant. Why should we flee to our colonies as refugees when we could arrive as conquerors? We must assert our dominance over the Green Sea, not act as beggars with our hands out. Our statures, knowledge, skill, and technologies far exceed anything in their world. I know Efrayim and the others. They will negotiate with Kemet because of the mutually beneficial arrangement they have established with their leaders. But if you were to control Pelasgoí, you alone would be king of the peninsula, then king of all the lands beyond as you conquer them."

The wizard's advice troubled Temen. He was no military man, no tactician. He had never even held a sword. "But Lykos," he protested, "what if Pelasgoí refuses to submit to my authority? What if they won't even allow our citizens to settle there after the bitter way our colony departed from us?"

"Then you crush them."

"I don't know," Temen responded as knots tightened in his stomach. "What if the citizens don't like it? One thing Atlanteans love above all is peace. Their goal is to lead a life of comfort, enjoying sumptuous meals, indulging in passionate love, and immersing themselves in a world of beauty. Our people don't want to go to war. It would be stark and hard, and many might die. If I propose we take back Pelasgoí by force, the voters could remove me from power."

Rhoxane's arms came around him in admiring support. "You are wise to consider these possibilities, my husband," she charmed. "But Atlanteans also like to be winners. We understand our place as the most advanced civilization on earth. If citizens were granted a choice between arriving as immigrants on the distant shores of lesser kingdoms, with their heads bowed and hands out, or marching in as triumphant victors ready to dispense compassionate judgment and teach the indigenous inhabitants the value and wisdom of our laws and rules, to establish our civilization with all its merits in a new place—which do you think they would prefer? I know which I would choose, even if it meant enduring the dangers of war."

"The last time we went to war, things didn't turn out so well," Temen reminded them. "There are still multitudes of folks who believe the whole reason the Conflagration happened was to punish us for our arrogance. Of course, you and I know it was a natural disaster caused by an errant comet, not the judgment of some supernatural being in the sky, but still ..."

This was troubling. Temen didn't want his homeland to flood. Nor did he wish to start over in some foreign land. Mostly, he was terrified of the prospect of war. There were so many things that could go wrong. And then there was the likelihood of death and destruction. What mindful Atlantean would willingly trade the near certainty of two or three hundred years of prosperity for the prospect of being killed abroad? He knew he wouldn't.

"I am king!" Temen announced in a robust voice.

"Indeed, you are," Lykos affirmed, bowing his head to Temen. "Which is why I am confident you will make a wise decision."

As Temen took a moment to settle his nerves and catch his breath, confidence sprang from his gut. The merits of Lykos's suggestion became clear. "Isn't it better to arrive as conquerors than refugees?" he voiced in consideration. "Wouldn't our citizens prefer to be masters than servants?"

"What a marvelous idea!" Rhoxane praised and kissed his cheek.

"When the people learn a great flood is coming, they will volunteer in droves to reclaim our old colony at Pelasgoí," Lykos assured him. "And under your capable leadership, our efforts shall not fail. The citizens will build monuments to you. Sculptors will carve your image on colossal statues to be remembered for all time—the king who saved the Atlanteans from the monstrous flood."

Temen stood, squared his shoulders, and lifted his chin. He reached a hand for Rhoxane, who took it and glided gracefully to her feet. "Come, my dear. Our evening awaits. I believe our course of action is set. Lykos, we can discuss particulars once this tiresome council session closes. Tonight, Rhoxane and I shall celebrate our pending victory."

His wife smiled, batting her lashes at him in promise, and Temen answered her flirtations with a kiss.

"As you wish, my king," Lykos replied with a bow. "Enjoy your evening."

A warm feeling of pride and satisfaction radiated from Temen as his eyes lustily raked over Rhoxane's stunning form. "I shall, Lykos; I certainly shall."

32

Diaprep, two days before departure

Ariel arrived at the coastal city of Diaprep with two unplanned companions. Well, she figured Oma might like to come along to reconnect with Noah after a couple of hundred years, but Ratiki had been a stowaway. After laying down the law about how dangerous the trip could be and that she would be busy working the whole time, he had given her a sad, pleading look, and then displayed his best begging behavior. It wasn't until after the air coach bound for Diaprep had lifted off its pad that she noticed something squirming around in her travel bag. Not wanting him to make a mess of her things, she fished him out.

I would miss you too much, he offered as an excuse, big round eyes peering mournfully at her while his little hands pressed together in supplication. *You never went anywhere without me before, but, lately, you keep leaving me behind. I promise not to get into any trouble.*

"Famous last words," she replied sarcastically. Though he had disobeyed her order, Ariel could hardly stay mad at one who displayed such love and devotion. Naturally, Oma found the whole situation utterly amusing.

Diaprep lay on a cheerful bay to the south of the Ring of Stones, where their meetings had taken place. On a clear day, one could see the gigantic white domes of the Azaes Fire Mountains to the northeast. Once or twice, smoke had puffed from one of them over the past thirteen hundred years, but they hadn't spewed massive amounts of fire, ash, and lava since the Great Conflagration.

When the three exited the station, they were met with an irritated voice. "You finally made it!" Noah rather resembled a mythical troll as he stood with his feet apart and fists propped impatiently on his hips while his long, cloudy beard flowed down his mighty chest. It always amazed her to recall his age seeing how robust a figure he presented.

"Noah, you old coot!" Oma reprimanded. "Is that any way to greet friends?"

When she stepped out from behind Ariel, Noah's caterpillar brows shot up and his mouth dropped open, widening into a smile. "Naunet! Why, you look as perky and whimsical as ever!" He wrapped his arms around her in a joyful hug.

"You're keeping in shape yourself, I see," she answered, hugging him back.

"It's the work," he answered modestly. "Let me introduce you to my lovely wife, Emzara."

"I'm so pleased to meet you both, and the cute little critter, too," Emzara greeted, shaking their hands with a welcoming smile. "You must come stay with us while you're in town."

Figures Noah could attract a younger wife.

"We don't want to be an imposition," Oma replied bashfully.

"Nonsense!" Emzara exclaimed while Noah hoisted their luggage. "We don't get visitors often, and Noah rarely talks about his younger days. I'm sure you've some stories to share."

Noah grumbled, "I'll not have you women flapping your lips with exaggerated tales about me." They all laughed.

Ratiki reared up on his hind legs and waved at Noah and his wife, his nose and whiskers twitching excitedly. "Ratiki says thank you, and do you have any pets for him to play with?"

"Our son Japheth has a hound," Emzara replied, "but I'm afraid it would chase the raccoon and scare it. We have some robins that live in our trees, though."

Ariel conveyed her words, and Ratiki wiped his hands over his eyes, dropped back to all fours, and ambled along beside them as they walked to Noah's sleigh. "He says birds are no fun to play with. They tease him and fly away. He'll be fine."

Noah gently shooed away a white gull that had landed on the raised roof of his charcoal sleigh, then helped the women into their seats. Ariel felt his vibrations of friendship, love, and foreboding when she touched his hand. Despite his grumpy exterior, it was evident that he possessed a kind and deeply compassionate nature. She realized how much he must have in common with her oma for him to have lived so long in an era with diminishing lifespans. *Few men care about trees these days, yet he wishes me to consult them and seek volunteers.* She was developing a genuine respect and appreciation for him.

Ariel had spent four days at the farm with her family enjoying a late Winter Solstice celebration. They had also discussed the drastic changes they would all soon undergo. Her brother and uncle agreed with a plan to keep a quarter of the grain harvest back stored in barns for the next four years to be loaded onto the arks. Her mother and daughter set the dates for their weddings in Gemini, when Ariel was sure to be back from Kemet.

"I should be home in time for planting," she had told them, "but surely, by Taurus. I will not miss your weddings."

More painful than the prediction of the flood had been the revelation about Temen. "I don't care," Sheera sniffed and sulked. "He is a stupid man with no feelings, and I hope I never have to lay eyes on him again. I will accept Taavi's proposal. My inner being tells me he loves me more than Mahmoud does and will remain faithful."

Besides crying about her father's cruel deception, Sheera lamented the fact all her dreams and aspirations would have to change. So much for becoming the premiere clothing designer of Evamont when the city would soon be under the waves of the ocean. Ariel tried to make it sound like a grand adventure, charging into the unknown, forging a new world, but Sheera wasn't taking the bait.

"At least we know in advance and have time to prepare. Taavi and I will discuss the destination proposals and decide whether we want to move ahead of the disaster or wait and travel with you on one of the arks. Don't worry; we won't broadcast it until the Council of Rulers makes it public, but we might travel around and see where we'd like to go."

Taking his responsibility as a guardian seriously, Mal'akhi planned to stay at his post until the last possible moment. He had thanked Ariel for confiding in him. "I think I should start seeking a spouse, as I prefer to marry an Atlantean," he had told her. "That way, we have a better chance of our child being gifted."

She had hugged her son and told him, "The most divine gift any human can possess is a truly compassionate heart. Don't be like your father seeking spectacular manifestations of energetic abilities, for you'll never acquire them from outside yourself. Find someone you love, who loves you, with whom you can laugh and enjoy life, for that is what all of this is for."

☦ ⛥ ✝ ✡

Diaprep was a thriving city, not unlike Evamont, with a pyramid, temples, theaters, a library, eateries, baths, homes, and marketplaces. Noah's house lay outside the walls south of the port between the metropolis and his shipbuilding camp. It was a single-story dwelling more resembling Mandisa's estate than her farm complex. The front faced east, toward the rising sun and the waters of the Ormo Poseidona. The patio had been built on the south side of the house instead of in front or back. Noah had fig, olive, and pear trees, all dormant now awaiting spring.

"You have a lovely home," Ariel commented when he showed them in.

"The bread is already baked," Emzara said. "It will only take a few minutes for me to put a meal together. Naunet, would you care to help?"

"I'd love to," Oma agreed and left Ariel in the front room with Noah. Noah showed her to comfortable seating in a spacious room flooded with natural light, while Ratiki occupied himself with investigating the new surroundings.

"Where are the forests you wish me to visit?" Ariel asked. The ride from town had been across a rolling meadow with only scattered shade trees.

"Between here and Lago Ursa, the gigantic lake to the west," he answered. "A canal extending from the lake to the sea carries logs to the shipbuilding camp. Vast forests lie on both sides of the canal. They're accustomed to us going in and carefully hand-picking a few trees at a time for the vessels I'm commissioned to build, but the sheer quantity required for the arks is unprecedented. I'll take you on a gondola after we eat. Emzara has invited our three boys and their wives to come meet you tonight. They're at the camp now, working on additional scaffolding we require before beginning the massive project."

"I look forward to meeting the rest of your family." Glancing over at the sound of something hitting the floor, Ariel commanded, "Ratiki, come here! You were to stay out of trouble."

He scampered to her feet, saying, *I didn't mean to knock it over. It's not broken. I'm good!*

"Sorry about that," Ariel uttered as she gave her pet a disapproving look. Then she patted his soft fur to assure him of her love.

"It's nothing," Noah dismissed. "He's a cute little fellow, but I'm glad Lysandra will put the animals to sleep. We don't know how long we'll be riding the waves until we land, or even if we'll end up where we intend to. This ship design is for carrying weighty cargo, not maneuverability." Hearing women's laughter, Noah scowled toward the side porch kitchen. "I wonder what they're saying about me that's so funny. Oma better not be telling her about that time we—oh, never mind. You don't need to hear about it either."

Ariel touched his arm with a heartfelt smile. "I witnessed a man die in Evamont a few days ago. A young man beat him in the head with a running board over a sleigh accident. I couldn't even sense the divine nature in his soul, as he had buried it so deep. You're a good man, Noah, wild oats or not. I can feel our connection and I know your spirit. Don't worry about Oma and your wife; they both love you."

He raked a hand through his hair and nodded. "I feel you too."

☥ ⛤ ✥ ✡

Hours later, Ariel ambled through the forest, playing a modal melody on her flute. Noah had brought her here and stayed with the gondola to entertain Ratiki so Ariel could focus her full attention on the trees. A rich, earthy scent filled the air, ripe with pine, cedar, decaying wood, and ancient bark. Various flora inhabited the woodland, from fuzzy moss to towering cypresses.

Knowing this would not be a comfortable conversation, Ariel primed her spirit with music. It seemed to please the grove as well. She sensed the trees reach out to her with satisfied vibrations, as if they were humming along, waving their boughs in a sedentary dance. Magnolias and dogwoods, void of their white flowers, were interspersed with tropical conifers and oaks in this mixed forest growing in a subtropical region of Atlantis that seldom suffered a frost. While the Capricorn air was cool and damp, Ariel found it far from cold and warmer than it had been at her farm.

Deep into the thicket, she paused and tilted her head back, observing the glimpses of blue sky peeking through the dense canopy of evergreens above her. A squirrel flitted its tail at her, and the songbirds sang their reply to her tune. Tucking her flute into its case hanging from a cord across her shoulder, Ariel closed her eyes and reached out her open palms, attempting to broadcast her message to every spirit surrounding her rather than a single tree. Through breathing and focus, she placed herself in a trance and radiated an entreating aura for the vegetation to receive.

The woods were distressed by her message. Ferns rolled in their fronds while small rodents skittered into holes. Leaves shook overhead and Ariel moved on toward the south, farther from the canal and Noah's boat.

"Archangel Barachiel, I call on you for a blessing," she prayed. "Lead me. Open the spirits of the trees to understanding. Jegudiel, bestower of love and mercy, remind the forest that we are all one."

Ariel passed through a clearing into a darker wood, almost entirely inhabited by cypress trees and their cousins, the gophers. She recalled the lumber of these trees was preferable for boatbuilding because of its resistance to rotting. It was also a soft wood, easy to plane and bend into curved planks. Reaching out with her intuition, she moved to a particularly broad tree in the middle of a grove. She gathered her energy, rubbed her palms together, and touched them both to the gopher's trunk.

A solemn exchange passed between them, and Ariel thanked the tree. She was the mother of this forest and wished to consult the other members. Ariel sat at her foot, took out her flute, and let the music take her.

When she sensed the tree trying to establish contact, she leaned her whole body against it, pressing feelings of love and appreciation into its woody fibers. Soon, she felt a peaceful blanket of oneness fall over her on the forest floor. She dug her fingers into the mulch that covered the ground until they touched the mother tree's root.

The Great Deluge is coming to drown us, but we are not afraid. We decree our lives shall not be lost in vain. The whole cypress forest agrees with the gophers and the junipers too. Take our tall, sturdy trunks and build the arks. Save as many as you can, but this one request we make—take our seeds with you and plant them when the waters recede. We will gladly sacrifice our lives to save our children. Guard them, nature speaker; keep them safe and we will live again through our seedlings. We are all one.

Ariel buried her face in her hands and wept with sorrow, joy, and relief, for it was a vast forest, many leagues in length and breadth.

"Yes, you have my word. I will take your seeds and convey them to the new lands. Your children will grow straight and tall and be one with the Creator and Creation for many centuries to come. Thank you, thank you, thank you."

Ariel pushed gratitude from the core of her being outward in a powerful wave that echoed through the forest, and the conifers waved their feathery needle-like leaves at her. "I'll tell Noah, and, because of your unselfish sacrifice, the name of gopher will be recorded and remembered for generations to come."

33

A week later, aboard the trading vessel **Orion**

Lysandra sat with Quetzal, Mandisa, and her husband Hashur under a canopy between the two masts of the ships while seamen manned the rigging and oars. Below deck was the cargo their host brought to trade for cocoa and coffee beans at the port of Cachitl on the Mayeb Peninsula. Hashur and Agathon had both insisted Mandisa shouldn't make the voyage alone, yet one of them had to stay and watch over the orchard estate. So they had tossed dice in a game of chance to determine who would go and the young athlete had won.

"I miss Agathon," he admitted as they lazed on pillows in the afternoon heat.

"I miss him too, honey bear," Mandisa said. "But you were so excited to be coming on this trip."

"I was," Hashur confirmed. "This part is dull."

"Dull?" Quetzal let out a laugh. "Just two days ago, Mandisa quieted a storm. That was exciting."

"And we saw a pod of whales," Lysandra added. "Ariel should have been here. She's been wishing to converse with a whale."

"She's probably halfway to Giza by now," Quetzal guessed, "cruising across the Green Sea toward the river delta."

"Land!" shouted a crewman. Lysandra jumped up and rushed to the front to see. Dolphins rode the vessel's bow as if they were guiding it to the shore. A gull swooped over her head as the image came into view. Unlike the shimmering mirages they had encountered earlier, it was solid and green. Eagerness and nerves rose to the surface as she wondered what would happen next.

"There it is, friends—the verdant jungle of Mayeb," Quetzal announced with a smile. He and the others pressed in behind Lysandra to watch their approach.

"I'm glad you studied Xi, Quetzal," said the captain, a diminutive man by Atlantean standards. "I usually fare well enough to negotiate our trade commodities, but it will be nice to express more complex ideas in their language with your help. Don't be surprised by the native inhabitants. We first established a settlement on the peninsula nearly six hundred years ago and, while a few passed on their height, most individuals who count themselves as Atlanteans are more Xi in their physical characteristics today. They are a delightful people, extremely hospitable and generous, but very different from us in culture and appearance."

"I look forward to learning from them," Mandisa said as they watched the coast grow near.

Hashur leaned in from behind her and wrapped a protective arm around her waist. The simple gesture of affection and support spurred an ache in Lysandra for Ariel's presence. Then, with a smile, she offered silent gratitude that they were together again, even though half a world apart.

After mooring at a worn wooden pier, the captain departed first and spoke to his trading contact. They exchanged pleasant words while a curious group of villagers headed toward the dock.

"All right, you can come now," the captain said, waving to them. "I'll make introductions and turn over communication to Quetzal."

Lysandra and her companions exited their ship via a wide plank, exhibiting friendly, grateful attitudes. The Xi were a smaller people whose heads barely reached Lysandra's shoulder. They all had black hair, with the men's cut in a bowl style and the women's longer. Most of them wore animal-skin loincloths over their tan bodies, though a few wore linen kilts. Tattoos appeared to be popular, and men and women had lines and swirls inked on their faces and around their almond-shaped eyes. The villagers' cheeks were smooth, and only the oldest men sprouted a few gray whiskers, while broad, flat noses and thick lips formed a prominent feature on their round faces. All had bracelets, anklets, necklaces, or armbands, some more than others, triggering Lysandra to suspect they served as status symbols.

A man in a natural linen kilt, a few thumbs taller than the others, with an abundance of gold hoops, stepped forward. The cut of his features suggested he was a descendant of the early Atlantean colonists. He bowed and greeted them in the Xi language. "We welcome you to Cachitl and are pleased to receive you with blessings."

Two children bounded forward with flower garlands for each of them. Lysandra chose a small hoop that fit perfectly on her head. Quetzal's was much longer and easily hung around his neck. She noticed how the people stared at them, especially Quetzal, with his powerful physique and bushy red beard covering almost his entire face.

Lysandra bowed in return, and the others followed her lead. "We are honored to be your guests," she replied in her recently acquired language. "Blessings of the Creator on you all."

The man, who seemed to be the leader, beamed a wide grin at her, then at the villagers to his left and right. They all bubbled with joy. He puffed out his chest and tapped it with the palm of his hand. "I am Kele, chief of Cachitl. You shall be my guests, eat my food, and sleep at my house. I am a carver of stone and would love to show you my art. What are your names and creative expressions?"

"I, Quetzal, am also a sculptor," Quetzal answered with an appreciative smile. "I would love to see your carvings, and we thank you for your hospitality."

"Kele, Kele!" A distraught young woman ran up to him with tears streaking her cheeks. "My mother sent me to get you. It's my little brother. He was playing and stepped into a scorpion's nest. He has many stings, and we are afraid he will die!"

"I can help," Lysandra volunteered and rushed to kneel beside the young teen girl. "I am a healer."

Kele glanced at the ship captain, with whom he worked regularly. The captain gave him a reassuring nod, and he turned his attention to Lysandra. "You can help the child?"

"Yes." Lysandra understood her knowledge and gift weren't tied to the physical location of her homeland. She could sense and weave energies wherever she was. She stood and took the girl's hand. "Take me to him."

Everyone followed. The vegetation was thick, the air heavy with humidity, and the heat from the sun reminded her of Daya in summer. The path was so narrow that she almost tripped on a root while a green broadleaf the size of an elephant's ear whacked her in the face. It didn't take long for a clearing to open, occupied by dozens of houses and several large stone buildings. Thatch roofs topped oval dwellings that employed mud bricks, wood planks, mud and stable, and logs grouped around a large well. The sight of fires and clay ovens outside the homes gave a sense of communal gathering and the practical aspect of keeping the heat away from the living spaces.

The anxious girl led her to a house that Lysandra had to bend over to enter. Thankfully, once inside, the pitch of the roof offered her ample headroom.

"Mama, I brought a healer who is here from Atla," she said. Releasing Lysandra's hand, she raced across the room and threw herself onto the floor, where a woman sat on a blanket, cradling a boy in her arms. "Kele says we can trust her."

Desperate brown eyes peered up at Lysandra through the dimly lit room and she approached with meek reverence to sit on the edge of the brightly colored woven wool blanket near the boy's feet.

"Your daughter said he stepped in a scorpion nest," Lysandra said. "Do you know which kind?"

"The bark-colored ones with black lines." Her full lips trembled, and fear strangled her voice. She showed Lysandra his foot and ankle, bearing at least ten visible angry red welts. "When one stings an adult, it is painful, but they recover. Yet these many stings on a child are often fatal. The poison already makes him hot and shake; his heart races and he struggles for breath. Please, healer of Atla, can you save my son?"

The boy's arm jerked in a sudden motion, and he uttered a feverish moan. A line of saliva from the corner of his mouth had dried on his jaw as he exhibited the serious symptoms of the venom.

Lysandra had none of her tools with her; they were all still in her bag on the ship. The only scorpions on Atlantis were a harmless variety of sand arachnid inhabiting the Menosus Isles. However, there were two kinds of poisonous spiders and one species of viper whose bites she had treated successfully. It was simply a matter of calling on the healing energies to aid the body's own defenses in fighting the toxin while drawing out as much of it as possible.

"Yes," she responded. "Please wet a cloth in cool water and cut the stalk of an aloe plant for me. We will use it to soothe the stings while I combat the poison."

The boy's sister nodded and dashed away.

"I thought you might need these."

Lysandra looked over her shoulder at the sound of Mandisa's voice to see she had brought her physician's bag from the *Orion*. While her procedure might have gone smoothly without her supplies, it was a comfort to have them. "Thank you."

Lysandra opened her bag, set her incense burner on a nearby table, and laid her ivory ankh on the boy's chest. She opened with prayers for Raphael's energy and the Creator's guidance. There was no magnetic assistance here like she enjoyed in the pyramid, and, without the proper acoustics, she didn't bother with shaking her sistrum.

While Lysandra focused her attention on directing healing energy to aid her patient, Mandisa helped the girl apply the aloe balm to the boy's foot and ankle. She sensed the battle in the child's veins and nervous system and bolstered the life-affirming chemicals and elements already working to save him by flooding his body with the spirit of health. The fragrance of her incense was mostly to calm the boy and his mother while she worked.

Absorbed in her ritual, Lysandra wasn't sure how much time had passed before his breathing and heart rate returned to normal. Fever left the child's body, and he became peaceful. Her concentration was broken when he sat up and said, "I feel better now."

Lysandra opened her eyes to see the swelling around the stings had subsided as well, leaving small red dots where the inflamed sores had been. "You must watch where you are stepping next time," she instructed with a smile.

Gasps sounded, and Lysandra glanced around to find the hut filled with concerned friends and relatives. They whispered excitedly among themselves, but the boy's mother addressed her alone.

"It's a miracle! Thank you so much. How can I repay you?"

"There's no need," Lysandra replied. "It was my pleasure, and it isn't a miracle. I'm a trained healer. This is what I do."

"But our healers can't do that," uttered the boy's sister in astonishment. "And so quickly?"

"She is a god!" exclaimed a man who pushed through the ring of onlookers to kneel in front of Lysandra. "You saved my son's life, took the poison from him, and now he is well. Only a god could do that."

"No, you are mistaken." Lysandra didn't know what to think of the response she received. She stood and bowed to the others. "See? I bow to you. We are all children of God, but I am no more a god than any of you."

She left with Mandisa and joined Quetzal and the others in front of a larger house near the trail to the pier. A crowd followed her, making her uneasy. The boy was with them, skipping and bounding as if nothing had happened. The villagers proclaimed to Kele what had transpired, and he was just as amazed.

"We will do for you whatever you wish," the village leader proclaimed. "You possess powerful magic."

"It isn't magic," Quetzal explained. "It's knowledge. Please come inside with us, for I have more knowledge to share with you. It is not good news I bring, but it is good that I bring the news, for it can save all your people and mine. Come, my friend, and I will tell you."

"My wife has prepared a meal for you and your companions," Kele said and pulled back the drape from his entry. "You will eat and drink and tell me this not good news. Then we will do whatever you wish."

Lysandra was glad to get away from the cluster of admirers. She had encountered nothing of the sort before, and the attention made her feel uncomfortable.

Kele showed them to pillows on the floor around a low table while his wife set baskets of mangos, papayas, boiled eggs, steamed shrimp, and unleavened bread before them. Then Quetzal told their host everything about the coming flood.

"Your peninsula is too flat and near sea level to be safe," Mandisa warned. "Are there mountains or highlands you could move to—at least until the flood waters subside?"

"To the west are the Tuxtlas Mountains," Kele said. "There is a lake and river for water, and we could take refuge in the highlands, but you may seek a higher, more sacred place to store your writings of knowledge."

"Do you know of such a place?" Lysandra asked.

Kele nodded. "We also trade with people from far down the coast. They tell of a city in the clouds and a vast lake so close to the moon and stars that the gods often wash their feet in it. I have not seen this place, but I trust the one who spoke of it. He comes every year bringing llama wool and potatoes to trade for our fruits and cocoa beans. It is far away to the southwest—too far for our village to relocate—but if you wanted your scrolls and tablets to be safe, I would store them there."

34

A week later, on the Giza Plateau

Ariel marveled at the great stone lion that oversaw the Khufu branch of the longest river in the world while Ratiki inspected a camel from a safe distance. The massive tribute to Leo rested in a bed of sand shaded by palm and date trees from the sun's rays. A thriving town created a picturesque scene along the calm water's edge. Ariel was surprised to discover Giza looked like any small town in Atlantis, except it didn't have a pyramid or colossal temple—yet. Broad, white marble steps descended between modest red obelisks to the dock where their ship was moored with other sailing or paddle vessels, and a paved boardwalk lined with lush yellow and pink flowering shrubs presented a lovely view.

On the opposite side of the channel, farms spread as far as Ariel could see across a fertile delta of black alluvial soil. Mud brick farmhouses with sprawling shade trees separated square plots of winter wheat with one in four left fallow. The area was far from the desert she had seen in her dream, even if it looked different from the plains of home.

Ptah stood a dozen cubits away, surrounded by a group of architects of both Kemetic and Atlantean origin. He pointed to a clearing behind the Sphinx's tail while holding a copper tablet filled with his calculations.

"Each of the four sides must be precisely four-hundred and forty cubits in length," he instructed. "I will mark the exact spot for you and stake out the corners. It needs to be two-hundred-and-eighty cubits high with a seked of five and a half palms. It is to be aligned perfectly with the cardinal directions of north, east, south, and west as they appear on the equinoxes and according to the North Star."

All Ariel had heard about for days was the first of three planned power pyramids that were to occupy the plain west of the town of Giza. Ptah was as excited as a squirrel with a pile of nuts over his new project, going on about what size to cut the blocks, what stone to use, and how many workers would be required to complete it in time. He marked down how many laser cutters to bring back with him, and the dimensions to cast the cradle for the mother crystal Céthur was acquiring for the project.

While she was sure Ptah found it all thrilling, she was far more fascinated by talking to the camel, a species she had never met before. By examining them, she was certain they were related to llamas, but the camel had never heard of a llama and didn't know they existed. He said his name was Abrax, and he and his whole family were domestic camels, though he knew of wild relatives who roamed the uninhabited lands of the vast continent, apart from humans.

Personally, I enjoy being pampered, not having to worry if there will be enough to eat, and, if a human annoys me too much, I teach him a lesson by spitting on or kicking him, Abrax explained. *Mostly, I give people rides or carry their sacks around. A comfortable tent, interesting travel—it's not a bad life.*

"What can you tell me of Kemet?" Ariel had asked. "I've never been here before. How much is desert and how much is green?"

Everything near the rivers and the inland lakes is green, Abrax recounted as he chewed his cud. He swatted at a fly with his tail and turned his head to the west. *Sometimes we go on a long caravan to Libya and there's some barren sand between here and there. My human complains when it doesn't rain, but I like the sunshine. People worry too much. There is enough water in the river; why do we need rain?*

"You're right that people worry too much," Ariel had agreed. "But you like to eat grass and leaves, right? Without enough rain, they won't grow except right beside the river. You and the other animals might not have enough to go around in the future."

While Abrax nodded that he understood, he still seemed unconcerned. *Scratch me behind the ear, will you?* He lowered his head so she could reach the spot. Ariel had laughed and was delighted to scratch and pet and brush him until he was a purring puddle of contentment.

The sound of a bellow and snort returned her to the present, and she glanced over to see Ratiki making a mad dash to hide behind her legs. "Abrax!" Ariel gave him a stony stare. "Why are you scaring Ratiki?"

He is a strange, fat rat who talks too much and annoys me, he answered. *I'm going now.* With a regal gesture of his proud head, the camel sniffed and ambled away.

He is even worse than llamas! Ratiki grumbled and sat back on his haunches to lick himself.

"Yes, yes!" Thoth's animated voice drew her attention to where he stood with his daughter, son-in-law, and three local dignitaries beside the Sphinx's right paw. "We need a vault to keep the library safe in case the river floods. If the pyramid is completed in time, people can also take refuge in it. We'll construct underground tunnels and large chambers and make sure the exterior doors are watertight. Ziusudra theorizes the flood waters won't reach this far, but we shall take no chances."

"And you want to put it under here?" The man in the red kilt appeared to have been born in Atlantis or of Atlantean parents because he was as tall as Thoth with a lighter complexion compared to most residents of Giza. He scratched his head, presenting Thoth with a confused expression.

"Where better to hide the most valuable information in history than beneath Leo's right paw?" Isis chirped. Today she wore a white chiton with a pale blue sash, and a silver headband pushed back black hair from her enchanting face.

"Thoth, if you draw up the plans for what you want, Isis and I can stay here and oversee the project while you and the others return to make preparations at home," Osiris volunteered.

Thoth patted his shoulder and smiled. "You are a worthy husband for my Isis." Then a frown wrinkled his face into concern. "But Isis, dear, that would interrupt your wisdom training. You should remain in school."

"This is more important, Father," she decreed. "Perhaps Osiris and I can divide our time between here and home."

Thoth nodded and kissed her forehead with a smile. "And you are a worthy daughter." Turning back to the man in the red kilt, he continued planning. "I'll want the walls of tightly fit stone. Ptah will be returning with more tools and workers in a couple of weeks. How many laser cutters and skilled laborers do you presently have?"

"We have a dozen laser cutters," he replied. "The problem is, they all need new power crystals to operate them. I could probably round up a hundred workers by tomorrow, a thousand by the time Ptah returns."

Thoth nodded. "He'll bring freshly charged crystals. I need a geologist to consult about the ground. Is there anyone still around who worked on the Sphinx?"

Bored with talk about the underground vault, Ariel whistled for Ratiki, who headed toward the river with a date in his mouth and gripping another in his little hand. "Stay by me," she commanded. "I don't want you eaten by a foreign crocodile."

His banded eyes widened, and he popped the second date into his mouth. *Why would we go somewhere I might get eaten?*

"I want to meet the new animals of Kemet," she replied innocently.

"I can show you!"

An enthusiastic young lad, not past puberty, popped out from around a corner to claim a spot in the road in front of her. He was all arms and legs, wearing nothing but a linen loincloth around bony hips. Black hair hung down to his dark, eager eyes that rounded in surprise as he pointed at Ratiki. "What's that?"

Ariel smiled at him. "He's a raccoon. You don't have a similar animal here. Hey, you speak my language."

"Yes!" He beamed with pride and jerked a thumb toward his bare chest. "I'm Huy, and I know three languages. You won't find a better guide, but I'm not cheap," he added with a look so serious that Ariel found it comical.

"Do you take Atlantean coins?"

"You bet! They're worth the most." The beaming smile returned to his narrow face, showing off big, bright teeth. "May I touch him?" He motioned toward Ratiki.

Ariel exchanged thoughts with her companion, and he waddled up to the boy, exhibiting a friendly yet curious expression. Huy squatted down and patted him. "He has hands like a person. Is he a type of monkey?"

"No." Ariel joined the lad crouched beside her pet. "Can you show me places to find the wild animals nearby?"

"There aren't many *really* nearby," Huy said, "because of the city, but we can go downriver and there are some meadows where giraffes and zebras graze, and in the river are hippopotamuses and crocodiles. We should ride camels," he suggested. "It will be faster—but will cost more." He narrowed his eyes at her, and she laughed.

"I suppose charging these huge fees is how you can afford camels."

"Well, they aren't *my* camels," he admitted. "They just live around here. I have the bridles, though. It won't take me a minute to round them up. You wait here."

Ariel picked up Ratiki and gave him a scratch. "Did you hear that? We're going to ride a camel, and you aren't to annoy it. I don't want to be spat at or kicked."

What are hippopots and gaffs?

"Hippopotamuses and giraffes," Ariel corrected, "and we're both going to find out."

Huy returned with Abrax and an older female camel who turned out to be his mother and they rode out of Giza to the northwest. They passed several shepherds tending vast herds of sheep, who gnawed everything down to the roots. Farther from town, the grasses returned, speckled with clumps of trees. Once the rooftops were completely out of view, small herds appeared on the meadow.

"You have elephants!" Ariel exclaimed at the site of a bachelor group. One tremendous male turned and faced her with a wary stance. Ariel soothed the bull with feelings of appreciation and conveyed to him their friendly intent. He nodded, waved his trunk, and flapped his ears. He plopped a pile of manure on the ground before approaching at a lazy amble.

"Yes, but that's a dangerous one." Huy turned the reins of his camel to move away.

"No, he isn't. He wants to meet us." Huy looked scared, and Ariel added with confidence, "I'm a nature speaker, one who talks to animals. He won't harm us." Ratiki climbed onto Ariel's shoulders and peeked around her head at the big bull.

These elephants differed slightly from those of Atlantis. They had practically no hair, with longer tusks and bigger ears, but stood no taller at the shoulder.

After exchanging pleasantries with the lead male, they rode farther into the meadow, passing a group of trees shading a species of ape Ariel hadn't encountered before. Then she spotted some black-and-white striped horses and the tallest llama-like creature she had ever seen. Its neck stretched far up to the treetops and its legs seemed as high as her camel.

"Those are the giraffes," Huy explained. "And the ones that look like horses are zebras, but they don't like people, so nobody tries to ride them. Can you really talk to the animals, and do you understand them?"

"Yes," Ariel answered. She called to a female giraffe with its yearling calf and the two moved her way in curiosity. "This mother is very proud of her son. She wants to show him off."

"Tell her I said he is handsome," Huy said.

Ariel conveyed his compliment and one of hers as well.

After a brief visit, Huy guided them to the riverbank where Ariel met the enormous hog-like hippopotamuses and the familiar-looking crocodiles, both of whom claimed to be kings of the Nile. The entire outing had been inspiring to Ariel, and she gushed with appreciation all the way back to Giza. There she settled up with her young guide.

"I thoroughly enjoyed my tour, Huy. Is this enough to cover your fee?" She handed him a trio of coins, one gold embossed with Poseidon's image, a silver Cleto coin, and a copper Atlas. It amounted to what a steep fee back home for an afternoon's service would be.

He stared at the coins in astonishment for a few seconds before he could speak while Ariel held the camel's reins. *Is the boy going to faint?* Abrax asked, *because I don't like it when they fall down. I'm afraid I'll step on them and get in trouble.*

"Shh, don't worry," she whispered to the camel.

"Lady, do you know how much this is worth here? Why, the Atlas alone could feed my family for a week."

"Put them to good use, Huy," Ariel advised. "Think of the future of your business. I will tell you a secret." She leaned over and he moved in close beside her to listen. "Soon, many visitors will come from Atlantis, and some might settle here. They will have many needs—discovering the best inns, houses or apartments to buy or rent, where the best places to eat are, and what occupations are hiring artisans or workers. You could provide the expertise they need, and they all will have coins like these. I'll bet not everyone in Giza speaks our language."

He shook his head and blinked, still too astonished to reply. Ariel patted his shoulder. "I can feel you are a good young man, honest and caring, and I wish you to be successful. Let the camels go, and come with me. I want to introduce you to someone."

Huy did as she asked, and Ariel took him back to the Sphinx where Thoth was still discussing plans with the man in the red kilt, Osiris, and Isis. At least they were now sitting in the shade at an outdoor table.

"Master Thoth?" Ariel didn't mean to interrupt, but how long could people work on construction plans without a break, anyway?

"Ariel!" He looked up at her as though welcoming the interruption. "Did you get to meet your animals?"

"I did, thanks to Huy," she answered and patted his shoulder. "Thoth, you need to establish a school here. Atlanteans who immigrate should learn the language, and the locals should be taught The Law. I know you can sense an open and willing spirit among many of the people of Giza. It isn't enough to build pyramids and erect power crystals. Those with aptitude need to be taught the mysteries, just like at the wisdom schools at home. I spent the last few days talking to people, at least the few who know Protelex, and they haven't even learned to read and write. You're the smartest person I know. Why just lock all the knowledge away in your vault when you can also lock it in the hearts and minds of the people who receive us with open arms?"

Thoth smiled at her. "I have thought of that, dear, and I intend to establish schools. But, first, we must get everything ready to receive the knowledge."

"Which includes preparing the residents of Giza," Isis added, patting her father's arm.

"We will need a count of how many Atlanteans plan to move here," Osiris stated. "And there are other towns up and down the Nile, so we needn't overburden Giza with all the immigrants. We must build new houses and craft shops to anticipate the influx of residents, and schools and temples too."

"Father, when Ptah returns with the workers and tools for the pyramids, try to send us an estimate so we can start preparing places for them all to go," Isis said. "We must leave some of the suitable land for the wildlife, but we'll need to establish additional farms to provide for the larger population. Ariel, what have you learned about the desertification?"

"Kemet is a large land, and I haven't inspected or received reports from all of it, but what I've gathered so far points to about half of the land still being green enough to sustain wildlife and nomadic herds. We saw some shepherds with sheep today. Rainfall has been on a steady decline for a few centuries and now they experience wet and dry seasons. Still, there seem to be barren wilderness areas between the lakes and springs that sustain plant growth and human populations west and east of the Nile. The best farming land runs a few leagues to either bank of the river for its entire length, though, if we built canals or aqueducts, we could extend it."

"Very good," Osiris said with a nod. "We'll discuss this all with the city planners after polishing Thoth's proposals."

"Look what we have so far," Thoth pronounced with pride and angled the papyrus with the schematic drawn on it toward her. It showed the spots for three pyramids, two temples, and a network of underground tunnels and rooms with various entrances.

"We are planning for above and below ground," he explained, "in case the people here need to take refuge. And here is where the Hall of Records will go, right beneath the Sphinx."

"Impressive," she agreed.

"Don't worry, Ariel," Isis consoled. "I'll look out for your new friend and can begin tutoring him if he likes. What was your name again?"

"Huy," the lad answered, seeming overwhelmed by the plans. "Ariel says I'll have lots of business when the Atlanteans start coming, and I want to learn."

"Then I shall be your mentor." Isis smiled at him.

His eyes went googly, a blush rose in his cheeks, and a dreamy look spread across his tan face. "That's wonderful."

Ariel mussed his hair playfully with her hand. "So, you can show me the best place to eat?"

35

Ryzen, a month after the Winter Solstice

Temen, elated to be home at last, lay between smooth, fragrant sheets with Rhoxane in his arms in his own bed in his own palace in his own city-state. Hobnobbing with the other kings and queens had been fun, but the meetings had ground on and on like a gyro that never stops spinning. Now he could get back to enjoying his luxury.

A servant holding a tray of delicious delicacies stood in the doorway and pulled a cord to ring a tinkling bell. Temen adjusted the sheet, so it completely covered his wife, and directed, "Bring it in and set it on the table there."

The manservant nodded and scurried in with the food and two drink cups. "Salutations, King Temen, and may you have a blessed day. Is there anything else you require?"

"No, thank you. We'll keep our privacy." Because he was in a good mood, he smiled at the fellow, who bowed and hurried away. "Darling, are you hungry?"

The most beautiful face in the world peered up at him with an insatiable quality. "It depends," Rhoxane purred. "What's on the menu?" She drew swirls on his chest with a delicate finger and fluttered her lashes.

For an instant, he remembered waking up next to Ariel. Temen hadn't thought about her in years until she was there in Atala yelling at him when he came out of his meeting. Now pangs of guilt needled him at the oddest times. He had to deny knowing her, and what was she doing there, anyway? *Forget her,* he told himself. *I'm with Rhoxane now.*

"You are a blue diamond, aren't you, my kitten?" Temen brushed his lips to hers, trying to decide in what order to quench his desires. Her moist lips and sizzling body were tempting, but so were the fruits and cakes on the platter.

"Temen, we must talk." The gruff voice and stomping feet of his wizard irritated Temen, and he huffed out a groan.

"What do you want, Lykos? And why don't you ring like everyone else? Can't you see Rhoxane and I haven't risen yet?"

"Then you should do so immediately." Lykos regarded him like a disappointed father would a worthless son. "You must sign the orders to commence building ships to convey our soldiers to Pelasgoí and we need to start a recruitment campaign. Traditionally, the king makes a speech upon returning from the Council of Rulers and that should happen soon."

"It can wait until we've broken our fast," he growled. "Go draw up the documents and post announcements that the speech will be tomorrow when I've had a moment to rest. I'll be out shortly."

"Yes, my lord." Lykos bowed with what Temen suspected was false deference and exited his chamber.

"Can you believe the nerve of him?" He turned to Rhoxane with fury on his face. "Why do I even need to keep him around anymore? I'm already king."

Rhoxane lifted a hand to caress his cheek. "Don't anger Lykos, my love. He could use his powers to remove you from power as easily as he used them to land you here, and neither of us wishes that. Besides, I'm a little afraid of him."

"Don't be." Temen kissed her and smiled. "I have power too and can have him locked up if necessary. Let's say when I settle all this business, you and I head off to Mestoria on vacation and leave him here. You, me, a nice beach, some fruity wine drinks in the sun?"

"It sounds delightful," she cooed.

✟ ☬ ☥ ✡

A full turn of the sandglass later, Temen marched into the room Lykos used as an office. "Don't ever intrude on my privacy with Rhoxane again," he shouted in his most commanding manner. Rhoxane had retired to the palace bath and wasn't near enough to hear his tirade.

Lykos glanced up from his seat at the table with an innocent countenance. "My apologies. I didn't mean to offend you, Temen, but, if you had your way, nothing would get done."

Temen huffed, but, to be honest, the wizard had a point. He brushed his fingers through his hair and glanced out the windows. It was already bright outside, and a trail of citizens were all moving in one direction down the street.

"What's going on today?" he asked and shifted to peer outside.

"Mandisa is back from her trip west, and people are curious to hear a story. Now, sign these and we can get everything under way for your army."

Turning back around, Temen walked to the table with a frown. "Are you sure about this invasion idea? I don't think we'll get any volunteers, and it will cost a lot of money to build the ships."

"We will need the ships either way, as our people must be conveyed to safety before the flood comes," Lykos insisted. "And they will volunteer in droves. Read this." He passed Temen a sheet of parchment. "I wrote a few points for you to make in your recruitment speech."

Temen glanced at the notes while satisfaction settled over him. The surge of confidence seemed to arise from nowhere, and he was suddenly certain the plan would be successful.

Setting it down, he signed the documents Lykos had drawn up without reading them.

"King Efrayim advised we should all start making preparations," Lykos reminded him, "and encourage citizens to relocate to our colonies in Kemet and Kush, or to Libya or Kaptara without sounding the alarm of impending doom.

But if we retake the rebellious Pelasgoí, we could move our population there. All the reports confirmed Thoth's predictions."

Temen pivoted and propped his hips against the side of the table, crossing his arms with a grimace. "I don't like it, Lykos. I don't want Atlantis to flood. Maybe the waters will only affect the north and we'll be safe here on Daya."

"Nobody likes it," he answered with understanding. "But Daya rests at a low elevation and is more likely to end up underwater than other parts of the continent. We do what we must, but let's be strategic about it."

More people passed by on the way to the big plaza in front of the temple, causing Temen to brood further. "This is a good time to make my recruitment speech. I want to distract attention away from Mandisa. She'll get folks interested in going to Maanu with her tales."

Temen jotted a few notes beside the ones Lykos had written, then returned to his chamber to put on a sash and his ring. A crown would be too much for this informal speech; he'd save that for the post-Ruler's Council address tomorrow.

"Rhoxane, darling, there you are," he said as she returned from her bath. "I'm going to appeal for volunteers for our new army. Won't you come to support me?"

"Assuredly I will," she said and squeezed her long hair with a towel. "I can be ready in half a turn of the sandglass."

☥ ☬ ✝ ✡

Temen took his time as he strolled with Rhoxane on his arm down the walkway to the grand plaza, waving at citizens, blessing them with smiles, and calling each by name. Her charm amplified his own and Lykos was trailing along too, doing whatever it was he did. A patrol of city guardians raced past them, heading in the opposite direction, while several sleighs and horse-drawn chariots conveyed their occupants to their destinations. *So many people,* he thought, *and it's up to me to save them.*

It almost surprised Temen to realize he wanted to save them—he truly did. He might not be the spiritual zealot Ariel was, but he was a good person, after all. *They look to me for leadership. I will deliver them safely to Pelasgoí as conquerors and rulers. We will build our new kingdom there, and those who rebelled against us will be our servants. Everyone will love me and erect statues in my honor. Lykos is right. I'm making the best decision for Ryzen.*

The crowds parted as the royal couple approached. Residents bowed their heads, and some reached out to shake the king's hand as he stepped into the generous plaza. The red, black, and white paving stones had been ordered in pleasing designs with benches and green plants in pots enhancing the attractive setting. Early flowers added color to the square where statues overlooked fountains and birds perched on lamp posts chirping cheerful tunes. The sun warmed the day, with the promise of spring not far behind. *Figures Mandisa could keep the rain away when she wanted to do something outdoors.*

Sure enough, the throng had gathered around to hear the woman's stories from her travels, and those two improbable husbands sat on the steps of the speaker's platform near her feet. Trying to appear interested, Temen stopped to listen with the others.

"Then a fisherman on the western coast ferried us south along a shoreline dominated by a towering mountain range he called the Copper Mountains," Mandisa recounted. "It took two days in the boat to reach the base of the peak we were to climb, and it took another two days to reach the city in the clouds. They called it Tiwanaku on the shores of Lake Titicaca that rests at an elevation so high Lysandra—the healer who traveled with us—had to infuse our lungs with extra air. It was so high, no trees could grow, but the people there still had farms and herds of llamas, sheep, goats, flocks of chickens, and other domestic animals. We were surprised to discover they already knew about The Law. They said in past times the energies had been especially potent at the top of the mountain, which is why they built their city there."

"Wasn't it cold?" someone asked, wrapping her arms around herself.

"Not when we were there, except at night," Mandisa said. "They called this their summertime, and they were picking berries and vegetables, though their grains weren't ready to harvest. It rained one day and even that wasn't cold, though it is much cooler than Ryzen weather."

"How big was the lake?" asked a man in the crowd. "As big as Lago Ursa?"

"Bigger," Mandisa reported. "And so many of the fish were foreign to our eyes, yet still tasted good when the locals prepared them. The Tiwanaku people offered us every hospitality and agreed to allow Quetzal to build a library there. They invited any Atlanteans who wish to come and visit their sacred lake and bathe in its energetic waters."

"Did you?"

Temen blinked in surprise when Rhoxane asked the question.

"Did you bathe in the waters of this lake?" his wife repeated in an interested manner.

"I did," Mandisa replied. "I connected to the energies there, and it was an invigorating experience."

"I'm sure it was," Temen confirmed with a nod. "And you likely have many more stories from your adventure to share, but I have an important announcement as well. May I?" He motioned toward the platform.

"Certainly, my lord." Mandisa stepped down, followed by her husbands, and Temen ascended the few steps.

"Tomorrow, I'll deliver the king's address in the primary temple to inform you of the issues we discussed at this winter's Council of Rulers," he began, gathering his sash over his arm in a regal gesture. "But one urgent item can't wait. These are troubled times, my friends. You may have noticed arguments and acts of violence are on the rise—even thefts. While I was in Atala, I witnessed a sight my eyes had never seen before, that I had only heard tales of from foreign lands—a dirty, ragged man begging on a street corner. Begging!"

Shocked gasps erupted from the crowd as people murmured to one another. Temen held up a hand. "I know, but I, King Temen, am determined to keep you safe, citizens. Atlanteans are known the world over for our excellent health, our art, architecture, and technology, and our unsurpassed prosperity. My promise to you was that foreigners would never take these blessings from you; I extend that promise to include any people from a neighboring city-state."

Men wrapped arms around their wives and children, nodding and agreeing with him.

"We can all sense the changes that have been happening," he continued. "Mandisa has even spoken of them—the rising temperatures, the failing coral reef, the intense storm patterns." Temen scanned his audience. "What if a hurricane was to break through, one so powerful even the greatest of air speakers couldn't turn it aside? Who will be on the front lines to defend you from the waves and winds? Who will keep order amid the chaos?"

The people looked at one another with questioning expressions of concern.

"On my way here today—this very morning—a squad of city guardians raced by to attend to an emergency," Temen reported. "We can't wait until we are thrust into a crisis to add to their numbers. Therefore, I am calling on the brightest and best, the most capable and loyal, the bravest and strongest among you, to volunteer for the new elite force I call the Ryzen Defenders. These valiant men and women will receive intense training—and handsome salaries—to learn every skill necessary to defend our city-state from any disaster, whether natural or manmade. Your families and neighbors are counting on you—and you know who you are," he added with a sweep of his pointed finger. "You feel the tug, the urge in your hearts and guts right now, at this very moment. You are being called, as surely as the energies call the gifted. Your gift is your courage. Supply that, and we can provide the rest. Ryzen is counting on you, my friends. Raise your hands, step forward, and one of my aides will record your names. It only takes one step to be a hero."

In no time, half the crowd had volunteered to join the Ryzen Defenders. Lykos clamped a proud hand onto Temen's shoulder and smiled. "See? I told you. They all want to be heroes."

"But what happens when the other kings and queens find out?" Nerves splashed in Temen's stomach and worried his brow.

Lykos leaned in to whisper in his ear. "They will follow your lead. A time of crisis is upon us, and all the rulers will need extra guards to keep the people in line once word gets out about the coming cataclysm. Everything you told the people is true, and, if we must go to war to regain a colony that was ours to begin with, then so be it. The other rulers needn't learn that part until it has been executed."

"But don't the Articles of Confederation stipulate that no city-state can declare war on a foreign country without the consent of the Council of Rulers?"

"You worry too much, Temen." Lykos stepped back and fingered his wizard's staff, its silver snakehead catching the sunlight. "All will be well."

36

Ariel's farm, two days before the Spring Equinox

Ariel walked alongside a sled, its iron plow churning the earth and releasing the rich fragrance of fertile soil. Planting had always been her favorite time of year as she imagined the crop that would arise from the seeds she buried in the earth. Farmers probably understood the Law of Sowing and Reaping more concretely than others because they put it into practice tangibly each spring and often again in fall. When she dropped a kernel of corn into the ground and covered it, she didn't have to guess, wonder, hope, or pray that corn would come up. Occasionally, a seed would be no good, or a rodent would dig down and eat it, but mostly, whatever she planted, she would harvest in great abundance. It was a sure thing, and so was its spiritual application.

She had returned from her trip to Egypt in plenty of time to help harvest the winter rye, and now all the old roots and stems needed to be plowed under to enrich the dirt before sowing the summer grains. As the weather warmed, she would plant her vegetable garden next. Besides being necessary to sustain life, gardening was therapeutic and was also engaged in by city dwellers with their small herb and flower pots on balconies or rooftops. Ariel perceived the energy inhabiting the ground, its vibrant elements that were absorbed through the skin, not to mention the soothing quality plants distributed into their surroundings. Mandisa would connect on an even clearer level with dirt and stones, but Ariel also knew the earth as a living entity. She loved her music and side jobs in nature speaker capacity, but Ariel couldn't imagine having a full-time profession other than farming.

Her brother Aram operated his plow a few dozen cubits to her right, and ahead, on the left, Uncle Menandros did the same. Her nephews and cousin were out to help with the plowing and, in the distance, the four immigrant workers cultivated another field. *I'll have to talk with them about being a stranger in a new land,* she thought. *Soon it's what we'll all be.*

Ariel smiled to recall how welcoming her family had been to the men and women who arrived from Trinacria, a large island in the Green Sea, to share in their farm. It was important to treat them with equity because of the culminating rule of The Law and Rules: *do to others what you wish to be done to you, for we are all One.* It was also planting a seed. Because they had been kind and treated immigrants fairly, she expected to receive the same welcome wherever they landed.

With everyone working together from sunup to sundown, the entire farm would be plowed in a day, and, tomorrow, everyone could go fishing. They would let the plant materials rot for at least a week before sowing the crop. Ariel's niece Mara brought out water, cheese, bread, and dried plums for everyone to keep their energy up, and they indulged in a few breaks, but it was a long, hard day of toil that left Ariel dirty, sweaty, and feeling fantastic.

As the sun hung low in the western sky, dipping behind the peaks of the distant mountains, Ariel and her family guided their sleds and plows back into the tool barn before dispersing to their dwellings. She arrived at her door at the same time Lysandra's sleigh pulled up in front. At the sight of her, Ariel's heart was filled with an incomprehensible delight, and she realized the immense joy that Lysandra's decision to move her practice to Evamont had brought.

Lysandra smiled when Ariel handed her out of the sleigh, but she could see that fatigue plagued her. "Welcome home, sweetheart," she cooed and brushed a light kiss to her lips without transferring mud to her esteemed physician. "I'm going to whisk into Elyrna for a bath before dinner. Would you like to come?"

"I would, but I think I need to lie down for a while," Lysandra exhaled. "There's a respiratory infection going around, and it seemed like half the population of Evamont wished to be treated for it today. I know plowing a field is strenuous work, but what I do drains me much more."

Ariel nodded, took her hand, and walked her to the door. "Once I'm clean and presentable, I'll come lie with you and send you a burst of my energy to help you recover. Mother has promised a hearty meal of tasty goodies for us."

"Thank you." Then Lysandra added in a hush, "Besides, when I get you naked in a pool of water, I don't want a dozen other village women around to make me behave."

Instantly, the memory of a youthful Ariel and Lysandra swimming nude in the pond near their farm flashed into her mind, filling her with desirous warmth. It was the first time she had seen Lysandra undress, and she had been so mesmerized and awestruck she couldn't speak intelligibly for the remainder of the day. After the swim, they had laid in a clover patch to dry, making chains of the flowers to pretend they were jewelry. Lysandra had looped a long chain over Ariel's neck, and she had settled a smaller hoop like a crown on Lysandra's head. They had been good friends for a while by then, but that day Ariel realized what she felt for Lysandra went far beyond friendship. Now she felt like it was finally time to reap the harvest from the seed planted that day long ago, one she had watered, fed, and nurtured, then put away with the belief it had died. It all came around in her mind now, as she recalled not all plants spring right up in a week; some take many years to produce their crop.

Ariel giggled. "You misbehave? I'm dying to see that! Rest, and I'll be back soon."

⚦ ☫ ☥ ✡

Lysandra dragged herself through the entrance, greeted by a fat raccoon and the savory aromas of baking bread and simmering herbs.

"Greetings to you too, Ratiki," she said when the household pet rubbed against her leg. "I don't suppose you want to take a brief nap with me," she suggested.

"Oh, good, you're home!" declared Sheera as she strode into the main room. "You look tired, Lysandra; you should sit right over here on the sofa and rest while you help me decide on which dress to wear for my wedding. Although Mother is adept at many things, she remains utterly oblivious in matters of style. Lucky for me, she reconnected with a woman who can appreciate fashion and grace. Now," she directed, guiding Lysandra onto the cushioned furnishing. "Sit here, put your feet up, and I'll be right in with the first option."

It was easier to give in to Sheera's request than to argue, so up her feet went as she reclined on the sofa. Lysandra wondered if being a nature speaker had anything to do with how Ariel's daughter turned out because Sheera was a veritable force of nature herself. As unpredictable as the weather, enough energy to release a volcano, and the vigor of a team of racehorses, there was little question about who dominated this household. To be honest, each of the women in Ariel's family was strong, independent, and talented, but Ariel possessed the deepest, calmest nature. Lysandra had little doubt her lover would replenish her energy when she returned from the village that evening.

Just as she was about to drift off, Sheera twirled into the room in a floor-length white tunic with a blue and green plaited waistband. A ruby heart pendant dropped into the cleavage above the scoop neck of the garment. Ratiki sniffed, and, being unimpressed, waddled past her toward the exit to the outdoor kitchen.

"It's lovely," Lysandra commented.

"I chose the green for fresh beginnings and the blue for truth and loyalty," Sheera explained. "The white speaks for itself. Make a good assessment." She walked across the room, spun, walked back, and twirled to show off all the angles of the dress. "The next one isn't quite as formal, but you'll see."

Sheera hurried out to change, and Philomena wandered in. "When you got back together with Ariel, did you know what you'd be in for?" she asked with a humorous smirk and a twinkle in her cocoa eyes.

"Sheera is a delightful young woman," Lysandra praised. "You wouldn't believe the poor attitudes that cross the door to my treatment room daily. I want to thank you in advance for preparing what I'm sure will be a culinary treat of the highest level. You are so welcoming and talented, and Ariel appreciates what you do for the family, as do I."

"Well." Philomena struggled against a bashful smile. "I enjoy creating new recipes, and they haven't always turned out as I imagined, but thank you. And I'll add, don't get used to it. I'm getting married in Gemini also and will be moving in with my new husband in Elyrna. After that, we haven't decided yet."

"Ariel said it would be a good thing for as many of you as possible to move a year or so ahead of the expected flood date to avoid the rush. Also, she says folks who wait until the last minute might be left without transportation. Of course, you and your husband can always come on the ark with us—"

"And all those smelly animals?" Philomena laughed. "We'll book passage ahead of time; you can be sure of it." She sat for a moment in the chair beside the sofa. "Have you two decided where you'll go yet?"

"She said Kemet was lovely and the inhabitants there were so open to spirituality, but I visited Maanu and met several groups of wonderful people there as well," Lysandra said. "Both places differ from home, and we long to discover a country with similar terrain and climate where our ark animals could freely roam and thrive."

"Not me," Sheera announced upon re-entering the room, this time in a knee-length floral print chiton, favoring pastel colors. "Taavi and I have already discussed it and he is fully onboard with my plan. He has a cousin who moved to Trinacria several years ago to open an inn, and now he has a thriving business. Taavi went to visit there once and said it's similar to here—has a volcano and everything—only without our technology. They have growing towns and will need a fashion leader to sew model clothing and set the trends. Taavi is a craftsman who throws and paints the best pottery around. He employs techniques the people there don't even know about and will instantly be the best at his craft. So, we're going to visit his cousin over the summer and, if we like it, we'll move there next summer after we've learned the language and had time to establish ourselves as a unit. By the way, Grandmother, since you're moving out, can we have your old room? It's the biggest and most convenient, being on the ground floor."

Philomena's mouth dropped, presenting Sheera with an incredulous look. "What if Oma or Ariel and Lysandra want my room? They're older and get first choice."

Sheera plopped a hand on her hip, returning an annoyed expression. "But we'll only be staying a year. Then they can have the room until the day the ice wall breaks. Anyway, Mother likes being up there where the birds pop in to say good morning and Oma says climbing the stairs every day helps keep her young. But later about that. What do you think of this tunic? Too colorful for a wedding dress?"

"It would certainly stand out," Philomena commented. "You're a pain in the ass, Sheera, but you are the most creative person with cloth I've ever known. How did all those flowers get on the fabric?"

"As you are aware, cloth is typically treated through bleaching, left untouched for its natural hue, or submerged in a dye vat until the desired shade is reached. Then, if the designer wishes to mix colors, he or she must cut and sew the cloth into the prescribed pattern and would never be able to cast an image like these flowers."

"You painted them on?" Lysandra marveled.

"Not exactly." Sheera winked, then spread out her skirt and peered down at it. "I had a metal worker in town make a press plate for me. It's two and a half cubits square, or about the size required for a short summer garment. I used slow-drying paint to draw the flowers onto the bottom panel, and carefully laid the piece of linen over it. Then I pressed down the top, latched it closed, and waited for it to dry on the fabric. Because I didn't use a water-based paint, it won't wash out at the laundry."

"That is—" Lysandra found herself at a loss for words. "Revolutionary."

Sheera shrugged. "It might not catch on. People are so accustomed to single colors, and, in my experience, change doesn't come easy. We'll see."

By the time Sheera was modeling her fifth, and last, dress—and Philomena was back to cooking—Ariel returned bathed, smelling of rose water and spice, wearing a clean tunic, ready to share the sofa and snuggle with Lysandra. "You didn't make it upstairs?"

"I was drafted as a fashion critic." She smiled and leaned into Ariel's embrace. "It's all good."

"Mother, you missed all the others," Sheera complained, "so your vote doesn't count."

"I still say you look gorgeous in this one," Ariel declared. It was a lovely cut in lemon yellow with spring green accents that showed off her long legs and gentle curves.

"Dinner is ready," Oma announced as she padded in to join them. "Philomena has outdone herself tonight, so let's all take our time and enjoy."

"I just need to make a quick change," Sheera responded. "Lysandra, which one?"

"Call me old-fashioned, but I think the first one, the formal gown, is most fitting. Save the others to wear on your trip to Trinacria, and the locals will be amazed."

"Thank you!" Sheera gushed and rushed out, her feet clomping up the outdoor stairs.

"Have I mentioned today how much I love you?" Ariel asked with an adoring smile. She stood and offered Lysandra a hand.

"You show me in big and small ways all the time," Lysandra answered from her heart.

"Ah, rekindled love," Oma sighed in delight. "Nothing is ever so sweet."

37

Spring Equinox at the Ring of Stones

Lysandra enjoyed the festivities, the dancers, skits, music, and food at the equinox festival. Thoth and Quetzal felt the celebration shouldn't be interrupted, so they planned their report and strategy session for the following day. It wasn't all frivolous partying, as the event had an added spiritual significance, reminding the people of the Law of Balance. *For each thing, there exists its opposite: hot and cold, light and dark, peace and conflict, male and female. Too much of anything is harmful, so seek balance in all your ways, both for the body and for the spirit.* Living a balanced life was necessary for a successful human experience, which, as the priest had pointed out in his message, included making time to enjoy oneself.

King Kleitos also gave an uplifting speech, encouraging summer travel for Atlanteans to visit places beyond their borders and learn to appreciate other cultures. While a few in attendance remained unreceptive to the idea, the ministry's pledge of free passage on Evamont ships to the destination of their choice resulted in much enthusiasm. The king still hadn't mentioned the looming disaster; none of them had, and Lysandra had only told her close friends Raffi and Helene. Raffi was concerned, but not surprised, and he volunteered to depart on a different ark from her to ensure a healer was on board. Helene had called in her husband Timoleon, and they discussed the matter at length before Lysandra moved away. She promised to keep them informed and Timoleon had volunteered the ship he served as first mate to convey them wherever they needed to go. "My captain is a reasonable old man who wishes to retire and leave the vessel in my hands," he'd said. They ended up taking Ptah, his skilled builders, and tools to Kemet so he could start work on the pyramids.

Because it was still cool at night and they desired privacy, Ariel had brought a tent this time and they pitched it far from the noise of the celebration, which continued long into the night. The event fulfilled its purpose, creating a high vibrational atmosphere of merrymaking and cheer, exactly what Lysandra thought of as excellent medicine for the citizens of Evamont. King Kleitos might have overindulged in his wine, laughing too loud and dancing so brazenly, but his light behavior set the tone for the masses to enjoy themselves.

"I had a wonderful time dancing with you tonight," Ariel said as she spread a pile of blankets for them to lie on. The joy Lysandra sensed radiating from her testified louder than her words. She laughed, "But I shouldn't have another bite to eat for days."

Lysandra crawled across the woven wool covers, feeling a mix of contentment and desire. "Me too." She sighed as she plopped down on a stack of pillows. "This was good for everyone. There will be enough trials in the months and years to come. Everything will be different."

Ariel settled in beside her and pulled the thickest blanket over them. "Different doesn't mean not as good."

"Yeah." Lysandra rolled on her side and stroked her fingers through Ariel's hair. "All that matters is that we'll be together."

"We'll bring your art supplies with plenty of extra paints and canvases," Ariel promised.

"Every country in the world needs farmers and healers," Lysandra noted. "I think women with our skills will be welcome wherever the sea takes us." She laughed. "Did you see King Kleitos hopping on one foot, belting out a tavern song around the bonfire?"

"Did you see my brother bounding along behind him, doing the same silly stuff?" Ariel's fingertips caressed Lysandra's cheek as her tongue played over her lower lip. "I can only think of one thing that could surpass tonight's revelry."

"A game of Twenty Squares?" Lysandra teased.

Ariel shrugged and drew her hand away. "If you prefer it to a game of twenty touches, see who can hold out the longest before she—"

"Hush your chatter and kiss me, Ariel," Lysandra demanded. "You know I want you."

⚧ ⯪ ☥ ✡

As the sun rose, a delicate spring mist settled over the meadow at the Ring of Stones, creating a mystical ambiance. Merrymakers had either gone home or were soundly sleeping off the effects of their celebration in tents littering the field when Lysandra and Ariel joined their chosen counterparts to begin their day. After their opening exercises, all eight closed into a circle, feeling the energy the monolithic structure produced and that of their own aligned bodies. Lysandra wondered what she might have sensed in the time before the Great Conflagration when the cosmic pulses had been more potent.

"Shipbuilding is underway," Noah reported. "I can't imagine the sacrifice for an entire forest to be cut down, but my workers have tried to spare the younger trees whose trunks are too small for planks." He wiggled a finger in his ear with a perturbed expression. "I guess it doesn't matter anyway, as the flood waters will wash them away soon enough."

"What do the residents of Diaprep say about the construction?" Thoth inquired.

Noah shrugged. "Nothing, yet. There are always ships being built and they pay little attention to me. My sons have told their wives who have told their families, of course, and they are all quite disturbed by the predictions, as you would expect. Ziusudra, did you find the rooftop of the world?"

"I did indeed, and it's a perfect place for you, Thoth, to establish a library. In fact, they have already started collecting sacred texts and writings in a cave," the aged astronomer enthused. "I met an enlightened master who could levitate, and we had fascinating discussions about The Law. Their version is slightly different but teaches the same concepts. Ériu was invaluable with her translations, but my vibrational connection with Boqin was such that we could often understand each other without words."

"It was a fascinating place, and the people were delightful," Ériu confirmed, "but I found the air too thin. It's not a location I prefer to move to."

"That sounds like Tiwanaku in the Copper Mountains of Maanu," Quetzal commented. "It's another exceptional spot to store knowledge, and the people of the lake would welcome settlers."

"Construction on the pyramids and underground complex at Giza has begun," Thoth said. "Ptah is absent from today's meeting because he is overseeing the Kemet project and doesn't need the interruption. My daughter Isis and her husband have moved there to help ensure everything goes smoothly. I've sent envoys to Kush, Kaptara, Trinacria, Pelasgoí, and Libya to warn them of the flood. One has returned from Malakopea in Anatola and reported their wise men formed a similar prediction. After the last cataclysm, they began work on an underground city to save their people from any pending disaster. My ambassador to Jerico thanked us but insisted their city walls would protect them. The Phoenicians are eager to engage in conversations and joint plans to protect both our cultures and populations. Being at sea level, they are concerned the water could rise there."

"What about Iberia?" Ariel asked. "I've heard there's a high plateau and mountains there north of the Pillars of Hercules."

"We'll make a list of all the countries we have contact with to see who is receptive to our message," Ziusudra answered.

"We'll all be occupied for the next few years," Thoth confirmed. "I shall see to the construction of three great libraries in Giza, Tiwanaku, and Kirāt to house our wisdom. Noah is busy with the arks and Ptah with the power pyramids.

Quetzal, what about the possibility of building pyramids in the west? Maybe we could ship a couple of mother crystals that way too."

"There is a quarry near Lake Titicaca the locals use," he said, "and we will already be cutting stones to erect Thoth's Hall of Records, so it's certainly possible. Also, in the north, the Xi seemed very receptive to our return. Because of Lysandra's healing arts, they think we are gods."

"Even if these pyramids aren't or can't be used to charge crystals, the structures themselves amplify restorative energies," Lysandra explained. "Their magnetic and acoustic properties will become invaluable the more our connection to healing frequencies wanes."

Thoth nodded.

"I've started packaging collections of seeds for the arks," Ériu said. "I'll make five complete sets, in case five arks are finished in time; although, depending on where each vessel lands, some plants may not survive in a harsh environment."

"Ériu," Ariel addressed, catching her attention. "I have special seeds to add. They are the children of the gopher trees who volunteered to become the arks, and I made a promise to save them."

"Certainly," she replied. "I'll make sure they are divided between the ark packs."

"Ariel, I suppose you'll call and select the animals for the arks," Noah supplied. "Like with the seeds, we can't know for certain if each vessel will end up in a land similar to their natural habitat, but, for survival's sake, each ark should carry a full complement."

"I agree," Ariel said. "But only including one male and one female of each kind may not be enough to ensure the continuation of the species."

"I feel certain many animals will seek high ground and save themselves," Thoth considered. "The Creator would not allow any to perish if it wasn't their time. We have drawings and records of species from thousands of years ago, some of which are no longer among us. Do not let your soul be burdened, Ariel. I know you love them all, but we can't save each individual."

"I have a suggestion," Lysandra said, feeling Ariel's pain. "What if when our citizens relocate early, they each take a few animals with them? Especially domesticated ones. My cousin would refuse to leave Atlantis if she's told her cats can't accompany her."

"The same with my sons' dogs," Noah added. "I don't see how that would be a problem. Many city-dwellers keep pets and rural folks have favorite horses or other livestock."

"That would help," Ariel confirmed, "but not with the wild beasts. I suppose it would make the most sense to include young adults of breeding age who have no blood relationship. Even then, if they don't find others of their kind, they'll be forced into incest, thus producing inferior offspring down the line. I'm not suggesting trying to fit an entire elephant herd, just for some, maybe two females to each male."

"Have them to the arks when we designate a day," Thoth decreed, "and we can see if there's room for additional females. Noah, what was it Archangel Uriel told you about the livestock?"

"For chickens, goats, sheep, cows, and so forth—the ones we depend on for milk, eggs, wool, and meat—to bring seven of each. I can't say why seven instead of six or eight, except it is a spiritual number that represents completion. Seven days of the week, seven chakras, seven colors in the rainbow, seven planets around our sun, the Pleiades. He said two of each kind of all beasts that crawl, walk, or fly on the earth, and seven each of those who are kept in our service, but I don't suppose we'd be in too much trouble if we find room for a few extra females. I think he meant that as a minimum."

"Thank you, Noah," Ariel responded.

"Lysandra, how do you feel about taking on some students?" Quetzal asked. "I have less time to devote to the wisdom school now and I suspect those sitting among us have friends or relatives with some talent and aptitude for healing."

"Me, teach?" Lysandra's eyes popped wide.

"Yes, you teach," Quetzal repeated. "You don't have to ensure they reach full enlightenment, just that they understand all the proper principles and can see with spiritual eyes enough to weave the healing energies. We'll need healers in our new lands, and you have been practicing successfully long enough to share your knowledge with others."

"Indeed," Thoth seconded. "Though my Isis has learned much, she could benefit from your added training when she comes back to visit. Why not stay in Evamont and take on a small class of apprentices? It would be most beneficial."

"My sister Fótla shows great promise,"Ériu spoke up. "I'll send her to you for instruction."

Ziusudra lifted a finger. "My wife Jatziri has aspired to practice the healing arts for years now. She understands the spirit world well enough to learn."

"Well, I might manage a few apprentices," Lysandra stammered, being left with no way to refuse their requests.

Lysandra barely heard anything else said at the meeting as her brain had shifted into frantic planning mode. *Am I ready for the responsibility of students? How do I explain to them my process when so much of it is intuitive? I've only started my practice in Evamont and am already overwhelmed with patients. When will I have time for students?*

The council ended with a plan to meet back in a year, if nothing major changed, since everyone had important work to accomplish. Ariel's arm around her waist, steering her toward their tent and sleigh, came as a welcome comfort. "You will be a marvelous teacher, my love. Our friends' loved ones will be in excellent hands."

"I appreciate the vote of confidence." Lysandra brought her arm around Ariel in reciprocation. "I know you don't want to leave any behind, and it will be agonizing to choose. Why not just ask the herds to decide for you? With five arks—assuming Noah can complete that many—that's five pairs of each species. The insects take up little room and will reproduce faster, and I dare say extra mice will get onboard even if you tried to keep them off." That got a chuckle out of Ariel.

"Noah showed me his plans," Ariel said. "The bottom deck is for the large animals—herbivores separated from carnivores by storage rooms and several walls. We also commissioned tanks for the freshwater fish to be housed on the lower level. Saltwater species should be unaffected. The middle deck is for the smaller mammals, the domestics, and the human passengers, leaving the top level for birds, bees, insects, small reptiles, and amphibians. I told him we'd need a bathing tub for sea lions and manatees and those who require being immersed a large part of the time. I'll start moving fish into the tanks first, as they can live there for many months. Then I'll need to collect insects and tiny creatures from the north and south who won't be able to travel fast enough to reach Diaprep on short notice. The others I won't call until it's time to go. Besides, who knows what will happen in the next four or five years?"

"Presuming Mandisa was correct, and we have that much time," Lysandra added. "Ziusudra suspects the Terrible Ice will break during the transit of Inanna set to occur in Cancer of 1361, four years from this Summer Solstice. All things considered, it's a solid prediction, but countless variables could speed things up."

"Let's not worry about that now," Ariel said and kissed her cheek. "Let's get you home and start planning for those students."

38

Ryzen, the month of Ares, spring 1360

Temen stood in the forum before the citizens of his city-state in elegant attire. Behind him on the platform were his wife, his wizard, and the general in command of his force of Ryzen Defenders. Like all the other rulers, he had encouraged travel, and foreign languages had become established courses in primary school curriculums, although Temen still didn't understand why they didn't just insist everyone else in the world learn to speak Protelex. Much had gone on behind the scenes over the past three years, and the date the Council of Rulers had agreed upon to inform the citizens of the looming disaster had come. Temen wondered if the other kings and queens had a wizard to soothe their emotions when the announcement was made.

"The Council of Rulers is a wise group of kings and queens whose primary goal is to keep Atlanteans healthy, prosperous, and safe from harm. It is through our efforts and those of our predecessors that we have done so since the beginning of the Third Age."

Scanning the faces of people whose names Temen knew, who had honored him with gifts and loyalty, he felt the weight of his office as he never had before. He entered this venture thinking he would spend all day lounging about the palace being waited on, only needing to attend the occasional meeting or function. His dreams of a life of luxury had come at a terrible price. Not only was their entire nation soon to disappear from the face of the earth, but now he was having to lead a war to secure the best possible place to move himself and his population.

Lykos had taken him and Rhoxane to visit Pelasgoí, which bore many similarities to parts of Atlantis. The highlands provided a haven from the rising water, and, although the terrain was mostly rocky, there was enough fertile land for cultivating crops and flourishing vineyards. Unfortunately, when he had brought up the possibility of immigrants moving from Atlantis, the leaders answered with a resounding, "No."

Temen didn't want to go to war. Wars were uncomfortable and there was always the chance they'd lose, but Lykos had convinced him it was the only alternative. Now he had to break the bad news to his followers.

"We kings and queens of Atlantis received troubling information several years ago and have been coordinating behind the scenes as we awaited the time to share this revelation with you. Today is that day." Temen straightened, summoning all his courage, and putting on a brave face for his audience. "The archangels warned us of another cataclysm to come so that we would not be caught unprepared like our ancestors. Behind the Terrible Ice, warming temperatures have caused a great thaw, and, within one to two years' time, the ice wall will break, and an ocean's worth of water will inundate Atlantis."

Temen raised his palms to quiet the frantic gasps and fearful murmurs that erupted from the crowd, even as he struggled to calm his own nerves. "Do not be afraid. We have been blessed to receive this warning in time to act."

"What do we do?" called out a woman from the crowd.

"How do we know this prediction is true?" yelled a man with a dubious look.

"Unfortunately, it is true," Temen stated. "I was skeptical myself at first, but the leading gifted and learned people have all studied the evidence and confirmed it to be so, even our very own Lykos." He motioned behind himself to the stately wizard occupying a seat of honor. Lykos gave a grim nod and twisted his staff in his hand.

"I will lead you and tell you what you must do. The government has been overseeing the construction of tremendous vessels to carry citizens and animals to safety when the waters descend on us, but we are urging people not to wait. Other kings and queens all have destinations in mind for their residents to journey to as refugees, but not me. The people of Ryzen shall arrive as revered, first-class citizens after your elite Ryzen Defenders quell the long-lasting rebellion in our Pelasgoí colony."

"But the colony was abandoned after the uprising more than a hundred years ago," an elder in the crowd pointed out.

Temen raised a finger. "Ah, but we have devised a foolproof plan to retake the peninsula and all its islands for Ryzen. We staked claim to that land a thousand years ago, and just because some colonists wished to separate from us in the recent past is no reason for us to give up our claim. They have grown fat and lazy, corrupt in every way. The rebellious lot in Pelasgoí have even forsaken The Law and Rules, which are our civilization's foundation. They steal, rape, pillage, and kill each other like savages. It is our duty to retake control and save them from themselves. And, besides, the population is sparse. There'll be plenty of room for us to settle, to bring our livestock and belongings, and to build new homes. The southern islands have a perfect climate for our citrus trees."

"What if Pelasgoí floods too?" cried out a young woman.

"Our experts predict any flooding there would be minor, as it is far beyond the Pillars of Hercules," Temen explained. "Even so, there are highlands we can take refuge in."

"King Temen, you can't be suggesting we go to war!"

He recognized that voice. *Mandisa.* She shouldered and hipped her way to the front.

"Our survival is at stake, Mandisa," he said in as calm a tone as he could offer the irritating woman. "I will do whatever it takes, even lay down my life to provide a safe harbor for the citizens of Ryzen. Or have you gained enough power to hold back the great northern ocean that lies behind the Terrible Ice?"

"You know I cannot perform such a feat," she retorted. "But war is never the best solution. I've been to the lands in the west," she expounded, spinning to face his audience. "Maanu is a vast continent with friendly people and a variety of climates in which to settle. They would welcome you with open arms."

"Yes, if you wish to live in a jungle infested with vile snakes and poisonous arachnids," Temen pointed out. "Or at the top of some treeless mountain where it's cold all the time. The land is wild and dangerous, and the people are primitive, where in Pelasgoí you will find cities and farms patterned after ours. Yes, the locals have lost their way, but they can easily be turned back to The Law. They will see us as saviors."

"But Temen, you don't have the authority, and to send our young people to war—"

"Silence, air speaker!" He glared at her with fury. "It is *King* Temen and I—not you—rule Ryzen. I bear the burden, the responsibility, and I will do what is best for our people. Hold your peace or leave this forum."

Even as Temen felt a cooling breeze brush through him, the gathering turned on Mandisa with angry words and vicious expressions. With her head held high, she made her way past the hostile crowd and through the exit.

☥ ⛤ ✝ ✡

It took Temen and Lykos a turn of the sandglass to finally settle the people and convince them everything was proceeding splendidly and all they needed to do was pack. Exhausted and depleted, he collapsed in the plush comfort of the palace sitting room, surrounded by the familiar company of Rhoxane, Lykos, and General Gershom. Over the past two years, since employing his service, Temen had come to respect the experienced leader, who had fought as a mercenary in Tyre's battle against Jerico, captained a ship, and spent decades serving as a city guardian. His broad stance, muscular build, and the scar cutting through his brown beard revealed a man who, at seventy years old, still exuded strength.

"You handled that brilliantly, my king," floated Lykos's smooth praise.

Temen grimaced. "I don't like it. We're going to get in trouble. Only by a majority vote of the Council of Rulers is a king allowed to go to war with a foreign nation."

Lykos responded in a scoffing manner. "Really? Temen, Atlantis is all but done for, everyone scrambling to find their own solution, and you're worried about getting in trouble with the council? A year from now, there may be no more Ryzen—no more Atala or Evamont. What kingdom will the others rule? But you will be established as King of Pelasgoí before disaster strikes. That makes you wise. Besides, what can they do—reprimand you? Ours is the only sizable army in Atlantis."

Anxiety plagued him like a swarm of irritating flies. "Mandisa will oppose us, and many people listen to her. Lykos, I know you influenced the gathering at the forum, but there are thousands of others, both in the city and spread throughout the countryside, who weren't under your spell. What if she turns the majority against us?"

"Why not have her arrested?" Rhoxane suggested.

Temen snorted and shook his head. "Like she would break a law or rule?"

"With a majority of the jurors' votes, you could pass a new city-state ordinance," Lykos mused, "one she couldn't help but break. What if it was decreed that a woman was only allowed one husband?"

With a dissatisfied frown, Temen answered, "Then men could only have one wife and there are plenty who would oppose such a directive. There's a juror with two wives, so there goes one vote immediately."

"What if the wording didn't forbid two wives, only two husbands?" Rhoxane supposed.

"That wouldn't be equitable," Temen argued. "Every woman in the city-state would rise up and demand equality, and there are several women jurors to appease."

"Not if you approach the issue with the correct logic," Lykos asserted. "If a woman has two husbands and becomes pregnant, how can anyone be certain which man is the father of the child? Sometimes a child strongly favors one parent or the other, but suppose her husbands had similar features? Then one leaves the marriage, and who is responsible for the child? There are many ways to present this from a legal perspective that have nothing to do with women's rights. Temen, you just have to be smart about it. I can always persuade a juror who is on the fence."

"So, if this new ordinance passes, would it extend to those already in a marriage agreement with two husbands?" Temen speculated.

"If you decree it," Rhoxane replied.

"Mandisa would never give up one of her husbands," Temen stated. He was certain of it.

Lykos shrugged. "Then she would have to desert her family's citrus orchard and move away from Ryzen. No more Mandisa, no more opposition."

"Or," Gershom noted lightly, as if in jest, "she could meet with an unfortunate accident."

Temen cringed. "I cannot condone murder. It goes against The Law and Rules in the strictest sense, and even my compromised morality can't justify such an act. Lykos, if you can draw up the proper wording, I'll present the proposal to the jurors tomorrow."

"Excellent plan," Lykos agreed. "With her opposition out of the way, we can proceed with our invasion plans."

"But, Lykos, what if we don't win? Or what if we do, but we lose all our soldiers in the process?" Temen raked a hand through his hair, feeling older than his sixty-four years.

"Don't worry about that, King Temen," Gershom assured him. "Our engineers have developed the most powerful laser cannons ever conceived. Our enemies will have no defense against them and will quickly surrender in the face of our superior weapons. I expect minimal casualties, even if met with heavy resistance after we land. Your troops are an elite fighting force, most of whom I trained myself."

"Laser cannons?" Temen felt the blood drain from his face as his rounded eyes jerked to Lykos. "You never mentioned laser cannons. You know the use of laser technology as a weapon is expressly forbidden since the disaster of the Second Age. We can't use lasers for our attack."

"Again, I say why not? Temen, this is the end of Atlantis as we know it," Lykos argued. "Thoth is building power pyramids in Kemet, and I've heard Quetzal is constructing them in Maanu. Wasn't our technology all supposed to remain on Atlantis? Yet they understand we must establish it in the regions our people will soon inhabit. That's why I've contracted a superior stone mason and architect to build your pyramid in Pelasgoí as soon as your forces take the peninsula."

"Thoth and Quetzal are building pyramids?" Temen took a moment to think and felt Rhoxane's subtle touch stroke his arm.

"The old rules don't apply anymore, husband. If honorable, enlightened masters like Thoth and Quetzal are bending the rules to meet the present circumstances, it is certainly allowable for a king to do so as well."

Though he quaked on the inside, Temen couldn't allow Rhoxane to realize the full extent of his dread. For years, he had yearned for a gift, to be someone special, admired, and respected. But when he heard the angel's call in the Opocalám Mountains that fateful day that changed the course of his life and followed it to Lykos' wisdom school, this was not what he had in mind.

"What's our strategy?" Temen asked.

General Gershom rolled a map out onto the little table between their couches. "We have ten newly constructed warships with twenty pairs of oars that will carry one hundred each, divided between oarsmen and marines. Behind them will be ten more passenger ships bringing horses and another thousand Ryzen Defenders—that's an army of two thousand. They have been divided into specialties of archers, footmen, and cavalry—if they're even needed. Each vessel has two laser cannons with crystals a cubit large to power them. They are also equipped with steel ramming bows if our enemies send crafts out to meet us as we approach. These are the most modern, excellent ships in the world. Even Atala hasn't their equal."

He pointed to a dot on the southern end of the peninsula and to another around the bend on an eastern harbor. "These are their most prominent cities. We'll capture Pelepus and Palaio Faliro. By then, the whole peninsula will have heard of our might—and surrender."

"I was there when the laser cannons were tested," Lykos stated. "They were extremely successful. One blast can level an average-sized building or blow a hole through the side of a warship. Their aim is accurate, and stone is no match for their power. You'll see, Temen. The leaders of Pelasgoí will raise a white flag and give their settlements over to you."

"Well, to General Gershom," Temen specified modestly.

"No, my king, to you," Gershom declared. "You'll be leading the assault from our flagship."

Oh my gods! His disbelieving gaze shifted between each of the three who surrounded him. "You don't think I—." He swallowed and squeezed his hands into fists to prevent them from shaking. "But I know nothing about warfare. I'd only be in the way." Panic roared through Temen with the intensity of a gigantic tsunami.

"Not at all," Lykos soothed. "Seeing you lead from the fore will be the inspiration to transform our fighting men and women into a legion of champions."

Temen bolted from their company to the nearest comfort station and doubled over in dry heaves. If his stomach had contained any food, it would have all been cast up. An uncontrollable dizziness sent him into a trembling heap on the floor beside the elimination bowl. For the first time in fourteen years, Temen wished he were back on the boring farm with Ariel.

39

Same day in Evamont

Ariel sat with her athletic, handsome son Mal'akhi and his attractive, petite fiancée Nymphe at an outdoor table on this beautiful spring day, feeling the warm breeze on her skin. She savored the crisp flavor of her lemon water, enjoying the young couple's delightful company. Ariel noticed fewer citizens filling the streets of the city, which seemed almost empty compared to four years ago. At least half of the urban population and a third of villagers had already moved away on transports carrying them to familiar destinations that welcomed new residents from the universally revered nation of Atlantis. Iberia, Libya, and Kemet were popular destinations, along with the island kingdoms of the Green Sea.

"We're planning our wedding ceremony for the Summer Solstice," Nymphe bubbled as she kept one arm looped around Mal'akhi's. "Captain Chanokh arranged a spot for us on the roster of weddings to take place at the festival—there's only five this year. Then he's giving Mal'akhi a whole week off for us to spend time together." With adoring, pale blue eyes, she beamed up at Mal'akhi, her golden spun hair cascading down to her warm, ivory skin.

A flashback of bliss tore through Ariel, raising her vibration so that any passerby might think she was the blushing bride-to-be. She and Lysandra hadn't wished to upstage Sheera's wedding, or her mother's, but they also didn't want to wait longer than necessary to declare their love to the world. Theirs had been a quiet ceremony, officiated by Quetzal in Elyrna's public garden, where the flowers joined their fragrant energies to celebrate the joyful union. Surrounded by a small group of family and friends, Oma had pronounced the blessing over them while Quetzal tied a cord around their joined hands in a symbol of the binding quality of their love. Yaluk, who welcomed Lysandra back into the family following a speculative trial period, sang a traditional love song, lending the beauty of her voice to the affair. Of course, Sheera had made a fabulous new garment for Ariel because nothing she owned was suitable for the occasion. Lysandra had never looked more radiant. Marrying the woman she loved had been the most incredible, transcendent experience of her life, and bringing those frequencies back into her heart made her feel like she was floating on a cloud.

"Have you talked about where you'll go?" Ariel asked, returning to the moment. "It's essential for you to start your life together somewhere you'll be safe and happy."

"I'm needed here, Mother," Mal'akhi said and laid a hand over Nymphe's. "King Kleitos even hired a hundred extra guardians to keep the peace and see to the orderly boarding of passengers on the departing ships. Tensions are already high, and we don't expect the flood for another year. So, we want to come on the ark with you and Lysandra."

"I'd love to have you both with us," Ariel rejoiced, "especially since Sheera and Taavi have already moved to Trinacria." Suddenly tinged with sorrow, she added, "I don't know if we'll ever see them again."

Ariel shook off the sinking sensation of loss and declared, "Nymphe, you must come to board our ark early. It's on scaffolding in Noah's shipyard in Diaprep. Mal'akhi, where will you be?"

"Probably at Lycia Landing near the Azaes," he answered. "That's where most of our transport vessels dock."

"But honey bear." Nymphe looked up at him with worry etched on her youthful countenance. "I don't want to be away from you. What if you don't make it to Diaprep to the ark and we end up thousands of leagues apart and can never find each other again? I must stay with you."

He pulled her to his side with a robust movement and kissed her forehead. "I want you to be on that floating fortress with my mother, do you hear me? I'll come to you. Somehow, someway, when the dam breaks, I'll get to you. But I must know you will be safe."

She buried her face in his neck and squeezed her arms around him. "You have to triple promise," she demanded.

"I triple promise," he said, smoothing her hair with a calloused hand. "Shh, there now. We were planning a wedding, remember?"

Ariel's heart went out to Nymphe. She regularly reminded Lysandra that she would be on board that vessel the moment they received word the first crack had formed in the ice. There's no way she could stand to be separated from the person she loved most, so she completely understood how the young bride felt.

"Mal'akhi is strong, smart, and reliable," Ariel confirmed. "If he says he'll be there in time, then he'll make it happen."

Nymphe sniffed and peered across at Ariel. "Where will we land? Where will our new home be?"

Ariel swallowed her sip of lemon water and set down the cup. "Wherever the sea takes us. Will your family come with us, or are they resettling early?"

"My cousin Racheal wants to come with us," she said. "My mother and stepfather are leaving for Kush right after the wedding and my father doesn't plan to go anywhere. He's joined a sect of folks who convinced him the flood is a hoax. He says we're all stupid and that the kings and queens have fabricated the disaster to seize citizens' property once they've left Atlantis."

Ariel let out a discouraged sigh. "I've run across some of those; sorry to hear your father was sucked in by them. Mal'akhi, those are the ones you'll have to watch out for when they decide they want on a ship at the last minute. Do you have a sleigh yet? How are you going to get from Lycia Landing to Diaprep?"

"I found a used sleigh for a good price," Mal'akhi answered. "I just don't have anywhere to park it."

"Of course you do!" Ariel declared. "At our farm, you silly boy. But you'll have to take it to Lycia Landing and keep it in a safe place. If chaos breaks out, some panicked person will steal it out from under your nose."

"I still don't like us being separated." Nymphe turned her worried expression back to Mal'akhi. Ariel would prefer they both stay at her side, but she realized it wasn't realistic. She was proud of her son's courage and loyalty to the citizens of Evamont.

"Well, it's time for me to get back on patrol." Mal'akhi pushed up from the table and presented his fiancée and mother with hugs and kisses before jogging across the street to join his squad.

"Be careful!" Nymphe called after him.

"He'll be fine," Ariel assured her. "I've got to get going, too, Nymphe. It's planting time, but you both are invited to dinner this weekend. We'll talk more then."

Nymphe hugged her and kissed her cheek. "I'm glad to have you in my life now. I see where Mal'akhi gets his strength."

☦ ☬ ✝ ✡

Ariel sought Oma when she returned to the farm. Her uncle and brother had planned to sow the spring crop tomorrow, so she was devoting today to getting caught up on her visits. The house was empty, as it often was these days. Her mother and her new husband Eadric packed up all their belongings and took a ship to Giza in Kemet after hearing Ariel's stories of her travels there. Oma still lived with Lysandra and her, but she spent a great deal of time traveling to see all her old favorite places across the continent. Ariel could hardly blame her.

This season would bring more work for those who remained at the farm. The immigrant laborers had all returned to Kaptara. Aram, Shemu'el, and Yaluk were staying to board the ark with Ariel and Lysandra, but their oldest son, Hevel, took a wife and moved to Trinacria. Uncle Menandros and Gamila promised to stay through the harvest, then were planning to follow their daughter Mara and her new husband to the settlement of Waset along the Nile upriver from Giza. Lysandra was too busy with students and patients to help with the crops, but everyone still in Atlantis needed to eat, so six of them would do the work twice as many had performed in the past.

Ariel found Oma in the meadow, a league from the house surrounded by friendly elephants. "There you are," Ariel called out. "You are a hard woman to track down."

"Adira has been missing me," she answered as she leaned against the matron's tremendous shoulder, stroking her trunk.

"Good afternoon, Adira," Ariel greeted. "Can I steal Oma away from you for a few minutes?" Never wanting to be left out, Ratiki bounded up behind Ariel to greet the elephants too.

You have been so busy lately, Adira mentioned. *You don't come to see us anymore. Why can't you stay here to visit Oma?*

Ariel stretched out her hand and brushed her fingertips along the wrinkled lines of Adira's trunk, peering into her understanding eyes. "I suppose you can hear what I need to say. It's almost time for you to choose a few outstanding males to go with you and your daughters on the arks."

Turning her attention to Oma, she said, "After planting, I'll be spending much of the summer collecting freshwater fish and crustaceans and housing them in Noah's tanks. We are supposed to have another year, but I can't just call the fish; I must bring them. I thought you might want to come with me and visit Noah and his family again."

"I would enjoy that," Oma replied, "but not collecting fish." She wrinkled her nose, making Ariel laugh.

"Have you decided to come with Lysandra and me on the ark with Ériu and her sisters and their family? Mal'akhi, Nymphe, and her cousin are joining us."

Oma scowled. "You don't know where you'll land. It could be on some barren rock."

"I promise, if we land on a barren rock, we'll shove the ship off of it and float until we find somewhere good."

"Shove the monstrous boat off the rock," she scoffed. "You can't do that. We'd be stuck in the middle of nowhere."

"Then please, Oma, go to Giza and find Mother or to Trinacria where Sheera is," Ariel pleaded. "You mustn't wait until the last minute."

There now, Naunet, Adira comforted, rolling her trunk around the old woman's shoulders, breathing softly on her. *Don't be upset. Ariel wants you to be safe.*

Ariel took Oma's hands. "Did you hear what Adira said?"

"No," she growled, "but I can guess. Elephants care about everyone. Once, a few hundred years ago, I watched an elephant rescue a baby lion from a sucking mud hole. Sweetie, all my friends are gone. Everyone my age has passed on."

"Not Noah," Ariel reminded her. "He's still around and older than you and not giving up. I need you, Oma. You mustn't lose your joy over a few changes."

"Ha!" She laughed, then let out a sigh. "I love you. Now, why have you come to trouble me?"

"To make sure you leave before the flood waters arrive," Ariel replied in irritation. "And to seek your wisdom. I wish to devise a way to extend my voice to the animal kingdom at a distance. We don't wish to load them all onto the vessels months prematurely, but, once the ice cracks, we'll have very little time to get them settled. I won't be able to travel to each habitat and call them in person."

"Have the pairs been selected?" Oma asked.

"Most of them," Ariel answered, "but I'll be talking to additional packs and herds this summer. I want to make sure unrelated bloodlines are represented, and creatures from other places than Evamont get to go. I've asked for matriarchs and patriarchs to select members of their herds and packs, so I don't have to. But then there are the solitary beasts, and so many I've met and know by name, but are they the best to bring? I hate this, Oma, I hate it! I don't want to choose who has a chance and who's left behind. It's too great a burden."

Feeling a wave of emotional exhaustion, Ariel sank to the grassy earth and dropped her head into her hands. She felt Adira's trunk nuzzle the back of her neck and felt her warm breath on her skin.

I know you want to bring me, but I must stay behind. I am too old to take up space. Take my daughters and I'll find suitable mates for them. Do not be sad, Ariel. We all understand.

"No!" Ariel spun her head around in distress. "You're my friend. I can't leave you!"

I don't want to go, Adira quipped and curled her trunk, casting her gaze away from Ariel. *I'm used to this world and would rather die here than start over in a new one. Long voyages on human ships are for youngsters, not matriarchs. You don't get to decide everything, Ariel. I choose to stay behind. Just look after my daughters, please. And don't despair. We all came from the Creator and will all return to the Creator. The Creator and Creation are one, just as you and I are one. Wherever you are, I will be.*

Oma quietly sat beside her and laid a gentle hand on her knee. "You have been tasked with saving lives, Ariel, but it's not your fault they can't all be saved. The other creatures are closer to the divine spirits than we are in many ways. They understand they can't all go on the arks, and they are at peace. You must be at peace about it as well."

"But Oma," Ariel began as tears filled her eyes. The thought of picking and choosing, leaving millions behind to perish, was gut-wrenching. Humans were different. They have a choice to believe the report or not and act as they see fit.

"Hush now, child. To call the animals from a distance, you will need a high vibration, not a low one of grief," Oma explained. "And you must amplify your energies. I suggest you sit in the Circle of Stones with Lysandra and any other gifted you can find to join you. Then you must do away with fear and regret. No guilt and no grief. Only when you radiate a powerful love will they hear you from afar."

40

Ariel's farm, three weeks later

Feeling refreshed, Lysandra returned home before dark, as the daylight had been lengthening toward summer. Her second set of students had completed their lessons, and she'd spent the day observing them perform treatments on the patients; therefore, her energy hadn't been depleted.

She smiled when Ratiki scurried to greet her and sniff her feet as she exited the sleigh. Green plants and flowers filled the square between the houses, and the olive tree near the well was full of white flowers, many of which littered the ground and bench under its boughs. She picked a big, juicy, red strawberry from a large clay pot to the right of their entrance.

When Ariel opened the door, she smiled, took a leisurely bite, and pushed the rest into her spouse's mouth. "I'm not too tired," she sang out with delight as she brushed against Ariel on her way inside.

Leaving the door open for a breeze, Ariel followed her. "Neither am I, and I want all the time I can get with you before I have to leave for the four corners of Atlantis, gathering fish and tiny creatures and informing species about the arks."

From behind, Ariel embraced Lysandra tightly, her lips leaving a trail of moist kisses along the nape of her neck. Her tantalizing touch sent shivers through Lysandra, sparking flames of arousal. "I suppose dinner can wait," she mused and turned in her lover's arms. Lysandra answered Ariel's advances with a deep, demanding kiss as her hands took hold of her slender waist.

Ratiki's chattering interrupted them and Ariel turned to glance over her shoulder at the threshold. "Are you expecting company?" she asked.

"No." Lysandra was more annoyed than curious. They may not qualify as newlyweds after three years, but she still yearned for the delirious pleasure she and Ariel gave each other as often as they could muster. With Oma away on an excursion to visit Echo Cave in the Opocaláms, they had the entire house to themselves.

Ariel pivoted and walked to the open doorway. "It's Mandisa and her husbands and—" Ariel turned a startled look to Lysandra. "A sled full of stuff."

With her curiosity and concern piqued, Lysandra hurried out to meet them. "Mandisa," she called. "We are happy to see you, but what happened?"

Hashur assisted Mandisa and then Agathon out of the sleigh, which pulled a sled stacked with boxes, crates, and furniture behind. "We are so sorry to arrive unannounced," Agathon quickly answered. "It's times like this I wish someone would have invented a device to talk at a distance."

"Mandisa?" Ariel came around Lysandra and hugged the beleaguered air speaker.

"Ariel, Lysandra, don't worry," Mandisa replied. "We brought food ready to eat when we realized we'd be arriving at dinnertime."

"We aren't worried about that," Lysandra scoffed and took her turn to hug their guest.

"Hashur, Agathon, come on inside," Ariel invited. "I've just brewed the tea we were going to have with our meal. There's plenty." With a glance at a damp, cloudy atmosphere, she added, "Can I help you bring your things inside?"

Mandisa closed her eyes and raised her face and palms to the darkening sky, remaining still and quiet for a moment. "It can wait. I must tell you both what happened and ask for your help."

"Of course we'll help," Lysandra declared, as they all made their way inside.

Agathon set a basket containing fresh berries, bread, cheese, and a jar of smoked oysters on the table.

"You won't believe what King Temen is doing," Mandisa grumbled. "Thank you both so much for your hospitality. It's just ... I don't know where to begin."

"I do," Hashur snapped. "With getting us thrown out of Ryzen because you presented an idea in opposition to his plans."

"What?" Ariel questioned in disbelief. She set cups of tea and empty plates out while the others settled in at the table. Then she took the vacant seat beside Lysandra.

Mandisa passed the basket, and they all filled their plates while she opened with a question. "Does your ex-husband have any experience in the military or strategic planning?"

Ariel's brows furrowed. "No," she scoffed. "He wouldn't even combat a spider and had to call me to get it out of the house. Once he ran from a chipmunk, insisting it had rabies. I mean, he wasn't entirely cowardly, but certainly not city guardian material. Why?"

"Because he's planning to invade Pelasgoí," Hashur huffed out.

"Invade?" Lysandra couldn't believe it. They hadn't been engaged in an actual war since the uprising in the Maghreb some five hundred years ago. After that, the Council of Kings adopted a policy of leniency toward colonies who wished to separate from Atlantis, which is what Pelasgoí had done.

"And use laser weapons to ensure their victory," Agathon added sourly.

"Laser weapons were forbidden by the First Council of Kings of the Third Age," Ariel recited as if she were answering a question in a primary school class.

"He became angry when I mentioned Maanu is eager to welcome immigrants from Atlantis to their shores as an alternative," Mandisa recounted. "Shortly afterward, he pushed a new city-state ordinance past the jurors, though I can't fathom why they voted to approve it."

"What ordinance?" Lysandra's nerves stirred, preparing her for what was sure to be an absurdity.

Hashur answered, his indignant fury hovering near the surface. "That while a man can still keep multiple wives, a woman is now restricted to only having one husband."

"What?" Lysandra and Ariel spat out in unison.

"That's completely unfair," Ariel grumbled. "And he never acted like men should for some reason have more rights than women. If anything, he was attracted to strong women."

"I believe there's more to it," Agathon said with a frown on his studious face. "His chief minister Lykos used to be the headmaster of the Southern Wisdom School and exercises several talents. I'm sure he exuded his influence in getting the jurors to agree, and probably in convincing the masses this war is a good idea. You wouldn't believe the cheers Temen gets."

"This morning as we were crossing the Skismengi Channel Bridge, thousands of citizens were attending a rally and Blessing of the Fleet event," Hashur groaned.

"Now it's starting to make sense," Ariel said and popped a ripe berry into her mouth. "This Lykos fellow is behind everything. Sure, Temen was interested in politics and had a wishful desire to be important, but he could have never engineered getting elected king or even performing administrative functions on his own. And plan a war?" She shook her head and let out a sad laugh.

"Still," Mandisa countered, "he announced he will lead the troops into battle alongside General Gershom, who is quite competent, by the way. Anyhow, to make a longer story short, I was given the choice of giving up one of the two best men on the continent or leaving Ryzen for good. You can see which I chose."

"All because you offered an alternative place for people to go?" Lysandra felt anger rising in her normally placid core.

"I agree Lykos is using his talents to sway votes and probably feeding Temen ideas," Agathon said. "But he could just dismiss him or say no to some of his suggestions."

"Temen was never a man for engaging in conflict," Ariel supplied. "Rather than ask for divorce like a normal human, he snuck off to Ryzen and left us to believe he had died, all because he didn't want to face me in person. If Lykos pressured him—and fed him enough rewards—he could get him to do just about anything, empathetic or telepathic powers or not. That pretty, young queen of his is just the kind of reward that would tempt Temen. I'm sorry, Mandisa. You are absolutely welcome to stay with us for as long as you wish. It's a big house and everyone else has left. If you don't mind making a few repairs, there's an empty dwelling across the square the workers from Trinacria vacated after last fall's harvest. And I'm sorry Temen did such a vile thing to such good people," she apologized.

"It isn't your fault," Hashur assured her.

"We don't want to impose," Agathon mentioned. "Mandisa just thought—"

"She was right," Lysandra declared. "It's good that we stick together this close to the coming calamity, anyway. You are no imposition, are they Ariel?"

"Not in the least," Ariel confirmed and smiled. "Having an air speaker to ensure our last crop receives the perfect amount of sun and rain means more food to carry on our ships. Besides, we'll love the company."

"Thank you both," Mandisa said. "We'll be very happy in the empty house and will repair anything necessary. How have you been faring?"

They chatted while they ate, catching up on each other's news. Lysandra could feel Ariel's tension and knew she was upset over Temen's actions, feeling responsible by association.

"I recruited three more nature speakers for the other completed arks," Ariel mentioned, "but I'm not sure if there even is another nature speaker to be found in Atlantis. Each ship will require one, as our job is vital to keeping the animals calm and behaving when they're awake. Lysandra has trained six physician students, four of whom have become initiates in the Wisdom as well. Every ark will have a healer, even if the fifth is finished in time, and they all know how to put the animals to sleep."

"I've connected with eight other air speakers, three of whom are quite gifted at weaving elemental energies and directing rain clouds," Mandisa said. "I also ran across Ériu's older sister, Banba."

"I met her when I visited Ériu to transport some seed containers to Noah," Ariel said. "Now there's a take-charge kind of woman," she added with a laugh.

"Even more so than Mandisa!" Hashur proclaimed.

It was good to see Hashur laugh after how angry he had been earlier in the evening. Lysandra realized he knew The Law and Rules as well as she did, but healers understood the physiological benefits of upholding them. One should never go to bed angry or hold bitterness or unforgiveness in their heart. Clinging to any negative emotion was harmful to their health and shaved years off their lives.

After their meal, Ariel turned on the outdoor lights, and she and Lysandra helped them bring their belongings from the sled trailer into the abandoned house. Ariel performed an insect and rodent purging. Lysandra wasn't sure exactly how she did it, since she was always saying insects didn't have any consciousness to connect with. It had something to do with producing a frequency they didn't like that drove them away from the area. However, apparently, mice were much more cognizant than she had imagined.

Then Lysandra lit sage and carried it around the dwelling in a cleansing ritual to dispel any destructive energy and attract healthy energies in their place. They left them with a portable lamp since the old house-powering crystal had died and needed to be recharged. On the way back to their home, Lysandra took Ariel's hand.

"Whatever Temen does or has done is not on you, sweetie."

"I know," Ariel muttered. "Then why do I feel responsible?"

"Because you take on too much. It's something I had to come to terms with years ago," Lysandra explained. "Even during the Second Age, when people's powers were much more attuned than ours, physicians couldn't save every patient. Sure, nobody suffered disease back then like they do now, but there were fatal accidents. Remember, I told you about the guy whose friends rushed him in last month? He was flying his sleigh at an altitude of around a hundred cubits returning from Lycia Landing when the power crystal gave out and he and the vehicle plummeted to the ground."

"Like what almost happened to us at the Terrible Ice," Ariel said. She closed the door behind them and enfolded Lysandra in her embrace. "His body and skull were too broken for you to repair."

"Yes, but he was still breathing when they brought him in, and I did all I could," Lysandra recalled. "Even the old masters could not have saved him. I've learned to accept my limitations and realize I'm not a god—not in that sense, anyway. You must accept there are things you can't control and be all right with it, Ariel. If you treated him even half as well as you do me, you were an excellent wife. Temen—and he alone—bears the responsibility for his actions."

"Yeah, and it will be his fault when he gets himself killed trying to be something he's not."

Lysandra met Ariel's lips with soft empathy, a comforting, supportive kiss of solidarity. Yet as Ariel responded, all the emotions of the evening solidified into driving need. Their clothing didn't make it to the bedroom but fell like breadcrumbs across the house. Ratiki, full from his portion of the meal, lay curled in a ball on the sofa, not bothering to track the linen crumbs to their destination. Lysandra kicked the bedroom door shut just in case.

41

Mid-summer on the Leo New Moon, off the shore of Palaio Faliro, Pelasgoí

The sun rose over the sea behind them, casting the rocky shoreline and high-walled city in pale, golden hues as the Ryzen fleet approached the east side of the peninsula. The salt air invigorated Temen's senses, as, with the captain, he commanded the stern of the gently rocking vessel, a hundred soldiers on board at the ready. Nine more ships glided in formation, ready to attack on his order.

Although nerves pricked at him like the feet of a thousand ants crawling across his skin, Temen had gained confidence after their initial victory at Pelepus yesterday. The laser cannons had been even more effective than Temen imagined, demolishing ships and stone structures alike, completely annihilating the harbor. General Gershom advised they not go ashore until after securing the second, more prestigious port. Then the marines would disembark to quell any further resistance. The Ryzen forces hadn't lost a single man.

Excitement built at the thought of his imminent triumph. *Everyone in Atlantis will hear of my conquest and, while they are scrambling to gain entrance to other destinations, I will be crowned king of Pelasgoí. My supporters will get the choice properties while my engineers build our pyramid. People will sing songs and tell stories of my leadership for generations to come. Lykos was right, as usual. I don't know why I ever doubt him. Rhoxane will be so proud of me, and I'll ensure she enjoys every luxury this new land offers.*

As the cozy town overlooking the docks stirred, Temen motioned to his trumpeter to sound his horn, sending the proper signal to the other ships. In short order, they formed a semicircle around the cove, hemming in all vessels moored there. The cannoneers aimed their weapons at the opposing ships first, to ensure they couldn't use them for an attack or escape. In the silence on board, Temen perceived the subtle hum of the crystals powering up the big guns.

His anticipation mounted, stirring Temen's blood like nothing ever had, even Rhoxane's creative attentions. This was different. Today, he held all the power. People's lives were in his hands. If he gave the thumbs up, the rebellious colonists could live to serve him. If he gave the thumbs down, they would die and make room for the citizens of Ryzen.

Before yesterday's attack on Pelepus, Temen had never seen a person die. He had attended the funerals of a few scattered relatives, but they had been old and already dead. This was different. At first, it was horrifying. Rushing men, women, and children had screamed and cried as the blasts sent tremendous stones flying, igniting fires where they struck. He watched from a distance and didn't witness the horror that must have filled their eyes nor smell the blood or hear their bones crack, but it was terrible all the same—terrible and awesome. A part of him was sick and wished to look away, but the other half couldn't turn his mesmerized gaze from the carnage.

It had taken no time at all for half the port and town to lie in ruins, and white flags waved vigorously. Temen had discussed the idea of leaving a ship with its complement of soldiers there, but they decided to bring them all to Palaio Faliro in case they faced tougher fighting. It would be easy enough to send half of their fleet back once this stronghold was under their thumb as well.

With his pulse beating in his ears like a massive kettle drum, Temen raised the sword he would never use in combat, paused for a breath, and then sliced it downward with a swipe of his powerful arm. The first laser cannon shot off its energy pulse, blasting an enemy war vessel in half. The sight and sound of it were like the sparks and noise-makers of a festival times a hundred, and his confidence soared.

The second cannon spat its rain of fire into a building at the bottom of the stair-step outcropping of rocks the town had been built on. He watched in fascination as men and women raced around yelling. The city guardians poured out wearing their uniforms and helmets, uselessly gripping spears, swords, or bows in their hands. He wished he was near enough to see the expressions of surprise on their faces. *They should have been more receptive to my visit,* he thought with smug satisfaction.

Temen waited too long for the next shots. Frowning, he marched to the rear cannon and addressed the two men who worked frantically on the mechanism. "What's wrong here? Why aren't you firing on them?"

"My lord, the power is out," reported the first man in a tense voice.

"What do you mean?" Temen thundered, even as a coil of dread tightened in his gut. "Insert a new power crystal."

"This is the new crystal," answered the second marine.

"Then get another one from the hold." Temen struggled to keep his voice forceful and not tinged with terror, but he feared his wide eyes might give him away.

A soldier rushed up to them with horror plastered on his face. "There aren't any more. That was the last one—I just double-checked."

"What?" Temen exclaimed in a pitch higher than he had intended. "Captain," he shouted, spinning to the bearded older man at the helm. "They say we are out of power crystals. How is that possible?"

"No one anticipated how quickly each would drain," he said. "We brought four for each cannon when one should have been enough to last through many battles. You there," he said, pointing to a man fussing with the inoperative laser cannon. "How many of these did you use yesterday?"

"Three, sir," he replied.

Temen's mouth went dry, and his palms sweated. "Three?" he screeched incredulously. "And nobody bothered to inform me or the captain? What's wrong with you idiots?"

"My lord, we didn't know there were only four crystals for each cannon," answered the man beside him. "And we sure didn't know they would give out so fast."

"It could be because we are so far from Atlantis," the captain uttered in retrospect as he heaved out a sigh. "There are no mother crystals for hundreds of leagues for them to draw from, no obelisks to boost the power."

"Shouldn't someone have thought of this before we left Ryzen?" Terror had gripped Temen, and he wondered if his heart would burst through his chest with its pounding effort. "Have the oarsmen guide us over to General Gershom's ship. He isn't firing either."

"None of them are, sir," observed a crewman behind him.

The captain nodded and gave the order. Temen's worried gaze turned to Palaio Faliro, where marines piled into vessels while others appeared to be wheeling a defensive weapon in their direction from a turret in the city wall.

"General Gershom!" he cried. "We're out of power crystals for our cannons!"

The seasoned leader acknowledged him with a grave nod. "Change of plans. We'll land and take the town on foot," he shouted back from his deck.

Temen shrank back and grabbed hold of the railing to steady himself. He didn't like that idea at all. "Don't you think we should retreat, come back later with more crystals? Wasn't the whole idea that we had a superior weapon? Without it—" He didn't get to finish.

A whooshing sound and the faint flash of a shadow from Temen's peripheral vision had him spinning to gape as a huge stone splashed into the sea only a few cubits from the side of his ship. As if coming from a distant well, he heard Gershom's firm words.

"We cannot abort the mission, my king. This is our only window, your only shot at glory. If we leave and return, they'll be ready for us. We can still win and take the day. Have courage!"

Temen nodded as his legs turned to jelly. He wasn't sure if he was more afraid of looking like a coward or of dying, as neither option appealed to him. The general barked orders for the ships to close in while Temen held on, swallowing the bile that threatened to come up.

Their foes continued to fire catapults at them while three ships gained speed, cutting through choppy water toward them. His captain pivoted their angle, protecting their flank from the oncoming vessel as their oarsmen dug in to increase their speed. Temen sat on a bench, worried the two ships would ram each other and knock him over the side. Although he knew how to swim, he would be far too vulnerable in the water.

General Gershom is right, he told himself. *We still have a thousand elite warriors with their traditional weapons, and we still have the element of surprise. We're Atlanteans; we will triumph.* He avoided remembering these people were mostly colonists with roots in Atlantean bloodlines too.

"Pull in oars!" shouted the captain, just as the nose of the enemy vessel scraped off their reinforced bow.

The Pelasgoí craft mirrored their own in design, except it only had sixteen oars instead of twenty and one mast rather than two. To Temen's horror, colonial warriors bolted over the railing and onto their deck with weapons drawn while a second row fired arrows into his marines.

"Get them!" Temen cried as he scurried to the opposite side of the helm behind the captain.

"Draw your sword, my lord," the captain demanded as he hoisted a harpoon in both hands. With a powerful thrust, he skewered two foes who rushed them.

Maybe jumping into the water isn't such a bad idea, he considered.

With a glance to his left, he noted two of their ships had made it to the dock, and soldiers who disembarked were immediately met by townspeople with hoes and rakes and iron pots and pans. From the tops of the walls, archers sprayed arrows. To his right, he spied one of his ships ablaze, with its crew abandoning their posts for the safety of the bay.

"King Temen, your sword!" growled the captain, as he fought off two more attackers.

Temen swallowed, fingered the hilt with a trembling hand, and squeaked out, "I don't know how to use it."

The burly, gruff man with his unruly tufts of beard sneered at him as if he were an underling instead of his ruler. "Stick them with the pointy end."

A third ship landed, and its Ryzen Defenders poured out into the fray. Temen still had a shot at victory, but not if he was killed here and now. "I'm going to find General Gershom," he stated resolutely. "Kick this rabble off my flagship!" As soon as the command left his lips, Temen leaped over the railing and splashed into the churning blue-green water.

He managed to swim to the rocky shore without being struck by an arrow, whacked by an oar, or run over by a ship's keel. His soaking blue tunic stuck to him like a second skin as he pulled himself out of the shallows, and his golden laurel still secured around his honey-brown locks. Between it, his ring, and two orichalcum wrist bracers, anyone who spotted him would know he bore a high station. Temen counted on the tradition of holding important leaders for ransom rather than killing them to hold, as he stumbled forward behind his battling army.

Temen glimpsed General Gershom at the fore, clashing with a determined-looking officer from the opposing force. Everywhere around him were deafening noises—steel and iron clanging, catapulted rocks smashing, grunts and yells from the combatants, horns trumpeting signals, and the roar of fires, both from burning ships and buildings near the docks. An odd, coppery odor mingled with smoke, salt, and seaweed in his nostrils. Temen recognized it as blood. His sandal slid in a puddle of it, and he barely regained his balance without falling.

The entire scene was surreal, like something out of a terrible nightmare that he would awake from at any minute. When the tip of an arrow grazed his upper arm, tearing his flesh and drawing blood, he realized that, while this may be a nightmare, it was no dream. Instinctively, he clamped a hand over the minor wound and gnashed his teeth together.

Temen scrambled onto a small boulder and turned a slow circle, surveying the scene in every direction. In the distance, he spotted the boats carrying their horses and reserves, and hope flared in his soul. Then he watched them turn and move away. Five of his warships had landed, three had been boarded, and two were in flames. There was no retreat. He would either win the battle, be captured and humiliated, or die.

Balling shaky hands into fists, Temen let out a curse. "Why?" he shouted to the sky as if the gods lived up there among the stars somewhere. They couldn't dwell inside him. If they did, why had he never been able to connect to them? He had watched Ariel do it hundreds of times, listened to her share a revelation from her meditations, and saw the peaceful look of satisfaction overtake her at the joy of being part of the One. Why didn't it ever happen for him?

"This was to be my moment!" With hot tears stinging his eyes, Temen gripped the hilt of his sword and yanked it from the scabbard that dangled from his belt. "There is no Creator!" he scoffed bitterly. "No spirits, no benevolent energies, no angels. It's all a lie. There's just struggle and disappointment, blood and sweat and tears. We live and we die and that's all there is!" With a grief-stricken grimace, he raised his sword and rushed toward the fray.

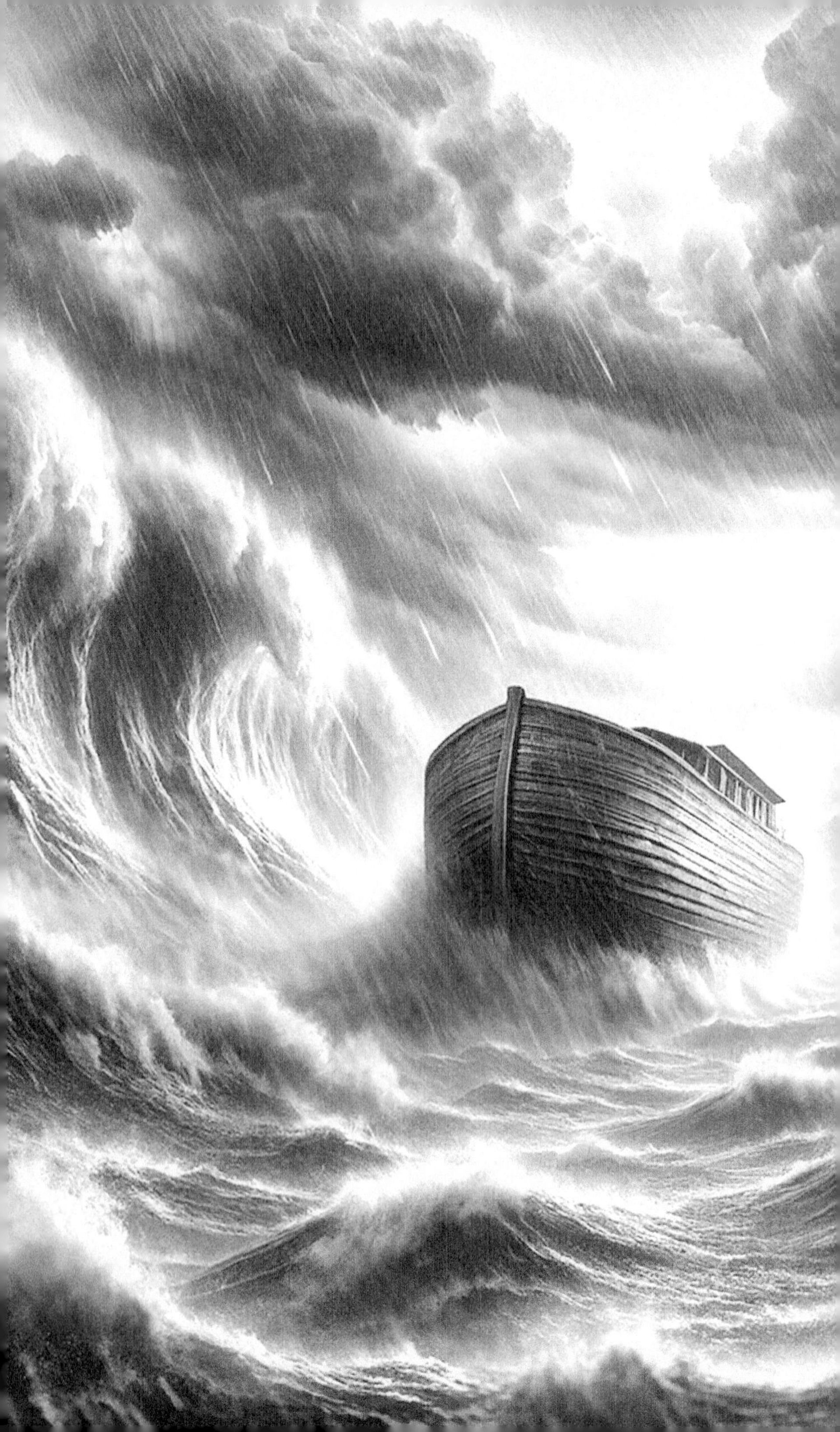

Part Three
Paradise Erased

42

Ryzen, a week later

Lykos lay between crisp linen sheets with the irresistibly beautiful Rhoxane in his arms, sated from a night of pleasures. He should have been satisfied, but a shadowy, foreboding feeling had niggled at him all week. There was every reason to be anxious where Temen was concerned, but General Gershom would have ensured everything proceeded as planned, even if the king prattled off some ridiculous command. Gershom had sworn to take his orders from Lykos, and nobody else. He would succeed. Unless ...

A smooth, feminine hand graced with polished nails, and the cool platinum and sapphire of her ring, brushed across his skin, teasing the hairs of his chest to stand on end. "A copper for your thoughts?" The seductive quality of her voice was almost enough to lure him back under her spell.

With a smile and a stroke of his fingertips to her exquisite face, he answered, "Just wondering how things went in Pelasgoí and when your husband will return." He chanced a tempting glance down at her rounded breasts with their strawberry nipples still responsive from their most recent stimulation. *No*, he told himself. *This window for us is closing fast; I can feel it.*

"I don't understand why you insisted I marry him." Rhoxane pouted and swirled her fingers in his variegated black and gray chest curls. "He isn't half the man you are. You never adequately explained why you couldn't just become king yourself. I don't mean to complain. At least he's clean and easy to manipulate, but it's so tiresome pretending to be madly in love with someone so clueless and self-absorbed. *You're* the man of power I desire to be with."

Lykos brushed a kiss to her full, ruby lips and trailed his hand to rake through her luxurious brunette strands. He recalled fondly how Rhoxane had come to him about six months before she married Temen, requesting he tutor her in honing her mesmerizing skill. She had been twenty-five, not too old to enter training, though she should have started after completing her secondary education. However, her prominent family forbade her to attend a wisdom school, as they thought it was a waste of time. They were grooming her to run a grand estate and perhaps pursue a career in politics, not spend years contemplating the stars or communing with spirits. If not for her gifted grandfather, who keenly recognized and dispelled her attempted hypnotic suggestion, she might have succeeded in entrancing them all into getting her way.

Rhoxane's gift had developed slowly without nurturing or guidance, but she possessed it all right. Lykos detected it on her instantly and knew he could use it to his advantage—if he didn't become enthralled by her himself. Lykos was known to the world as an astronomer, an alchemist, and a master of knowledge. He could weave energies in ways that affected emotions, yes, but he also had talents he had not revealed to another soul—including telepathy and mesmerizing. Why would Lykos want anyone to know he could make them do whatever pleased him? Such a skill would be perceived as a tremendous threat, and he could have been banished. So, he used it sparingly and kept it to himself. But Rhoxane, who also practiced the art, was so adept at falsifying emotions that Lykos—with all his vibrational insight and awareness—couldn't discern her genuine feelings toward him. Did she love him or only his abilities? Or did she merely love what she could glean from him?

Intrigued by the only other person he had ever met who was as proficient at curbing and eliciting emotions from others as he was, Lykos had taken Rhoxane under his wing—and to his bed—before concocting the plan to use her to help him control Temen. Temen. Where to start?

Twelve years before Thoth, Ziusudra, Quetzal, and their helpers put the clues together to predict what was about to occur, Lykos had arrived at the realization that Atlantis had little time left before the next great natural disaster caused their ultimate destruction. He made a spreadsheet of ideas, possibilities, and schemes to come out on top when the mountains crumbled and the sea washed away his beloved homeland. He had considered making himself king, but what if something went wrong? There would be no one else to blame. Also, being a ruler would take too much of his time away from honing his calculations and fine-tuning his predictions. Lykos had established a reputation as a scholar, not a politician, and the two seldom overlapped. Besides, pulling a puppet's strings was so much more fun.

The first candidate he tried was a local athlete from Ryzen who was popular and extremely easy to control. Regrettably, he was also young and reckless and made the ill-fated choice to engage in alligator wrestling while Lykos had been away communing with the cosmos. It was then he sent out a wide message on a frequency specifically aimed toward a marginally competent individual absorbed with ambition and delusions of grandeur. He felt Temen on the opposite end of his telepathic call all the way from the Opocalám Mountains. It was so delicious to discover his stooge was on a vision quest. Lykos pretended to be an angel, showing him the path to seize his destiny.

Temen had been easy to mold and manipulate, though there were times Lykos had wished his malleable clay had been less intellectually dense. He explained to his pupil that he could give him all his heart's desires if he would be diligent and follow his instructions to the letter, although it would take time. One doesn't just arrive in Ryzen and be crowned king the next week. Honestly, Lykos couldn't have been more pleased that Temen turned out to be handsome and charming, with a knack for remembering names and making people feel at ease. It's possible he could have even become king on his own one day, but Lykos made sure all the sheep of the city-state rallied behind Temen.

Sure, he couldn't mesmerize everyone. Men and women with robust connections to the spirit world and those who were exceptionally strong-willed resisted even his most powerful suggestions. But he didn't need everyone's support—just a majority.

Temen was easy to keep in line as long as he had nice things, good food, and a beautiful companion. Lykos learned his type. While Temen experimented with a few young men and pretty boys, he gravitated toward powerful women. Unfortunately, he had trouble keeping their interest. Add that Lykos needed someone to watch over Temen and keep him in line when he wasn't around, Rhoxane showed up at just the right time to fill that role in his plan.

As he gazed at the beautiful, enticing woman less than a third his age tingling with desire for him, he felt a tinge of jealousy toward Temen. Yes, this had all been his plan, but he still didn't like sharing Rhoxane.

"Do you really?" he asked with a raised brow and allowed his fingers to trail down her neck to her throat to her collarbone. "Are you my plaything, or am I yours?"

"Why can't it be both?" she answered smoothly. Her hand wandered lower as a corner of her mouth quirked upward with a beguiling flare. "We are special, you and I, and while our powers don't work on each other, I think we make a stellar team."

"I'm not always convinced of that, my love," Lykos admitted.

Rhoxane play-sulked, stilling her exploration of his body. "You don't think we make a good team?" She lowered lush lashes at him.

Lykos laughed and brushed back her hair to catch the look on her captivating face. "Not that part, silly. For all I know, you have me completely bewitched, just putty in your talented hands." He won an infectious laugh at his comment.

Just as her roaming hand was about to find its mark, the bell to their chamber rang. Lykos groaned while Rhoxane giggled, slid out of bed, and quickly wrapped a robe around her breathtaking nude form.

"Who's there, and what do you want?" Lykos barked.

"Your servant Eshkar, master," a trembling tenor voice replied. "We have news from the war, and you will wish to hear it—now, I think, most powerful one."

Eshkar's trepidation made Lykos grimace, and he furrowed his brow. Ever since another servant ruined his favorite kilt at the laundry and he punished him by putting the fellow into a trance and suggesting he perform a sexual act on a ram, the entire palace was terrified of him. The careless domestic hadn't been physically harmed by the incident ... much—rams can be testy—but when the mesmerizing effects wore off and everyone in town was whispering about him, ogling him with shocked expressions, and awkwardly avoiding him, his dignity took quite a hit.

Not wishing to risk a chance on gossip, Lykos motioned for Rhoxane to use the secret passageway behind a tapestry back to her chamber. She blew him a kiss and silently mouthed, "For luck," and slipped away.

"I'm coming," he grunted. "I haven't dressed yet as it is barely dawn."

"Yes, Master Lykos," Eshkar confirmed. "I'll have your breakfast waiting when you are ready to eat. The messenger is in the main hall." His footsteps tapped away, and the jagged teeth of anxiety gnawed at Lykos's gut again. This would not be good news.

Lydos strode into the main hall in a crimson tunic cinched with a black band to meet a haggard sailor he recognized as Captain Jabari, the man he selected to lead the support team. The captain in his seventies, though not as well-maintained as Lykos, turned a grief-stricken, bearded face and haunted gray eyes to meet his.

"Captain Jabari," Lykos addressed as he approached with his hands clasped regally behind his back, chin high, and posture erect. "I sense a dismal report to come."

Lowering his gaze, Jabari nodded.

"Here, let us sit down." Lykos showed him to a bench along one wall between a bust of some former queen on a pedestal and a tall, leafy plant extending from its bulbous, painted pot. He stared across the room at the canvas of the kings jumping the bull Temen had brought with him to hang in the palace. A tinge of loss mingled with the other emotions as he realized he would miss the man. He had been quite pleasant and could truly turn a phrase. People enjoyed being around him, even if he wasn't everything he pretended to be. Lykos locked the feeling away and stiffened himself for the words to come.

"At first, everything was perfect, just as we had planned," the captain began nervously. His shaky hand didn't know where to be as he brushed it through his hair, and then wiped it down his beard. "Pelepus fell before the sun moved far across the sky. The laser cannons worked perfectly, and the demolished port raised a white flag of surrender. General Gershom ordered we all move on to Palaio Faliro and come back for a land invasion after the second harbor was secured, you know, so they couldn't launch their warships to hem us in." He waved the restless hand in animation.

"What happened at Palaio Faliro?" Lykos prompted, knowing it inevitably ended in defeat.

"I'm not entirely certain," he admitted, "but from my vantage point, half a league behind the attack force, the laser cannons didn't work. They fired off one volley and then nothing. The warriors of Pelasgoí bombarded them from the city ramparts, sent ships to engage them in the bay, and then some of our vessels landed and tried to take the city on foot. We waited at a safe distance, but we didn't have laser cannons, and I didn't want to risk losing all our soldiers, horses, and vessels. Our cargo liners were bigger and less maneuverable than the warships, and, if they were being set on fire and boarded, I knew we would fare no better. Neither the king nor the general were there to give me an order, so I did what I thought was wisest and protected our assets."

Lykos inclined his head with brooding consideration. He would have preferred Jabari had sped into the fray to support the marines, but he understood the captain's reasoning. "What of King Temen and General Gershom?"

"We waited to see if they would prevail. If we had gotten a sign, if a flag had gone up over the city, I would have rushed in with aid, but ..." Jabari huffed out a frustrated sigh of regret, lowered his gaze, and shook his head.

Lykos gave him time to compose himself. When the captain raised his chin, a somber expression solidified his countenance into stone. "They sent an envoy to inform us that the general and King Temen had been captured. He promised no harm would come to them until all the leaders of Pelasgoí convened and decided what to do. They gave me this as proof." The captain withdrew a ring from his pouch and handed it to Lykos, who quickly recognized it as Temen's. "Although they didn't say so, ransom is customary, isn't it?" he added with a hint of hope.

Why didn't the laser cannons work the second day? Lykos puzzled. "What of our warriors? Did he say if they were taken captive as well?"

"No, sir, he didn't say. Did I make the wrong call? Could my men have turned the tide?" His remorseful eyes searched Lykos's gaze with doubt. "I'm ready to accept whatever punishment you deem fit."

What a predicament. This should have worked. We should have taken the port and the peninsula. "You said the laser cannons demolished Pelepus but, what, they malfunctioned at Palaio Faliro?"

"From what I witnessed, yes."

Lykos rubbed his temples, closed his eyes, and took a deep, calming breath. For a week, a sense of unease had troubled him, likely triggered by the vibrations emanating from the failed attack. He had avoided using clairvoyance to see the events because he wanted to be wrong. He wanted to believe it was just nerves and not a sign. Weaving the subtle connections through the ether, he focused his awareness on Temen's wavelength at the time and place the battle would have occurred. The talented wizard eased himself into a trance and allowed the sounds and images to materialize in his mind. As soon as he saw it, his consciousness bolted back to the palace hall, his eyes flying open in alarm.

"The power crystals failed! It wasn't the weapons themselves," he revealed to Captain Jabari. "We purposefully used much larger, more powerful crystals than were necessary to avoid this very problem." Lykos was suddenly assailed with worry and a tinge of guilt. He should have foreseen this. With the fading of energetic connections and the need for power boosting here, the effects must have been much greater at such a distance. The sun's potency harnessed in the crystals had been consumed more rapidly than any of his collaborators anticipated. He should have taken that into account.

Lykos shook it off. There was no point belaboring the failure. He could take measures now and devise a new strategy. "Eshkar!" he bellowed, then leveled his gaze on Jabari. "Secure the remainder of our fleet and grant the soldiers shore leave. Then please return to share your account with the jurors."

Relief rolled off the captain as he bowed and exited the hall. *A severe reprimand would serve no purpose*, Lykos reasoned, *and I may require his services again soon.*

"Yes, my lord?" Eshkar raced in and bowed before Lykos, then raised an expectant gaze, vibrating with desire to please the wizard. His snowy tunic and matching headband contrasted with his tawny skin and walnut brown hair, and his thick midsection proclaimed he missed no meals. Eshkar had served in the palace for thirty years, faithfully performing his duties regardless of who ruled. Lykos had found him acceptable and loyal, avoiding the gossip that so many staff members thrived on.

"Inform the jurors of an emergency meeting to take place in two turns of the sandglass," he instructed. "And make this hall ready to receive them. Then don't disturb me until they have all arrived."

"Yes, my lord," he stated with sharp assurance, pivoted on his heel, and marched out barking orders to other palace attendants.

Now, to inform Rhoxane she is about to become the acting queen of Ryzen.

43

Lykos subliminally suggested every person in residence assist Eshkar so he could discreetly enter Rhoxane's chamber. Having dressed for the day, she met him with an anxious expression, and the two clasped hands. "Just tell me," she demanded.

"The invasion failed, and Temen was captured." Frankness was kinder than platitudes.

When Rhoxane pressed against his chest and squeezed him, Lykos could sense her dismay and displeasure, though he couldn't tell if it was over losing the battle or her husband.

She straightened and wiped an unexpected tear before meeting his gaze. "We will pay his ransom, won't we? I mean, he's gentle and comfortable and I never wished him any harm."

"Yes, my dear," Lykos promised, kissing her forehead as he steadied her with firm hands on her shoulders. "We'll negotiate for his safe return. Of course, he'll have lost the people's confidence and will be voted out as king, but in a year it won't matter, anyway. Right now, you'll be taking over leadership. We'll have to make different arrangements for our citizens' safety, perhaps in Kemet or Kush."

"Of course," she agreed. "What about Maanu, though? Mandisa said—"

"There's plenty of land and friendly locals," Lykos agreed. "If people wish to go there, we'll send passenger vessels to transport them; however, it doesn't appeal to me. Maybe Ur," he mused. "Pelasgoí would have been perfect. I have foreseen it will be a great empire one day."

"Don't worry, Lykos," Rhoxane soothed and pressed her lips to his.

He raised his fingers to caress the smooth, damp skin of her matchless face and noticed something odd. Backing away, Lykos stared at her, scrutinizing her features. There was the slightest shimmer, perhaps brought on by the unfamiliar appearance of tears. He had never seen her cry for real, only fake to-get-her-way weeping. He took her chin between his fingers and tilted her head from side to side.

"Stop it!" She slapped at his hand, anger flashing in her expression as she pulled away.

Lykos's mouth fell agape as astonishment shot through him. "Well, bury a spoon!" spilled from his lips and his eyes rounded. "You're using a glamor!"

Rhoxane whirled away, turning her back to him, and hugged her arms around herself as she paced across the room. "I don't know what you're talking about."

"Yes, you do, clever sorceress. Show me." He caught up to her, grabbed her shoulder, and spun her around, peering at her intently. "Show me your real face."

"This is my real face, you impertinent scoundrel!"

"Rhoxane, I am so impressed, humbled even," Lykos admitted. "I caught just a glimpse, when you were being emotional just now—honest emotions, for once. It's so hard for me to read you, to know when you are being false with me. Is everything between us a lie?"

"No," she snapped and jerked away again.

Sensing her vibrations, Lykos followed with, "I didn't mean to offend you. But if anything has ever been genuine between us, please, for the love of Poseidon, lower the veil, just for me, just for a moment. I swear I won't regard you with less esteem; on the contrary—more."

She hesitated. "Damn emotions," she muttered in frustration. "I don't know why I care about that fool, Temen, but so you know I'm committed to you ..."

Rhoxane sucked in a raw breath and released her illusion just long enough for Lykos to get a peek. Her hair wasn't a glossy brunette, but mousy brown, her perfect features marred with inadequacy, her flawless complexion splattered with freckles, her lush lashes and sensuous lips ordinary. In an instant, her stunning looks were sealed back in place.

"Satisfied?" she growled.

"More enthralled with you than ever," he confessed. "I mean, the face you were born with is cute, attractive enough—"

"But common," she snipped. "I heard my parents talking behind my back as a youth. How could a daughter with such a common appearance ever become the face of their noble clan? 'Sure, she has the brains for it,' they would admit, then sigh in disappointment. At age fourteen, I decided, why settle for a fate of flawed inherited traits when I could create any aspect I desired? After all, we are slivers of the divine on the inside; why not elevate our physical bodies to match?"

Rhoxane resumed her air of nobility as she promenaded around her bedroom, with her customary confidence renewed.

"Teach me how to do that," Lykos bade. "How did you change your look?"

"I don't know if I can teach it, and why would you wish to change your look?" she asked in suspicion. "You are strikingly handsome for a man of any age—your robust physique, noble chin, symmetrical features, piercing eyes, and the brush of silver in your hair give you a distinguished appearance. I'm completely attracted to your natural face."

"It could be a useful skill," he shared, struck by inspiration. "What if I go somewhere and don't wish to be recognized?"

Frowning, Rhoxane said, "I use it as an enhancement. Don't you possess enough skills of deception already? I don't want you to become so powerful that you no longer need to keep me around."

Lykos approached her with a warm smile, gently took her hand, and pressed a soft kiss to her fingertips. "Never. So, how do you do it?"

He sensed Rhoxane was weighing him, seeking to determine his measure of sincerity before revealing more. With a twist of her wrist, she caught his lower lip between her painted nails. "I'll tell you when I believe I can trust you not to use the illusion on me."

"But our skills," he began, then went silent. The illusion, as she called it, had worked on him for years without a hitch, until she became distracted by introspective concern for Temen's life.

She smiled and wiggled her brows at him when she caught the realization in his gaze. "This skill, as you call it, isn't applied to another, but to oneself. Therefore, it doesn't have to work on anyone else. As long as you hold it, everybody will see what you want them to see. Now, we should deal with the crisis at hand."

"Fair enough," Lykos agreed. "I will strive to earn your trust, my lady, but now we have an important meeting to prepare for. I'll join you in the main hall when the jurors arrive."

☥ ⊛ ✚ ✡

Lykos ate the breakfast Eshkar had prepared for him and changed into something more suitable than his bold red for the assembly. Then he entered the hall, taking his usual seat in the advisor position to the left of the king's spot. Captain Jabari occupied the witness chair and the nine jurors had all settled into their places when Rhoxane strode in last, gracefully gliding into her seat to the right of the empty throne.

"Ladies and gentlemen of the jury," she announced, "Captain Jabari of the Ryzen Defenders has brought us a troubling report this morning, which requires our immediate attention. It is with a heavy heart that I give him the floor to speak."

The captain stood and recounted his testimony. Lykos pulled out Temen's ring and passed it among the jurors for examination.

"Has a ransom been issued?" an elder asked.

"Not yet," Lykos replied. "However, I suggest we start collecting treasure, so we'll be ready when the time comes. We must endeavor to save our king."

"Why did we try to invade Pelasgoí in the first place?" asked a distraught woman, as though she had been unaware of the plan. To be fair, Lykos had hit her with a stronger dose of mesmer than the others because of her initial opposition to the idea. Perhaps she didn't recall that session.

Lykos rubbed his chin and shook his head in a distressed manner. "King Temen had the best interests of Ryzen at heart, Syrene," he explained. "I advised against it, but General Gershom convinced him the scheme would succeed. None of us could have guessed such huge crystals with so many to spare would burn through their reserves in a few turns of the sandglass."

That, at least, was an accurate statement. But this is what he needed Temen for, to begin with—somebody to take the fall when things went awry.

"We find ourselves facing our darkest moment with no ruler to guide us, no one elected by the people to take on the responsibility of arranging safe travel for our citizens to acceptable destinations before the flood comes. That is why I propose we vote unanimously to appoint Queen Rhoxane as interim ruler until King Temen has been safely returned to Ryzen. Don't let her youth fool you. Rhoxane is a shrewd and capable woman whom the people greatly admire. They will look to her now for leadership. Therefore, we should make it official."

The jurors discussed the matter with nods and gestures, while Captain Jabari, having completed his role, excused himself from the hall. After a few minutes, a juror with a deep, earthy complexion raised a question. "Queen Rhoxane, are you willing to accept this grave responsibility? We all know the reputation of your family is beyond reproach, but haven't they already departed for the Green Sea?"

Rhoxane seemed tired, and more tense than Lykos could ever recall. He wasn't certain if it was because an instance's lapse in her façade had allowed him a glimpse at not only her ordinary appearance but also at her extraordinary talent. He suspected—even without that disruption—having all their plans crumble into defeat would have been cause enough.

"Yes, my family has emigrated to Phoenicia," she answered in a steady tone. "They have friends there, trading partners they have known for decades. However, as you can see, I remained here by my husband's side to lead and defend the residents of our great city-state. I intend to complete that role. I'm honored to accept this burden and shall not board my transport until every citizen of

Ryzen who wishes to leave has safely embarked on their vessels. It will require swift work and dedication, but I believe we can make the necessary adjustments in short order. I appreciate your vote of confidence."

They conferred for a while longer, then turned back to Lykos. "It is agreed," decreed the elder who first spoke. "Queen Rhoxane shall serve as interim ruler until King Temen's return or until we have all safely departed for our new homes."

☥ ⚛ ✝ ✡

Lykos escorted Rhoxane outside, where Eshkar rang a large bell to attract the people's attention. The jurors filed out and surrounded them in solidarity. When a substantial enough crowd had gathered, Lykos raised his hands, and the men, women, and children, all with bright curious faces, quieted. He gave the solemn news of the military failure and King Temen's capture, then introduced Queen Rhoxane as their responsible, caring ruler. She engaged the crowd with assurances until a heckler leading a squad of disgruntled people in rural attire interrupted.

"You don't have the right to send us away!" shouted the severe woman wearing a kerchief with a basket on her hip and three stair-step children at her side.

The man beside her pointed and sneered. "We know about your ploys to steal our land! The flood predictions are a hoax, you hear me? Don't let these nobles and politicians trick you into leaving Ryzen. You heard her—she's not going anywhere until we're all off to Kemet or Maanu or some such foreign land."

"Yeah," added the gruff voice of a mountainous fellow in a worker's kilt. "They just want to trick us. Well, I'm an Atlantean," he proclaimed, jerking a thumb toward his bare chest. "Why would I wish to go live among inferior races?"

With what Lykos perceived as genuine concern, Rhoxane stepped forward, reaching an arm toward the crowd. "It isn't a hoax. I'm not lying to you.

My family owns a quarter of the land in Ryzen already; what would we do with more? And if that were true, why would they have already resettled in Phoenicia? Please, neighbors, I implore you to take this threat seriously. When the flood waters rush in, it will be too late. Book your passage now."

"Bah!" The big man waved a dismissive hand at her and spun away.

The residents radiated a mix of fear, hopefulness, and distrust, and Lykos did what he could to soothe them. It wasn't that his powers were weakening—hardly. It was the level of anxiety the public faced. Now he had to come up with a new strategy as well. Where would he go to live comfortably in a position of respect and admiration, where he could practice his gifts and have other scholarly wisdom thinkers to associate with? And what was he going to do with Temen once he was rescued?

Glancing at Rhoxane, who glided into leadership like it was a glove made especially for her, he faced his biggest question of all. *What will I do about Rhoxane?*

44

Same day in Evamont

"This procedure requires intense concentration and not all physicians can perform it," Lysandra explained to her students, Isis and Ocotlan. Ériu's sister Fótla and Ziusudra's wife Jatziri had completed their training and returned to their respective towns to practice until it was time to board their arks. While Lysandra considered Isis her most talented apprentice, her constant traveling between Atlantis and Giza had put her behind the others. A year ago, she was joined by Ocotlan, a local young man with promising potential who had glued himself to Lysandra's side, eager to learn.

Her clinic was on the middle floor of Evamont's main pyramid, where the generated magnetic energy could be focused, and the harmonic acoustics used to full advantage. Several other healers also operated from rooms on the same level. Aloe, lemon balm, and lavender plants occupied pots in the cozy chamber decorated with Lysandra's paintings and illuminated by a sloping, square window and light panels. The candles served a more ceremonial purpose. Incense lightly floated around the room along with the vibrations of the cymbal and sistrum.

A burn victim lay on the cushioned treatment table Lysandra had brought with her from Atala while she stood with her students beside him. She had already administered an herbal sedative and put him to sleep because of his severe pain.

"We will use the ankh as a focal point, even though it's possible to regrow skin without it," she tutored. "This is more akin to channeling, like the process used to regrow a severed limb. It requires completely opening yourself to Rafael's healing energies to flow through you like a conduit. Empty your mind of self and connect fully to our Source of spiritual power. It will take a long time, which is why I canceled my other appointments for the day when his friends brought him in. Questions?"

"What do we do with our hands?" Ocotlan asked as he held them up. They were smooth, slender hands attached to the arms of a gangly teen who had excelled at his academy studies. He wore his brown hair shorter than most young men and sprouted no beard at all, even though he was in his eighteenth summer. Lysandra had immediately sensed in him the most important ingredient to becoming a talented physician—a tender, loving soul. Ocotlan would never be an athlete or guardian or stonemason, but he could become a wonderful healer.

"If you were working alone and without an ankh, you would hover them over the injured flesh," Lysandra said. "For now, extend your palms toward the loop in the ankh's top as I focus it on his wounds. Your heart should radiate love for the particles and waves of his skin, encouraging it into rapid reproduction. If your brain must exercise thoughts, they should adhere to well-being and restoration. Today, as with everything in life, love is the key."

"But isn't it hard to swell with love for a stranger?" he asked.

Lysandra exchanged a glance with Isis. She had been present for this lesson on an earlier occasion. "Actually, Ocotlan, it is easier to exude love for strangers than someone you know. They are a blank slate, a person formed in the image of the Creator. When looking at people we know, our memories can get in the way—an argument or disagreement, an opinion we've formed, can hinder pure love from flowing. Likewise, if the patient is someone we care about—a close friend, relative, or lover—anxiety and worry for them can interrupt the flow of positive energies. That's why it's best to avoid treating those you love most for a serious illness or injury if it can be avoided and there is another capable physician available."

The young man nodded, rolled his shoulders, closed his eyes, and extended his palms toward the ivory ankh. Lysandra held it over the worst portion of the patient's burnt flesh. She wasn't certain what had caused the angry red and black insults to the left side of his body, but, for her art to unfold, it didn't matter.

"Take a deep breath, relax, and empty your minds of thought," she instructed in a peaceful tone, leading by example. "Reach through the ether and call on Archangel Rafael, progenitor of healing power. Picture bright pink skin, fresh like an infant's covering his form. Give thanks that it is done. Let the frequencies flow from the heavens, through your heart of love, through your hands, as we all focus our Jjeevan Shakti through the symbol of eternal life and into Reuven's body. Encourage his healing pathways to form the new skin with joy and affection, as you would encourage a baby to crawl or take its first steps. Now, I will be silent."

Lysandra dropped into her meditation and started weaving energies from the ether and her own life force with those of their patient, Reuven. Both her hands and the ivory ankh became vibrant and warm, tingling with infinitesimal electric sparks. After a while, she backed off from her exertion and opened her senses to assess how her students were doing. Ocotlan tried too hard, as if he could heal the man through the power of his will. She sensed tension rather than relaxation in his muscles. Still, his efforts contributed to the whole.

Isis, on the other hand, seemed to have mastered the art of allowing energies to flow through her like an aqueduct. Lysandra detected a powerful talent in Thoth's daughter, causing her to smile and offer thanks to Rafael, the ancestors, the Creator, and all the spiritual beings. It pleased her to know Thoth and his family, along with Ariel's mother and all those who had or were moving to Giza, would have a gifted healer to meet their needs.

Several turns of the sandglass later, Lysandra oversaw her students applying a balm of aloe to the regrown skin to soothe and nurture it. "Isis, you may wake him now."

Isis selected the correct pungent herb and snapped it under his nose. "Reuven, wake up," she commanded gently into his ear. He fluttered his lids until he could hold them open, then glanced around.

Ocotlan smiled and waved to him. "How do you feel?" he asked excitedly.

Reuven wiggled his fingers and toes and held up his arm to admire the new skin. Then he peered down at his side, hip, and thigh. With a broad smile and sleepy look in his appreciative eyes, he uttered, "Better. Instead of unbearable pain, there's an odd tingling sensation. And no hideous scarring!"

"You'll have to take it easy for a few days and keep applying this salve," Lysandra instructed, handing him a small jar. "To ensure your healing is complete, you are to avoid direct sunlight, offer daily prayers of thanks, entertain only positive thoughts, and stay away from fires. Your new skin is quite sensitive and needs time to mature. If you do that, you'll be playing push toss again in no time."

"Thank you, Lysandra, Isis, and you are?" he inquired.

"Ocotlan," her younger apprentice beamed with satisfaction.

"Thank you all so much. My mother said you could repair the damage, but I never imagined I'd be as good as new. I was so scared, and it hurt so bad."

"You must also thank Archangel Rafael, the Creator, and all the spirits," Isis added. "Growing new skin for you was a joint effort."

"And I appreciate it more than I can say," Reuven declared. He sat up and swung his legs over the edge of the table, careful to hold the modesty cloth in place over his groin.

"We'll leave you to dress now," Lysandra said and turned toward the exit to give him privacy.

She and her students were surprised to find Quetzal waiting. A quickening of fear shot through Lysandra like a flaming arrow. "Ariel!"

"Is still in Ampherium collecting fish, bugs, and tiny creatures as far as I know—safe and sound," he assured her.

Lysandra's heart-thumping eased. "Thank the stars," she exhaled. "Then what?"

Quetzal glanced at Isis and Ocotlan. "My students," Lysandra said. "You know Isis, Thoth's daughter."

"Oh, yes, Isis. I thought you were in Kemet," he said.

"I returned to complete my training," she replied.

Lysandra smiled at her. "Which you have just about done."

"Thank you again," Reuven said as he departed the treatment room, fully dressed and skipping like a giddy schoolboy. He waved, and they all responded in kind. "Don't worry, Lysandra. I'll do as I'm told."

"Take care," she bade him, then looked to Quetzal. "Would you like to step into my clinic for a moment and tell us what's happening?"

The brawny scholar nodded, and they entered the room, closing the door behind them.

"This morning, I received a telepathic message from a friend at the Southern Wisdom School in Ryzen," he reported gravely. "Ryzen ships and marines attacked our former colony of Pelasgoí using forbidden weaponry. After causing much damage and loss of life, they fell to the colonists when the crystals powering their lasers failed. King Temen was taken prisoner."

A collective gasp erupted from the trio of healers at the shocking report. "Mandisa told us he was planning to recapture Pelasgoí so his citizens could all move there and keep his kingdom together. Ariel said he wasn't capable of leading a military operation; it seems she was right."

"I heard General Goshen, a respected officer, was in charge and Temen had gone along to rally the troops—probably to accept the locals' surrender and declare himself king of Pelasgoí. I don't think their defeat was his fault, but he should have never undertaken such an action to begin with. People are getting scared and desperate now that all the rulers are openly telling them to abandon Atlantis and go somewhere else. I fear you physicians will see more violence victims before it's over."

"Oh, this is such horrible and distressing news." Lysandra leaned her hip on the edge of the treatment table, feeling more exhausted than she had in days.

"What will happen to the people of Ryzen now?" asked Isis with concern.

"My friend said Queen Rhoxane has been granted temporary authority in Ryzen and is busily lining up transportation for everyone who will leave to the friendly ports of their choice, but, like here, there are those who don't believe a flood will happen."

"I have an uncle and cousins who are deluge deniers," Ocotlan said. He crossed his arms and grimaced. "They won't listen to me. They think I've been brainwashed and, what's more, don't believe the Great Conflagration even happened. Some self-proclaimed prophet has been going around preaching that the Third Age founders made it up as an excuse to seize power and establish limiting rules on society—like no laser weapons. What were the Ryzens thinking?"

"That they wanted a choice location to settle and that Atlanteans, the most advanced civilization on earth, should have their pick, whether or not it's currently occupied by another nation," Lysandra concluded in frustration. "Do you know how to find Ariel? Someone should tell her."

At that moment, Lysandra longed to hold her beloved in her arms, to share in her distress, to know she was safe. While she sometimes had prophetic dreams or heard messages from the cosmos, Lysandra had never possessed a telepathy gift. Even if she could talk to Ariel at a distance, she yearned for a physical touch. So much of the time since they had wed they still had to spend apart, performing their missions to prepare for the coming cataclysm. Her stomach tensed and churned at the thought of getting separated from Ariel when the ice wall burst and the sea engulfed their home. What if Ariel was away in Gadlan or down on Daya and they ended up taking refuge on different vessels? How would she ever find her soulmate again?

Quetzal rested a broad, affectionate hand on her shoulder, soothing her anxiety with his touch. A smile spread between his fuzzy lip and fuzzier chin, and his intuitive eyes crinkled. "I can find her, and no—you won't be parted forever. We'll know when the Terrible Ice cracks and will have a few days to put everyone into place and fasten the ark doors. Just pray all the residents have taken their transports by then. We only have room for those whose places have been reserved. Don't worry, Lysandra. Ariel will be there watching over you and her menagerie."

She nodded and sent appreciative vibrations to Quetzal.

"And you, young lady," he added with a wink, pointing at Isis, "need to get back to your husband. Is she ready to begin her own practice?" he directed to Lysandra.

"Give us another week, and yes," Lysandra agreed, "she's ready."

"Very well. I'll leave you youngsters to do your thing and go track down your spouse. Everything will work out as it should."

Quetzal departed and, as Lysandra had sent all the other patients away earlier, she told Isis and Ocotlan to go home and enjoy their evenings. She wasn't looking forward to the long sleigh ride back to an empty farmhouse. But Yaluk had invited her to dinner and Oma was due home anytime. *Tonight, maybe?* Lysandra had always been fond of Ariel's great-great-great-grandmother, but, since moving in with them, her appreciation for the extraordinary woman had grown.

I'll have to tell Mandisa what happened, she thought. Eventually, the night would boil down to her being alone in their bed, hugging a pillow stuffed into one of Ariel's tunics so it would smell like her when she snuggled it. *We will not be separated*, she repeated to herself. *I must trust and believe. It's all about trusting and believing—so simple and yet so hard.* Shepherding her thoughts, Lysandra sang uplifting songs to herself on her commute home.

45

Immortal Glade, in the forests of Ampherium, the next day

Ariel sat on a pillow of thick moss and moist leaves skirted by lush ferns and primrose, listening to the warble of a birdsong. Somewhere, a woodpecker hammered away at a tree trunk, its tapping providing a percussive beat to the music of the forest. The scent of fungi reached her through the still air, as slow, wet drops rolled down from branch to branch of the giant redwoods whose arms stretched to the sky. The warm humidity made her tunic stick to her body while fallen needles poked at her legs, neither of which affected her love and appreciation for this forest. *This could be the last time I commune with the Immortal Glade, dig my fingers into this earth, hear these songs, and touch the Oldest Tree.* Ariel wanted to remember every aspect of the woods.

Twenty or more small boxes she had fashioned with wooden frames and mosquito netting spread around her in a broad arc as bugs and beetles of all descriptions marched through their openings in rows of two—two grass crickets, two dung beetles, ladybugs, fireflies, leaf beetles, and more. Ratiki watched the procession with intrigue, twitching his whiskers and flicking his tail. Ariel pulled the flute away from her mouth, holding it in place.

"Don't bother them, play with them, or get the bright idea they are a snack," Ariel warned with a glare. He kept his busy hands to himself, allowing the bugs to move around him with nothing more than a curious sniff.

Can't I help put them in the boxes? he asked, glancing at her over his shoulder.

I want to help.

Ariel smirked. "You can help by deciding on a female to join you on our ark. I swear, Ratiki, you can't make up your mind."

Giving her a sheepish grin, he turned back to watching the insects.

Ariel had already collected the spiders and ants and secured them down by Largo Ursa in her staging area. She didn't bother to gather flies, ticks, and fleas, as plenty of those would come aboard with no invitation. Her assistant Balam, a fellow about half her age, stayed with the fish tanks and cages already loaded onto cargo sleds to ensure their safety.

Quetzal had sent him to help her after he discovered the budding nature speaker down in Mestoria working as an entertainer and "animal trainer." He had explained to Balam how special his gifts were and what a vital role he needed to play. Gaining his confidence, Quetzal brought Balam to Ariel for tutoring. He was a pleasant young man who loved animals, and his muscles came in handy.

She played softly on her flute, trying not to clash with the birds, as the tiny creatures she had assembled, using a pleasing frequency to draw them near, crawled into their boxes. Then she closed their doors and latched them shut. Picking up the containers, she stacked them on a smallish sled and secured them with a strap so none would fall off on the trip down to the lake. Deciding he had walked enough for one day, Ratiki climbed onto the sled, squeezed himself between crates, and licked his feet.

Before leaving, Ariel set her palm against the bark of the Oldest Tree to tell her goodbye. She sensed a message coming from the staggeringly wide sequoia. *I survived the last cataclysm; I shan't make it through this one. Gaia says the time is near. It has been nice communing with nature speakers through the centuries. I appreciate knowing some humans see me as more than wood for their house or boat. I'm glad to know we are all One.*

"I will take some of your seeds with me on my ark so that your children may grow in a new land."

Ariel relished the vibrations she and the tree exchanged. It was impossible to bring full-grown living trees on the arks, but they had all seemed satisfied with knowing their seeds would be saved. She received the Oldest Tree's gratitude and smiled, keeping her thoughts light so she wouldn't descend into tears at their farewell. Bending over, she scooped up several cones and dropped them into the pouch on her belt. When she looked up, she spotted a friendly black bear and two six-month-old cubs. Ratiki scrambled to the top of the containers on the sled and chattered nervously.

"Hush, Tiki! This bear is our friend." She turned her attention to their visitor.

Is it time? the nervous mother asked.

"No, not yet. I must gather the tiny creatures early, for they cannot travel as fast."

The mother bear stepped closer while her cubs romped and tussled, pawing at each other playfully. She barked and gave them a sharp stare when they tumbled too near Ariel's sled. Obediently, they settled down.

Will you take my cubs? A boy and a girl. I wish I could promise they would behave.

"They would have to go on different ships and never see each other again," Ariel explained.

The bear looked at her cubs, who bounded up to rub on her, and she sat back on her haunches to hug them. *I understand. I feel something is changing and it will be soon.*

Ariel was troubled by both the Oldest Tree and now the mother bear saying they sensed imminent danger when, according to Ziusudra, they should have almost a year more. Theirs hadn't been the first hints she had received, adding weight to the concerns.

"Bring your children to the other side of the great lake. Near the mouth of the Abzu River is the human town of Diaprep where the ships are. Wait in the closest forest until you hear my call. Then your cubs will arrive first, but they must go on different arks. I love you, my sister. I wish I could save you all."

By saving my children, you are saving me. I have enjoyed blueberries and honey, trout and grubs. I have known the pleasure of mating and enjoyed affection with my children. I have splashed in the river and bathed in the sunshine. Mine has been a wonderful life. Will there be those things where you are going?

Ariel didn't respond at once. She wasn't sure what climate and terrain they would arrive in. "They will have food and water and a mate where they go, but I can't say what the new land will look like."

The mother cocked her head and flicked her ears, then licked the nearest cub's head. *All will be well. Blessings on you, nature speaker. I will take them downriver and await your call.* She rolled to her feet and lumbered away, the two rascals trotting to keep up.

As Ariel watched them go, she smiled at the wisdom of bears.

☥ ☬ ✝ ✡

Upon returning to her base camp—a tent, campfire, and cargo sled stacked with tanks and crates beside the peaceful, picturesque waters of Largo Ursa—Ariel was surprised to find Quetzal talking and laughing with Balam.

"Well, look what the puma dragged up," she teased as affection for the wise man warmed her heart. "I wasn't expecting to see you here." Ratiki scampered off the sled and raced to greet his old friend.

Quetzal waved and Balam trotted over to take charge of the small sled. "I'll get these secured. Quetzal has news for you."

She flicked a gaze, sharp with trepidation, to her red-haired guest. A stirring in her gut warned her it wasn't a cheerful message he brought.

Ariel strode forward, warding off anxiety with calm steps, and motioned to two folding chairs that were set by the fire. He inclined his head, then gave her a hug when she drew near. "Ariel," he murmured into her ear. "Lysandra is well."

"Good. Now I can breathe," she uttered in return. They took their seats, and she offered him refreshment from a pitcher she drew from an ice chest beside her chair. "Lemon water? There's wine in the tent."

Seeing Quetzal brought no treats for him, Ratiki wandered off to dig in the grass near the sprawling lake.

With a smile, he held up a hand and shook his head. "I'm fine, thank you."

Quetzal's story about the attack and Temen's capture was disturbing yet not unexpected. In the months since Mandisa came to live with them, Ariel had resolved any feelings of responsibility for or concerning her ex-husband. Though she felt empathy for his ill-fated predicament, she knew his actions were his own and not applicable to her.

"I'm sorry to hear of it," she responded, "especially the lives lost. Ryzen will pay his ransom, and, if not, the Council of Rulers will, if for no other reason than to save face with the rest of the world. They can't allow a king of Atlantis to languish in the hands of rebellious colonists forever. What concerns me more is our timeline."

Quetzal leaned forward, his elbows on his knees, and quirked a brow at her. "What have you learned?"

"The Oldest Tree and several cognizant forest creatures are nervous," she answered. "They are sensing more pronounced changes coming from Gaia and have been hinting the time is near."

"Eleven months is practically immediate where the earth is concerned," he stated. "She's millions of years old. Even the age of humanity is but a blink of an eye to her. Yet, I must admit, I often experience an unexplained tingle running up my spine, tickling my consciousness, screaming at me to run. How soon will you be done collecting the fish and tiny creatures?"

"I still need to go to Gadlan for those unique species, but I could be done in a week with Balam's help."

"Of course I'll help!" The eager young man trotted over upon hearing his name.

"Can I trust you to transport these to Noah and then bring the big sled up to Gadlan?"

He gave her a disappointed, offended expression. "If not, what good am I?"

Ariel reached out her hand to him, and Balam took it. She smiled at him and squeezed his hand. "You know I'm bad about wanting to be in charge of everything myself."

"I need to go to Diaprep anyway," Quetzal said, pushing out of his seat to stretch. "Balam, would you accompany me in case I get lost on the way?"

Dimples creased at the corners of Balam's mouth at his broad grin. "Certainly, old man!" Balam stepped away from Ariel to shake his hand.

"Don't forget to aerate the water in the tanks," Ariel instructed, as she stood to see them off.

"I won't," Balam answered with a laugh. "Can you strike this camp by yourself?"

Ariel gasped in feigned outrage. "I was setting up and taking down camps before you were a twinkle in your dada's eyes, you little squirt."

Noticing something new was happening, the inquisitive raccoon raced back into their midst. Sitting up, balanced between hind legs and tail, he waved his hands in the air and twitched his whiskers. *I can help Ariel take down the tent.*

They all laughed, and Quetzal moved to her for another hug. "Lysandra is worried about the two of you being separated," he whispered.

"Lysandra worries about too many things," she replied. "Let her know I'll be home soon and promise not to leave her side until we land in our new country."

A sudden ache formed in Ariel's heart. *If only I had telepathic abilities! How I long to talk to Lysandra while I'm away from her, to reassure her all is well, to enumerate the many ways I love her. I only hope the emotion I emit from my heart reaches her from a distance.*

46

One week later

Ariel gazed through the window of the cargo sled's cab at the sprawling landscape below. Rectangles of green, brown, and amber fields spotted the central plain as Balam steered the craft safely between ground and cloud levels. Interspersed were deep green splotches of forests and swathes of blue water reflecting the sky—or did the sky reflect the hue of the water? She couldn't remember. In the distance to her right rose the stately, rocky summits of the long, winding, western mountains, low, misty clouds ringing them like ethereal kilts or a spirit lover's embrace. To the left loomed the immense snowcapped domes of the Azaes, making everything else in the world appear small. She recalled Oma's story of meeting Methuselah there when she was young and hearing the stories of life on Atlantis before the Great Conflagration. A smile crept across her lips.

The city of Evamont was visible from their height, though she hadn't been able to make out her specific farm amid the myriad. She knew herds would be grazing on the meadows—Adira and her family—even though she couldn't see them. Ariel shot an arrow of love vibrations toward the lea and thought about all the happy moments she spent with them and other animal friends. They passed over the long, lazy ribbon of the Abzu River as it dipped and curved, cutting through the terra like a slithering snake.

Four paws and a lump of weight climbed into her lap as Ratiki squirmed over her to peer out as well. *What is so interesting out there? I'm in here. Pet me.*

With a snicker, Ariel ran her fingers through his plush fur and tickled him behind his ears. *I'm memorizing the beauty of our homeland, Ratiki,* she conveyed to him alone. If she spoke aloud, Balam would join the conversation, and Ariel remained in a contemplative mood. For tens of thousands of years, her ancestors had dwelt on this land, reaching upward to the heavens to converse with angels, spirits, and the Creator, reflecting inward to heal their bodies and commune with their inner beings, and extending outward in fellowship with their neighbors, even to distant, foreign lands. They excelled in creative crafts, appreciating beauty, and working to maintain it in all aspects of their extended lives.

Nearly a thousand years, she marveled, having personal knowledge of Methuselah's age when he passed on. While at fifty-six Ariel felt young and strong, she realized she'd not remain even half that long on this earth. Noah was the oldest person she knew of, and she figured he must have inherited the tendency. All Atlanteans once reached such advanced ages. They were giants among humanity, not in size, necessarily—though they were taller than many other races—but in their achievements and spirituality. Still, everything changes, and this was no exception.

Casting her gaze wistfully through the pane, Ariel clung to this moment, committing it to heart memory. Atlantis, the land of dreams, would soon be only a memory, and, as time rolled on, even the memory of her home would fade into myth or be forgotten altogether.

⚲ ⚛ ✟ ✡

Excitement bubbled in Ariel's core as they flew around Diaprep and approached the shipbuilding camp from the ocean side. It had been a long time since she had been here, and the enormity of the scene took her by surprise. To the right of the canal lay a vast clearing, at least as large as her grain farm, with four tremendous, enclosed vessels occupying spots on land and one moored in the water, which seemed to consume the entire harbor. Planks enclosed all the sides with only the small upper decks bearing windows. There were no oars or oar holes, no masts or sails, and, even hearing Noah spout off proportions, she hadn't imagined how massive they would be until seeing them for herself. They were breathtaking to behold.

Ariel didn't wait for Balam, or for the cargo sled to pull to a complete stop. As soon as she saw Lysandra standing on the landing pad, she slid off, bending her knees to absorb the shock as her sandals hit the ground. They locked eyes and, in an instant, rushed into each other's arms, the feeling of overwhelming joy and relief at being reunited washing over them. Showers of kisses followed, and Ariel was reluctant to ever let go.

"Uh, excuse me." Balam's voice was timid and small. "Where do you want these?"

Ariel glanced over Lysandra's shoulder at her assistant guiding an antigravity mover with a tremendous fish tank riding on it.

"Go take care of your fish," Lysandra said, with an adorable smile, her face flush with radiance. "There's a meeting over dinner in two turns of the sandglass. A veritable who's who of dignitaries are here, and, once we're done hashing out the details, I get you all to myself."

Feeling fur brush her bare leg, Ariel chuckled. "Almost all to yourself. I'm really ready for that," she uttered with a sigh. "You look good." It was so hard to drag her hands from Lysandra's waist when she wanted them on her hips, her breasts, and everywhere else on her luscious body. Duty came first.

"I'll save you a spot at the table beside me in case you're late," Lysandra promised, then added, "but don't be late."

Ariel laughed, happy and relaxed to be in the same place as Lysandra and their circle of chosen leaders. She glanced back at her spouse in time to catch a view of her shapely bum snug in a short, white chiton swish away. Then she placed her hand to the side of the tank.

"There are four this size, one for each ark," she told him. "There are eight of the next smaller size and twelve of each of the other sizes, all labeled with an ark number. They go in the aft quarters of the lower decks. Use the central lift shaft to take them down."

"Father sent us to help."

Ariel spun around to see two strapping men, one around her age and the other appearing younger. *Noah's sons.*

"I'm Japheth," smiled the stockier one, with curly brown locks and a three-day beard shadowing his once clean-shaven face. He extended a hand for her to shake. "And this is my little brother, Ham."

Ham shook her hand next, looking as if he'd rather be anywhere else. He was a handsome fellow with straight, ebony hair cut above his shoulders, a trim jawline beard, and a thin mustache. Both were tanned with healthy physiques. "Pleased to meet you," Ham offered, though his tone begged to differ.

"I'm Balam," her assistant grinned and shook the men's hands.

Ariel smiled at the brothers. "I'm Ariel and we welcome your help. Noah speaks highly of all his sons. I presume Shem is working on Ark Five?"

"Yeah," Ham grumbled.

"Where you should be?" Ariel raised a brow, then looped her arm around his to escort him to the cargo sled. "Anyone can cut a board or hammer a nail, my fine fellow. But these tanks of fish and crates of tiny, crawling creatures are why you and your father and brothers are building the arks. Everyone's favorite animals will come later, but these are important too. Every species the Creator brought forth on the earth is valuable and we want none to be lost."

"I suppose you're right," he agreed in a less disgruntled manner.

Japheth piped up with enthusiasm. "My wife loves animals. She wanted to come with us, but Mother said she needed her to help prepare the meal since there'll be so many people."

"My wife is an excellent cook," Ham praised. "You can meet Shem and his wife, Nahalath, at dinner. Nahalath is a nature speaker like you, and she's expecting a child."

Ariel's eyes lit with interest. "I didn't know Noah had a nature speaker in his family. I have two grown children," Ariel added conversationally as they helped her load tanks on an antigrav skid. "Are either of you fathers yet?"

"We decided to wait until our ark lands to start a family," Japheth said.

"Which is smart," Ham added. "My wife and I only recently married and plan to do the same. Wow, you've got a lot of fish," he commented. "And are the bugs really necessary?"

Steady hums, buzzes, and chirping sounds originated from the crates and boxes. Ariel laughed. "Yes, they are."

"We already put the beehives onboard, and they're the most important, right?" Japheth asked.

"Yes, but they're all important, just like Noah's sons."

Ham laughed and slapped Japheth on the back. "Hear that, big brother? We're all important!"

Support trellises and braces secured three arks on the beach, one floated in a deep-water pocket inside the harbor, and a fifth was still under construction a short distance from the shore. The pounding of hammers and din of muffled voices echoed through the work yard, while the scent of fresh-cut lumber was overpowered by the pungent odor of pitch that coated the outsides, casting the wood in a charcoal color.

Japheth pointed to the closest boat. "We named the arks after archangels. This one is *Michael* or Ark Two. The one that's already been launched is *Uriel*, Ark One, because he brought us the message. Over there are Ark Three, *Gabriel*, and Ark Four, *Barachiel*. The incomplete one is *Jegudiel*."

"Very impressive," Balam commented as he gazed up at *Ark Michael*. "We only brought fish and bugs for the four that are ready. How long do you think it will take to finish the fifth?"

"Another six months maybe," Ham replied.

"I hope we have six months," Ariel muttered, but she doubted it.

Japheth and Ham helped her affix antigravity skids under the tanks, and they guided the precious cargo up a wide ramp into an opening in the side of the colossal vessel that towered above them. Ariel made a quick inspection of the doorway and gave it an approving nod. *Plenty wide for elephants and even the giraffe could have fit through, though it may have needed to duck its head. Still, an easy fit for our big mammals.* Ratiki shuffled along a couple of cubits from her feet; he had learned long ago how to avoid getting stepped on.

"This is the middle deck," Japheth said, giving them a brief tour on the way to the lift shaft. "We've already packed Ériu's seeds in this storage room." He gestured to the right as they turned toward the vessel's rear. "We sealed all the containers with wax to make sure none of them get wet. Over there," he motioned across the central corridor, "are stacked bags of milled flour, dried herbs, vegetables, and fruits, and sacks of whole grains for porridge and soups. Father says to wait for the signal to add apples, lemons, and other fresh foods."

"Where will the people be?" Balam asked. Ariel didn't know which arks they would be assigned—one reason for the meeting, she supposed—but Balam would be going with Quetzal and Mandisa.

"In the forward section of this deck," Ham said, pointing behind them. "We can show you on our way back up. The antigravity lift is toward the stern and the staircase is in the front half. The kitchen is up there too and there are comfort stations front and rear on all decks, but Father says to just go over the side when the seas quiet down because—you know—less unpleasant work." Everyone laughed.

They passed more storerooms stacked with hay and straw, barrels of fresh water, a wine cell, and some empty cubbies before reaching a central shaft rising and lowering from their deck. Since they built it large enough to fit two elephants side by side, Balam and the biggest tank made it in place with room left for Japheth and the aquarium he guided.

"I'll send it right back up," Japheth said, then pressed his palm to the copper plate and pushed a lever to lower the metal platform.

Beyond the lift shaft, the interior layout changed to incorporate two aisles with small animal containment cubicles in three banks spanning the width of the ship. Each enclosure had been prepared with straw strewn inside, creating a comfortable bed for the animals, and a water bucket and food dish had also been provided. In the exterior rows, the habitats were stacked two high while in the center were smaller ones affixed three high.

The empty platform rose to meet them, and Ham and Ariel brought their fish tanks onto it. "We aren't sure if the lifts will still work after the flood, once we're far from the mother pyramids," Ham noted as he pushed the lever. "But we're bringing plenty of charged crystals in the hopes it will. After we've landed somewhere, we won't need the arks anymore, so we can always chop a hole in the side to get the big animals out." The metal plate stopped at the lowest level, which was dimly illuminated by sunlight shining down the shaft from the airy top deck high above them. Dust and hay particles floated in the sunbeam as if suspended in a glass of water.

"We have old-timey lanterns that burn oil," Ham said as they moved out of the stream of light into shadows, "and regular light panels, but we don't want to burn through our crystals."

"Where do you want these to go?" Japheth asked. He and Balam had waited in the hallway for them to arrive.

"These are heavy but won't move around like horses and elephants," Ariel said. "I thought they should go right in the middle of the hold." She pointed to an open, roped-off space running down the center of the deck. "The insects and tiny creatures go up top with the birds and fowl."

"Father installed sliding barn doors and storage rooms to section off the front portion for the predators," Ham said, "and their enclosures are equipped with metal bars."

Ariel nodded. "Excellent." They secured the huge aquariums in place and returned to find a dozen unfamiliar faces ready to help.

"Noah sent us," a workman in a kilt with a fuzzy chest and fuzzier chin announced. "He doesn't want you to be late to the conference."

"Thanks!" Ariel praised. "Balam, you know where they're supposed to go. Take a third of these fine fellows with you to load Ark Three—uh, I mean Gabriel—and if some of you will help me take the containers marked 'One' across the plank to *Uriel*. Japheth, Ham, can you each be in charge of the other arks, since you know where to place the tanks?"

Japheth exhibited a modest smile and swiped a hand through the air. "Nothing to it. We've got this. Mother will have our hides if we're late for dinner. Come on, fellows; let's get these loaded up."

Guiding an enormous fish tank on its floating skid, Ariel led her team to the massive vessel that gently bobbed in the water beside the shore, noting many birds and gulls had already taken up residence in the covered loft resting on top. *They know,* she thought and silently wished for more time.

47

The clanging of a large bell alerted Ariel and her helpers it was time to gather for the dinner conference, even though they hadn't started securing the insects and tiny creature containers yet.

"Don't worry, Ariel," Japheth assured her with a friendly pat on the back. "We'll return to help you after Father and the others are done with us."

"Thank you," she answered and wiped the sweat from her brow. The group marched in a clump to a shady spot in the grass outside Noah's house, where several long tables and chairs had been arranged to accommodate the crowd. Someone had set up a wash basin and hand towels for the guests' use, and Ariel's entourage stopped to wash their hands. She wished she could bathe properly since, between exertion and the heat of the afternoon, she was covered in perspiration. This would have to do.

With a glance up, Ariel scanned the tables where over fifty people sat chatting, laughing, and drinking cool liquid from their cups. She was grateful when her gaze fell on Lysandra, who joined with Quetzal, Mandisa and her husbands, and a few others Ariel had yet to be introduced to. Being thirsty and tired, she rushed to take the seat Lysandra had reserved for her.

"So sorry to be late," she said, hoping her odor didn't offend anyone. At least Lysandra would be pleased by it—or so she had often said. Ratiki curled around her legs and tugged at the hem of her tunic to remind her of his presence. She absently stroked his head, assuring him he would be fed too.

"No problem." Quetzal beamed at her. "I want you to meet my brother, Demetrios, and his husband, Malah. They are actors with the Pisces Players, and quite excellent ones, if I may brag on them."

"You may indeed," Ariel allowed after swallowing a long draught of water.

"I saw them a few years ago, and, Ariel, they were so entertaining," Lysandra gushed.

Demetrios blushed and flitted a humble glance at Malah.

"And one of the few troops still performing anywhere in Atlantis, as most have already moved overseas." He motioned to the woman on his other side. "This is Queen Zamná of Diaprep, our most honored guest."

Now Ariel really wished she could have bathed and put on clean garments. "Your Highness," she uttered and lowered her chin in respect. Not as elaborately adorned as she would expect a queen to appear, the woman presented a striking picture and displayed a quiet, regal manner. Although she may not have possessed Lysandra's singular beauty—to be fair, she had to be over a hundred—neither was she plain, with her black hair plaited and pinned atop her head and dark almond eyes with lids bearing chic lines and hues reflecting a popular style.

"I am so pleased to meet the nature speaker in charge of saving our precious animals from the looming deluge," she stated in a genuine tone.

"The pleasure is mine," Ariel replied. She'd never met a ruler of Atlantis in person before—well, except for Temen. She briefly wondered how he was doing and if he'd make it back before there was nothing to come back to.

The group chatted away happily as they indulged in a sumptuous three-course dinner reminiscent of a holiday feast. They shared humorous stories from their pasts, laughing and enjoying their wine as if they hadn't a care in the world. After the dessert was served and the dishes cleared away, Thoth stood to address the gathering. A hush fell over the yard such that even the birds quieted, and squirrels and monkeys sat still on their branches. Deciding dinner was over, Ratiki padded off in search of something interesting while the people talked.

"Thank you all for being here today," Thoth began in a robust voice so everyone could hear him speak. "I'm sure by now you know about our neighbor Ryzen's failure in their attempt to reconquer Pelasgoí. While Queen Zamná and the other rulers don't condone King Temen's course of action, they understand his desire to secure a safe, suitable place for his people to live, as they wish to do for all Atlanteans. You who have gathered here, along with other relatives not in attendance, have volunteered to wait until the Terrible Ice breaks and ride aboard Noah's arks to safeguard the seeds and animals until the waters have receded and dry land is found. It is of the utmost importance to protect every species going forward. Today we need to decide who will occupy each of the five arks to ensure a suitable mix of abilities and genders on each."

An urgency chewed at Ariel's gut, and she was about to say something when Noah stood from two tables over and angled himself toward Thoth. "I can't guarantee the fifth ark will be finished in time." He motioned toward the colossal vessels. "Birds have already built nests on the upper decks and wild beasts gather at the edge of the woods when Ariel hasn't even called them yet."

With Noah breaking the ice, issuing concerns, Ariel pushed up from her chair. "The Oldest Tree said she senses the changes intensifying rapidly and other animals feel them as well."

Noah nodded to her over his shoulder before continuing. "I propose we select passengers and caretakers for the four completed arks while continuing to build *Jegudiel* as a safety net for stragglers and deluge deniers who rush to us when the flood waters come. Even in its current condition, it should float."

Ziusudra strolled up beside Thoth. "When I look to the stars, I still see signs of my earlier prediction," he stated. "We should have until next summer's solstice."

"Yes, the moon and stars influence happenings on Earth," Mandisa added, though without moving from her seat. "However, our sun produces the most potent impact, and this summer has been the hottest yet. I agree with Ariel and Noah. We must be ready at any moment."

"Certainly, any prediction can be flawed," Ziusudra admitted. "Queen Zamná, what is your council on the matter?"

Ariel returned to her chair as the queen glided to her feet. "Four rulers of Atlantis have already taken their families to safety in one of our colonies abroad. Temen is in captivity awaiting his ransom to be paid, while the remaining five—myself included—intend to board the arks after as many of our citizens have left as wished to. It has long been my policy that, if I must err, it should be on the side of caution. Therefore, I must agree with Noah, my chief shipbuilder, and a most wise elder. We should prepare our places on the crafts that are ready now. If the last one is finished in time, all the better, but we simply can't presume."

Upon concluding her statement, the regal woman sat back down beside Quetzal.

Thoth's gaze followed her to him. "Quetzal?" he asked.

"I've walked around inside them," he called out. "There's plenty of room in the passenger quarters for twenty or more people to have space for comfort—thirty if cramped—and Noah and his family have filled each with food Ariel and Ériu helped secure. Let's just divide into four groups, like they said."

Ariel glanced around to see Ériu and her clan, who took up an entire long table, nod in agreement.

"Very well," Thoth concurred and inclined his head. "Each ark needs a nature speaker, an air speaker, and a healer for certain. Would all the nature speakers please stand?"

It was fortunate they decided to only outfit four ships today, as there were only four nature speakers present: Ariel, Balam, Hypatia—an older woman from Autopolis whom Ariel had met before—and a younger woman from Noah's table, whom she supposed to be Shem's wife Nahalath. If the demure brunette was pregnant, she wasn't showing yet.

"Noah?" Thoth inquired. "I presume you wish Nahalath to be on your vessel. Since you built them, which one do you call yours?"

"*Uriel*," he answered. "Ark One, bobbing in the harbor there with the long gangplank."

They assigned those with talents and special skills or knowledge to the different arks so that all had an eclectic arrangement of caretakers. Noah and his three sons led the four teams onto their respective vessels and showed them around. They were instructed each could start stowing their belongings in a storeroom beside the passenger quarters but were required to travel as light as they could.

Lysandra took Ariel's arm as they walked behind Shem, Noah's middle son—a rugged fellow with sandy hair—up a broad ramp into the belly of *Michael*, Ark Two. He pointed out the privies, lift, and staircase, and took them up top where there was an open portion of the deck for getting fresh air. Indeed, birds had taken over about half of the available spots. Then Shem showed them the human quarters on the middle deck, which consisted of a common area with a kitchen and seating, and four semi-private sleeping nooks equipped with hammocks and bunks.

Ariel had told Thoth that six family members were joining her, as her uncle, aunt, and young cousin had left a week ago for Melitē in the Green Sea, where many of their friends had moved. He paired them with Ériu's group of six, Khafra the air speaker, and King Masadu of Gadlan and his three family members. She had hoped Mandisa and Quetzal would be with Lysandra and her, but they had to spread their chosen gifted leaders among the arks plus balance out the numbers of relatives and rulers. Ariel hoped they ended up landing near each other; it could happen.

"Well, now, who'll be taking charge of *Michael* here once we're all adrift in the ocean?" Banba stood in the middle of the common room with fists on her hips. The tall, slender woman wore a summer-green tunic that brought out the hue of her keen eyes. She resembled her younger sister Ériu, except her long wavy tresses were a golden blonde instead of ginger red and her smooth, ivory skin was void of endearing freckles. Every measure of her person projected strength, confidence, and an aspect of command.

Ratiki, who had been quietly trailing Ariel since they left the eating area, stepped forward, nose first, to inspect the new human acquaintance. While others stepped aside, the formidable Banba held her ground, presenting the raccoon with a challenging stare. He raised up and gave her a friendly wave.

With her stance set, the woman didn't budge. In fact, none of the new people crouched to beckon him or extend him any affection.

I don't think they like me, he sulked and waddled back to squeeze between Ariel and Lysandra's legs. Ariel sent him consolatory vibrations and counseled that now was not the time.

Céthur shrugged and raked thick fingers through his acorn hair. "My guess is, that would be you."

Ériu laughed while her other sister, Fótla, sucked in a breath and nodded. She twirled her fawn hair nervously around a finger and stared at the knotted wood planks. "While I've trained a bit as a healer, I'm mostly just a vintner and brewer who enjoys dancing."

Their husbands looked at each other helplessly. "I'm a farmer," Fótla's husband Téthur answered. He was a wiry fellow much smaller than Céthur with cherry-wood-tinted hair tied back in a band. "And Fótla is the best dancer in Elapus, not to mention makes a fine cup."

"I'm a stonemason and builder," replied Banba's more substantial husband, Éthur. "If anything breaks, I'll repair it, but I know nothing about running a ship."

"I assumed Ariel would be in charge since she's bringing all the animals," Banba asserted, cocking her head inquisitively at the nature speaker.

Ariel discerned the noncommittal vibrations in the room—all but Banba's. With a subtle smile, she said, "I'll take on the task of supervising and nurturing the menagerie, confirming their needs are met. Lysandra will oversee diet, nutrition, and daily meditation exercises to ensure we humans remain healthy as long as we're aboard. Ériu will manage her seeds and teach us all as many languages as time allows. Khafra will deal with the sea and winds, so we may avoid violent storms. And I surmise King Masuda is the most experienced leader in dealing with aspects of administration and conflict resolution."

The king took his wife's hand and nodded cordially to Ariel. "I agree to let each person be in charge of his or her area of expertise. Banba, what is your specialty?"

"My wife reads the tarot and served as an Elapus city guardian for twenty-five years rising to the rank of commander," Éthur stated. "Since the sisters' mother passed, she has taken over as the matriarch of their clan. So, I guess you could say she's part prophetess, part warrior, and part boss."

Extending an arm to the side, King Masuda made a modest bow to her. "I don't mind taking a break from bearing the mantle of leadership for a while. There are nearly a thousand residents of Gadlan who refuse to leave, insisting nothing will happen. And while I must admire their sense of rugged individualism, their lives and deaths are a heavy burden to my soul. My wife and sons elected to stay to the end with me while the rest of our family members embarked for Maanu at the beginning of summer. However, Banba, I am at your service should you require my strength, knowledge, or experience."

"Well now, fellows," Banba smirked and flipped a strand of her hair back. "I ne'er thought I'd see the day when so many powerful folk would lay their authority at my feet. I dare say so small a group won't even require a leader and I wasn't fishing for a crown—nor would I accept one. But King Masuda, if you wish to take a sabbatical, I certainly understand. One of our young'uns was being a might bit stubborn about leaving himself."

"How did you convince him?" asked Masuda's wife, whose name Ariel hadn't caught.

Humor played over Banba's expression, and she shifted her arms to wave expressively. "I got him thoroughly drunk and told his husband and sister to carry him onto the transport. Off they sailed, and he didn't wake up for two days. By then, there was no turning back."

Everyone laughed at her story. Ariel would have liked to visit longer, but she had to excuse herself to finish loading the fish, bugs, and frogs. Once they were all safely stowed on the arks, she gathered the nature speakers and healers to discuss the care of the creatures. Lysandra had already taught them how to make the sleeping potion.

It was late when Ariel and Lysandra returned to *Ark Michael* to find it placid and void of occupants. Like its namesake, the sturdy planks emanated a sense of protection that set Ariel at ease.

"Shall we enjoy our first night in our new home-away-from-home?" Lysandra asked.

Ariel's eyes sparkled at her. "I will certainly enjoy the privacy." For the first time in weeks, her mouth demanded Lysandra's in a passionate kiss of reunion and release. Allowing her hands to roam where they may, she delighted in her wife's nearness, her taste, her touch, and lingered in her embrace until need swelled like a surge of the sea.

"Shall we claim a bunk for the night?" she murmured, her voice husky and low.

"*You* may claim a bunk," Lysandra teased with a gleeful gleam in her gaze. She tangled her fingers in the front of Ariel's tunic. "And *I* will lay claim to every bit of you." One kiss led to another as they shuffled their way toward the nearest sleeping spot, and Lysandra's tone turned ardent. "I missed you, Ariel, and am so relieved and grateful to have you back with me where you belong."

"I'm here, my darling," Ariel breathed. "And we'll stay together for the duration."

48

Ryzen, the month of Virgo, one week before the fall equinox

Lykos stood at the Ryzen dock office wrapped in an oiled cloak, while the wind gusted and torrents of rain fell in sheets. Palm trees outside the window bowed their heads to the sandy shore as the power of nature roared. He regretted having forced Mandisa to leave. *Was she protecting us from this all along, or have the storms merely grown worse as the time of cataclysm nears?*

He didn't have an answer. Lykos had tried to ward off the hurricane himself, but, regrettably, his mesmerism and powers of suggestion didn't extend to the winds and waves that thrashed wooden crates, barrels, and small crafts about outside the secure structure while an ominous howl whistled through the windows.

Four soaking wet Ryzen Defenders draped in short, red capes set down trunks laden with a substantial treasure while two more stood by armed with spears. Lykos had received the ransom demand at last, but, because of the approaching weather, the envoy from Pelasgoí had departed right away to the south, not waiting to receive the payment. "Send your own ship," he had snarled.

"We won't be able to launch until this storm has subsided," declared Captain Jabari.

"I can see," Lykos grumbled. "It should be past us by this time tomorrow. You were wise to anchor our ships farther out in the bay where they wouldn't get smashed."

Startled by a crash, the dock sergeant turned to see a red roof tile shatter into pieces on the paving stones outside the partially open door. "Is this it?" he asked with grimaced lips and bulging eyes. "I planned to leave with the next transport, but I'm too late. Heavens help us!"

"No, man," Lykos rebuked him. "This is a normal storm, not the predicted flood." Though it was bad enough. "Jabari, can you secure a trustworthy captain and vessel to convey this hoard of silver, gold, and orichalcum to King Temen's captors as soon as it's safe? These brave volunteers will protect the ransom from pirates. I want you to stay and captain the king's craft when we depart for Ur." He had discovered Ur in the Valley of the Two Rivers beyond Phoenicia and found it promising. Rhoxane was agreeable to the location and Agriculture Minister Kishar planned to accompany them when they left. "Bring your family and settle there too, my friend."

Captain Jabari gave a slight bow. "I would be honored to serve you and the king and queen in the land of Ur; however, I don't know the language."

"Two delegations from Ryzen have already arrived there," Lykos related, "including Minister Ofira. I received a telepathic message from my fellow wisdom master Nikanor that the land flows with milk and honey and is sparsely populated by nomads. We shall build our own city and keep our language."

"I wish to come!" shouted the dock sergeant over the thunderous wind and driving rain. The twiggy, younger man peered hopefully at Lykos. "Let us send off this ransom and then sail for the new land."

Lykos shook his head. "We must wait until King Temen's return, if possible. The astronomers agree we should have until next summer's solstice." Though Lykos wasn't convinced of the prediction. He didn't have a better one, but he had experienced troubling dreams and noticed a more pronounced fading of the energies. Last week, his powers of persuasion hadn't even worked on an uneducated palace servant. Then there had been the birds flying north when they shouldn't have been, with autumn approaching. Grateful for receiving Nikanor's message, he feared it could be the last report he'd hear from a distance. Long had he dreaded this moment. If only things had worked as he had planned.

"Courageous Defenders," Lykos addressed the guards. "Watch over these treasure chests and guard them with your lives. As soon as the weather clears, load them onto the proper ship, and bring back King Temen safely." He realized he had used Temen as a pawn in his scheme, and yet he honestly cared about him. They could work out something where Rhoxane was concerned, and it's not like he had meant for any harm to come to Temen. He had given the man everything he ever desired, hadn't he?

The guards snapped to attention and saluted. Lykos nodded. "Well, gentlemen, I must brave the elements and return to the palace. Queen Rhoxane is likely to be anxious about the tropical storm."

"I'll secure the best ship and captain remaining," Jabari promised. "Be careful a tree doesn't blow down on you as you return."

"I will." Lykos took one last glance at the men who had vowed to ride out the squall in the security of this stone structure. If the tidal surge wasn't too high, they'd be safe here and so would the ransom. At least Lykos was assured no thieves would be out in this weather. Thieves. There never used to be thieves. He popped the hood of his cloak over his head, pulled it tighter around his tunic, and took off into the torrent.

⚤ ☬ ✟ ✡

Lykos unlatched the heavy oak door, and the gale blew it wide as if it were a leaf of parchment. Employing his substantial might, he forced it closed, dropping a puddle of water inside the threshold. Eshkar rushed in with a mop and dry towel, which Lykos traded for his dripping cloak.

"Thank you, Eshkar. Has the palace sustained any damage or leaks?" He toweled himself, deciding he would need to change clothes before going to talk to Rhoxane. Lykos had jogged through the sideways driving rain to and from the dock office because it wasn't safe to operate a sleigh in the squall. He had passed downed trees and smashed roofs. Wooden sheds and the few market carts that remained in the city had blown away, shattered into stone walls, or strewn about in pieces like leaves. Residents of Ryzen had departed in droves once word of Temen's defeat reached them, and Lykos could hardly blame them.

"The palace is secure, my lord," the servant assured him. Glancing around, Lykos noticed how empty the royal residence seemed. His footsteps and their voices echoed around the chamber walls and the high ceilings.

"Who remains here?" Lykos had been so busy with other matters that he hadn't noticed the shrinking staff.

"Sarah—Queen Rhoxane's handmaiden—Ahkin the cook, two guards, and me," Eshkar replied.

Lykos nodded. "Tomorrow, the ransom leaves for Pelasgoí, which means King Temen should be back in about two weeks. Be ready to depart by then. Do you wish to accompany us to Ur, and do you have relatives or friends to bring?"

"I have nobody," he answered. "Well, that hasn't already left or doesn't wish to. Ur is as good a place as any that isn't Atlantis, I suppose."

"Very well. Please inform Ahkin and the guards. The queen and I would like our dinners in two turns of the sandglass."

"Yes. I'll see to that."

Lykos started across the hall, then turned back with a considering gaze at Eshkar, who was mopping the puddle by the door. "Eshkar," he addressed, drawing the attention of the tubby yet reliable man. "You have served Ryzen well and I'm pleased to have you accompany us to our new home."

"Thank you, my lord." Eshkar's smile beamed as if he had just been awarded the top prize at the summer games, and Lykos supposed it was the first time he had praised the man. But he had stayed when almost everyone else had gone, so he deserved it.

Lykos went straight to his chamber and changed into a black and white garment with sharp, geometrical lines tied with a red sash. He ran a comb through his salt and pepper hair and neat chin beard, studying himself in the reflecting glass. He had considered taking a bath since he was already wet but didn't want to wait for the water to heat. The sounds of the howling wind were barely noticeable inside the secure palace, though a glance out his window reminded him of the savage storm. *How does Mandisa do it?*

Satisfied with his appearance, Lykos set down his comb and walked around the hallway to Rhoxane's proper chamber entrance. He rapped a whimsical knock rhythm and waited.

"Come in," Rhoxane called, and he was happy to do so.

Sarah stood behind the queen, brushing her long, silky brunette strands that shone like a polished onyx gem. "Good afternoon, Minister Lykos," she addressed. "Has my husband's ransom been secured and sent?"

"Secured, my lady, but not sent until the weather lifts," he answered formally.

"Thank you, Sarah, that will be all," Rhoxane dismissed.

"Yes, my lady."

When she moved to pass Lykos, he stopped her. "Sarah, we will all be leaving the palace as soon as the king returns. Do you wish to travel with us to start over in the Valley of the Two Rivers across the Green Sea, and do you have relatives who wish to go with you?"

The young woman with honey hair blinked incredibly big blue eyes at him. "My sister is still in the city. My parents have gone to Melitē and my grandparents refuse to leave. I don't have a sweetheart, I'm afraid. But—" She bit her lower lip and glanced over her shoulder at Rhoxane.

"I'd love for you to stay with me," the queen answered her unspoken question.

Peering up at Lykos, Sarah smiled. "Yes, please. Thank you. I'll tell my sister to get ready."

"Have her move into the palace," Lykos commanded. "It's almost empty."

Beaming, Sarah scurried off and Lykos closed the door. Rhoxane's eyes danced at him, and her lips curved in a playful smirk. "You act like nobody knows about us, my love, when the truth is they always have. Neither Sarah nor Eshkar would dare utter a word, but they aren't blind, and I truly don't think they care."

"Still, I shan't have your reputation tarnished, especially with all the work you've put forth to save our citizens. In a matter of weeks, you've pulled off a miracle, Rhoxane," he said in sincere admiration. "More than half our residents have reached their destinations safely, and most without overly complaining. When I picked you to be Temen's wife, I had no idea what a fabulous ruler you would make on your own merit."

She rose from the chair at her dressing table as Lykos crossed the room to place a kiss on her lips.

"I knew about you since I was in primary school—Lykos the astronomer, Lykos the alchemist, Lykos the wisdom teacher."

This time, he took her in his arms and kissed her deeply, with heat radiating through his body. He brushed back a strand of her luxurious hair and cupped her cheek with his palms. "Tell me how you do it, please? I would find you the most amazing woman even if you looked like a crone, but, honestly, your parents were far too critical. The glimpse I saw of your face wasn't the one I'm accustomed to, but it wasn't unattractive either."

"You want to know, do you?" she teased seductively, fingering the collar of his tunic. "How about tit for tat? You teach me something new, and I'll return the favor."

Lykos never grinned, but, at her suggestion, he couldn't help himself. He slid his hands down her body to land on her hips while he thought of a response. "Are we talking energy magic or ...?" His grip roamed to her buttocks, and he squeezed the delectable flesh through the fabric of her gown.

Rhoxane laughed, flopped her forehead to his shoulder, and shook her head. When she looked up at him, her cheeks were flush, and tiny tears squirted from the corners of her eyes. It took her a moment to catch her breath. Lykos hadn't thought his suggestion had been that funny.

"You?" she uttered, visibly trying to rein in her reaction. "Teach me something about lovemaking? Something I don't already know?"

Lykos drew his lips and brows together in dissatisfaction. "It could happen," he huffed, pulling his hands away. Rhoxane grabbed them at once and slapped them back onto her body.

"I'm sorry, Lykos. I didn't mean to offend you. You are so much more creative than poor, sweet, clueless Temen. Now, where were we?"

Lykos would have given up all his secrets to learn Rhoxane's true feelings for him—something that might never happen. "You were about to tell me how you change your appearance."

"Yes, right." Hilarity back in its box, Rhoxane slipped from his grasp and paced her bedchamber while her nervous fingers wound about each other. "I started when I was about fourteen or fifteen years old. Nobody taught me," she explained. "One day I peered in the reflection glass and pictured how I wished to look. Day after day, week after week, I continued to only see myself the way I wanted to appear—smooth, flawless skin, perfectly proportioned cheekbones, nose, chin, and lips. I would close my eyes and imagine my shiny, dark hair and sensuous curves to my breasts and hips. I dreamed—both awake and asleep—that everyone turned to look at me with appreciation in their gazes. With my new self-image, I began to carry myself differently, with more confidence and grace, like I imagined a beautiful woman would. Each morning, I went to the reflection glass and focused on my new aspect until it was all I saw before leaving my room. Soon my parents noticed, and people complimented me for my beauty." She shrugged and turned to lock gazes with Lykos. "After a while, I didn't even have to concentrate on creating my look; it just came naturally."

She took timid steps toward him with a hesitant expression, drawing her folded hands up to her chest. "Only when I'm overly emotional or my attention is too intense on something else does the illusion waver, and, in the past ten years, it's been rare. I don't even think about it anymore, really."

"It isn't an illusion," Lykos declared and reached for her. She sighed and leaned into his embrace. Running his fingers through her hair, he said, "Each person is who he or she believes they are, and all manifestation begins in the imagination. You saw yourself as beautiful; therefore, the rest of the world saw you the same way. We all create our realities, at least in the way we view ourselves, others, and the world around us. If I could, I would imagine we were back in the days of old, during the Second Age, when Atlantis was at its zenith. Everyone would live a thousand years, aging slowly and in good health. We would all be able to move objects with our minds, talk at a distance, self-heal, influence the weather, and talk to animals. We would lie down, close our eyes, and traverse the stars while our bodies rested. We could walk on water or through fire, commune with angels, and converse with our ancestors. The Law would rule each person's heart, and no one would contend with his neighbor."

Stroking her back, Lykos brushed kisses to Rhoxane's brow, cheeks, nose, chin, and lips. "You are not only beautiful but also clever and talented."

"And you are wise and skilled at getting your way," she replied with one eyebrow raised, as if suspicious of his praise.

Lykos shook his head and lowered it to rest against hers. "I've always believed that The Law was only for our people, that Atlanteans were the true children of God, heirs to eternal life, and other races were something less. After all, they couldn't do what our ancestors could, or even what we can today. We live twice or more as long and many with gifts are still born among us. I truly believed we were the chosen ones in all the universe, but now ..." Weary, his voice trailed off and he pressed his cheek to Rhoxane's, letting out a long, somber sigh.

"You can read the stars, Lykos, but you can't control their movements," her consoling tone murmured in his ear. "Gaia is a living, breathing entity, not a dead rock. She moves and grows, shifts and changes. Mountains rise and continents fall. One species wanes while another thrives. It's just the way things are." She leaned back, bringing her arms around his neck, and brushed a kiss to his lips. Pinning him with an intrepid gaze, Rhoxane stated, "You interpreted the signs, tried to secure us the best alternate place to live, and who knows? Maybe Ur will be even better than Pelasgoí. In your zeal, you may have bent The Law and Rules, but you didn't break them. Atlanteans *are* the children of God. It's just ... maybe everyone else is too."

49

Ariel's farm, three days before the fall equinox

Sunshine beamed from the east over the distant treetops, grazing meadows, fields of grain, and the little hill behind Ariel's house on a beautiful late summer morning without a cloud in the sky. With Lysandra, Oma, Nymphe, and Mandisa by her side, Ariel felt a deep sense of contentment and tranquility as they harvested vegetables from the garden before the day grew hot.

Oma hummed an old, popular tune while Ratiki busied his paws digging feverishly in the tilled soil. "Stop it, Ratiki," Ariel rebuked him lightly. "You'll disturb the roots."

I'm helping, he replied in his defense. *There's something down there—a mole or big bugs, one of those with all the legs, or maybe digging crickets. I can hear them and smell them down there. They're the ones hurting the roots. I'm saving the vegetables!*

Ariel gave him a sideways, suspicious look. "Uh huh. Just be careful, please. You like peas, so if you ruin them—"

I won't ruin them! He flashed her an offended gaze that made everyone laugh. Burrowing with his nibble fingers, Ratiki pulled out a wiggly grub. *See?* He held it up and waved it around before shoveling it into his mouth.

"What a delightful animal friend," Nymphe cooed as she carefully laid lettuce leaves atop summer squash in her basket.

"Delightful and pesty!" Ariel smirked at Ratiki, who chewed and blinked innocent eyes at her.

"He's inquisitive and quite adept at opening drawers, trunks, cabinets, and anything with a lid," Lysandra supplied.

"He reminds me of Ariel when she was three or four," Oma added with a wink before shuffling over to the tomatoes. She plucked a fat, juicy, green caterpillar as big as a mouse from a half-eaten plant and scowled at it. "Ariel, you didn't include tomato hornworms in your collection to save, did you?"

"Of course, Oma," Ariel replied, horrified her great-great-great-grandmother would suggest such a thing. "They transform into beautiful moths and are an important part of the food chain. I've stored them in their cocoons, and the moths won't emerge until early next summer."

"Well, since the species is safe ... Ratiki, do you want this?" She dangled the engorged larva out between her thumb and forefinger, offering it to him. He bounded over and examined it before accepting the treat and running off to play with it—maybe eat it too.

Everyone laughed again, and Ariel shook her head with an amused expression. As the sun sparkled off the dew, a gentle breeze carried the enticing scent of celery and peppers, delighting Ariel in the simple pleasure. She rocked off her heels to sit on the ground momentarily, her knees drawn up under her arms, to close her eyes and breathe with appreciation. A bumblebee hovered close, defying physics just to remind her that anything was possible. A robin and cardinal in a nearby shade tree competed to see whose song was the most beautiful, and people she loved surrounded her.

As she relaxed in wonder and gratitude, connecting with the plants and animals with whom she shared the garden, Ariel experienced a sudden pang of alarm. Her eyes shot open, and she glanced around. Everything appeared as it should.

"Mandisa, did you feel something?" she asked in a tense voice. The women stopped picking vegetables and opened their awarenesses. Mandisa sunk her fingers into the soil, turned her face to the sun, and closed her eyes. Oma stretched, retrieved her basket, and meandered toward the house with a resigned sigh.

"What is it?" Lysandra's hand gripped Ariel's arm with concern.

"I could be," Mandisa answered after a moment and locked eyes with Ariel. "I want confirmation, though."

"Confirmation for what?" Nymphe asked, passing a nervous gaze between the older women. "What's happening?"

"As do I," Ariel concurred, ignoring Nymphe. She suspected Oma's reaction had been all the confirmation she needed. "Oma, where are you going?"

"To put my travel bag into the sleigh. We're bringing all these nice vegetables with us. Lysandra, dear, go tell Yaluk and Aram it's time."

Ariel pushed up and spread her palms skyward, sending a call for the albatross she had spoken with four years ago. She couldn't be certain if he was still alive, if he was nearby, or if he would even hear or respond to her.

"The Terrible Ice?" Lysandra's voice tightened and Ariel felt tense vibrations coming from her.

"We think so," Mandisa said in a small voice. She pulled a few more turnips and potatoes and squared her shoulders. "I sensed a tremor in the earth, but I would need to touch the ocean to be sure. There could be an earthquake in the far distance, or an underwater volcano disturbing Gaia; I can't be certain from here and we're nowhere near the sea."

"Isn't it too early?" Hope lingered in Lysandra's question, but Ariel had talked with her about her suspicions. When no one responded, she slumped her shoulders and set down her basket. "I'll go tell Yaluk and Aram."

"Wait." Ariel was making contact with the large aquatic bird. "Look at the Terrible Ice," she instructed from her trance as her farm faded from her awareness. "Do you see a crack? Is there water coming through?"

☥ ☱ ☩ ✡

While Ariel tried to communicate with a distant albatross, Lysandra felt a prick in her own intuitive nature, as though Quetzal was reaching out to her like they had practiced decades ago in wisdom school. She relaxed and allowed his energy to wash through her. It was a salty, white-capped, crashing wave of warning, and she knew.

"The crack in the ice," she uttered at the same time Ariel did. Pulling out of their altered states, the two stared at each other as they processed the warning. This is what they had been working toward for four years—this very moment—yet now that it was here, it seemed unreal.

"Now? Already?" Nymphe's frantic words came out an octave too high, and she shot up from her station in the beans. Even Ratiki came running at all the nervous energy flying around the garden.

"I'll get Agathon and Hashur," Mandisa said. "We'll accompany you to the Ring of Stones."

Ariel nodded, then clasped Lysandra's hands. "Tell my brother to take his family to *Ark Michael* and get settled in now. Noah will know. We'll go call the animals and once I'm sure they're on their way, we'll join them."

Lysandra hugged her fiercely, trepidation growing in her belly. This was it—the beginning of the end. Images of giant waves overturning and sinking ships popped into her imagination and she had to drive them away. *No, not the arks. They are too big and specially designed to remain upright and afloat.*

She swallowed and relinquished her hold on Ariel. "I'll tell them to be gone within the hour. Everything will work just as we have planned." The words of encouragement were as much for herself as for Ariel.

Nymphe's face paled, and her chin dropped. "Mal'akhi! I have to tell him."

"We will," Ariel assured her. "We have a few days before the great northern sea breaks through, and I'm certain word of the crack will spread quickly. Don't worry, Nymphe; I'm not leaving my son behind."

Lysandra knocked at her cousin's door as she struggled to tamp down the rising flood of dread inside. Aram answered with a broad smile and his hands stained orange from working pottery clay. "Good morning, Lysandra," he chirped. Upon seeing her trepidation, his cheery countenance fell. "What's wrong?"

"It's time to go. Where are Yaluk and Shemu'el?"

He pressed his lips together and nodded. "They're in the barn milking the cow and goats. Is Oma going with you all?"

"Yes. She's going to help Ariel call the animals and we'll probably get to the ark tomorrow, but don't wait, Aram. I'll go tell them."

He nodded, then pulled her into a firm hug. "Into the unknown, hey? It'll be an adventure."

"You are amazing, you know that?" Lysandra gave him a squeeze around the ribs before letting go.

The barn door stood open, letting the light and fresh air stream in. Shemu'el would be in his last term at the Elyrna Secondary Academy if it hadn't closed a year ago. Trying to make up for lost time, Lysandra had devoted many hours to Yaluk and her sons and knew Shemu'el grew more restless and bored with each friend who moved away.

"Look, you silly goat," Shemu'el groaned while the buff and brown goat danced and kicked at the bucket. "Be still, or I'll roast you for dinner!"

"Don't threaten poor Zoe," Yaluk demanded as she squirted streams of milk from the cooperative Leah, a black and white spotted milk cow, into her pail. "She'd be still if you'd put a pan of cut apple in front of her."

"I shouldn't have to bribe the ornery nanny just to do her job." The sandy-haired young man glared at Zoe. He had grown so much since Lysandra arrived and now stood taller than his mother—when he was standing. Squatting on his stool with irritation radiating from him, he reminded her of a small child who was tired of being teased. She had also noticed how the changes had affected his demeanor as he had transformed from a happy-go-lucky lad to the image of a sulky teen Hevel had been when he was this age.

"Yaluk, Shemu'el?" Lysandra hated to intrude on them, knowing Shemu'el would be embarrassed she had witnessed this side of him.

Yaluk glanced up. "Oh, good morning, Sandy," she bade, using her childhood nickname. "It's a lovely day, isn't it?"

Shemu'el hunched over his bucket, trying to settle his goat. Hopefully, he threw out, "Is there something you need me to do, Aunt Lysandra?"

"Yeah, sweetie." The words dropped from her lips in disappointment. She had enjoyed living at the farm with Ariel and reuniting with her only remaining family. Sometimes she could kick herself for not reaching out sooner. *Why had I been so afraid? The world as we know it wouldn't have ended.* Now it would.

Her nephew twisted his head over his shoulder with a questioning expression. "You can pack up your sleigh and go to the ark now," she said.

Leaping from his stool, Shemu'el grabbed Zoe's lead rope and reached a shaky hand to stroke her head, ears, and beneath her horns. "What about our animals?"

"We talked about that," Yaluk reminded him. "We're cleared to bring the cats, a milk cow, three hens, and a rooster, and a buck and two does from the goats. Noah said we need to have extra domestic animals and a few others are bringing theirs as well."

"Yes, but—" He lowered his gaze to Zoe who danced on his feet. "Ouch," he muttered in a hush. "My trunk is packed, so I'll get Leah, Zoe, and the others we decided on loaded onto our livestock sled. Have fun managing your cats." He rolled his eyes, trying humor to relieve the tension.

"Your dada built a travel cage for them," Yaluk said. She rose from her stool with the bucket in her hand. "It's really time? I didn't feel anything, and it's such a beautiful day."

Lysandra's nod was grave. "It's time. We're off to call the animals and will meet you tomorrow. Quetzal said we only have three days, so leave now. There's still much to do when you get to Diaprep."

"We will."

Lysandra met her cousin halfway and hugged her with as much emotion as when she had first offered her apologies for ignoring her for decades. "Everything will work out," she promised. "We're under Archangel Michael's protection, after all."

"We'll be waiting when you get there," Yaluk avowed. "Don't be late this time."

With a laugh, Lysandra pulled away and fingered a tear out from under her eye. "I promise not to take thirty years."

50

Lysandra stood with Hashur, Agathon, and Nymphe as they leaned against a monolithic stone facing the trio of women who sat holding hands in the center of the observatory. They had left a pesky raccoon climbing all over the luggage in the sleigh, no doubt trying to open latches to see what was inside. *As long as it keeps him busy and he doesn't bother Ariel*, Lysandra thought.

They had packed her art supplies and dozens of blank canvases in case there were none where they landed. Oma and Ariel arranged all the fresh produce into crates and barrels to eat before starting in on the preserves and grains. Lysandra had comforted Ariel when she gazed longingly over her almost ripe fields of barley. They had already sent loads of dry corn south to store onboard, but most of this year's crop would be swept away with the houses, barns, trees, and—*Adira*.

The thought of her elephant friend pricked Lysandra's heart with an inconsolable pain. She had brought her portrait, and her daughters stood by, waiting to be called, but she'd never see the old matron who elected to stay behind again.

Lysandra knew she should push such anguish from her mind and soul. There was nothing wrong with feeling honest emotions; it was part of the human experience. To not express sorrow meant one didn't care, and Lysandra cared very much about losing her home and the people and animals she loved. Quetzal, Mandisa, and Raffi would be safe, only not necessarily in the same part of the world as she and Ariel. Her friend Helene and her husband were probably still engaged in ferrying folks from Atala to ports in the Green Sea, though she wasn't sure. *Helene's husband has a ship; they'll be all right.* There would be time enough to worry and grieve when they were drifting about at sea. Right now, Ariel needed to be surrounded by high vibrations to broadcast her message.

"How do they do it?" Nymphe whispered, her youthful face beseeching Lysandra. Gazing at the gifted women, she wondered the same thing.

In a hush, she replied, "I have a talent for healing. I can easily find the right frequencies to repair what's wrong with people's bodies. Ariel has accessed the ether waves sent out by plants and animals since she was a child and can interpret their meaning, while Mandisa does the same with water, air, and earth—maybe a little fire; I'm not sure. Everything in creation has a vibration; it's just most people are no longer aware of them."

The young bride with the golden hair leaned against her, likely seeking comfort. "I wish I had a special ability," she murmured.

Lysandra put a motherly arm around Nymphe. "You do. You make Mal'akhi happy. Have you any idea what a challenge that presents?"

Nymphe giggled, nestling into Lysandra's shoulder. "We make each *other* happy."

Returning her attention to the circle, Lysandra listened to their low chants and hums and sensed the stone at her back vibrate. Though she couldn't make out words, she felt a powerful burst of energy radiating from the talented trio, amplified by the Ring of Stones. Overhead, a flock of ducks changed direction and veered south. Deer, gazelles, wildebeests, and wild horses raced across the meadow. It had begun.

☥ ⚛ ☩ ✡

Ariel reached for specific creatures she had talked to on her travels—Moonshadow, the black jaguar, Ixquic, the matron alligator, the mother bear, the sloth, the monkeys, and Adira. She knew her friend wouldn't come, but she still wanted to touch hearts with her one last time. The surge of warmth that struck her boosted Ariel's energy as she radiated the call. The four pairs of animals chosen—a few by her, most by their societies—should hurry to Diaprep to board the arks. *This is the time. Come,* she broadcast. *Come now.*

This feat was only made possible by Oma and Mandisa lending their energy to hers, giving her reserves to draw from, and adding their spirit voices to the chorus. The high she experienced was unlike any Ariel had known, and she wondered if this was how Lysandra felt engaged in her exercises at wisdom school. She lost all attachment to her body, exchanging it for a rushing stream in the ether, vibrations forking out like the roots of a mighty tree to reach the beasts being called. In her mind's eye, she saw each one as it leaped up from its rest and raced toward the staging area. She perceived some were already there, waiting for her to guide them into the bellies of the monstrous ships, where they would be conveyed from death to life over tumultuous waves.

In her transcendent state, Ariel perceived stars racing by and saw visions, unsure if they were of the past, future, or simply another place. A profound sense of love enveloped her as her consciousness became unmistakably and intimately connected to everything. Mandisa and Oma, the earth and the sky, were all part of her, and she was part of them, like ingredients in a recipe that were both themselves and fractions of the whole. This was the divine One, Creator and Creation, unrestricted by time and space, that simply was. It was glorious, and she never wanted the flow to end.

Then Lysandra sat over her with her hands on her face and words coming from her mouth. "Sweetheart, are you all right?"

As Ariel blinked, trying to focus blurry vision, she realized she was lying sprawled out on the grass. Oma peered over Lysandra's shoulder. "She's fine," she quipped and moved out of Ariel's line of sight. Mandisa took her place.

"That was awesome, Ariel," her friend declared with a grin. "As long as I live, I'll never forget it." Then she too moved aside, leaving her and Lysandra in the center of the observatory.

"I guess I overloaded on energy," Ariel squeaked out. Her mouth felt suddenly dry, and tremors ran through her tingling body in waves. Yep, she was back.

"You were glowing," Lysandra murmured and brushed a kiss to her forehead. "We saw birds and grazing animals take off toward Diaprep. I'm certain you got the message out to them."

Ariel closed her eyes in pure bliss and contentment, relishing the gentle caress of Lysandra's hands on her skin, and smiled.

"You don't have to get up yet," Lysandra's voice purred. "I'm right here with you."

Finding the strength to move one arm, Ariel reached for Lysandra and felt her warm hand clamp around her tingly one. "I love you. I love everything and everyone, but I especially love you, Lysandra. Now I understand how you lost track of time without forgetting me. It was like you were riding the waves with me inside my heart." Her lids fluttered up, and she noticed the sun hung low in the west. "How long have I—"

"Shh, it's all right." Lysandra's lips brushed Ariel's. "The other two woke up long ago, but you exerted the most energy. It's still today, if that's what you mean."

"We've got to get going." Ariel tried to sit up and became light-headed. "In a few minutes."

Oma's face peered down at her again. "We're putting dinner together and will spend the night. There's plenty of time if we get an early start tomorrow." The corners of her eyes crinkled, and Oma crouched down on Ariel's other side. "Thank you, pumpkin, for giving an old woman another ride around the universe." She kissed Ariel's cheek, radiating love and appreciation, before she moved off again.

Ariel lay in the grass holding Lysandra's hand and decided this was the new best day of her life.

☥ ☬ ✛ ✡

The next morning, as they were readying to leave, Ariel found Oma sitting on the running board of her sleigh with her arms crossed over her chest and a defiant look etched into her features. "Come on, Oma," Ariel said, reaching to give her a hand up. "We're going to see Noah and lead the animals into the arks."

A stubborn face peered up at her. "Take me to the Azaes," she demanded. "I want to go to Methuselah's cave."

"Oma, we don't have time for more sightseeing. We're needed at the shipyard. The flood will come any day now." When Ariel took her arm, her oma pulled away and scowled at her.

"If you won't take me, I'll walk." The old woman grabbed the edge of the sleigh and pulled herself up. "I might make it before the ice wall breaks and water swooshes through."

"You're being unreasonable. What's so important about Methuselah's cave all of a sudden?" Ariel didn't have time for this. She needed to get her party to safety, make certain every animal made it onto an ark, and then ensure her son got out of Lycia Landing. But the port was close to the volcanoes, so maybe …

"That's where I'm going to ride out the deluge," she pronounced with her chin held high.

"What?" Ariel grabbed her by the shoulders and stared down at her in disbelief. "No, you're not. I need you. You're coming with us on the ark and that's final."

"Take your hands off!" She wiggled away from Ariel and the others stopped packing and arranging the pull-behind sled, all wearing as astonished expressions as she did. "I was making decisions for myself long before you were born, young lady. You aren't in charge of me."

"Oma." Her great-great-great-grandmother's sincerity struck her like a fist to the gut and anguish swirled over her akin to a coiling python. It was like with Adira, only worse. Surely Ariel could talk some sense into her.

"I'm old, honey, and Noah has a wife and family—Thoth and Ziusudra too," she let out with a sigh. "Atlantis is my home, and I don't want to start over somewhere else. I'm tired and set in my ways, and yesterday, child, you showed me things I used to marvel at when I was young. The feeling called me home—not here, not to the farm, but to my true home. I'm ready to join the ancestors and the angels, to be absorbed back into the One. I don't want to bob around inside a giant box and wash up on some foreign shore where I'll wither with age and ache with pain."

"I won't allow that, Oma," Lysandra promised as she glided to Oma's other side. "I've kept patients healthy who were older than you." Though Ariel couldn't name one. "And my abilities worked fine on the Mayeb."

Oma offered her a bittersweet smile. "Precious Lysandra, so kind and giving, take care of Ariel for me. We can't know if any of you will keep your connections to the energies after another cataclysm. I lost mine over time and you'll be far away from our homeland. The world is shifting and there's no place in it for me. I'm ready to go, my dears. And, besides, Methuselah's cave is high on the eastern volcano's side. It may not even flood up there. What if others who stay behind take refuge in the mountains? What if some survive? Who will look after them? Who will teach them the wisdom? I would rather my body die here while I transition into a spirit and ascend into the cosmos. I've had a wonderful life full of adventure, never shying away from a fresh experience, and loved every minute of it—even the sad or painful ones, because they taught me to have empathy and compassion for others. Now, Ariel, prove to me that you aren't selfish. Extend your love to me by letting me go."

Ariel struggled to breathe as the weight pressing against her chest grew more oppressive. She loved her mother and daughter and daily offered prayers of thanksgiving that they were somewhere safe; at least she could live the rest of her life believing it, even if she never saw them again. But Oma was special, and they shared a unique bond. She touched her palm to Oma's chest to feel her emotions, just to make sure she wasn't afraid of being a burden.

"This is what you really want?" Ariel phrased it as a question, but she could sense the honesty of Oma's words and intentions.

"It is!" Oma seized Ariel in a fierce hug and they both wept as they clung to each other. "You're a big girl now and don't need Oma to teach you anything more. Go, fly the way you were destined to, and allow me to do the same."

Ariel should have suspected this, but she had been blindsided. It was one more heartache that she didn't want to bear. She arrested her thoughts when the "Whys?" began. *Trust*, a voice spoke to her heart in comfort and support. *All is well.*

"I love you, Oma," Ariel declared as warm tears fell. "I'll take you to the Azaes if that's what you truly want."

51

The party took turns hugging Oma and pronouncing blessings over her on the side of the massive volcano. Methuselah's cave was two-thirds of the way up, its broad entrance draped with snow. Agathon and Hashur unloaded her trunk while Mandisa and Nymphe piled baskets of fresh food inside for her. Ariel checked for bears and found none. It was too early for hibernating and there wasn't much for a bear to eat up here, although she came across a few bats.

Mandisa started a fire with some old wood and dead shrubs she found in the cave. Agathon asked, "Where will you get wood to keep your fire going?"

Oma grinned at him and patted his cheek. "I don't think I'll need to worry about that but, if need be, I'll burn my trunk and the crates."

"I brought an ax," Hashur said. "We could fly down the mountain, cut some wood, and bring it back up."

"You are kind, but you all need to hurry now. Old Naunet will be just fine. I can sense Methuselah's presence. He'll keep me company. Besides, I have blankets to stay warm."

Ariel wrapped her arms around the stubborn woman and sighed. "Are you sure you won't change your mind? We—"

"Will be fine without me," Oma declared and stepped back. "I've seen almost everything there is in this world to see. Now I want to see this giant wave you all have been talking about for the past four years. Don't worry, child; I'm not afraid."

"I'm afraid for you," Ariel admitted. "And sad to lose you."

A knowing smile lit Oma's eyes. "You'll never lose me, dear. I'll always be with you," she vowed, pressing her palm to Ariel's chest. "Now, go on," she ordered with a shooing motion. "I wish to meditate."

Ariel rubbed her hand under her eye to wipe away a tear. She hugged and kissed her oma for the last time, then released her into the Creator's hands. "And I'll always be with you."

"I know that, sweetie. Now go."

Without a word, the group of six humans and one raccoon climbed into two sleighs, one pulling a trailing sled, and lifted off the flat spot outside the cave entrance. Mandisa didn't have to tell Ariel it was probably a lava shaft that stretched deep into the earth's crust. If it erupted like it had during the Conflagration, Oma wouldn't drown. Ariel pushed the image away and tried to appreciate the beauty of the trio of white-capped domes and the lush valley surrounding them. Gazing back from the sleigh, they were fantastic to behold, with the ocean wrapped around the triangular peninsula. How many thousands or millions of years had they ruled over the surrounding land? History taught her that Atlantis was once much larger and there were more of them nearer the ocean that now lay underwater. The continent had more resembled a large pear than the elongated string of islands she had known. What would it look like after the deluge?

☥ ☬ ☥ ✡

When only a few leagues from Noah's shipyard, Lysandra's company had to stop in Diaprep to swap out power crystals on the sleighs, finding the city nearly empty. Most of those who remained were filing onto the last transport vessels. The sight of the once vibrant metropolis, now devoid of activity, struck Lysandra as strange and unsettling. Trash littered the streets and decorative plants were either overgrown or wilting for lack of care. The market square was abandoned, and no music played.

"Let's go," Lysandra urged, while Ariel plugged the new crystal into its slot.

"Well, if anyone needs to use a comfort station, this would be the time," Ariel suggested.

Figures a mother would think of that. With an eerie shroud of unease clinging to her, Lysandra opened the door to her side of the vehicle to climb back in, when seemingly, out of nowhere, a gang of four desperate men raced toward them.

"Out of the way!" yelled the first one, wild-eyed with long hair flapping around his shoulders.

"We're taking those sleighs!" shouted the biggest one, a rough-looking fellow who could have made Quetzal seem small.

Lysandra gasped and slammed the door behind her. Little protection *that* would be as the roof was down and the aggressors could easily vault over the side.

Hashur jumped from his sleigh to meet them with determination chiseled into his fair features. Brawny and athletic as he was, Lysandra doubted he could hold off four ruffians while they made their escape. Besides, Mandisa would never leave him behind.

In a blink, all four frantic men were upon them; only Hashur didn't stand alone. Slender, bookish Agathon had armed himself with the axe from the sled and Mandisa and Ariel flanked them on either side, creating a defensive line between the would-be thieves and the sleighs. Ratiki scrambled onto Lysandra's shoulders, grabbing the hair on the top of her head as he raised up to rebuke them. She could picture him baring his teeth—from a safe distance, of course.

Everyone is calling their bluff while I sit here with a raccoon on my head! she thought in disgust at her lack of courage. To be fair, in all her years, Lysandra had never witnessed a violent act. It was shocking and terrifying to see Atlanteans behaving like savages and made her tremble to think of what life in a foreign land would be like—wild, savage, dangerous? Oh, why didn't the ark come with a rudder? If only she could be assured of landing in Giza!

"Back off!" Hashur growled at them. They didn't comply. Lysandra could feel their fear from her seat in the sleigh.

"Diaprep has loaded the last ship!" the smallest of their attackers shrieked.

"There are no more transports, and I must get my wife and child to safety," cried the largest brute. He grabbed hold of Hashur's shoulder. "Step aside and I won't hurt you."

Really, Lysandra groaned to herself. *You didn't think about making plans sooner? No, you wait until the waters are almost here, then turn into a madman.*

"We aren't going anywhere, and you can't have our sleighs," Mandisa declared. "We have families too."

The big man wrenched back a fist and swung it at Hashur, who ducked and followed through with a punch to his attacker's gut. Agathon shook his axe threateningly, though Lysandra doubted it intimidated anyone. The other three rushed at Ariel and their friends.

"Let's help them," Nymphe called as she climbed out of the back seat. "My husband is an Evamont Guardian," she shouted with a surprising measure of authority.

"This isn't Evamont," snapped the long-haired fellow, then he took a swing at Ariel. Lysandra cringed, but her amazing wife blocked the punch and sidestepped his next one so that his fist slammed into the front of the sleigh. "Ow!" he hollered and shook his stinging hand.

Lysandra realized these weren't normally violent men. They didn't even seem to know how to fight. They were just scared and low on options. A crash drew her attention, and she spun her gaze to the man who had assaulted Mandisa. Wearing a stunned expression, he lay in a heap with a toppled bench and a potted palm strewn across him. Mandisa's hands were outstretched, and a blast of wind still curled around them.

She summoned the wind to knock him down! Lysandra surmised. Admiration and no small measure of glee crackled through her, tugging up the corners of her open mouth. Just as Nymphe whirled around to join Ariel, Lysandra spotted a pack of dogs racing down the street. They let out vicious barks that startled the men who attacked them.

"Let's get out of here!" one cried. An instant before the pack was upon them, the four rushed away, taking refuge in a nearby empty building.

The dogs leaped and clawed at the closed door, barking and snarling, completely ignoring her party. Then another wave of wonder hit Lysandra. *Ariel! She called the dogs to defend us.*

Before she had time to comment, Ariel and Nymphe were back in the sleigh, with Mandisa and her husbands clambering into the one behind them. "Let's go!" Mandisa called. Ariel pressed her palm to the copper plate and pulled a lever. They climbed into the air above the despairing scene and sped south toward the shipyard.

Lysandra took a moment to catch her breath while Ariel operated the controls. "Thank the gods you're all right," she said. "Nothing like that's ever happened to me before, and I must admit I was frightened. But you were amazing."

"You really were," Nymphe seconded.

Ariel shrugged. "They were much more scared than we were, and I can hardly blame them. We were supposed to have more time to transport all the people to safety. They only wanted to survive."

"Yes, but they could have simply asked for a ride," Lysandra countered. "They didn't have to go all barbarian on us."

"Is that what people in other parts of the world will be like?" Nymphe queried as she leaned in between them from the back seat. Worry pulled her brows in, and she nibbled her lower lip.

"I don't know," Ariel replied as she steered around a tall grove of treetops. "We aren't responsible for how other people act, only how we respond. I don't wish those men ill, and I hope they can get their families to safety. That doesn't mean I was going to let them steal our sleighs and leave us stranded. The dogs didn't hurt them, just chased them away. Lysandra, Nymphe, it's all right to be afraid; this is a crisis, after all. But we can't let fear control us. Look there," she pointed ahead. Lysandra, who had been watching Ariel, turned her view to the front. The enormous clearing came into sight, dominated by the five arks. They still rested in the same spots as a week ago, only now the surrounding space was filled with bustling activity.

Ariel landed the sleigh at the same time Agathon set Mandisa's down. A slightly older woman trotted over from one direction with Ariel's student Balam and a young woman rushing in from another. Lysandra and Nymphe followed Ariel out of their sleigh to meet them.

"Mandisa," Ariel called. "Meet Balam who will serve as Ark Gabriel's nature speaker."

The eager young man smiled and shook her hand. "Nice to meet you." Then, swinging toward Ariel, he excitedly proclaimed, "The animals are gathering!"

Lysandra had to cover her mouth to hide a hushed laugh at the sarcastic expression Ariel sent him.

"Pleased to meet you," Mandisa returned. "Ariel has had good things to say about you." He blushed and hopped from one foot to the other.

"And this is Shem's wife Nahalath," Ariel continued with the introductions. "I haven't had the pleasure of working with her yet, but Noah assures me she is skilled enough to converse with the animals."

"Yes," she confirmed, shooting Ariel an uncertain glance. "But I'm not so successful with plants."

Ariel rested a hand on her shoulder and smiled. "That's all right, Nahalath. You merely need to reassure the animals and keep them calm. The plants on-board are all seeds who can't communicate yet, anyway."

The pretty young woman smiled back at her in appreciation. "And this is Hypatia from Ampherium who will supervise *Ark Barachiel*. While I wasn't privileged to receive a formal education in a wisdom school, Hypatia taught me much when I was your age, Balam."

Lysandra hadn't met the older nature speaker before. She stood as tall as Ariel with a lean body, but that's where the similarities ended. Her skin was like brushed copper and her black hair cut short. Rich, brown eyes shone from between inky brows and a broad, flat nose.

"I'm ready to do my part," she said, making eye contact with each person in the group.

Ariel sucked in a deep breath and slowly exhaled. "We need to proceed as quickly as possible while keeping an orderly procession. Residents of Diaprep are becoming frantic and order is breaking down. I worry they might descend on us, demanding space onboard the arks."

Nahalath raised a timid hand. "Noah has employed a troop of city guardians to protect us from harm, promising them room on the arks. We wanted to save everyone, but so many didn't take the threat seriously."

"Everyone thought they'd have more time," Hypatia uttered in regret.

Ariel nodded and turned to Lysandra. "Can you get Ratiki and our belongings settled on *Ark Michael*?"

"Certainly," she answered.

"I'll help," Nymphe said.

"Mandisa, Hashur, Agathon," Ariel called their names. "I wish to see you all to bestow upon you blessings before—"

Mandisa stepped forward and took her hands. "There will be time," she promised and kissed Ariel's cheeks. "Bring the animals in."

Ariel returned the kisses and pivoted to her nature-speaking crew. "You heard the boss—let's bring the animals in."

52

Ariel took up her position by the expansive ramp leading into *Ark Michael* while the others moved to their respective crafts. While *Uriel* bobbed in the cove, the others still rested in their braces near the shore. Noah had plans to move them out into the bay or beyond once all the passengers—human and nonhuman—were secured aboard, hopefully, to avoid the inundation from smashing arks into each other.

Shaking out her arms and shoulders, Ariel adjusted her posture to one of optimum alignment and cleared her mind. This wasn't the time to grieve over Oma or Adira, to worry about Mal'akhi, or to wonder if she'd ever see friends and family again, save those who would travel with her. She couldn't fret over agitated townspeople who might burst into the shipyard at any time or speculate about the future of technology. Ariel must focus on love, radiate a compassionate invitation, and allow Source energy to flow through her to perform a miracle.

She lifted her arms, palms up, took a deep breath, and bade them come. It was a general broadcast, not trying to pick specific individuals. The animals knew who they were, and who they were supposed to line up beside without her micromanaging the Creator's intent. She and the others were there to moderate, encourage, and soothe. *All is well,* she transmitted. *Come with me.*

A tremendous, churning ball of bright, warm energy moved in Ariel's chest until it encompassed her entire body from head to toe. Radiating outward, it signaled the cattle and beasts to leave the meadow and forest's edge. Four lines, almost a league long each, formed of their own accord, winding their way to the arks, from the largest to the least. To assist the massive aquatic manatee, Ariel had brought them aboard ahead of time on anti-gravity skids and helped them into large tubs of brackish water. Miracle or not, they couldn't have made the trip overland this far.

Elephants led the way as the animals marched two by two. The great aurochs came next, followed by bison, moose, and elk. Mighty brown bears and their smaller cousins, the black bears, behaved themselves and didn't frighten the horses or llamas who moved purposefully behind them. The shaggy-maned plains lions, sleek pumas, jaguars, tigers, and other big cats, wolves, coyotes, foxes, hyenas, and wolverines walked peacefully near deer, gazelle, pronghorns, mountain goats, sloths, and beavers. Bunnies hopped, and the jaws of alligators didn't snap at them. From the bulky bull elephant to the humble shrew, they all crossed up the ramp and through the threshold into the arks while overhead, from the largest condor to the tiniest hummingbird, more birds winged their way into their roosts under the canopy of the top deck.

It was truly a spectacle to behold, eliciting gasps and awe-inspired responses from all who gathered around to watch. Ariel was aware of others' presence near her while keeping her attention on her task.

"Well, bury a spoon," dropped from Lysandra's lips with astonishment.

"What does that even mean?" Ariel asked the question she'd posed dozens of times without thinking.

"It comes from an old fable." Ariel shifted her gaze at the sound of Noah's voice, and she peered at him in curiosity. "Oh, don't let me interrupt. Watching the parade of animals is probably the most spectacular thing I've ever witnessed."

"No, please," she said, looking back at the procession. "I want to know. It won't divide my focus too much."

"I've never heard it," Lysandra entreated. "Please tell us."

"My great-great-great-grandfather Methuselah used to tell me this story when I was a lad—which was hundreds of years ago—so, if I get a detail wrong, I apologize."

"Quit teasing us and get on with it," Ariel implored.

Noah laughed. "Once there was a man named Yack who lived happily in a little villa with the wife he loved." He launched into the tale with the inflections of an expert storyteller.

"One day, while they were eating oyster soup for dinner, his wife laughed at something he said, choked on an oyster, and died. He tried to revive her but couldn't. Even the town's best healer was unable to help. Yack was so devastated by grief that he took the spoon she had been eating with and buried it in the yard, so he would never have to look at the offending utensil again."

Pricked with a sudden pang of empathy for poor Yack, Ariel's vibration dropped, and some monkeys started misbehaving. Reminding herself it was just a fable, she mentally commanded the monkeys to settle down, or they'd be left behind.

"After tossing and turning, mourning her loss, Yack awoke the next morning to find a tremendous vine had grown outside his window from the very spot where he had buried the spoon. Deciding he had nothing better to do, he began to climb it. He climbed and climbed until above the clouds he reached an orchard. The boughs of the trees hung low, burdened with a crop of golden apples.

"Excitedly, he picked one and raced down the vine to where his wife lay awaiting the burial procession to arrive. Yack bit off a piece of the apple of the gods which was supposed to grant immortality and placed it in his wife's mouth. The magical properties of the fruit brought her back to life and Yack rejoiced with exceeding gladness. Then she bore him children to love and cherish, and Yack and his adored wife lived happily ever after."

"Yes!" Lysandra exclaimed as if she had spent years in the dark and someone finally switched on a light. "I forgot. My mother used to tell me that story when I was a child. I never thought to connect it with the expression, but it makes sense.

People say it to mark an extreme—terrible like losing one's love, or marvelous like bringing her back from the dead."

Noah's lips twitched between his gray beard and mustache and his eyes twinkled as he leaned on his walking staff and turned his gaze back to the phenomenal display. "Bury a spoon indeed."

☥ ☬ ✟ ✡

All the creatures, great and small, were secured in their pens, roosts, or cages before sunset. Ariel was exhausted, but completely overflowing with satisfaction. When she thought the day couldn't get better, Lysandra walked into the bunk space where she lay bearing a steaming bowl of something that smelled divine. She pushed up on an elbow and smiled at her.

"You were amazing, and I know you're spent," Lysandra cooed as she nestled her bum in beside her. "It's how I feel after performing treatments all day."

"Did you put them to sleep yet?" Ariel asked as she scooted up farther to have both hands to hold her bowl.

"I thought they'd want to settle in a bit," she answered. "Will you come with me after we eat?"

"Certainly." The first bite tasted as good as it smelled, and Ariel took her time to savor the flavors.

"Shemu'el, would you be happy with this hammock?" Yaluk asked as Aram and his family carried their belongings into the space partitioned off by blankets hanging from ropes overhead.

"Sure, whatever," he muttered and plopped down on the trunk he had been lugging.

"Ariel, can we assign Mal'akhi a hammock too?" Aram requested. "We thought the younger folks would be comfortable up there."

Alarm struck Ariel, thrusting nervous energy through her veins. "He isn't here yet?"

"We haven't seen him," Yaluk replied.

"Nymphe!" Ariel glanced around without spotting her daughter-in-law.

"She went out to the landing pad to wait for him," Lysandra said. "Eat, Ariel. There's plenty of time still. Eat, we'll put the animals into their sleep, and if he hasn't arrived, we'll go talk to Noah about sending someone to get him."

"If he isn't here by then, I'll go get him myself," Ariel declared with an iron conviction. She realized her son was a grown man and an experienced city guardian, performing a vital role in saving lives; she also recalled the ruffians who attacked them and tried to steal their sleigh. *Anything could have gone wrong up there.*

"Come on, sis," Aram consoled. "You think the archangels orchestrated all of this, but they can't see that Mal'akhi arrives safely?"

With a sigh and a nod, Ariel confessed, "You're right, of course. Still." She ate her food, renewed her strength, and headed off with Lysandra to put the menagerie into hibernation.

⚥ ⟁ ✟ ✡

Lysandra gave Ariel a dense cloth mask soaked in Frankincense oil diluted with water. It wouldn't do for them to breathe in the tranquilizing fumes and fall over, passed out in the carnivore corner.

"This is great, Lysandra," Ariel praised. "I almost wish we could all get put to sleep and miss the horrific wave that will descend upon us. Even with all my focus, I doubt I could keep the animals calm during that."

"Thanks, but we must stay awake in case we need to take some defensive action." Lysandra fixed her mask around her nose and mouth, then lit the sedative mixture. She had piled cups full of the herbal and narcotic blend into a large clay incense bowl that hung from a trio of thin cords tied together at the top. As they strolled through the lower deck, Lysandra swung it back and forth, allowing the sweet smoke to pass over all the creatures. Ariel laced her fingers through those of her empty hand, bringing a smile to Lysandra's lips.

"It looks like it's working," Ariel commented, as a pair of donkeys curled their legs under their bodies and lowered their heads.

"Are you afraid?" Lysandra asked. She had tried to stay busy for the past many months so that she wouldn't have time to think about floods or losing the only homeland she'd ever known. She had seen the Terrible Ice and the thawed ocean swelling behind it and comprehended exactly what was about to transpire, yet she couldn't imagine it truly happening. The slow nausea of dread stirred in her stomach—or maybe it was just fumes from the drug getting through.

"I take it seriously," Ariel answered in a steady tone. "I'm more worried about Mal'akhi arriving in time than anything else."

Lysandra squeezed her hand. "I know, sweetie. He'll be here. This has been a day to remember."

"It has at that. So many highs and lows—too much emotion. I feel like I've been marinated in spices and fried over a hot cooktop."

"You need to rest, to get some sleep," Lysandra said. "You'll feel better tomorrow."

"I'll sleep when Mal'akhi is on this ship," she vowed. "I need to go talk to Noah, find out if anyone's gotten word." She stopped walking when they passed the base of the staircase. "Can you finish this without me? I can tell it will take a long time just to walk up and down every deck of this monstrous floating barn, and I need to know where he is. My nerves are about to get the better of me, especially since I've been pushing them away for a couple of days straight."

"Sure, I can. We've finished all the big predators and I'm not worried about any of the others."

"Do the birds, insects, and tiny creatures, too," Ariel said as she took the first step. Her hand trailed out of Lysandra's until their fingertips fell apart. "Shem and a few carpenters should be coming by soon to secure the folding blinds around the top row of windows to keep any from falling out when the wave hits."

They locked eyes for a moment and Lysandra nodded. She could feel Ariel's stress, though she tried to maintain a businesslike exterior. "We've got each other, my love, and we've got this."

Ariel's eyes crinkled in a smile. "I love you," she professed and jogged up the steps.

Lysandra watched her rush off to assume even more responsibilities, but she couldn't blame her. She wanted to be sure Mal'akhi was safe too. *What if the water comes while she's off the ark? What if I'm left here with lions and bears to care for and she's swept away by the giant swell?*

An ache tore through her soul at such a horrific thought, begging Lysandra to run after her. But she had a job to do, and surely Aram had been right. *The archangels wouldn't have orchestrated all this just to let Ariel be lost at the last minute. All will be well, Lysandra. All will be well.* She held onto that hope as she finished her rounds to lull the animals all to sleep.

53

Noah was busy answering questions, making decisions, and directing people where to go by torchlight near the hectic landing pad between his house and the shipyard when Ariel broke in line to speak with him. "Mal'akhi," she exhaled, breathless from running the many hundreds of cubits from *Ark Michael* to the staging area. "He hasn't made it to the ark yet. Is he—"

"I haven't seen him," Noah rushed to answer. "Did you check with Nymphe?"

"She's looking for him too. I'm going to go get him."

"No, Ariel, you can't leave now," Noah stated with authority. "We're about to move the arks into the bay. Besides, what do you think you can accomplish that your guardian son can't do for himself? Do you want to shatter his self-esteem with his mother rushing to his rescue?"

"Better that than have him drown in the deluge," she snapped, tension getting the best of her.

Noah spared a moment to wrap an arm around her and turn her back toward the arks. "Have faith, my friend. Your prayers are more powerful than your body. Even if your sleigh was to reach Lycia Landing, it might not have enough power to get back. He's a man, not a little boy. Let him be a man."

Ariel hung her head and leaned into him. "Oma refused to come. She made us leave her in Methuselah's cave."

Noah nodded and pressed her shoulders in tighter. "I heard," he answered in solace. "I may have done the same if not burdened with this task."

"Noah, King Efrayim wants to talk to you," a woman interrupted.

"We have the antigrav lifts in place," Japheth reported, reminding Ariel how busy Noah was.

"Has everyone else on the arks' rosters arrived?" Noah twisted to ask the woman holding a scroll.

"King Basilius and his family have boarded *Ark Barachiel*, and Thoth has taken charge of them," she replied. "Ham divided the carpenters who stayed to work on *Ark Jegudiel* between the other four vessels, and Shem is overseeing the last of the fruits and vegetables being carried aboard. So far, the only reserved passengers not accounted for are the twenty guardians you have posted on protection detail, Zosar's daughter, who's on her way from Menosus, Queen Shifra from Mestoria—although she never replied with a confirmation that she's coming—and ..." The woman flitted a nervous glance at Ariel. "Mal'akhi."

"Thank you," Noah replied. "Keep a close watch for them and let me know the minute they touch down. Japheth, sound the horn. As soon as everyone milling around here goes inside and the produce has been loaded, we'll seal the doors and move the arks into the bay."

"Yes, Father," his obedient oldest son replied, quickly stepping away to avoid deafening those around him with the horn's blast.

"Ariel, find Nymphe, and you two go back to *Michael*. We'll make sure he finds the right ark."

Feeling defeated, Ariel nodded, lowering her gaze to the ground, and trudged away, dragging her feet as she moved. She wanted to go get her boy. *Maybe it would be humiliating for him, but who knows? He could be grateful. What if—*

"I guess this is goodbye for now." A familiar deep voice roused Ariel from her inner argument. Quetzal and Mandisa stood in front of her. The burly man grabbed her in a bear hug and brushed kisses to her cheeks. "Take care of my favorite student, now, you hear?" he charged with a grin, though a sting of regret touched his eyes. Ariel would miss him too, as she had grown fond of the man who had become a father figure to her. She hugged him back, letting out a sigh.

"You know I will. But who'll take care of you?"

"I've got grandchildren accompanying me, and this formidable force of nature." Releasing his embrace, Quetzal motioned to Mandisa.

Before Ariel could respond, Mandisa threw her arms around her neck, kissed both cheeks, and then surprised her by planting one on her lips. "If one good thing has come of the entire situation, it has been getting to know you and becoming friends. Remember me when a gentle rain falls, or a cool breeze refreshes you on a hot day."

"Likewise," Ariel said and kissed her back. "And remember me when you hear a bluebird sing or smell the blooms of wildflowers. I will miss you both so much," she confessed.

Quetzal shrugged. "Unless we wash up on the same shore. Then you'll get tired of us!" he laughed.

"Never!" Ariel meant it. While she knew their spirits would always stay connected, sometimes she just wanted to see a goofy grin or enjoy a human touch.

"Noah wants us to get moving now," Mandisa said as she seemed to struggle to hold back tears.

"Blessings on you both, and I'll give Lysandra your love. Hugs to Hashur and Agathon," Ariel bade them, supposing they had already made their farewells to her wife in person. She had to forcibly yank herself in the right direction, as she still itched to grab a sleigh and go after her son.

Moon and starlight lit her path back to the colossal ship. The air was still and not even crickets chirped. Nature perceived what was coming as surely as Ariel did. *Would it be tonight or wait for daylight? Tomorrow or the next day? Soon. Very soon.*

☥ ☬ ☦ ✡

The next morning, Lycia Landing

Mal'akhi's guardian blue and white uniform had become dirty and tattered over the past few days. Ever since people learned of the crack in the ice, Evamont had been in turmoil. About a third of the million-plus residents remained and most of them had rushed to Lycia Landing and tried to bribe or bully their way onto anything that floated. Fishermen were accosted at knifepoint for their boats, and fistfights had broken out in lines to board passenger vessels.

King Efrayim stayed in the city as long as he could. Still, he had left the previous afternoon at the urging of the guardians after looters broke into the palace hauling off with whatever valuables they could carry. It made Mal'akhi sad to see society fall into such disarray, and it was all he and his squad—one of the few remaining—could do to keep folks from killing each other.

Most of the looters were deluge deniers who had now gathered in a hateful gang on a hill overlooking the docks. They shouted jeers and insults at the men, women, and children who feared for their lives, and occasionally tossed rocks or rotten produce at them. The red smear on his vest wasn't blood—thank goodness—but a splattered tomato.

"I'm sorry, but you can't take that," Mal'akhi said, pointing at a tubby man's trunk. "There isn't room. It's people and handbags only."

"But I don't want to leave with nothing," he argued with a beleaguered expression.

"You're leaving with your life," Mal'akhi's friend and associate Pamphilos told him and took the trunk handle, pulling it aside.

Mal'akhi had become a squad leader with the few remaining service men and women now under his direction. He couldn't help but feel grateful for his dark-complected mate, who had been by his side since he first joined the city guardians years ago.

"Move along, now, or you'll lose your spot," Pamphilos advised. The fellow hunched his shoulders and stepped onto the gangplank.

The ship's first mate cupped a hand to Mal'akhi's ear. "Only four more can fit on this vessel. Then we're putting out to sea."

Mal'akhi faced him with a grave visage. "Then what? There are hundreds, if not over a thousand, people in this line." He glanced around the harbor. "There, that warship," he declared and pointed.

The first mate shook his head. "It's already full. There's a trading vessel down at the end of the pier and the captain is charging a thousand gold Poseidons to each passenger."

Mal'akhi's muscles twitched, and his jaw stiffened as he glared down the dock planks at a big cargo ship with a short line. "King Efrayim forbade price gouging."

"Yeah, well, King Efrayim's not here today. Four more," the mate repeated. "We're overcrowded as it is."

Counting off the next four in line, Mal'akhi whispered to Pamphilos, "Stop after this one; the ship is full. Then stay here and maintain order while I go check something out."

"Will do," his friend affirmed, and Mal'akhi marched down the planks. Disappointed grumbles, angry shouts, and fearful cries singed his ears as righteous wrath boiled in his gut.

"Where's the captain?" he demanded, standing tall with a sword at his side and a spear in his hand.

"Here!" called a fancily clad older fellow standing on a platform on the vessel's aft, holding onto a rigging rope. "What does a lowly guardian want with me? To beg for passage?"

"No, you worm-ridden snake!" he snapped. "I have sworn to uphold the laws, rules, and ordinances of Evamont. I heard you are charging a thousand gold pieces per passenger."

"It's my ship," he retorted, raising his chin. "I can charge what I damn well please."

"No, you can't. By King Efrayim's decree, nobody is allowed to raise their fares. Thousands of citizens need space on a ship, and you wish to cater only to the very wealthy? You don't have room for all that gold. The weight alone could send your rig to the bottom of the harbor."

"Nonsense! This craft carries shipments of ore across the Atlantic every month. And, besides, who's going to make me let that riff-raff aboard?"

"These people deserve as much of a chance as anyone else, and I will enforce the law as is my duty!"

The captain motioned to four brawny armed men, who hopped over the railing onto the pier to force Mal'akhi away. He gripped his spear lightly in both hands, assuming a practiced stance.

The men drew their swords and crept closer, testing thrusts and jabs. Mal'akhi batted their blades away with his spear, then swirled and swept the closest one off his feet. The planks shook when the man's substantial weight landed on them. While he rolled to his hands and knees and gained his bearing, two others tried advancing from different directions. The reach of Mal'akhi's spear and his years of training gave him an advantage, but it was his anger over the captain's inhumane actions that fueled his strength. With a flurry of spins, he knocked one foe's sword away into the water and then struck the second in the head with the butt of his pole, rendering him unconscious.

"Quit dancing around and get rid of that guardian!" the captain snapped.

Then Mal'akhi felt thunderous vibrations rumble through the wood, the soles of his sandals, and up his legs. Making a defensive swing, he spun around to see the entire line of desperate people who didn't get on the passenger ship stampeding their way toward them. Men and women clung to their small children while elders exercised amazing strength in their determination to board something that would float. *Well, good luck getting them to pay you,* he thought, and dove into the water just in time to avoid being trampled.

Keeping hold of his spear—because he may well need it again—Mal'akhi kicked and paddled his way back to the shore. Pamphilos was there to give him an arm up. He shook his head with a stupefied expression. "Glad to see you haven't lost your reaction time."

"Yeah," he said with a laugh and slung wet hair out of his eyes. He passed a despairing glance around Lycia Landing. Long oars pulled the passenger vessel they had just finished loading away from the dock. Several smaller crafts were heading out to sea, and, in the distance, he spotted the warship's sail. A commotion and a loud splash to his right drew his attention. So many people piled into a fishing boat built for eight that they were pushing each other out. Clouds obscured the sun, and the air reeked of fear. The gangs of deluge deniers laughed from their perch on the hill.

"What a bunch of idiots! You'll all kill each other and then no flood will come."

"I don't think there's anything else we can do, Mal'akhi," Pamphilos admitted seriously. "Look, the rest of our squad is leaving."

"But the people," he lamented.

"There are no more boats. What can you do?"

Inspired by a fresh idea, Mal'akhi jogged over to the vacant harbor office and kicked in the door. Pamphilos had caught up by the time he exited with a large, cone-shaped talking horn. Mal'akhi climbed the ladder to the roof and hollered into the instrument as loudly as he could.

"There are no more boats! Citizens, head south, up into the Azaes Mountains. Take refuge in the heights of the volcanoes." He repeated the message several times. Some people simply stood about as if waiting for an airship to appear out of the sky to carry them away, but others started walking toward higher ground. Then he climbed back down, responsibility weighing heavily on his heart.

Pamphilos slapped a hand on his shoulder and grinned. "Good thinking. Now, what about us?"

"I've got a sleigh hidden in the underbrush about two hundred cubits that way," he said, pointing down the shoreline away from the village. "My wife and mother are probably frantic, but still." He hesitated and glanced back at the dismal scene around him.

Something vibrated deep in the earth. Mal'akhi didn't need special talents to sense it. An impression of foreboding overwhelmed him, and he peered to the north. He couldn't see anything on the horizon where the sky met the ocean, but flocks of wildly screeching birds filled the air above them. The sound of a distant roar rumbled, sending a shiver down his spine.

Flashing a terrified glance at Pamphilos, he commanded, "Run!"

54

By the time Mal'akhi and Pamphilos reached the third-hand sleigh he'd bought cheap and kept hidden from prying eyes, he detected terrified screams while droves of Atlanteans raced through trees and underbrush up the gently sloping base of the nearest volcano. As they threw branches and a green coverlet off the vehicle, Mal'akhi spared a glance across the bay to the north.

The monstrous wall of water towered above the earth, gulping everything in its path. As he fell still, staring in disbelief at the dark swell approaching at terrifying speed, Pamphilos shook his shoulder.

"Come on, man—let's go!"

Not bothering with doors, they both leaped over the sides onto the bench seat and Mal'akhi pressed his palm to the start plate. Nothing happened. Shock battered his brain, practically rendering him witless. He slammed his palm into the plate again. "Come on, you blasted piece of junk!"

"Try a new crystal," his friend cried as he fiddled with inoperable levers and pedals.

Yes, a fresh crystal! Mal'akhi dug through a box under his seat, tossing out gloves, a hat, an empty cup, and a dirty rag, at last fishing out a pouch full of power crystals. "These were all charged last week, and I haven't used any of them," he said, pouring out four sharp-cut clear quartz gems.

His fingers trembled as he jerked out the dead one and tossed it over the side. Pamphilos shoved a new one into the slot, and Mal'akhi tried the power plate again. Still nothing.

The din of the tidal wave grew louder in his ears before his throbbing pulse drowned it out. Mal'akhi had just started a life with Nymphe and didn't want to leave her a widow so young. He wanted to have children of his own, to love and nurture them, to teach them the wisdom of The Law as his mother had imparted to him.

Pulling the useless crystal loose, he jostled another from the bag into place. Rather than plead and beg, Mal'akhi followed his mother's instructions and example. "Thank you, Archangel Michael, for your protection. Thank you, Creator God, ancestors, and spirits, Source of all love and power in the universe, that this sleigh will start and carry us safely to the ark you have provided for our deliverance."

It's not enough to say the words, Ariel's tutoring resounded in his mind. *You must exude the emotions of trust and appreciation and believe in your heart what you say is true.*

Closing his eyes, Mal'akhi drew in a slow, deep breath, ignoring the abysmal din of approaching doom and blocking out the shadow the mammoth crest cast over the harbor. He blocked out images of death and destruction, fear and anguish, and, with deliberate calm, placed his palm on the copper plate. The power hummed on and Pamphilos yanked the control bar and punched the acceleration.

They zoomed upward as fast as the sleigh could muster. Mal'akhi felt the spray and chanced to glance over his shoulder. Behind them, he couldn't make out anything resembling land as the immense surge of water inundated everything in its path. Shifting his view to the right, he witnessed the wall of water splashing about, frothing with white foam at each wave peak, as it swallowed forests, meadows, and the port village of Lycia Landing like they were children's toys in the wake of a life-sized tidal wave. It was terrible and surreal, and Mal'akhi felt his stomach catch in his throat as they continued their rapid ascent.

"I'm glad you have a solid line of prayer, brother," Pamphilos squeaked out while he pushed and pulled the sleigh to its limits, "or we would have been goners. Still not out of the woods."

Below them, Mal'akhi couldn't spot the ships he had helped load in the harbor. *Did any make it or were they all swamped?* he wondered. The water stretched as far as the east was from the west, from horizon to horizon. His mother told him it would obliterate their entire part of the earth; however, Mal'akhi had found such a prediction hard to fathom—until seeing it with his own eyes.

Keeping a tight grip on the bar, he turned his attention to the front. The peaks of the Azaes lay ahead, and Pamphilos guided them through a wide gap between two summits. Mal'akhi doubted any but the fastest sprinters outran the onslaught of the soaring flood waters, but he couldn't worry about it now. Beyond the snowy domes, the land below them appeared tranquil and normal, lulling him into the dreamy idea that the danger had passed.

Then the sea burst through the valleys, gaps, and passes of the Azaes with the force of a waterfall, swirling and churning, cutting a path like surging rapids around rocks in a stream. He covered his ears to block out the wailing roar that sounded too much like the cries of dying men and women. Taking one more glance back, he noticed that at least the highest tops still pushed above the swells, though their snowy caps slushed off like flavored frozen cream on a hot day in Ryzen.

"Push it, Philo," he shouted. "We've got to stay ahead of it. It's almost a hundred leagues to Diaprep."

"Everything's wide open," he replied. "We're on the straightest course—should only take a couple of turns of the sandglass. We'll beat the wave by a minute or two," he promised, "if the power holds out." Mal'akhi closed his eyes and resumed his prayers.

☥ ☬ ✝ ✡

Ariel stood on the open portion of the top deck, white knuckles around the railing, searching the air to the north for a sleigh. She had tossed and turned last night until Lysandra did something to her that forced her into sleep. At King Masuda's advice, everyone else remained below, busying themselves by securing furniture and tying barrels to posts and other such preparations. Lysandra and Nymphe wanted to join her topside, but Ariel had insisted they stay back with the others.

"It only takes one set of eyes to watch for him, and I can't be worrying about either of you getting washed overboard when the flood wave arrives."

Lysandra had grabbed her so tight it hurt and demanded in the most forceful voice she'd ever heard her use, "And we can't be worrying about you getting washed over either. Maybe you can talk to dolphins, but you can't swim like one. You're being reckless!"

"I should have gone after him yesterday like I wanted to instead of listening to you and Noah," she had snapped.

She promised Lysandra she'd tie a rope around her waist as a precaution—which she did—but she regretted the argument. Ariel didn't want to die knowing the last words she'd said to her wife had been spat out in anger. *She knows you love her,* her inner being reminded her.

Glancing around the bay, Ariel took in the sight of four massive vessels resting in the water with long distances between them, anchored in place to prevent them from drifting into one another. *Uriel* was the farthest out, nearly clearing the end of the peninsula. Her *Ark Michael* was next, with *Gabriel* and *Barachiel* spread apart but nearer to land.

Last night, they had raised the arks and carried them out into the bay with anti-gravity lifts. No sooner than Noah had pulled his guardians and sent them to board their vessels, a horde of panicked residents had swarmed into the shipyard. Some grabbed up parked sleds and sleighs and took off flying south, while others rushed to the grounded ark. Ariel watched as hundreds of people without transportation piled into the unfinished *Ark Jegudiel.*

Although Ariel empathized with their predicament, she was too worried about Mal'akhi to dwell on it. Looking back across the peaceful bay, she spotted someone in a gray robe and long beard patrolling *Uriel*'s top deck. *Noah*. Everyone had made it except Queen Shifra and Mal'akhi. *They weren't sure the queen was coming*, she recalled. *She may have arranged other passage*. It comforted her to know Noah also watched for her son. There was nothing to do now but wait.

Winds gusted and fell calm. Birds winged by and a pod of harbor porpoises appeared tiny as they glided along the length of the ark. Ariel sent them friendly vibrations. *What have you heard? What do you feel?* she asked.

One answered, *The ice cracked. The flood will come anytime now*. Nothing Ariel didn't already know. She nervously paced back and forth between the boarded-up aviary and the railing as far as her safety rope would allow.

Stopping herself, she said, "This isn't helping anything. I should be in deep meditation, thanking the real Michael for my son's safe arrival, praising the Creator for his unfailing love. I should remember that we never truly die, that our years on earth are but a blink of an eye, that Mal'akhi and I have always been and will always be together."

Ariel tried to purge herself of doubt and worry. Never in her life had doing so proven so difficult. Whether it was the weakening connection to the energies or the overwhelming stress of the cataclysm, she couldn't be sure.

An eagle soared overhead, with regal wings outstretched. Before Ariel could ask, he conveyed a warning. *The ocean is flowing over everything. All the trees are gone and I've nowhere to land to rest my wings. I'm heading south.*

It was more confirmation than a surprise. Ariel had sensed a shift early that morning that woke her from Lysandra's induced sleep, though she couldn't be sure until now. As the moment of truth crashed down on her, Ariel felt an otherworldly peace, beyond her ability to comprehend, and she knew—not hoped, not believed, but knew—Mal'akhi was safely on his way.

"Thank you, thank you, thank you." The thrill of victory filled her soul, and she lifted her hands in praise. Moments later, Ariel felt anxious vibrations slam into her, and she resumed a diligent stance, scanning the horizon to the north. The faraway rumble of something tremendous reached her ears before she saw the league-high wall of ocean rising on the horizon.

For an instant, peace and praise were consumed by an awesome sense of how small and helpless humans truly were. The temperature dropped and a salty gust blew back her hair. Ariel suddenly wondered if the arks would be capsized by the towering wave.

"Strike the anchors!" Noah shouted. "Ariel, get below, now!"

She waved to him, but she wasn't going anywhere. Somewhere out there, her son's sleigh was speeding toward them. She had to make sure he landed with her.

A glint of light reflected off something in the air just ahead of the massive surge and Ariel's heart leaped. She waved her arms and yelled, even though she knew he couldn't hear her. "Mal'akhi, over here!" Acting as if he were an animal, she reached out with her energetic frequencies and called for him. She wasn't a telepath—not for human communication—but it couldn't hurt. Maybe he'd sense her and move the right way.

The ominous surge roared behind the rusty sleigh like the hungry jaws of a mythical leviathan. "Hurry!" It was a superfluous command, as he was surely flying as fast as possible. Ariel waved some more, and, to her relief, the sleigh veered in her direction. It raced toward the ark much too fast, jolting a flaming arrow of fear through her system, but Mal'akhi had no choice as the colossal rise of the sea matched his speed. There wouldn't be time to land and get sealed below deck. Scrambling to make her hands fly, Ariel rearranged the rope around her waist to pull all the slack to one end, then double-knotted it to the railing.

The wobbly vehicle tipped left and right, speeding toward her like a flying racehorse. Ariel gripped the wooden bar tight in one hand and waved with the other, cringing, and gritting her teeth, every muscle taut. In an instant, the sleigh swooped in a few cubits above the deck with a mountain of roaring seawater only seconds behind. Mal'akhi and another young man tumbled out of the hurtling sleigh and rolled across the gopherwood planks while the vehicle crashed into the far side of the deck, tipped up on its front end, and tumbled over the rail into the abyss.

"Quick, quick!" Ariel screamed, motioning as the end of the world hastened to catch them.

Her son and his friend clamored to her, feet slipping, hands grasping for purchase on the smooth, wet surface. Ariel couldn't breathe, and her heart pounded like a thunderous stampede of elephants. She thrust out a hand and grabbed his.

"Tie yourselves in!"

Relief and terror wrestled in Ariel's emotions as the massive wave sped toward them. Mal'akhi had made it; he couldn't be swept away now.

Her son and a fellow she recognized but couldn't pull his name into her flustered brain made quick work of their knots. "We made it, Mother!" Mal'akhi huffed out between rapid breaths.

"Hold on!" She braced herself.

Time seemed to crawl as the mighty swell lifted *Ark Michael* to its salty breast. Ariel glanced around to see Noah's ark rise on the wave, tipping back and forth, yet righting itself with each rocking motion. To her other side, she watched the wall of ocean devour the shipyard. It plucked up the unfinished fifth ark, filled with screaming people, and pushed it along and up like a bobbing cork in a great tub of sloshing water. The scene turned more surreal as the errant vessel tipped on its side, with a gaping mouth sucking in the sea while it careened toward *Ark Barachiel*.

They didn't get the door closed, she realized in shock. *Jegudiel*, filling with water, rose and fell, and bowled on its side, its top crashing against *Barachiel*'s sturdy bow. The collision spun *Ark Barachiel* about as the gigantic wave carried them all higher. Ariel could feel the anguished cries more than hear them over the breaking crests. Her body was aware of the motion of her vessel being tossed left and right, the pushing and sinking as first bow then stern topped a swell. In the distance, the unfinished ark with its gaping opening in its side bobbed on a rolling wave once, twice, and then she saw it no longer. The other four arks—those protecting her friends—all seemed sound. This is what they had been built for. They may have no sails, oars, or rudders, but they stood up to the turmoil of the deluge, preserving the lives of all inside.

As the violent shaking, pushing, and surging continued, Ariel dared not try to move to the hatch. They would have to remain here, tied to the railing until the waters calmed. She was so wet from the spray that she hardly noticed when the clouds opened and torrents of rain pounded them from above. Although the weather had been warm, Ariel shivered with a chill. The wind howled around them, and the ice melt felt far colder than water at a beach.

"Are you all right?" Mal'akhi asked. He slapped one hand over hers, clamping them both to the rail.

"Yes, just cold and—" Ariel couldn't put words to how she felt in that moment. "I knew you'd make it!" Despite everything, she could slap on a joyful grin that her son was with her and safe.

"I couldn't let you down," he replied cheekily. "Hope you don't mind that I brought Pamphilos."

"I'm so glad to see you both. The more the merrier," Ariel responded with an amazed delight and overwhelming release.

Although her side of the craft initially faced the oncoming doom, they had been spun around many times and now it overlooked the south, giving her a view of what was to come. She watched in awesome horror as the surge poured over the islands of Menosus, rendering the tallest lighthouse in the world a mere speck to be snuffed out. Poseidon's temple and the largest pyramid in Atala, all the lakes, rivers, forests, plains, hills, and mountains disappeared beneath the impervious sea. The only world Ariel had ever known was gone. And yet, her family and friends and representatives of all the animals had been saved.

Oma. "Mal'akhi, did you see the Azaes? Did the deluge cover them?"

"We flew through them," he answered, as soaking wet as she was, if not more. "The ocean poured between the peaks as if they were fingers trying to hold it back. At the last glance I had, the tops were still above water. Why?"

Ariel closed her eyes and reached with her senses to find Oma. She felt her words touch her soul. *You'll never lose me, dear. I'll always be with you.*

Shaking her head, Ariel decided to wait to tell him. Maybe the water hadn't filled Methuselah's cave, and, if it had, Oma was where she wanted to be.

55

Ryzen

"Pardon me, are you in charge?"

Lykos recognized the aged Queen Shifra of Mestoria, although she must have forgotten him. Her flowing white toga and abundance of jewelry were as out of place as a shark in the desert, much like the regal woman herself standing halfway down the busy dock where Lykos employed his abilities to keep calm and order among the crowds boarding the last ships in Ryzen.

"I'm Minister Lykos. What are you doing here?"

"My husband, daughter, and I were flying to Diaprep to be carried away on one of those enormous arks the other rulers are taking when our sleigh just puttered out of energy and dropped to the pavement about half a league out of the city. We had to leave all our belongings and walk. Your citizens are so rude and unhelpful," she complained. "Nobody could fix our sleigh, nor did they offer us a ride."

"Well, Your Highness, in case you didn't notice, we're in the midst of a crisis," Lykos quipped in an impatient tone. While they had been waiting for Temen's return, Rhoxane had sent almost everyone away in a steady stream of transports, most heading east through the Pillars of Hercules. There were only a few hundred residents left now, besides the deluge deniers who lined the port heckling them and boasting of how they had elected their own king.

She jutted up her chin and turned down her nose in offended defiance. Lykos pointed. "You see that vessel at the end of the pier, the *Trident*? Take your family and board it now. Captain Jabari will assign you a spot and you must tie yourself in. We're about to shove off."

"Really, Minister Lykos," she scowled and folded her arms over her chest.

Lykos didn't have time for the likes of fastidious queens. He peered around her to spy a well-dressed man of her age and a younger, mature woman. "Sir, if you wish your family to live, put them on that ship now," he ordered, his voice brimming with grave warning. A jolt in the energies woke him that morning, and Lykos had embarked on a brief clairvoyant journey to the Terrible Ice. With spirit eyes, he had witnessed the unfathomably tremendous ice wall break apart and slough off in shards the size of islands. The flood surge was rapidly speeding south, erasing their entire civilization in its wake. They could no longer wait for the return of their king.

No sooner than the sun had risen over the channel, Lykos had ordered Eshkar to clang the temple bells and announce the last chance for citizens to leave. He had hurried Rhoxane and her maidservant to get settled in on the *Trident* with one piece of luggage each. While expecting Rhoxane would protest, Lykos was greeted with her complete understanding. "All we need is each other," she had said. "Everything else is replaceable." Still, he read the regret and unease in her concerning Temen's fate.

"If it is what we must do," Queen Shifra's husband remarked and moved a hand to the small of her back to herd her along. "Shifra, hurry now. I believe we are out of time."

"But our belongings? And we're supposed to be on a big, safe ark, not that open-air military boat." She frowned, waving toward the *Trident*.

"Come along and stop being difficult," the sensible man insisted while the long-legged daughter breezed past them.

"I won't be left behind because you two are slow," she snapped and strode down the planks.

With a huff, the queen allowed her husband to escort her away.

Agriculture Minister Kishar approached next. "The seeds for our spring crops are sealed in crates and tied down in the hold."

"I've packed the most important documents in this trunk," announced Minister Dareios as he joined them, motioning to a chest two brawnier men carried. "I wish we would have had more time."

"It is what it is," Lykos sagely replied. "Stow them onboard and then secure yourself. We need to leave *now*." He turned to the beefy, hairless man beside him, dressed in a guardian's uniform. "Namazu, is my household all aboard?"

"Yes, my lord," he replied in a formal bass timbre. "Queen Rhoxane, her maid-in-waiting Sarah and her sister, your man Eshkar, Ahkin the cook, and the mighty Tukumbi."

Lykos nodded, picturing the formidable woman warrior who had the courage to remain in Rhoxane's service when all but two of the palace guardians had fled the city weeks ago.

"Lykos, it's time for you to come on board so we can get a head start." Namazu gently took hold of the wizard's upper arm, urging him to move.

Instead, Lykos turned to the captain of the trading vessel that was currently being boarded. "Captain Platon, do you have this in hand?"

"Indeed, Lykos. Go on now and blessings upon you."

"Blessings on you." Lykos gave him a farewell wave and started down the pier with his muscle-bound guard. At once, a terrible dread seized his heart, and a vision of gruesome death and destruction flashed before his eyes. In his mind's ear wailed thousands of horrified cries, and his knees gave up their strength, causing him to stumble.

"My lord, are you all right?" Namazu easily lifted Lykos back to his feet as a tremor shot through his senses.

"Run," he uttered, clinging to the big man's bulging arm.

The sound was that of a distant waterfall as vast flocks of birds screamed overhead, speeding past the harbor. Heavy, portentous clouds filled the sky, blocking out the sun, and rumbling vibrations rippled through the planks.

"I'll get you to the ship, Lykos," Namazu's deep voice thundered in his ear. A firm grip dragged him forward while Lykos struggled to keep his feet under his reactive body.

They were still a dozen cubits from the *Trident* when Lykos shouted, "Cast off!"

At the sound of a collective gasp, Lykos ventured a glance to the north. The mammoth surge was still leagues away, but now everyone saw it coming. Strong arms thrust him over the gunwale into the ship, followed by the rocking motion of Namazu's bulk landing with his jump. Crewmen raced to untie the mooring ropes, and Rhoxane threw her arms around his neck.

"It's so much bigger than I had imagined," she whimpered, trembling in his arms.

"Captain, look!" a crewman shouted. Lykos glanced toward him, wondering why the fellow was so far behind everyone else spotting the giant swell. He wasn't pointing at the ocean but at a frantic gang of people stampeding their way down the dock. Screaming and yelling, half of them bolted onto the already full cargo ship, leaping, scratching, and clawing their way onboard despite protests. The crewmen and passengers fought back while a few oarsmen tried to maneuver the vessel out into the channel. The other half charged toward Lykos's warship.

"Those stupid deluge deniers," Lykos grumbled. Narrowing his brows in disgust, he couldn't help but yell at them, "Do you believe me now?"

Unfortunately, they posed a new and more immediate threat to the *Trident*. The vessel designed to hold a maximum of a hundred people, counting oarsmen, crew, and soldiers, was already over capacity at a hundred and ten. They simply couldn't take on more.

"Push off, now!" commanded Jabari. The rowers on the port side locked their oars into their slots and shoved them through, extending the distance between the side of the ship and the pier. Still, the gang kept coming. Those who arrived first made daring leaps, trying to land on the deck. A couple made the distance, while others fell shy, grabbing onto the gunwale, or crashing onto outstretched oars. Lykos heard a crack, and his jaw stiffened.

The next wave of panicking citizens dove or jumped into the channel and swam for the *Trident*, crying and wailing frantic pleas to save them. All the while, the looming tower of seawater rushed nearer.

Lykos enjoyed many things. He liked being the smartest person in the room, manipulating others into doing his bidding, and generally treating the world as his plaything. Like Temen, he loved delicious food and delectable women, art and music, and power. What he did not enjoy was destruction, suffering, and death. Lykos was a student of the wisdom, an adherent of The Law. He understood the power of compassion, the necessity of forgiveness, and, above all, the value of life. He also realized his power had limits. Lykos couldn't save these people.

The craft lurched to one side as dozens pulled on the railing, trying to climb on while crewmen looked helplessly from the interlopers to their captain.

"There isn't room!" Rhoxane shouted to the desperate swimmers. "Strap yourself to planks from the dock," she ordered. "Get onto one of the little boats and tie yourselves in!"

Either no one heard, or they refused to obey.

"We can't let them swamp our ship," Captain Jabari barked. He took a swing at one, landing a powerful punch, and the trespasser tumbled overboard with a splash. Various crewmen contended with others while the oarsmen struggled to move the *Trident* out to sea. And still, the thunderous wave approached, its crest high enough to block out the sun if it wasn't already behind thick clouds. Lykos felt raindrops strike his head and face.

Then he perceived the warm, tender touch of Rhoxane's hand on his cheek and turned to gaze into her eyes. He felt her support and encouragement, her compassion and permission to do what she understood he must. He took her hand away and kissed it. "Buckle yourself in," he instructed. Instead, she locked her fingers in his, sending her energy streaming to him like a molten lava flow.

With his other hand, Lykos braced himself against the mast and sent out a powerful blast of soothing, suggestive vibrations. Everyone stopped fighting. Those who grappled at the sides or tugged on oars ceased and turned around to swim back to shore. The frantic gang who had jumped aboard the *Trident* leaped back into the darkening waters and paddled away. An eerie calm fell over the ship.

"Thank heavens!" exclaimed Queen Shifra from her seat in the forward section.

Rhoxane squeezed Lykos's hand and murmured, "Better to save some than for all to perish."

Lykos nodded, sorrowful at what he had to do, and glanced over her shoulder. His eyes rounded in terror. If only he could subdue a deluge so easily.

There was no more time. Lykos grabbed a rope from the mast rigging and wrapped it around Rhoxane and himself, tying a quick knot. Jabari shouted, "Port side, row—starboard, pull oars!"

Seeing the monstrous wall of water looming over them, Rhoxane's eyes shot wide, and her mouth fell open in a silent scream. She clung to Lykos, and shrieked, "Is this it? Are we done for?"

"Maybe not," Lykos answered. "Captain Jabari is turning into the wave, so it won't roll us over. There's a possibility we can ride it to the crest."

As the bow swung perpendicular to the swell, Jabari ordered, "Pull in all oars and hold on!"

"Rhoxane, give me your energy again," Lykos bade her. Salt spray from the towering ocean mingled with hard, fat raindrops to soak them through. In his mind, Lykos slowed time. He noticed the rough, splintery wood of the mast, the flapping of the sail overhead, the scratchy hemp fibers of the ropes, and the smooth perfection of Rhoxane's skin next to his. He stared intently into her eyes and felt her electric jolt again as her vibrations joined his in the dance of a lifetime.

The wizard couldn't command physical elements or call whales to steady their ship, but he could employ the power of his imagination. The floor pitched and its incline rose as the surge pressed against their keel, pushing the vessel onto its tail. Lykos blocked out the surrounding screams and trunks sliding down the aisle; he didn't look at passengers and crew members who had failed to strap themselves in tightly enough tumble into the roaring depths. Instead, he pictured the *Trident* sailing on tranquil waters, the sun beaming overhead. He imagined sitting on a beach with Rhoxane sipping iced orange water from decorative glasses. Reaching into a future possibility, Lykos visualized their children—a boy and a girl. They were young, active, healthy children who ran about playing with a little dog when not seriously engaged in their studies. They had a nice clay brick house in the lush valley of Ur, with fig, date, and olive trees. Lykos taught at the village school and Rhoxane played the harp, looked after the children, and, of course, served as the local magistrate.

As he clung to the mast and Rhoxane, visualizing his desired future, Lykos was struck with a powerful realization, one he had been hesitant to entertain before arriving in this life-or-death scenario he had worked so diligently to avoid. The words spilled out of his mouth without thought or hesitation.

"I love you, Rhoxane. Not because we might both perish before our next breath, but because you're a remarkable woman worthy of being loved. You don't have to say it back," he added as water poured over them. "I know I'm much older than you and have an ego—I'd have said the size of Atlantis, but that's past being an apt metaphor."

Despite the devastation and certainty of death, Rhoxane laughed at his joke. "You might be a little late with your declaration, but it's nice to hear you say it. You must know I love you, even if you are a power-crazed manipulator. Maybe next time."

A powerful burst of love filled Lykos's heart, making him feel as light as a feather. Nothing else mattered—not the storm or the crushing swell, imminent death, or even the end of his civilization. He had spent eighty years seeking to understand all the mysteries of the universe; only now had he grasped the most important one of all.

"No, this time!" A ferocious grin spread across his typically sober face, and he shouted to the ocean, "You can't defeat me—I win! Somebody loves me! Thank you, thank you, thank you!" Appreciation multiplied in his soul, and he radiated it with such brightness as to rival the sun. The next thing he realized, their craft, battered and creaking from the stress, floated atop the massive flood waters, riding the current—and they were alive.

Sounds and frequencies of relief vibrated all around him as Lykos's chest heaved up and down.

"All right, boys, that's the way to ride a wave!" came Jabari's jubilant cry. Tensions eased and muscles relaxed. They were still being whirled around in the middle of a larger ocean than the one they'd known before, but the worst was behind them.

Lykos unwound the rope that had latched him and Rhoxane to the mast while the captain made a headcount. The finicky old queen and her family were safe, and many others, although about thirty of their number and all their food and water, had gone overboard. Lykos couldn't find his cook Ahkin or Namazu, which was perplexing since he figured if anyone was strong enough to hold on, it would have been his faithful guard.

"How will we survive without food or water?" fretted Minister Dareios as he shivered in the cool wind.

Lykos smiled and wiggled his fingers at the forward section of the ship. "How can you think about food, man?" exclaimed Queen Shifra. "Our lives were just spared from certain doom, and you're worried about your belly?"

Rhoxane giggled. "You can make them believe they are full and satisfied, can't you?"

He shrugged. "For a few weeks, but, hopefully, it won't take that long. Captain Jabari will get us back on course. We can always pull in at various ports along the way. Why, the queen's jewelry alone would outfit us all for months!"

They laughed, and Rhoxane brushed a kiss on his cheek. "I meant it, you know," she confessed, catching his gaze. He instantly knew what she was referring to.

"So did I." His eyes danced at her as he caressed her hand.

An unsolicited thought interrupted Lykos's affections, bringing a frown to his face. "What is it?" Rhoxane asked with a tinge of worry.

"What if there aren't ports along the way anymore? Just how far will the flood waters reach?"

56

Palaio Faliro, Pelasgoí

Temen grumbled, pacing the eight steps back and forth across his stone and iron-barred cell. It was musty and undecorated, and all he had to occupy his time was counting bricks and staring out the window overlooking the harbor, the scene of his miserable failure. His captors had moved General Gershom to a more secure facility after he had attempted an escape, so he didn't even have him to talk to anymore. He rubbed at the scruff on his face in irritation. These people wouldn't even allow him a razor to shave his scraggly half-beard. It itched.

Sitting on his bunk with a sigh, Temen wondered how much longer it would take for his ransom to be paid and for someone to come to get him. Would they come to get him? Surely they would. The leaders of Pelasgoí hadn't demanded an unreasonable amount—steep, yes, but certainly attainable with the coffers he left in Ryzen.

If Temen was honest, he had to admit he hadn't been abused during his stay. They gave him nutritious meals and wine, allowed him to bathe, and no one beat him, although he was occasionally the butt of the guards' jokes. The town magistrate treated him with respect, for which he voiced appreciation.

Still, Temen found it painfully difficult to reach a level of appreciation when deprived of all the beauty and comfort he had grown accustomed to. He never understood how Ariel could be grateful, even when there was nothing to feel gratitude about. One autumn, their crop yield was puny, Sheera and Mal'akhi misbehaved and were sent home from school, and a rabid fox she had tried to save bit her, and yet there she was, standing out on her little hill, raising her hands and giving thanks. It made no sense. Conversely, being king, having beautiful things, excellent entertainment, a stunning wife, and the admiration of all the people—those he had been grateful for. Only, without them, he felt ... empty.

Temen was restless and bored and frustrated. It had been three moons since he was captured; what was taking so long? He and Rhoxane should be celebrating the fall equinox with a festival and feast, yet here he sat waiting. All right, so the magistrate told him the ransom and conditions had only recently been agreed upon and his demands were sent to Ryzen just a week ago. He knew the travel took time, but still.

He pushed up from the plain wooden bunk with its thin padding, worn covers, and solitary pillow and paced to the window. The iron bars were cool and smooth in his hands as he held them to peer out. People milled about the pier and along the boardwalk below while some fishers unloaded their haul. A group of workers had been noisily refurbishing his warships for Pelasgoí's use for weeks. Off to the side, a pyre of rubble burned, the faint scent of smoke reaching his nose. He regretted the entire incident. Why had he let Lykos talk him into this? So many of his soldiers, men whose names he had committed to memory, were gone now, and no one would tell him what became of the survivors. Their fate weighed heavily on his soul.

Hoping to spy a ship approaching, Temen lifted his gaze far out to sea, across the dark waters to where the sky touched the waves. A flock of gulls sailed along in a V, screeching their call to herald their flyover. A glint of sunlight caught his attention. He shaded his eyes with a hand to examine the anomaly to the southeast. *Not a ship.* Hope sank. *Merely a large swell reflecting the sunbeam.*

He stared at the distant wave, watching it grow larger and larger until it seemed to tower above the waters of the bay. Whitecaps foamed at its crest and a mountain of sea rode its wake. Temen's jaw dropped, and his eyes widened. Terror seized his chest as if a mighty brown bear had ripped it open and clawed at his beating heart. A small part of him had hoped that Mandisa and the others had been wrong. But Atlantis was supposed to flood and their plan to move to Pelasgoí was to keep them safe. It shouldn't reach this far into the Green Sea.

At first, his rigid fingers couldn't release the bars and his frozen feet were incapable of moving. *Did Lykos know? Did he send me here just to be rid of me and take the throne for himself? No, he could have done that at any time. Why is this happening?*

Temen swallowed a lump the size of an elephant and rushed to the door of his cell, frantically beating it like a drum. "Guard! Help! Let me out—the flood is coming!"

A disgruntled, scruffy man whose belly hung over his belt in an unseemly fashion waddled over to him with a scowl. "What are you hollering about? There's no need for—"

"Quick, Erastos," he addressed the guard, hoping it would give his words the urgency they carried. "A giant wave is heading for the harbor. You must let me out and warn the magistrate!"

Moving with an uneasy gait, Erastos dragged his feet to the nearest window on his side of the cell. "Great Poseidon, we're all going to die!" he shrieked in horror. Spinning on his heel, the guard sped from the tower, with Temen yelling after him.

"Wait, you miserable coward! Let me out!" It was no use. Neither Temen nor anyone else in confinement would receive help. There simply wasn't time.

With his heartbeat racing, his breathing shallow, and a pounding in his ears like the clang of a temple bell, Temen rushed back to the window to stare helplessly at his impending doom. The colossal swell drove toward the shoreline like a writhing mountain, producing a roar now audible in Temen's ears. Although his cell lay on the third floor of a corner tower in the city walls atop an outcropping fifty cubits above the beach, there was no doubt the sea would swallow him.

Residents and workers below screamed and ran, leaving everything behind, pushing their way up the steps to the open gates of Palaio Faliro. They looked like ants scurrying from danger, darting this way and that, crawling over others who moved too slowly. The total scene was surreal, and, for a moment, Temen removed himself, as if he was watching a play at the theater. Surely, he wasn't about to die.

Then panic set in as, in horror, he realized this was indeed happening and he would spend his last seconds on earth locked in a primitive cell alone. He cast his frantic gaze around the tiny chamber and dashed to his barred door. "Help! Is anyone there? Is anybody else up here?"

His hysterical cries were met with silence while, beneath his window, the distant din of frenzied screams was almost drowned out by the approaching crest. With the fear of being alone overwhelming him, Temen rattled the bars, kicked the solid wood, and even tried throwing the small table at it. Reason told him, even if he got out of the cell, he'd never make it a safe distance away in time. Instinct insisted he try.

The king beat clenched fists on the stubborn door, sobbing in anguish, though it refused to yield. *How much time do I have?* Until a few minutes ago, he would have answered, "At least a hundred more years."

Temen zipped back to the barred portal, his stricken gaze stretching up, up, up at the terrible crest, and sucked in a deep breath. Destruction was upon him.

The force of the water knocked him across the room and into the stalwart door, which was at last ripped from its hinges. Sea water filled every crevice of the tower, jutting him upward until his back hit the ceiling. In that instant, events from Temen's life flashed through his awareness in reverse order—his victory at Pelepus, jumping the bull with the other rulers, his coronation as king, making love to Rhoxane, eating breakfast with his family on the farm ... holding his infant son for the first time.

Then Temen was a little boy. Consumed with distress, he ran to his mother and was encircled by her loving arms while he rubbed a fist in his eye to wipe away tears. "Mama, my boat. I was playing with it in the stream, and it washed away. Now I'll never find it!"

"Shhh, there now, Temen; it's all right," his mother soothed as she cradled him. Despite being submerged in saltwater, he smelled her apricot and lily perfume and was enclosed in her comforting presence. "It's only a toy. We can get you another one."

Suddenly, Temen was aware of the burning in his lungs and the stinging of his eyes. He had held his breath as long as he could. He didn't want to open his mouth, but his body's struggle was too great. Pushing and paddling, he sought a pocket of air for one more breath. If he could just draw one more breath. There was none. Against his will, his mouth flew open, gulping in the warm water of the Green Sea that still spun him about with its unruly churning.

Terror gave way to sadness and regret—regret for all his mistakes and shortcomings, regret for not having enough time to enjoy his life. As he sputtered and coughed—which only allowed more water down his throat—grief and remorse slid silently into acceptance, and everything went black.

Temen ceased struggling against the inevitable and hung suspended in the deluge that filled the tower, alone, in the dark. Presently, a bright light poured over him, as brilliant as the sun gleaming on snow. He squeezed his eyes shut against its radiance, and yet the light consumed him. In the stillness, he heard a voice—not with his ears, but in his mind. It was his mother.

Temen, you are not alone. You were never alone.

A tremendous sense of peace enveloped him, driving away the remnants of loss. He became aware of luminous beings surrounding him and instantly recognized his mother, although she didn't look the same as he remembered. Each glowed, radiating love and acceptance toward him, filling him with more joy than he could ever recall. Wave after wave of vibrations washed through him, each revealing a long-lost truth. It was a most euphoric, unearthly feeling. Glancing about, Temen realized he wasn't on earth anymore.

"Welcome home." That shining being was his great-grandfather. Others in the welcome party seemed familiar, though he couldn't place where he knew them from. Temen felt groggy, like waking from a long, intense dream.

"Did you enjoy your ride?" one of them asked. They all smiled and projected affection toward him.

"I—" he started to say when another revelation struck him. Temen laughed and shook his head in embarrassment. "I was so silly! Why did I think and do such stupid things? Why did I strive so hard and believe I wasn't enough, that I had to be more? Why didn't I understand who I was all along?"

"You didn't fare so bad," his mother answered with a smile, reaching an arm around his waist. "There are many who do worse."

"What about Rhoxane and Lykos, Ariel and my children, all the people I love back in Atlantis?" Temen was still shaky and unaccustomed to his new body. He felt light, but awkward when he moved.

"They will be along to join us when it is their time," his great-grandfather said with an endearing smile. Temen recalled going fishing with the old man and other good times, but he sensed more memories of him lurking in a fog that hadn't quite cleared.

Then, flashing through him like a bolt of lightning, came the awareness of the divine portion of his being, the connection with the Creator that had eluded him for the past sixty-four years. Yes, yes, yes! Blinding joy erupted from his core as Temen realized he was home, back with the One and the spirits of those who had gone before him. At the edge of his consciousness, he could feel every soul ever born, both human and animal. He sensed the stars and planets and faraway galaxies, and everything was good.

A truth awakened amid his delirious delight. *There is no light and dark, good and evil, love and hate. There is only light and the absence of light, good and the absence of good, love and the absence of love. For when the Creator set into the void the heavens and the earth, they were pronounced good. There is only one Source, and it is light and love, which can never be extinguished.*

57

Three days after the Deluge

Mandisa stood on the deck with Quetzal, Hashur, a brawny stonemason named K'an, and two of the five Diaprep city guardians who were assigned to Ark Gabriel. The waters were much calmer, but they still encountered waves of twenty cubits or more from time to time. To the north, south, east, and west stretched nothing but the opaque depths of unsettled sea.

"Can you tell which direction we're headed?" K'an asked. His coloring matched Mandisa's, his physique rivaled Quetzal's, and he quoted poetry like Agathon—to her surprise.

"The first two days, the flooding carried us due south," Mandisa answered. "But today I've noticed a slight movement to the west."

"We can't expect a stable current after such upheaval," Quetzal explained. "In a few weeks or months, the ocean will find a new rhythm, though not the same as before."

"I haven't spotted any of the other arks since we closed our great door," mentioned a stalwart guardian.

Quetzal nodded as a serious expression filled his ruddy face. "When the massive swell descended on Diaprep, it could have knocked us all in different directions, like pins struck by a ball in a game of lawn knockdown. I kept contact with Thoth, Ziusudra, and Lysandra for most of the first day, so I know they all survived the initial encounter. I suspect we are too far apart for my telepathic powers—weak as they are—to be of any more use."

"I think you wanted to move toward Maanu, anyway, didn't you?" Mandisa asked.

"It was my preference," Quetzal confirmed. "I helped Thoth move tablets and scrolls to his new library in Tiwanaku where he left several of his students. And we got along so well with the Xi people of the Mayeb. However, I am of the firm belief we will land precisely where we are meant to."

"Hey, I think I see something!" called Hashur. Knowing him to have sharp eyesight, Mandisa hurried to his side. Without a rudder, their vessel floated leisurely along at an awkward angle, the rear moving forward and slightly sideways. He peered over the railing, using his hand as a sunshade as he scanned the rise and fall of the waves.

"Over there," he pointed. While Mandisa strained to see, the others all gathered around.

"There's a person out there," Quetzal cried in astonishment. "I feel human vibrations. K'an, go fetch Balam and Raffi."

"Right away!"

As he raced off, Mandisa glimpsed something floating in the ocean about a hundred cubits off the side. "I think you're right, Quetzal."

"I'll get some ropes," Hashur offered and hurried into the aviary on the top deck to search for them.

"How will we reach him or her?" asked the concerned guard.

"The ropes," Mandisa said. "I'll use them to repel down the side of the ark and tie one around the survivor—if he or she is alive—and you can pull them up."

Quetzal shook his head. "I sent for Balam so he can call dolphins or an orca to push his raft over to us. Then one of the young men can climb down."

"You think—" Mandisa began in a sharp tone, slapping fists to her hips.

Holding up a palm, Quetzal broke in. "It's not that you're a woman or getting older or any of that, so don't be offended. It's a dangerous assignment and I can't lose you."

"We are twenty-six Atlanteans," she stubbornly replied. "None of us are expendable."

Hashur returned, dragging volumes of rope. "Here we are. Now what?"

"Measure how long they are," Mandisa instructed. "We'll probably need to tie several lengths together."

Quetzal cursed and rubbed the back of his neck, a pained expression pulling his face tight. "Now the waves are taking it away."

"You called?" Balam jogged up, panting for breath after his sprint.

"See that raft?" Quetzal pointed. "Call some marine animal to push it towards us."

"I'll try," the young man said and started his ritual.

"Here," Hashur reported. "I tied them all together."

"Good. Now, tie one end securely to this railing," Mandisa instructed. When he immediately complied, Mandisa supposed he was so used to taking orders from her that he didn't even bother to ask what for. "I love you, Hashur," she repeated for the millionth time. "I don't mean to bark commands at you, it's just—"

"I know." A slight blush lit his sweet face. "It's just that you know what you're doing. I trust you, my love. There. Test it."

She did and smiled at him. "Thank you."

"Where are we coming with those whales or dolphins?" Quetzal asked impatiently.

"Well, master, there have to be some in the general vicinity for me to reach them—a few leagues or nearer. I can't call them from the other side of the ocean, plus it would take them too long to arrive. The terrible deluge has knocked them out of their usual haunts. Besides, I don't even know where we are. I tried—no one answered."

"Be ready," Mandisa said. She took hold of the rope and climbed over the side.

It had been a long time since she'd done any climbing or water walking; she felt more confident about the second. She hadn't taken time to find gloves, and the rope was rough in her hands. With her focus on the refugee who needed help, Mandisa walked her feet down the sides of the ark. *I could stand to exercise more often,* she reminded herself.

She stopped when her feet sank into the churning sea below, still holding onto the rope, and opened her energies to flow between herself and the water. It was confused, its regular patterns and composition disrupted from being inundated with unfathomable tons of fresh water. Using her gift, Mandisa spread a calming influence through each drop until the area surrounding *Gabriel* became smooth. Then she pulled on the tiniest droplets within droplets, bidding them to squeeze tighter and denser together. The water obeyed.

As soon as she felt the surface solidify under her feet, Mandisa released the rope and cast her gaze over the water, spying the small raft. Inhaling a deep breath, she asked the wind to blow toward her, bringing the survivor with it. A stiff breeze struck her, blowing back her long, ebony braids and faded yellow tunic. Together, the elements guided what she could now perceive as a ripped-off section of dock planking toward her at an easy pace. A figure lay still atop it. *Quetzal said he felt a person's life force, so they couldn't be dead already.*

When the object was less than fifty cubits away, Mandisa spread a hand toward it, imagining the surface of the ocean was as stiff as a board. She allowed compassion for the person in need to fill her body and spirit until it was as tangible as dough to be kneaded into a loaf. Letting the emotion guide her, she confidently set one foot in front of the other and walked over the tranquil sea to meet them.

This wasn't the first time she had walked on water, although the practice required immense focus and energy and wasn't to be taken lightly or used as a magic trick to impress. The flow of energies employed to create worlds wasn't to be called upon in vain. While still holding all the other frequencies, Mandisa added grateful appreciation to the mix.

Upon reaching the makeshift lifeboat, her eyes widened, and her heart extended even more radiance. Lying on the wet planks, she found a young mother with a baby cradled in her arms. She had tied herself on with a cord and both seemed to be alive and breathing.

Pivoting, she shouted up with her hands cupped around her mouth. "Quick! Send down a litter or large basket. It's a mother and infant!"

Leaving her friends to obey her command, Mandisa returned her attention to the survivors. She crawled over the boards and laid a gentle hand on the woman's shoulder to roust her. "You are safe now," she said. "We've got you and your little one."

Slowly, the woman stirred, opening tired eyes to her. She blinked, then wiped water drops from around her eyes as amazement blossomed on her face. She tried to speak, but only a squeak came out.

"Shh, it's all right," Mandisa soothed. "There'll be time for introductions after our healer treats you and your little one. Your prayers are answered. You're safe, sweet one." She stroked a hand over the young woman's scraggly, damp hair and cold cheek, sending affectionate vibrations to warm her.

Once the others were pulling up the platform carrying mother and child to *Gabriel's* safety, Mandisa held out the hem of her tunic, lifted her face toward the sky, and coaxed the wind. Creating an updraft per her request, the vibrant movement of the air elevated her to the top deck to join the others.

Quetzal gaped at her in astonishment. "Mandisa, that has to be the most extraordinary thing I've ever witnessed!"

The corners of her mouth turned up, and she batted her eyes at him. "Doubtful. You saw Ariel, Balam, and the others call the animals onto the ark, and healers like Raffi and Lysandra grow back patients' severed limbs. And I'm certain you've astrally traveled the universe, so … we all have our gifts. We're like parts of a body, each performing its function, none more or less worthy than the others. I appreciate your leadership, Quetzal, and your praise," she said with a broadening smile. "But I think I'll go lie down and rest now."

He scooped her up in a hug before handing her over to Hashur, who put an arm around her and helped her downstairs.

☥ ⛤ ✝ ✡

Twenty days later, in the West Atlantic

Mandisa sat across from Agathon at a little table in the human quarters of Ark Gabriel engaged in a game of Twenty Squares. She rolled the dice and moved her piece. On Agathon's turn, he passed her, gaining the advantage.

"You know, occasionally the rolls should go in my favor," she commented.

He leaned back in his chair, fixing her with an amused grin, and laced his fingers behind his head. "I've got to be better at something."

It had been a long Libra, and Mandisa grew bored being confined to the ship. She had a couple of storms to deal with and had encouraged a cloud to form on an exceptionally hot day, but there was little to occupy her time. To make matters worse, their living arrangements allowed for limited privacy. She, Hashur, and Agathon were accustomed to delighting in frequent evenings of pleasure, and they hadn't managed to squeeze in more than the rare, brief interlude.

What she had enjoyed was getting to know the remarkable men and women on Ark Gabriel. Demetrios and his husband Malah ensured there was entertainment every night as they performed songs and dances, jokes, and acted scenes from their theater productions. Raffi's granddaughter played the flute and would often join Agathon's lyre and Mandisa's drum to play for the others. Queen Zamná was a classically trained dancer whose movements were beautiful to behold. King Tecuani, who joined them from Ampherium after sending his citizens away, was a talented artist who had graced the ark's interior with his painting. The city guardians, stonemason, carpenters, and others she had never met before boarding, all shared their creative expressions as well—including the king's wife, who prepared more delicious meals than the best restaurants in Atala could boast.

"I want some fresh air," Mandisa announced and pushed up from the table before taking another move in the game. "Let's go join Hashur on deck."

He gave her a sly look. "Not being a sore loser, are you?"

"Never," she quipped. "I'm just restless and bored. Maybe we'll spot land today."

"Sure," her sweetheart of a husband agreed. "Fresh air would be nice." He took her arm, and they strolled the dim passage to the stairwell. The ship had already burned through half of the light-duty crystals, so they were now held in reserve for use only during the first hour after dark and to operate the cooktop when the seas were too rough to safely use the wood-burning oven. Some light filtered down during the daytime and candles were in plentiful supply. Mandisa didn't find any of these measures an inconvenience.

Quetzal, Hashur, and King Tecuani patrolled the top deck with K'an, his girlfriend, and Raffi's granddaughter. The weather was pleasant, and the fresh breeze was invigorating. "Where are we?" Mandisa asked. Agathon strolled over to Hashur's watch post, falling in shoulder-to-shoulder beside him at the railing.

"According to my calculations, we should be on the Mayeb peninsula," Quetzal replied. He rubbed the back of his neck with a broad hand and shook his head.

"At least that's where you wanted to go," Mandisa answered, not sure what to say. Instantly her thoughts turned to the Xi people they had met here. They had been so friendly and hospitable. Then she remembered the Tuxtlas mountains they had mentioned and encouraged herself by imagining them safe in the highlands.

"Why don't we send out a bird?" asked one of the young women. "It can relay a message back to Balam if it sees land."

"We could do that," Quetzal considered. "But even if it spots something, we can't steer the ark."

"No," Mandisa agreed. She caught his gaze with a sparkle in her eyes and joy dancing on her lips. "But I could encourage the wind and current to push us in the right direction."

His burly face lit with delight, and he slapped a hand on her shoulder. "You are so handy to have aboard."

"Hey, I see something!" Hashur shouted from his perch near the bow. *Gabriel* faced northwest today.

Everyone rushed to gather around him. "I think I see it too," seconded K'an as he leaned over the rail with a hand shading his eyes.

"Mandisa, why don't you do your thing?" Quetzal suggested with a hopeful grin.

☥ ⚛ ✢ ✡

The next morning, twenty-four days after the Fall Equinox of the year 1360 of the Third Age, *Ark Gabriel* came to rest against a mountain on a high plateau in an area of Maanu northwest of where the Mayeb peninsula should be. The occupants opened the enormous door in the ark's side and lowered the ramp to find themselves surrounded by a verdant landscape spotted with large gray stones, tropical plants, and the loud call of big, colorful birds. As Mandisa gazed across it, taking in the vista, she detected a lovely waterfall that splashed from over a hundred cubits into a lagoon pool below cast in a hue reminiscent of Ariel's eyes. A curious group of short, brown-skinned people gathered to greet them, filled with awe and a little fear.

Quetzal stepped out first, waving and smiling at the people. The others followed, exuding friendly auras and faces. He spoke to them in the Xi language, hoping people here knew the tongue.

"Greetings, friends." He extended open palms to them, as was a traditional practice. "I am Quetzal of Atlantis, and these are my friends. We have traveled across the great water to escape the Deluge."

A skinny fellow with his black hair cut in a bowl wearing a white kilt and no shoes pointed excitedly and answered, "Quetzal coalt!" which meant Quetzal from Atla, the Xi people's name for Atlantis.

Mandisa recognized a taller man who pushed through the crowd with an exuberant grin consuming his features. Kele, chief of the village Cachitl, held out his arms in welcome.

"Quetzal! Mandisa! I'm so glad you made it to us. Your warning saved my people. After your visit, we moved up here and, when the flood waters came, not a soul was lost. You are most loved and appreciated, dear Quetzal and friends. Stay with us and teach us. Be our leader, and we will be your people."

The two men embraced while cheers sounded from the villagers. The mother and her son, whom Lysandra had healed from the scorpion poison, rushed to hug her. Her son was much bigger now, and immensely curious about the ark.

"There are animals inside," Mandisa told him. "Do you want to watch when we bring them out?"

"Yes!" he answered excitedly.

A warm sensation of belonging flowed through Mandisa's spirit. She pictured many adventures to share here with Hashur and Agathon and all the new friends she would make. It wasn't Ryzen or Evamont, but, for now, it was home.

58

The Green Sea, twenty-eight days after the Deluge

Thoth sat in his secret hideaway in a cubby on the lower deck, reading a book by candlelight. Sometimes he just needed to get away from everyone, and he found the spot next to the manatee tub relaxing. The two sweet-natured, meaty sea cows snored softly, their heads on sandbag pillows while the rest of their bulk lay suspended in water inside the oversized tubs.

Hypatia had been recently checking on the animals and told him the otters were awake to eat and get some exercise, if he wanted to join the others to watch them play. While tempting, he felt like a little peace and quiet. Hypatia had rolled her eyes at the scroll he had with him: *A Philosophical Treatise on the Second Age,* though Thoth found it fascinating.

He had just embarked on Heron's interpretation of the Law of Cycles when a forceful bump jarred the vessel with an unexpected jolt, knocking over his candle and extinguishing its flame. It nearly threw the librarian from his stool as water from the manatees' habitat sloshed over the rim, creating tiny streams in the dirt and straw littering the floorboards.

The vibrant and always ready-for-action King Basilius popped his head around the stairwell and shouted, "We hit something!"

And I wanted to reconsider Heron's hypothesis, he thought regretfully as he rolled the scroll. "I'm coming," he called in reply. Taking a glance at the fat, lazing aquatic mammals to ensure they still slumbered peacefully, Thoth paced through the dim passage and climbed the stairs.

It seemed he was the last to arrive, as a frenzy of activity met him up top—as did a close-up view of mountains. They had drifted through a much wider version of the Herculean Channel two days ago, and Zosar had been keeping a close eye on a ridge to the south. The air speaker's primary responsibility was to move their rudderless craft toward Kemet and the mouth of the great Nile River, but Thoth hadn't recalled seeing any mountains in the vicinity on his last visit.

Ark Barachiel, named for the chief guardian angel and archangel of blessings, had floated in an enormous circle for weeks—first south, then west, north, and finally east, bringing them through the pillars into the Green Sea. From what Thoth's body perceived, they weren't moving anymore.

"We've run aground on these cliffs," King Efrayim informed him. "The water of the Green Sea is much higher than the last time I traveled this way, as there used to be a broad beach and gentle slopes before reaching the mountains."

"The flood waters have extended beyond the Pillars of Hercules," Thoth reasoned. "Can we dislodge our ark and continue east?"

Ptah strode over to him, bearing a serious manner. "I've been examining the jagged rocks and the way the vessel's keel hung up on them. Come, I'll show you."

Thoth followed the master builder, whom he trusted to know his business. Ptah, wearing a black and gold Nemeš to cool his head, extended an arm toward the offending peaks. "An errant wave lifted the ark and splashed us this way, headfirst, into a narrow dip between the rocks on this side of the ship and that rise on the opposite side."

As Ptah pivoted and motioned across the breadth of the ark, Thoth realized they were wedged between two points.

"Perhaps at high tide," he began.

Zosar, a slender fellow even older than Thoth, shuffled over, wearing disappointment like a shield. "It *is* high tide."

"Weren't you supposed to prevent things like this from happening?" asked a frustrated Efrayim. The king let out a sigh and ran his fingers through salt and pepper hair that had lost a bit of its former luster.

Straightening and taking on a defensive posture, Zosar spoke boldly. "Air speakers cannot control the winds and waves. We aren't magicians. I did the best I could, but do you spend all day and night on high alert, exuding your energy to maintain order? Were you able to convey every citizen of Atala to a safe port before the Deluge came?"

"That will be enough." Thoth's voice was soft with compassion and understanding. "We may carry a sliver of the divine in our souls, but we still operate as human beings. We have horses, oxen, donkeys, and llamas, along with a sufficient amount of wood. Let's build chariots and wagons and journey across the Libyan valley to Giza, where Isis and Osiris wait for us. If any wish to stop at a town along the way, they are welcome to. At least we found dry land, and that is a blessing."

Thoth turned, raised his hands, and called out in a robust voice to the two dozen people who stood around, fretting at their dilemma. "Friends, countrymen, let us gather and give thanks! Let us rejoice that we have been safely delivered from death to life, that we have found the land of the Maghreb. We have plenty of provisions to see us to Kemet. Be thankful and of good cheer!"

"But, Master Thoth, this isn't where we planned to land," Zosar responded with even more disappointment. "I did the best I could, but—"

Thoth stepped to the old air speaker and rested a hand on his shoulder. "All is well. If we unintentionally came aground, there must be a reason for it."

"We should call them the Nuisance Mountains because they have created an annoyance for us," King Basilius suggested with a half laugh.

"No," Thoth mused thoughtfully. "From this point forward, they will be known as the Atlas Mountains because they are where the Atlanteans came ashore after moving to this new continent."

Hypatia and Efrayim's wife agreed it was a marvelous idea. On that day, they set to work, using their remaining crystal energy on anti-gravity skids to move goods, materials, and animals that couldn't navigate the rocky terrain farther down the southern slopes into a lush valley cut by a river with ample volume for the freshwater fish they carried.

☥ ☬ ✝ ✡

Giza, thirty days later

Thoth's vibration raised on eagle's wings at the sight of sunrays gleaming off the shining top of the great pyramid in the distance as if it were the brightest of stars. While most of the journey took them through grasslands and scattered forests harboring plenty of streams and ponds, he was glad Zosar had redeemed his reputation by finding water in the dry areas they passed through. The wild beasts had danced for joy at the chance to stretch their legs and kick up their heels. The alligators, beavers, and otters headed straight for the river at the base of where the ark had landed. Grazing animals feasted on the grasses and leaves of the green valley and Thoth was almost sad to say goodbye to the manatees when they embarked on the long, overland trek.

Joy swelled in his heart at the thought of hugging his daughter and son-in-law again, and of seeing his completed library. Several of the city guardians who rode *Barachiel* with him had stayed in an oasis village that was conspicuously short on male residents, for which they received much teasing from Basilius, Efrayim, and the others. The rest of his party whooped and hollered and Hypatia sent vibrations of urgency to their animals, who picked up their pace.

They brought goats, sheep, pigs, chickens, and several sorts of cows along with the horses, llamas, oxen, and donkeys that conveyed them across the vast plains. A wagon filled with seeds of every variety trailed behind, and Thoth suspected most would grow on the fertile banks of the Nile. They had traded some trinkets for a couple of camels, and the honored librarian entered Giza riding atop one. Not as comfortable as a sleigh; however, considering the recent energy crisis, more reliable.

The procession was met with the sounding of trumpets. Residents rushed out waving palm branches and cheering. Women presented them with baked goods and men shook their hands, offering to carry their loads.

"This way, Master Thoth," enthused a lanky lad whom he recognized as Huy, Ariel's entrepreneurial tour guide. He must have grown half a cubit since the last time he'd seen him. "Isis and Osiris are coming to greet you."

They turned down a sunny street that led toward the Great Sphinx where Atlanteans who'd traveled ahead of time gathered with colonists and indigenous dignitaries. Nearing the delegation, Thoth commanded his camel to kneel and, with Huy's assistance, slid off to the paving stones. Isis rushed past the others and threw her arms around his neck, showering him in kisses. As tears of joy welled in her eyes, she was too emotional to speak.

Osiris joined her and offered genuine greetings. After extending him a manly embrace, the young man stepped back, glowing with appreciation.

"Thoth, these people have turned out to honor you because your vision saved them all," Osiris praised. "A couple of moons ago, the Nile flooded much more expansively than any can remember, and we knew what caused it. Isis hasn't ceased her prayers for your safe arrival from that terrible day until now."

The local city planner Thoth had worked with to design his library and position the pyramids stepped in beside Osiris. "We all took refuge in the completed pyramid and underground tunnels you designed and waited for the water to recede. Ptah, you are most honored as well," he proclaimed, gesturing toward the big architect. "Without your expertise, there would be no pyramids."

"Osiris had a vision," Isis said, still clinging to her father's arm, "so the farmers all harvested their fields early. Now their land is richer than ever with the fresh layer of sediment."

"Come friends, new and old," called the jubilant city planner. "We will have a feast tonight to celebrate your arrival, complete with singing, dancing, and gaiety. Let's laugh together and exchange stories. You shall meet my family and

I will embrace yours. This is a day of triumph, signaling a new era of prosperity for Giza and all of Kemet with Thoth as our leader."

"Well, I was ready to retire anyway," chuckled King Basilius. "I always wanted to try my hand at engraving."

"Now, don't be hasty." Osiris slapped a hand on his shoulder with a grin. "The old man knows just about everything, but he's not exceptionally organized. I feel sure he'll need you and King Efrayim's help if we are to establish New Atlantis on the banks of the Nile."

Thoth had to admit his daughter's husband was right. Besides, he didn't want to rule; he just wanted to collect knowledge and dispense it to the people.

"I'll leave the ruling to younger folk," Thoth responded as he beamed with pleasure in the shade of the mighty stone cat. "Ptah has more pyramids to build; Zosar and Hypatia have seeds to plant and beasts and rivers to tend to. I'm sure my children can benefit from Kings Efrayim and Basilius's experience. I place Kemet in their capable hands. Just leave me to study the stars and teach reading and writing to our new neighbors."

Cheers resounded, for Thoth had learned of Isis's and Osiris's popularity in Giza. He shook hands, tried to remember names, and itched to descend the stairs into his amazing Hall of Records beneath the Sphinx's paw. Stepping aside, he took a moment to savor the sights that stretched before him. Thoth soaked in the picturesque view of the vibrant river, the grandeur of the architecture, the tranquil ambiance of nature, the warm rays of the sun, the comforting shade, and the infectious enthusiasm of the people, and gave thanks.

59

The Green Sea, thirty-three days after the Deluge

Clouds still covered the sky, even though the latest rain had stopped, and a muggy dampness hung in the air like a heavy, wool cloth. The entire month of Libra had passed without sight of land, save when *Ark Uriel* passed between the pillars. Ziusudra had been moody and cross because his instruments and calculations proclaimed one thing while their eyes beheld another. Noah had assured him all would be well, but even he had begun to wonder. *Did the whole earth flood? Where are the islands of Melitē, Trinacria, and Kaptara? Why haven't we seen the land of the Maghreb or Pelasgoí?* He hoped and prayed the waters of the Deluge had not washed away the Atlanteans and indigenous inhabitants who lived in the Green Sea, but he couldn't be certain. It seemed to him as though those who were carried in his ark were the only humans remaining on the earth.

Ziusudra had assured him that wasn't so, that others had survived. They were certain their sister arks made it safely through the initial calamity, only they hadn't seen nor received energetic signals from the other chosen, gifted leaders in weeks.

"What do you want to do?" asked Noah's daughter-in-law, Nahalath. It was now noticeable that the reserved brunette was with child, as a cheery baby bump bulged under the band of her creamy chiton. Shem stood beside her, a steadying hand pressed to the small of his wife's back, also awaiting the patriarch's instructions with an expectant expression.

Noah had been brooding all morning, despite realizing it served no purpose. Even if Ziusudra could provide him with the exact location of dry land, he had no power to guide the vessel. Lifting a helpless gaze at the dense clouds, he asked for clarity and guidance.

"Send a raven," he instructed. "Tell it to make an outward wide circle looking for any sign of land and return before getting too tired. Have it report back to you anything of promise."

"That's a good idea," Shem replied optimistically.

Nahalath nodded and woke the snoozing raven. Giving it proper instructions, she told the group, "She promises to do her best." Then she lifted the bird and gave it a boost into flight.

"Nothing to do now but wait," grumbled Ziusudra. "Until these clouds break up, I can't even consult the stars to determine our location."

Emzara stepped closer and took Noah's arm in a supportive gesture. "We should divide our time between merriment and meditation," his wife suggested. "We can't let the dreary weather bring down our spirits. Shem, gather your brothers and the others in the common room and break out some wine. We'll play a game of Guess What or Guess Who."

"Wonderful, Mother," Shem agreed. "Come on, Father. You like wine and you're good at games."

"You all go along and, Nahalath, you go with them. I'll stay here and wait for the raven."

"When did you learn to communicate with birds?" she asked with a teasing smirk. "Emzara is right. You need to raise your vibration. Now, go relax and enjoy yourself. I'll let you know the minute the raven returns, regardless of the news she brings."

Noah expelled a sigh and patted his wife's hand where it lay on his arm. "Very well."

The games and drink helped ease much of Noah's tension temporarily. While he chatted with the air speaker Tirzah's husband about farming and forestry, Emzara and her sons' wives—except for Nahalath—prepared the evening meal. They took turns with Ziusudra's family and the others on board, performing all the chores. Someone had to sweep floors, empty chamber pots, help Nahalath care for the animals, and do the washing. Counting Ziusudra's wife, his brother and his family, Tirzah and her husband, and a group of guardians and carpenters, twenty-six people were riding *Uriel* to who knew where.

Tempting aromas rose from steaming pots and unleavened bread baking in the coal-burning oven, arousing Noah's hunger. Emzara insisted he had lost weight during the time they'd spent on the ship from not eating properly. Noah took a moment to feel gratitude for his wife's loving concern. Then Nahalath slid onto the bench beside him.

"The raven found nothing today, but we can send her mate out tomorrow," she reported. "It won't be long now, and, even if it takes weeks, we still have plenty of supplies."

"Thank you, dear," Noah replied and kissed her forehead. "How are you and baby Noah feeling?"

She giggled with an infectious grin. "I've been a little nauseous at times, but Jatziri is taking excellent care of us."

"At last, some good news. I'll give thanks for you and my grandchild—and your mother-in-law's cooking. Let's eat!" While a part of him wanted to wallow in despair, allow worry to suck him into a mire, and entertain thoughts of worst-case scenarios, Noah rallied and kept his spirits high. It was easy to become lost in serious contemplations as long as Thoth and Quetzal were making all the decisions, but these people looked to him as their leader—even Ziusudra, though he was equally capable. Therefore, he did his best to set a good example.

☥ ☬ ✝ ✡

Forty days after the Deluge

Over the past week, there had still been no sign of land. They had sent the ravens out several more times without a sighting. Nahalath had also talked to a pair of long-finned pilot whales. They reported having passed a long shoreline a few days before but couldn't tell them how to find it. "We got all turned around when the flood came," one had told her. "We aren't from the region and are just trying to navigate our way back to familiar waters," the other expounded. At least they had seen the land, so it was out there—somewhere.

That morning Noah ambled along the top deck, grateful for the sunshine, as he performed his morning meditation. It saddened him that connecting with the spirits and energies wasn't as easy for him now as it had been hundreds of years ago. He recalled persuading a walking catfish to leave its pond and dance on the bank to entertain a girl he had been sweet on. Naunet and he used to make a game of sprouting wildflower blossoms across vast meadows. Until eighty years ago, he could use telepathy to talk to friends at a distance. Best of all, when he was calm, contented, and resting in perfect peace, he could recall the feeling of joining his spirit to all of creation, experiencing the awesomeness of being whole with the One. In a bygone era, he had truly known the wonder of being an Atlantean. Now he only caught glimpses of glory, as if he resided in a thick fog that blocked out his most valuable senses. It was frustrating bordering on depressing, yet, understanding The Law, he realized the paradox: belief precedes manifestation. While other societies said, "Seeing is believing," The Law taught just the opposite—believing is seeing. *As above, so below; as within, so without,* he recalled as he fingered the six-point star pendant that hung around his neck.

"Why is it so much harder now?" he asked to whatever angels or ancestors might be listening. His steps were slow and deliberate, as was his intentional breathing. Holding out his palms at his side, he said, "I'm listening, ready to receive a word of wisdom." No voices sounded in his awareness.

"Why? Ziusudra said it's the natural cycle of the stars and heavenly bodies, that our planet has moved into a thinner place in the ether. He says Gaia is a living body with cycles like a woman, and it warms and cools, jutting up mountains in one place and sinking land into the abyss in another because it's nature's way, but surely Infinite Intelligence and Unwavering Compassion could intercede to prevent disasters that cost so many lives."

He strolled some more, keeping to himself when Nahalath strode out onto the deck. Seeing her made him smile. *Soon I'll hold my grandchild. I will bestow on him a blessing at his naming ceremony. All right, or hers. Either way, I'm happy.*

Allowing genuine joy to light his soul opened a door of inspiration, and Noah had a thought. Picking up his pace, he moved to join her by the birds housed in the long, open-air, covered shed.

"It's a beautiful morning, isn't it?" Her bright smile lifted his spirits even higher.

"Indeed." He peered out over the railing one more time. Still seeing nothing but sea, he suggested, "Let's send out a dove today. It will bring us a sign."

"Why not?" Nahalath chirped. She held the white dove gingerly between her hands, cooing at him until he understood the instruction, then launched him into the bright, clear sky. She took Noah downstairs for breakfast, and everyone chatted about the first thing they would do once they were off the ark.

"Soak in a real bath," Emzara said.

"Roll in the grass," Japheth mused dreamily.

"Kiss the ground," laughed Ham.

After a while, Noah returned to the top deck to find the dove perched beside its nest. Though sorely tempted to entertain negative emotions, he resisted. Cradling the bird in his rough hands, he extended vibrations of a patient love. The whales had seen land; it was out there somewhere.

"You can do it, sweet little turtledove. Go find a sign." He released it into the air, only this time he stayed, reciting the comforting words of The Law and imagining the bright new world they would soon discover. In addition to the stockpiles of seeds, Noah had brought a young olive tree with its roots tied up in a sack of dirt. He pictured himself and Emzara planting the tree beside their new home so his grandchild could play in its shade.

It hadn't seemed a long time when the dove returned with—of all things—an olive twig in its beak. "Nahalath, come quick!" he yelled.

She came, and trailing behind was the entire party. "What's wrong?"

"Nothing," Noah answered excitedly. "The dove came back with an olive branch, see? We must be near land."

Ziusudra checked the position of the sun and the moon's reflection on the sky while everyone babbled with excited voices.

"It's this way!" Nahalath pointed to the northeast.

"Tirzah," Noah instructed. "Speak with the elements about generating wind and a current. "Nahalath, can you find those whales again to give us a push?"

"Not those whales, but ..." Stepping to the railing, she closed her eyes and breathed deep, sending out vibrations even Noah could detect. A happy breeze fluttered the runaway strand of her dark hair that had escaped the band holding it back. Then she smiled. "How about him?"

An enormous gray sperm whale, with its square nose and tiny dorsal fin, surfaced, spraying a fountain into the air. He appeared small beside the colossal *Ark Uriel*, but he was powerful enough to nudge them in the right direction.

Everyone onboard cheered and Nahalath extended their gratitude to the whale. By dusk, *Ark Uriel* landed on the side of a mountain. Noah and the others spent the night on the ship, celebrating and making plans for the days and weeks to come. Ziusudra calculated that they were now in Anatola. From the measurements he had taken, the flood waters were receding at a rate of twenty cubits a day. While the highlands looked desolate to Noah, Nahalath assured him that grass and wildflowers were springing back to life.

After conferring with her, Tirzah, and Ziusudra, Noah determined it was best to keep the animals asleep until enough of the land was exposed for them to disperse to adequate distances.

Ziusudra pulled out a map of the region. "These lines show the boundaries of the Green Sea before the flood," he said, pointing. "And these show where I suspect they'll be from now on. The coast cities here and there no longer exist, along with those low-elevation plains, after being wiped out by the flood. But over here to the east of Jerico should provide lots of places to choose from.

There's also Anatola itself, Pelasgoí to the west, and Kemet and Kush to the south."

"Aren't there already civilizations in these areas? What if they aren't agreeable to us living among them?" Jatziri asked in concern.

Noah, remembering Quetzal's tale from the Mayeb, said, "I wouldn't worry about that. One demonstration of healing from you, and every tribe and city-state will beg us to join them. It's not Atlantis—nothing else ever will be—but I believe we can make a life for ourselves and our children in this land. After all, it and its inhabitants were also fashioned by the Creator. We shall consider it an exciting adventure, one to pass down through our family histories."

"Yeah," Ham interjected in an amused manner. "Listen, everyone, and let me tell you about the time we put all these animals onto Noah's ark and floated the ocean for forty days and forty nights after the great and terrible Deluge."

They all laughed at his delivery. Then, with a knowing smile, his mother added, "And what a story it will be!"

60

North Atlantic Ocean, fifty-seven days after the Deluge

Ariel scratched behind the mama bunny's ear while she busily nibbled on a carrot that was sadly past its prime. "What were you thinking getting all happy with your mate in the one afternoon we woke you up to eat? Here you are with babies and now Lysandra can't put you back to sleep."

The rabbit wiggled her nose, twitched an ear, and swallowed her bite. *Are stale carrots all you've got? And aren't we supposed to reproduce and repopulate the earth?*

With a laugh, Ariel replied, "No, we have hay, grain, and some onions and garlic and you could've waited to go hopping around with 'Sleepy' over there until we landed."

She rubbed her tiny bunny hands over her whiskers, down her mouth, and under her chin to make sure she had ingested every morsel. *I suppose it will have to do. Wait until we land somewhere? As if! You know rabbits don't live as long as humans, don't you? I can't waste my youth on your sailing trip.*

She had a point. It had been almost two months. The mice—the ones they knew about—already had two litters. She wondered if they even needed to be awake to do it. "Don't worry, Cleo. I'm sure you'll live long enough to hop around and nibble sweet grass in the new world." *If it has grass; if it's not a desert or frozen wasteland.*

Ariel turned her attention to the animal carrier atop the bunnies. "All right, you squirrel—don't get any bright ideas. You have one more turn of the sandglass before Lysandra puts you back to sleep and enough nuts to keep you occupied. This isn't a nursery, you know." She pointed an accusing finger at the pair of common gray squirrels, and they responded with innocent expressions.

Us? Behave like promiscuous bunnies? How dare you, air speaker! chattered the female, as if Ariel's suggestion had offended her.

Her mate reached into the bowl for another hickory nut. *Don't look at me—I'm just eating and pooping.*

Despite her weary anxiety, Ariel couldn't help but laugh at the pair. *These were the lottery-winning squirrels? Of all the rodents in the animal kingdom, they were selected as the best of the best?*

Continuing to check on the small animals who were taking their turns to be awake, Ariel's concerns resurfaced. Their ark had been all over the place. At first, it was carried south, then east, then west, and north, and now east again. With no astronomer aboard, Banba's card readings and Khafra's impressions from the sea and air were the best indicators they had to go on. Considering the angle of the sun and the biting cold in the wind, Ariel suspected they might be north of where Atlantis should be or near Gadlan. With that idea, she left the menagerie to find King Masuda.

She discovered the burly, yellow-haired giant of an outdoorsman parading around the top deck in nothing more than a tunic and short cape. Meanwhile, Ariel tugged her forest-green woolen wrap snuggly around her shoulders. *Maybe all those muscles and hair keep him warm.*

"Good morning, Masuda." He had insisted nobody use his title anymore; it reminded him his kingdom lay at the bottom of the ocean. "It's a bit brisk up here, don't you think?"

"A refreshingly bracing day," he replied with a broad smile that didn't reach his eyes. "Have you come to seek the counsel of whales or men?"

"Both would be nice," she admitted. He met her at the railing near the stern end of the boat that spun in lazy circles as the tides carried it along. "I didn't think our journey would last so long. The big animals need to move around. I've taken them out a few times in small groups to parade around their respective decks, but they need sunlight and fresh air. I can't bring them up here—they could fall overboard."

"I understand," he answered as he gazed out across the endless sea. The surface was choppy from the wind, but not so unruly as to rock the ark. "There's only so much deck walking and storytelling I can engage in. My arms itch to swing an axe or hammer, to build something, to do something other than sit around. I didn't want to believe it at first. You could say I was a deluge denier for about a year, questioning, and finding other explanations for the evidence brought forth by your team and other experts." He let out a sigh, and Ariel rested a hand on his arm.

"None of us wished to believe it," she consoled.

Just then, Masuda's young boys raced out onto the top deck, laughing, and launching a piece of canvas affixed to a cross with a string tied to it into the air. Colorful rags dangled in a knotted row, forming its tail. Ariel was amazed when the breeze caught the contraption and lifted it high in the air.

"Look, it's flying!" squealed the pre-teen boy with reddish hair and rosy, freckled cheeks as he bounded beside his taller, sandy-haired brother who held tight to the string.

"What is it?" she asked, having never seen such an oddity.

"Fáelán calls it a papyrus raptor because it swoops up and down without flapping any wings," the ginger-haired younger boy said, his broad grin displaying a gap in his pearly teeth. Ariel tried to recall his name, but her mind was too full.

Suddenly, the ship jolted and lurched, shooting the bow up by fifteen degrees. The boys slid and struggled to keep their footing while the papyrus raptor blew away. Masuda hastened to grab his sons before either could be thrown overboard with another impact.

Gripping the rail, Ariel's wide eyes searched the surrounding depths, seeing no sign of land. Using her senses, she quickly deduced it wasn't a whale or other living creature. She was alarmed when the ark stayed at this position and didn't rock back the other way or upright as it would if struck by a massive wave.

"We hit something," Ariel assumed.

"What?" Masuda recoiled. "There's nothing here but ocean."

"Let's go below and check on the animals," Fáelán suggested, as he wiggled from his father's hold now that he was steadier on his feet.

"Come on, Dada, Ariel," the younger child prodded, taking Masuda's hand and tugging on it. "What if the elephants rolled into the lion pen? What then?"

"That couldn't happen," Ariel replied. "But we should go check on them and try to discover what the problem is." By the time Ariel and Masuda reached the stairs, the two boys had downed three flights ahead of them. The pair ran into Aram coming up to meet them.

"You've got to come quick," he urged in alarm. "There's a hole in the bottom of the ship and water's pouring in."

Ariel left her brother and Masuda in the dust as she flew down to the lowest deck where the carnivores and big creatures were housed. She spied Lysandra kneeling on the floor, tending to Fótla's husband, Téthur. He had a bleeding gash on his head and a swollen arm, which she supposed could be broken.

"Lysandra," she said, laying a hand on her shoulder with concern.

"I'm not hurt and Téthur will be fine once I treat him. Go make sure the animals don't drown."

At her urging, Ariel ran uphill toward the gushing spray, her feet sloshing through a trickling stream of icy water. She arrived at the scene at the same time Khafra did, and they both gaped at the jagged shard of stone that had punctured the ark's hull. Not only was water coming in, but the vessel was soundly stuck. If it was suddenly pulled away, unplugging the rock over five cubits in diameter, *Ark Michael* could sink. The horrifying thought pierced her soul with terror.

Before she could catch her breath, Banba stood behind them, surveying the damage. "Éthur, you and Céthur get some spare wood and some hammers and nails. Be ready to quickly patch this hole when I say."

Without questioning, they rushed off to find the required materials. "You others milling about, take cups and buckets down there and start scooping water into an empty barrel for now. Khafra, can you make it stop?"

Khafra was a slender fellow around Ariel's age, with smooth hands, and flowing black hair. Despite his maturity, his thin chin beard and willowy hair spotting his upper lip looked as though they could belong to a youth. He scrunched eyebrows more delicate than hers over dark, almond eyes that betrayed his lack of confidence.

"I will try." He reached out open palms and inhaled a relaxing breath, then spread his hands over the spray that pushed its way between the surface of the stone and the splintered edges of broken floor planks. Closing his eyes, he started to work.

Ariel caught Banba's gaze. "I need to start moving the animals out of the stern where all the water is collecting," she said. The big cats snoozed near the hole, but the large herbivores were the ones in more danger. If they were suddenly awakened, they would be confused and scared, not remembering where they were. She would have to carefully bring them back to awareness one at a time and lead them to a safer place.

"No." Banba's sharp command surprised Ariel, and she blinked at the woman. Pointing, she directed, "You need to go out there and find some sea creature that can get us off this underwater mountaintop, and I mean right now. The elk won't be the only ones drowning if we don't get this leak under control immediately."

"You're right." Wishing she could do both, Ariel had to concur and jogged back to climb the staircase to the top. Banba had decreed the lift wasn't to be used except in the case of an emergency to conserve the power in its operating crystal. It was a smart rule; however, rushing down and up three long flights of stairs, set at an angle, no less, had Ariel panting by the time she reached the top deck once more. She suspected the mountaintop—which neither she nor Masuda had seen looming below the surface—hadn't always been beneath the ocean. It could very well be a high peak in southern Gadlan according to her earlier guesses.

Standing in the stiff wind, her cloak whipping about her, Ariel concentrated on reaching out with her energetic frequencies for a pod of whales, dolphins, or other large sea mammals who were easy to communicate with. She received no answer. Maybe it was her anxiety or maybe they were so close to where the Terrible Ice broke that all the marine mammals who once lived here had been washed south. Ariel quieted her mind and tried again. After several minutes, still nothing.

"Do you need any help?" asked Ériu, who had come up to check on her.

"Get me a long rope," she said. This wasn't going to do. Water transmitted vibrations much farther and with more intensity than air did. She had to go down there where the creatures were.

Ériu returned, lugging lengths of rope across the slanted deck. "What do you need these for? You aren't thinking about getting into the water, are you?"

"I have to," Ariel replied as she unfastened her wool wrap. She handed it to Ériu, simultaneously taking the coil from her.

"But Ariel, the water is freezing," Ériu cautioned, taking hold of her arm. "There must be another way."

"We've come too far for too long to let this vessel sink, and I know Archangel Michael will provide deliverance. Something is telling me to get in the water and call again, so that's what I'll do. If my body freezes, Lysandra can thaw it out again."

Ériu blinked. "She can do that?"

Ariel's lip curved and her eyes danced at her friend. "I once witnessed her revive a man who hadn't breathed for ten minutes after having his chest crushed by a stone in a construction accident in Evamont. The only things beyond her talent to heal are a traumatic brain injury and a severed head. Trust me; I'll be all right."

"If you say so. But I'm not strong enough to pull you up. I'm going to fetch Mal'akhi and his friend."

With a nod, Ariel consented and finished tying off her knots.

"Well, here goes nothing," she said. Then she climbed over the rail and lowered herself into the frosty waters over twenty cubits below.

When Ariel was only a few cubits above the choppy waves, she jumped rather than take time to acclimate to the temperature. The impact stole her breath, and she had difficulty regaining it as the pain of a thousand needle-pricks bore into her chest and belly. She shook it off and focused all her attention on breathing. *In and out, slow and controlled*, she reminded herself. Her body shivered of its own accord. *Oma, I need you now.*

61

Ariel reached out to her oma and mentor through time and space, picturing her mischievous, laughing eyes that let her know she was up to no good, her sweet spirit, her acquired wisdom, and her intense loyalty. *Help me, Oma. Wherever you are, you said you'd always be with me. I need to find a sea creature who can get us unstuck from this rock, and the water is so cold.*

She closed her eyes, recalling Oma discussing the Law of Attraction with her. "You don't attract what you want; you attract what you are. Like attracts like."

"Wait, I'm confused," Ariel replied to the dream Oma. "I'm supposed to be a whale?"

"If you beg and plead like a needy person, the Universe acts as if you enjoy being needy since that is your focus and will respond with more lack. That is why we give thanks for what we do not have as if we had it. You know all this, foolish child. Has the icy water stolen your wits along with your breath?"

Ariel's eyes popped wide. Oma wasn't just in her memories—she was communicating with her right now. The revelation sent a surge of joy through her that overpowered the crisis at hand. Oma *was* with her!

"Assume the heart of the whale, pumpkin."

Heart of the whale. Ariel, still holding the rope, paddled a few cubits away from the side of the ark and shifted all her attention to her heart energy. *Whales have tremendous hearts.* She imagined her heart increasing in size with every beat. It outgrew her chest and kept swelling with love and appreciation. *I can still talk to Oma, even though we are far away.* The thought caused her chakra energy to radiate even wider.

When Ariel was so fixated on the visualization of her expanding energy that she no longer felt the stinging pain of the cold or entertained a single thought or feeling of loss or fear, she heard Oma whisper, "Listen!"

She felt an impulse to lower her head under the water and followed it. Everything sounded different under here—the subtle slap of the ship planks interacting with the mountain peak, vibrations from fish she hadn't noticed from above the surface. There came a distant thump. Wondering what it was, Ariel zeroed in on the low frequency that reminded her of the biggest of drumheads being struck with a slow-moving mallet. She counted two of her own heartbeats between each sound as it maintained a steady rhythm.

At once, Ariel knew. She poked her head above the water to catch a breath and lowered back in to send signals to the whale at least a league or two away. *I'm Lahun and I'll help you if I can,* came a genuinely compassionate reply. It was a female blue whale. She had been scooping up krill in the cold, northern waters, reluctant to go south for the winter because of suffering depression over losing her infant calf.

"We appreciate you so much," Ariel replied with her head above water again. Now that they had established a link, she didn't have to be under to reach the whale. "I'm so sorry to hear about your baby. Do you want to talk about it?"

We were near the Terrible Ice when it broke, crashing in gigantic sheets, and water shot out from behind it in torrents. My baby was swept away and not strong enough to swim against the powerful onslaught. I sped after her, trying to find her. Everywhere around me were strange currents. An albatross was announcing the end of the world. I finally found her body floating motionless the next day. She had drowned and I couldn't save her.

Empathy and compassion flowed from Ariel to Lahun with a force to match that of the Deluge. "I know how you feel. I couldn't save all the people and animals I wanted to either. There's so much we can't control."

I know she rests safely in the bosom of Creation, part of the One, but I am sad because I miss her. I won't get to enjoy watching her grow up. Her life was cut short and mine is incomplete. But I am happy to help you.

The massive blue whale surfaced on the other side of Ariel from the ark. *I've never seen a boat bigger than me before,* she commented. Although the splendid creature was the largest that had ever lived on the earth, it would have taken four of them lined up head to tail to match the size of *Ark Michael*. Having completely forgotten the frigid water and the imminent danger, Ariel swam closer and touched the gentle giant, caressing its skin with comforting strokes.

"I love and care about you," she conveyed from her expanded heart. "I am here with you and share in your mourning. You should also share in our joy. We still have many years to live. You will have another baby. It may not be the same but will be just as worthy and loveable."

"Hey, Mother, what are you doing down there?" Mal'akhi yelled over the railing above them.

Recalling why she was talking to the whale in the first place, Ariel threw back her head to peer up at him. "Tell Khafra and the others to get ready. This kind whale is about to push the ark off the rock. It might tear a bigger hole, but we won't be stuck anymore."

"I'll send Nymphe with the word," he hollered back. "Pamphilos and I are pulling you up."

"All right, but just a moment." Ariel turned her attention back to Lahun, transferring memories, thoughts, and emotions in a speedy conveyance, like logs shooting through a flume.

"Be at peace, my sister," Ariel told her with a pat to her side.

Shall I push the big boat now?

"Yes, please. The one at the railing is my child, my grown son. After he pulls me up, push us free from the snag. I hope to meet you again. We are connected now."

Yes, I would like that, nature speaker. There are so few humans left in the world that I can talk to. Hurry now, before your boat sinks.

Ariel smiled from her soul outward, kissed Lahun's salty skin, swam back to the side of the ark, and tugged on the rope. "Now!" she called up. Mal'akhi and Pamphilos hoisted her up and, once she was over the railing, she released word to the whale to push. In three heartbeats, the powerful creature had liberated them from their unwanted anchor in the middle of the ocean.

She sent warm wishes to her new friend even as she recognized her teeth chattered and goose bumps covered her skin. Mal'akhi threw a dry blanket around her. "Let's get you warmed up."

"Yes, of course, but first we must go check on the hull," she insisted, shivering uncontrollably. "I have to make sure no animals drown. I have to find Lysandra and help—"

"All right," he interrupted, turning her toward the staircase. "I get the point. I'm sure between Masuda and Ériu's clan, they'll have the hole boarded up by the time we get there."

He was probably right, but she had to be sure.

"Good job," Banba declared as she supervised her husband and the others spreading pitch into the cracks to seal the last trickling leaks. Ariel's feet splashed through only a few thumbs of water in the affected section of the craft, while an efficient line of helpers scooped up what remained. "None of your animals perished. Lysandra took Téthur upstairs, and she says he's almost fully recovered." Passing a discerning glance from Ariel's head to foot, she added, "I think you may need her more than he does."

"There you are," Aram announced. "How'd you get us off that ridiculous rock?"

Ariel tried to smile, but it felt like every muscle in her face was frozen. "It was Lahun, a great blue whale, who aided us."

He started to hug her, then retrieved his arm at seeing how wet she was. Making a second try at a greeting, he kissed her forehead. "Go warm up. We're all anxious to hear the ensemble piece you've been working on with Shemu'el, Khafra, and Fáelán."

"And Fótla is going to dance," Masuda added with a grin, which earned him a stern look from his wife, who stopped bailing water to glare at him. "Just saying." He held up his hands in innocence, and her glare morphed into a smirk.

Ariel left the others to finish the repairs and clean up and went to find Lysandra.

"Come here this instant," she commanded upon spotting Ariel looking like a frosty treat. Téthur lay sleeping in his bunk and Lysandra rushed from his side to embrace Ariel.

"First you say come, then you—"

"Hush, you impossible woman I love!" Lysandra kissed her. "You're so cold you're turning blue. Out of those wet clothes this instant and let's dry you by the stove."

Ariel allowed Lysandra to shuffle her across the common room and strip off her soaking tunic and undergarments. She draped a dry blanket around her, then slapped her palms together, swirling them to form a healing energy ball. When Lysandra's hands roamed her body, rubbing and caressing every thumb of naked skin, Ariel felt a sensual heat rise along with the therapeutic one. Bit by bit, her flesh roared back to life, and the color returned to her lips.

Once they could form a smile, she shone it at Lysandra. "I talked to a blue whale," she marveled in delight.

"Oh, sweetie, that's wonderful," Lysandra enthused. "You've been wanting to for so long. But couldn't you have done it from inside the ark?"

Ariel laughed and brushed a kiss to her lips, then a nibble, a lick, and she was falling prey to passion.

"Later, I promise," Lysandra responded with an adorably seductive look. "Someone could walk in at any moment."

"I just saved us from being stuck on a rock in the middle of nowhere for eternity. I dare them to disapprove of us," she challenged. Reluctantly backing away, she quipped. "Can you blame me? When you put your hands on me, it's the most powerful magic in the universe."

Lysandra laughed and took a last bite of Ariel's lower lip. "Get dressed." She pointed Ariel at their sleeping cubby and marched her behind the curtain.

"Yes, master," Ariel said in an exaggeratedly submissive tone. While she pulled a fresh tunic over her head, she asked, "Did you remember to put the rabbits and other small animals back to sleep?"

Lysandra froze, and her eyes went wide. "You woke them up?"

"It was their turn. That goofy female rabbit just had a litter of kits, so she'll have to be left awake, but the male—" Realization set in, and she dropped her jaw at her wife. "You didn't! Damn, she'll be pregnant again! The squirrels and hedgehogs, the chipmunks and marmots. If we don't watch them, they'll be reproducing like—like bunnies!"

With an endearing laugh, Lysandra settled a cloak around Ariel's shoulders and smacked a quick peck to her lips. "I'll take care of it right now. You have a recital to prepare for."

☥ ⚛ ✞ ✡

Ariel drifted between dreams and memories, reliving the awesome day—or had it been yesterday? She could still feel the tingle of the deliriously magnetic touch Lysandra had used to warm her body by the stove. Knowing they could be walked in on added a spark of excitement. To Ariel's relief, the others had all wandered off to try lawn knockdown on the deck by moonlight after dinner and the recital. What a ridiculous idea since the motion of the ship would make the ball impossible to control. Still, it had worked out well since she had gotten Lysandra all to herself for a while. Ariel had shared her experience with Lahun before engaging in a more intimate activity with her desirable mate.

She never tired of making love with Lysandra, giving and taking, indulging in mouthwatering morsels, and drawing sighs and moans of ecstasy from her partner. She had memorized every bump and freckle, every sensuous curve and erogenous zone, every ticklish spot. The knowledge only fueled her desire to visit them over and over again. She fell asleep in a blissful cloud of heavenly pleasure, holding Lysandra close, feeling their oneness all the way through her core.

Floating toward consciousness, Ariel inhaled her wife's fragrant scent, unmarred by the lack of a bathing pool. They all took turns with a washbasin and foot tub set up with a privacy curtain to bathe themselves. Ariel sniffed again—saltwater and seaweed. *Is that me?*

She shot awake in horror, realizing she spent the night cuddled with the most wonderful woman in all the world smelling like a hermit crab. *Jumped in ocean, turned to ice, Lysandra warmed me up, ate, played the recital, made love to Lysandra ... no bathing. Oh, sweetheart, I'm so sorry!*

Gently, Ariel disentangled herself from her wife, crawled out from under the coverlet, and slipped her tunic back on. Aram, Yaluk, and Shemu'el lay sound asleep in the hammock and bunk a few cubits away. She tiptoed past them, picked up a towel, and paused in the opening to the common area. Something was different.

Ariel listened with all her senses, trying to determine what was wrong. The sliver of light filtering in from the stairwell end of the deck's main hallway informed her dawn had broken and yet everyone still slept. *They were up late merrymaking,* she remembered. *And Ériu's family loves their alcohol.*

No sounds came from the monkeys, sloths, porcupines, badgers, or other middle-sized animals that shared their level of the ark. What she did hear was the call of gulls and the slapping and sloshing of waves in a soft, lulling rhythm at about the pace of an elephant breathing. Their rise and fall, in and out, was soothing, even tranquil.

It hit Ariel in an instant and her heart thundered in her chest. Could it be? She had to make sure. She realized what had changed—they weren't moving!

Dropping the towel, Ariel raced up the steps, in her excitement taking them two at a time. Bursting onto the top deck, she was greeted with a spectacular sunrise. Bold yellows and pinks streaked the eastern sky with brilliant rays of near-white light radiating from a gleaming ball of gold on the horizon. Scattered paintbrush strokes like pulled cotton spotted the pale blue, while to the west, the sky clung to its navy hue.

Tiny feet scratched up the steps behind Ariel, and a fat raccoon rubbed against her leg. *Why are you up so early? What do you see?*

In speechless wonder, Ariel picked up Ratiki and held him to her breast as she surveyed the vista before her. Fifty-eight days after the Deluge, *Ark Michael* had drifted ashore on a pristine white-sand beach personalized with several half-sunken boulders. Sea oats splayed out around a rotting log, their seed heads ripe and drooping from their weight. To the left, a cliff striped with light and dark layers of rock rose to a plateau overlooking the sea. To the right, away from the shore, stood a grove of young trees—juniper, birch, and hazel—with shrubs interspersed. And in front of her, and the bow of the ship, lay lush, rolling hills of verdant green, covered in grasses, clover, and heather. A small group of red deer grazed at a distance, paying them no mind.

As she marveled at the scene before her, trying to take it all in at once, a russet brown wren with little white spots on its wings landed on the railing near Ariel, tilting its head with curiosity, its short tail standing erect. It blinked, and Ariel perceived its thoughts.

"I am Ariel, and this is Ratiki," she introduced. "We are going to be your new neighbors."

The wren was so startled that it began hopping and almost fell off the rail. *I can understand what you're saying! You answered my question! What are you, a sorceress? Humans can't talk—they just make irritating noises.*

Ariel laughed and explained. "I'm a nature speaker. I have a gift to communicate with plants and animals."

Oh, a druid. Then you're the most powerful druid I've ever heard tell of.

"Do other people live around here?" she inquired.

The wren displayed negative body language, and Ariel read its thoughts. *Long ago, there were people; then the big ice came, but it's been warming for a while, so they came back. They live way over there,* it indicated by flicking its beak. *They aren't like you, though. They don't have big floating houses or strange animal friends with ringed tails. Enjoy your stay. I'm off to eat insects now.* The wren flitted its tail, and, with a jerk of its head, flew away.

Are we going to open the big door now? Ratiki looked up at her with an eager expression. *I want to romp in the beautiful green meadow!*

Smiling at him and absently petting his fur with fond strokes, Ariel gazed over the picturesque land with appreciation and gratitude. Though the morning air still bore a nip, everything was green—not a desert, not covered in snow—and living things seemed to have slowly been returning since the Great Conflagration that had almost destroyed the world. There were other people here, too, though not so many that they were everywhere.

She couldn't wait to run downstairs and share the wonderful news, that their prayers had been answered, and Archangel Michael had delivered them to a promised new land. They would explore first, find fresh water, and determine the best places to release the animals. Banba and Masuda would probably decide on where they would build their village and erect their monuments while she, Aram, and Téthur would select the prime farmland. Ériu could plant her seeds and learn the native tongue, and Céthur and the carpenters would construct their homes and workshops. Fótla could plant her vineyard and continue to practice healing with Lysandra. *If we make friends with the other people, they may need a healer, too. And both Ériu and Lysandra can teach wisdom principles to whoever wishes to learn. Masuda's sons and my nephew will have a safe, lovely place to grow up. I wonder what we'll call the new island. Is it an island? We'll see when we explore.*

Yes, Ariel was anxious to share this with her wife, brother, and friends, but, for right now, this instant, it was all hers—the inviting beach, the majestic cliffs, the burgeoning forest, and the emerald meadow, untouched and unspoiled ... the deer and the wren ... the gulls and the ebb and flow of the tide. Ariel would embrace the moment to appreciate and give thanks for all that lay before her and dare to imagine a new land of dreams.

Laws

1. The Law of One—The Lord our God is One with all and we are one with the Divine Power. All creatures and substances in the heavens and on earth spring from the same Source and are connected by invisible cords. Therefore, you are to love your neighbor as yourself because you and your neighbor are one.
2. The Law of Gratitude—In all things, give thanks, thereby creating more to be thankful for. Appreciate creation, offer praises, and speak blessings always.
3. The Law of Frequency—All things vibrate at their frequencies, whether living or still, seen or unseen. Tune your body and spirit to the frequencies you desire.
4. The Law of Attraction—Like attracts like. What a human thinks, feels, does, and is draws more of the same to him. Therefore, be mindful and meditate on what is worthy.
5. The Law of Reflection—As above, so below. As within, so without. The physical reflects the spiritual.
6. The Law of Sowing and Reaping—Whatever a human sows, that will he reap. Look at nature and learn. Thoughts, words, and actions do not return void but bring in a like harvest.

Laws

7. The Law of Energy—Everything is energy. Creation is complete and nothing can be destroyed or recreated; energy and solids can be changed in form and often are.

8. The Law of Cycles—Natural cycles control patterns on Earth and in the heavens. The constellations process across the sky, seasons turn, the sun rises and sets, the moon moves through its cycles, and the tides flow in and out.

9. The Law of Balance—For each thing, there exists its opposite: hot and cold, light and dark, peace and conflict, male and female. Seek balance in all your ways, both for the body and for the spirit.

10. The Law of Compassion—Do not judge yourself or others and practice forgiveness. None is without flaw; therefore, forgive so you may be forgiven, give that you may receive, love that you may be loved. To have compassion is to have understanding and with understanding, wisdom.

11. The Law of Cause and Effect—Everything happens for a reason. Identify and master the cause and achieve the desired effect.

12. The Law of Harmony—When vibrations work together, beauty like music emerges. Sunshine and rain, plants and animals, air, earth, and fire all work together. So must people.

Rules

Observe the following rules under penalty of jury:

I. Do not commit murder.
II. Do not steal.
III. Do not destroy your neighbor's property or animals.
IV. Do not break vows.
V. Do not falsely accuse others.
VI. Do not borrow and fail to repay.
VII. Do not charge interest above five percent on loans so you do not burden others or indenture them as slaves.
VIII. Do not eat or drink or do anything to excess lest your days be short upon the earth.
IX. Do not let the sun set on your anger, but make peace with your Creator, yourself, and your neighbor before you lie down to sleep. All are One.

Rules

X. Pay laborers a fair wage agreed upon by the majority.

XI. Honor your parents and all elders, for they are worthy.

XII. Love and nurture your children, brothers and sisters, husbands and wives, and those who have none.

XIII. Practice daily thanksgiving, meditation, mindfulness, and prayer, remembering you are a spiritual being.

XIV. Take one day out of seven to rest from labor for your body and soul require it.

XV. Be mindful of what you desire so that your heart remains pure, and you do not draw evil to yourself. Do to others what you wish to be done to you, for we are all One.

Follow these laws and rules that you may live long, prosperous, happy lives in peace.

AUTHOR NOTES

Before I introduce evidence and explain how I arrived at the theories presented in this novel, I want to clarify a few terms that differed in their meanings and concepts from the ancient world to the modern one.

Race. Throughout the story, I describe people with varying skin and hair tones living in Atlantis and then have some characters asserting opinions of racism that appear inconsistent with current society's understanding. This is because the word "race" meant something entirely different before the Common Era. The concept of a "nation," and by extension a "nationality," is a modern one, and the terms didn't exist in the ancient Mediterranean world. Instead, people who lived in Egypt, regardless of their color, were considered to be of the Egyptian race. The same for Greece, Persia, and other civilizations. White, tan, brown, and black people all inhabited the region, and nobody thought anything about skin tone. No one believed people were superior or inferior because of their melatonin's deepness. Therefore, in this book, the word "race" refers to anyone who is a native-born citizen of that country and has nothing to do with the modern construct.

Homosexuality. In antiquity, there was no word equivalent to "homosexual" in use. Even the original Hebrew, Aramaic, and Greek texts that became the Christian Bible didn't have a word for a person who engages in sex with members of the same gender. In most instances, the King James and subsequent versions of the Bible inserted the more modern term with all its accompanying condemnation in the place of the original word for a male prostitute. In Greek, the word "eros" applied to romantic love or sexual attraction and could be expressed toward a person of the opposite gender, as was more common, or the same gender, as was still accepted in society. Many people engaged in relations with both men and women—Alexander the Great being a notable example. All evidence points to same-sex relations not being viewed as unusual or improper.

Gender Roles. These vary throughout ancient history from place to place. Some societies were matriarchal while others were patriarchal, often changing back and forth over thousands of years. At the time of the Greek empire and before, for as long as written and pictorial records exist, men and women wore the same types of clothing, with none being designated for males or females. An oddity of both Greek and Egyptian culture was the elevation of women in lore and literature while denying them equality in their societies. Goddesses were as powerful as gods, female warrior heroes of old were exalted, and a woman could become pharaoh if she assumed the identity of a man, even though ordinary women of their civilizations had very little say. This supports Plato's claim that Atlantis practiced gender equality. Therefore, stories about people who lived thousands of years before his time portrayed men and women as equals.

Religion. In this book, the term religion is never used. The sources I consulted all describe Atlanteans as a deeply spiritual people; however, they did not practice organized religion as we know it today. Their beliefs are well spelled out in the novel along with the supplemental pages containing The Laws which govern the entire universe, and the Rules humans are called to live by to maintain a peaceful, orderly society. The concepts contained in them readily apply to most of the world's current religions.

The Big Questions

With that out of the way, we turn to the four big questions people ask about Atlantis: 1) Was there a real Atlantis? 2) Where was it? 3) What was their society like? 4) What caused Atlantis's destruction?

I spent long hours studying books, watching documentaries, and listening to podcasts to piece together the most credible sources and reports possible to answer those four questions, and I haven't the time or pages in this index to list all the information I uncovered. Therefore, I will briefly address each question with sample evidence and relate how I incorporated it into *Atlantis, Land of Dreams*.

1. Was there a real Atlantis?

The primary text source for the existence of Atlantis remains Plato's Dialogues *Timaeus* and *Critias*. While some critics insist the story of Atlantis is an allegory meant to teach readers a moral lesson, others believe he wrote about an actual place that had been destroyed in a cataclysmic event. The dialogues claim to quote Solon—a Greek senator—who visited Egypt between 590 and 580 BC and translated Egyptian records of Atlantis from about nine thousand years before Plato's time. At best, Plato's writing was a third-hand account. Still, there is much to believe about his story, and, centuries later, interest in Atlantis reemerged.

In 1627, Francis Bacon, the English scientist and philosopher, published a utopian novel titled *The New Atlantis*. Like Plato, Bacon portrayed a politically and scientifically advanced society on an unknown island. Then in 1882, Ignatius L. Donnelly, a former U.S. Congressman, published *Atlantis: The Antediluvian World,* which ignited a string of works attempting to locate the lost continent and glean wisdom from prehistoric Atlanteans. Donnelly theorized an advanced civilization whose immigrants had populated much of ancient Europe, Africa, and the Americas, and whose heroes had inspired Greek, Hindu, and Scandinavian mythology.

Archeological evidence, such as the construction of pyramids on continents that supposedly didn't know each other existed, strongly supports this hypothesis. Giant monolithic structures in South America, Asia, the Middle East, and the British Isles defy common reasoning. How could people with only stone-aged tools build such monuments? Likewise, the occurrence of the same symbols crops up in diverse locations worldwide. The Celtic Cross is the same as the Egyptian ankh, the Celtic trinity knot and the Vesica Pisces, the spiral, alpha and omega signs, and the widespread representation of a cross long before Christianity are but a few examples. Logic would point to a common source of origin and a civilization with advanced technology to cut enormous stones with such precision and move them into place despite their monstrous weight. After the archeological discovery of the city of Troy featured in Homer's *Iliad*, suggesting the story could have been a true historic event instead of a myth as previously supposed, the idea of Atlantis also being an actual place gained new momentum.

In the twentieth century, American Edgar Cayce, known as "The Sleeping Prophet," channeled visions of life on Atlantis while performing psychic readings. Because scores of his clairvoyant readings proved to be so accurate, many people believe his work is a credible source. There are many other authors, psychics, and Atlantis hunters I could list, but won't for brevity.

In more recent years, dozens, if not hundreds, of people have come forward worldwide claiming to recall a past life in Atlantis, including scholar Matias De Stefano. How much can one recall from a past life and how accurate are those recollections? Since many of these witnesses disagree on details put forth by Edgar Cayce's or Plato's previous testimony, it's hard to say. But there are certain big-picture points they all agree on, and those are the ones I've chosen to include in my book.

Was there a real Atlantis? As we follow through with answering the other questions, let's consider for the time being that one or more advanced civilizations could have existed in the distant past that affected peoples on both sides of the Atlantic Ocean, that their technology could explain the unexplainable, and that we truly don't know everything.

What about aliens from space? The theory about Atlantis being seeded by extraterrestrials, though popular with some people, is not one I explored in writing my novel.

1. Where was it?

Plato places Atlantis "beyond the Pillars of Hercules," or somewhere west of the Strait of Gibraltar. This description is rather vague, and, for hundreds of years, explorers and treasure hunters have sought to discover its location. Whenever ruins that might date from pre-diluvian times are discovered, the first question raised is, "Could this have been Atlantis?" Sites from Africa to Europe to the Bahama islands have given rise to speculation, and many have been debunked. The most widely accepted theory—and the one I built this book around—is that the continent (or large island) was located along the North Atlantic Ridge, currently beneath the waves of the ocean between Euro-North Africa and the Americas.

Being at the bottom of an ocean makes exploration extremely difficult, not to mention the probability that after, so much time, between erosion, corrosion, shifting tectonic plates, ocean currents, the activity of sea creatures, and the catastrophic events that caused it to sink, there could be nothing left to find even if an advanced culture once built cities on the spot. We've seen the devastation of earthquakes, volcanic eruptions, floods, and tsunamis in modern society. We're also talking about structures and relics from approximately twelve thousand years ago. Buildings of brick and wood would be long gone under the best of circumstances and even stone erodes and crumbles into pieces with the ravages of time.

Recently, tools like sonar and satellite imagery have revealed some mysterious grid like formations in the Atlantic that give the appearance of being manmade because their parallel and perpendicular patterns are not typically found in nature. Unfortunately, we do not possess enough information yet to positively determine if they are the streets of an ancient city or something else. Perhaps one day we'll have sophisticated enough equipment to discover evidence from the ocean floor convincing enough to sway the experts. In the meantime, other indications such as similarities found in stories (the arrival of Quetzalcoatl in Mesoamerica with his light skin and thick beard), symbols, and monolithic structures like pyramids linking the Americas to the Old World going back long before even the Vikings' explorations remain the strongest evidence for the location of Atlantis—well, and the fact the ocean itself was named for the place.

1. What was their society like?

All the sources I consulted agree on certain aspects of Atlantean culture, from Plato and bits and pieces of other ancient texts mentioning Atlantis to the modern past-life stories. These include that the people were extremely moral, spiritual, prosperous, creative, long-lived, democratic, and possessed technology more advanced than other contemporary civilizations. Let's examine three pervasive components of their society: spirituality, government, and technology.

Documents describe Atlanteans as connected to the divine and, in some cases, tout them as gods themselves because of the miracles they could perform. Some sources claim they were giants, although the word could mean in ways other than physical height. Having no remains we can point to and say, "This skeleton belonged to a person from Atlantis," we can't say for sure what they looked like. It is doubtful they were ten feet tall with blue skin and other such portrayals I've seen in fantasy art. The native Atlanteans in my book look like anyone else one might find in the Mediterranean world—Europe, the Middle East, and North Africa—with a few resembling Celtic or Nordic peoples. What united them other than their place of birth was their culture.

Accounts include their ability to connect to Universal Consciousness, use telepathy, telekinesis, see future and past events, self-heal their bodies, astral travel, contact the spirits of those who had moved on, and interact with angels and archangels. Today, we would say they possessed psychic powers. Remnants of these abilities have turned up occasionally throughout history and today in individuals we consider special, but seemingly all Atlanteans had them—until they didn't.

In the novel, Atlanteans are losing their powers and not living as long; however, occasionally individuals are born with or develop gifts. While most are what we would consider "ordinary" people, others can talk to plants and animals, interact with the elements and influence the weather, work healing energies on others, affect other's emotions and train their thoughts, or act as mediums, telepaths, clairvoyants, or mesmerists.

Testaments describe Atlanteans as artists and musicians who surrounded themselves with beauty. They were highly imaginative people who delighted in creating exquisite pieces to enjoy. And since their level of prosperity didn't demand they work all day, every day, they spent much of their time expressing themselves through artistic pursuits.

They also reportedly lived for hundreds of years. Biblical ages of nine hundred years and more are prevalent among characters before the great flood, after which they shrink down to a maximum of a hundred and twenty. The theory that people before the flood counted time and therefore their ages differently is popular, but no more provable than if they actually lived nine hundred of our years. And did everyone before the flood live that long or only Atlanteans who understood how to regulate and renew the cells in their bodies through meditation, healthy diets, and proper exercise? Was it their spiritual connection to the Creator that granted them longer lives, or conditions on the planet during that window of time?

While we don't know what clothes Atlanteans wore, their hairstyles, or their architecture, I based my representation on ancient Egyptian and Hellenistic societies. While Plato describes the Temple of Poseidon, we know little about what other buildings might have looked like. Some artists portray sleek skyscrapers more futuristic than ours, but I kept their architecture in line with what was popular in the Mediterranean world. It's clear from period sources, the closest connection existed between Atlantis and Kemet, or ancient Egypt. I also studied Minoan society, one that could have easily arisen from Atlantean roots centuries after the lost continent's demise. I represent Greek-style theaters and buildings similar to those found in all three places.

By all testimony, the civilization was prosperous and abundant in resources to the extent nobody lived in poverty. They valued human life and nature, living in harmony with the planet, partly because they believed in the Law of One—that everyone and everything in the universe is connected. Many indigenous peoples around the globe share similar beliefs, that the earth, plants, animals, water, mountains, etc. all contain spiritual energy the same as humans do. Therefore, they took great care in managing natural resources and avoided polluting the planet.

Are you sure Plato wasn't just describing the image of a perfect world, not one that truly existed? Possibly, but consider this: a man who lived in an extremely misogynistic society stated that men and women operated as equals in Atlantis. Wouldn't he be more likely to propose a perfect society run by men with women obediently and happily doing as they were told?

Plato wrote about Atlantis having ten kings, implying ten subdivisions like city-states united in a confederacy. The kings would meet every year to discuss issues and agree upon a course of action. He described their bull ceremony and other details, such as the layout of the capital city in circular rings. Plato also mentioned Atlantis having democratic principles. Therefore, I compromised by giving them a system of representative democracy ruled by an oligarchy of kings and queens who were elected locally. Along with the necessary department heads, I depicted them with a council of elected jurors who had to approve any measures the ruler wished to impose, thus a check and balance on royal power. The jury would also give verdicts in trials, but, because crime was so low, trials rarely occurred.

Atlantis was a nation of law, and The Law seemed to play a very prominent role in their society. Plato's version states The Law was etched into orichalcum plates posted on the great columns of Poseidon's Temple and that life in Atlantis revolved around following The Law. Yet nowhere is it recorded exactly what those laws were. Drawing from the Ten Commandments and the spiritual laws of the Universe, I composed my vision of what these most sacred laws would have been. Then I added rules for the smooth operation of society to cover the key points.

Perhaps the aspect of Atlantis that attracts the most interest and curiosity was their advanced technology. Various accounts include things such as flying machines, submarines, lighting, and "harnessing the power of the sun," often depicted by giant crystals soaking up the sun's energy. While there was no part of my book requiring submarines, I imagined their flying machines using antigravity and gyros with small, charged crystals as a power source, like our modern batteries. Atlanteans would never have burned fossil fuels in mass because it would have created pollution which they would not have abided.

Atlanteans were reported to be superior forgers, making advanced alloys from metal ore, such as steel and orichalcum. While Plato describes the unique and valuable metal, it's never been found elsewhere for real—except possibly in the cargo hold of an ancient shipwreck in the Mediterranean Sea. That's because unlike copper, silver, and gold, orichalcum isn't an element, but an alloy unique to Atlantis produced by combining other precious metals—perhaps gold, silver, tin, and mercury by some speculation.

Where were their telephones and computers? Well, here's the thing ... for most of Atlantis's history, they could communicate at a distance with their minds. Likewise, having a link to Universal Consciousness meant they could access any information at any time. But as they lost those abilities, a written language was created and information was recorded in scrolls and on metal plates, like the famed Emerald Tablets, reported to contain vast wisdom from the Atlanteans. Because few sources mention a telephone-like device—and it played nicely into my plot—I didn't supply them with long-distance talking instruments.

However, one advanced tool they must have possessed was the laser cutter. How could stone-aged people fashion such perfect, smooth, tightly fitting stones requiring no mortar to hold them together? Not with a hammer and chisel, but with laser cutters. And how did they lift the monolithic stones into place? Anti-gravity technology. Are you sure they weren't aliens who brought technology from another planet? Hey, human ingenuity is pretty good all on its own. We're talking about a two-hundred-thousand-year history here. Who knows how many times advanced civilizations rose and were destroyed, having to start over from scratch?

What I found to be a gaping inconsistency in Plato's account was the supposed attack on Athens, in which Plato asserted the whole Atlantean military attacked prediluvian Athens and lost, returning home in defeat to be destroyed by the gods in retribution. Honestly, if they were so advanced and had terrible and powerful weapons of mass destruction, how could itty-bitty Athens (which, by the way, wasn't a city in 9,600 BC) have turned away their forces? I chose to include the attack on a port (which was submerged by rising water and rebuilt along the new shoreline after the flood) near the Athens of Plato's time, but not by all of Atlantis. In my version of events, one city-state sends a small fleet equipped with laser cannons (banned by the Council of Rulers) to retake their rebellious former colony so they would have a place to go to escape the coming catastrophe. Unfortunately for them, they suffered a power failure as their crystals couldn't hold a charge so far from a mother pyramid. This gives Plato an event to reference in his account while providing a valid explanation as to why Atlantis lost.

Plato wrote that, as long as they possessed a divine nature, the people of Atlantis enjoyed a utopian society, "but when the divine element in them became weakened," things started to go wrong. Most critics point to the moral failings of Atlanteans—they became greedy and corrupt and wanted to take over the world. But is that what Plato's words truly mean? How is it that an advanced nation of spiritual giants whose existence was based on powers they received from heavenly energetic forces, who had been around for tens of thousands of years enjoying peace and prosperity, just woke up one morning and discovered lust, jealousy, hatred, and gluttony for the first time? "Oh, wow, everything is so perfect! I think I'll abandon what we've been doing since time immemorial in favor of depravity." It makes no sense. Temptation would have always been around; it didn't just suddenly show up. But what if another factor changed, one which weakened their link to their divine nature and put a short in their spiritual connection?

1. What caused Atlantis's destruction?

A popular version depicts Atlantis's advanced technology as causing their demise—or maybe weapons of mass destruction that backfired on them. The evil wizards who tried to enslave the world received their just rewards. The gods punished them for daring to attack Athens, or something like that. In my book, I propose a much more scientific explanation for what brought about Atlantis's downfall while still including aspects of Plato's account.

The Younger Dryas was a period of tremendous upheaval and climate change with an onset approximately 12,900 years ago, lasting for between 1300 and 1400 years. Then, in approximately 9,600 BC, the massive flood event, often referred to as Noah's flood, ended the period by raising sea levels about four hundred feet from where they had previously been. There is extensive evidence for this, including sunken cities near modern coastlines and geological impacts from tons upon tons of rushing water in a short time.

While theories abound as to what caused the "mini-ice-age," evidence points to a catastrophic event producing such rapid temperature drops that the frozen body of a mammoth was discovered in Russia with green vegetation still in its mouth. Concentrations of nanodiamonds and impact craters have been uncovered in sites across North America and Europe corresponding to the period 12,900-12,800 years ago (allowing for approximation) that are only surpassed by those dating back 65 million years and the extinction of the dinosaurs.

The most prevailing and credible theory is that the northern hemisphere was struck by some sort of space junk, probably the tail of a comet. A direct hit by such an object would have caused greater devastation, but a scattering of meteorites or the debris found in a comet's tail would have caused huge upheaval, including massive earthquakes, and volcanic eruptions, and the dust cloud from the impacts would have blocked out the sun's rays for at least several years. Additionally, a comet consists mostly of ice, resulting in the sudden onset of temperatures that could freeze a mammoth solid.

In ancient sites all around the world, we see images carved into stone that represent a great serpent in the sky. Could these be representations of the killer comet from antiquity? Perhaps, but wouldn't the astrologers and astronomers from back then have predicted it? We know even the oldest societies on earth studied the stars and assigned great meaning to cosmic events. Wouldn't they have seen it coming and done something? Maybe they tried, but not knowing exactly where or if it would strike the earth, the best they could do was to construct underground shelters for protection. There is evidence in Derinkuyu, Turkey, and other sites that they may have done just that.

Alternatively, there may have been no approaching object in space to watch if the asteroid belt between Mars and Jupiter had once been a planet that exploded 12,900 years ago, sending pieces flying into space. Situated between two strong gravitational fields—Jupiter and the sun—some debris and icy chunks could have struck Earth on their way to the sun. But whether it was a comet, asteroid, or something else, the strongest evidence points to our planet being hit by something, resulting in an increase in the tilt or polar axis of the earth from 16.5 degrees to the current 23.5 degrees.

The northern hemisphere was more powerfully affected than the southern, but the whole earth had to adapt and deal with violent changes. A prevailing theory regarding our most recent ice age is that of an ice wall that spread across parts of North America and the Atlantic Ocean through Scotland to Scandinavia. Behind it was a gigantic ice sheet. As temperatures warmed—possibly aided by solar flares—the ice behind the wall thawed, until one day it shattered, causing the greatest deluge in recorded history.

The Biblical account of the flood isn't the only one, and this probably wasn't the only significant flood event. Almost every civilization in the world has a flood story: Native America, Mesoamerica, South America, Mesopotamia, China, all over Asia, Australia, Polynesia, and Europe. Likewise, many of these stories tell of someone with a boat who survived and repopulated the earth. Other myths describe advanced people arriving on their shores on a ship from far away. I incorporated several of these characters into my story—those who seemed to fit with an Atlantean origin.

But didn't Plato say Atlantis was destroyed in a single day? Yes, but which Atlantis? Atlantis of the Third Age in this book was swept away in a day by the terrible deluge that flooded much of the world, but the real devastation happened about 1360 years before with the comet—the Great Conflagration. This event coincided with the start of the astrological age of Leo and the end of a twenty-six-thousand-year cycle of our planet's movement around our galaxy.

What changed that disrupted the ideal civilization of Atlantis? Let's see—hit by comet debris, knocked into a steeper tilt on our axis, moved into a different portion of space, and possibly increased solar flare activity. These would disrupt the magnetosphere and the flow of energetic waves. It could have changed the amount of radiation affecting the planet or how much more penetrated our atmosphere. Certainly not enough to make conditions uninhabitable, but maybe enough to advance the aging process, affect psychic abilities, and introduce static in the lines of communication between humans and spiritual beings and forces outside our dimension.

Isn't this all pure speculation? Technically, yes. But, if true, it would answer a lot of questions no branch of science has been able to. Science is constantly evolving. Only recently have we discovered that matter exists as particles and as waves, that everything is energy, and that space and time are intricately intertwined. Quantum physics is a wide-open field, and we're still exploring the mysteries of DNA.

How do you turn a story about the end of the world into a happily ever after? By extending the possibility that one day we might reclaim our Atlantean roots and reestablish a peaceful, prosperous world where everyone gets a place at the table. After all, isn't that the real reason our generation is so enamored with finding the lost civilization of Atlantis?

INDEX

Calendar and Measurements

The Atlantean calendar in this novel is based on the Zodiac. They counted twelve months, each corresponding to the astronomical constellations dominating the sky. The winter and summer solstices were important days to mark the passage of time, with the winter solstice marking the end of the year and the first day of Capricorn serving as New Year's Day. The equinoxes were also important dates for planning planting and harvesting and were celebrated with festivals. Their months would roughly correspond to these modern dates:

Capricornus (Goat): December 22–January 19
Aquarius (Water Bearer): January 20–February 18
Pisces (Fish): February 19–March 20
Aries (Ram): March 21–April 19
Taurus (Bull): April 20–May 20
Gemini (Twins): May 21–June 21
Cancer (Crab): June 22–July 22
Leo (Lion): July 23–August 22
Virgo (Virgin): August 23–September 22
Libra (Balance): September 23–October 23

Scorpius (Scorpion): October 24–November 21

Sagittarius (Archer): November 22–December 21

In my book, turns of the sandglass measure the passage of time in the day. If you need a point of reference, you could equate one turn of the sandglass with an hour.

These Atlanteans, like other people of the ancient world, also used longer astrological ages based on what part of the galaxy the earth was in during a given time. A Great Year ranges from 25,800 to 27,000 years of precession (depending on who is making the calculations) and is divided into 12 zodiac signs. Each is around 2,250 years long.

Age of Capricorn 21900 BCE 19650 BCE

Age of Sagittarius 19650 BCE 17400 BCE

Age of Scorpio 17400 BCE 15150 BCE

Age of Libra 15150 BCE 13000 BCE

Age of Virgo 13000 BCE 10750 BCE

Age of Leo 10750 BCE 8600 BCE

Age of Cancer 8600 BCE 6450 BCE

Age of Gemini 6450 BCE 4300 BCE

Age of Taurus 4300 BCE 2150 BCE

Age of Aries 2150 BCE 1 CE

Age of Pisces 1 CE 2150 CE

Age of Aquarius 2150 CE 4300 (completing a cycle)

For measurements, I used the most ancient designations I could find recorded in the Mediterranean region of the world. The longest was the league, approximately three miles long. For smaller measurements, the cubit was about 18 inches or half a yard or meter. The exact length of cubits seems to fluctuate between centuries and countries, but 18 inches is a suitable comparison. The thumb was initially the length of a person's thumb, but, in order to codify the term, I assume a thumb to be an inch long. "Seked" is an ancient Egyptian term describing the inclination of the triangular faces of a right pyramid.

The talent was a commonly agreed upon term for weight in antiquity; however, exactly how much it weighed varied between centuries and locales. In this book, I have struck an average of a talent weighing about 50 kg or 110 pounds.

Currency in this Atlantis is a creation of my imagination based on coins common to the period, which I have represented in three denominations. The most common, least valuable, is the Atlas—a copper coin. Next is the silver Clito, and the most valuable is the gold Poseidon. Because of the rates of inflation and exchange with other currencies, I don't assign a "dollar value" to these. Merely understand that a gold Poseidon would represent a far larger sum than a copper Atlas coin.

Where in the world are we?

Atlantis, Land of Dreams, takes place about 9,600 BCE in the real world; however, few of the places were called by the same names we use today. I reached back to find the oldest place names I could for spots around the world referenced in this book, though I may not have uncovered all the same ones used that far in antiquity. After much searching to find pronunciations for these, I came up empty; however, pronouncing them the way they appear to sound is a reasonable bet.

Below is a place-name reference chart, so you know where my characters are in the world.

Story place	Modern name
The Green Sea	The Mediterranean Sea
The Pillars of Hercules	The Strait of Gibraltar
Kemet	Egypt; some sources say all of Africa was known as Kemet
Giza	Giza, Egypt
Waset	A Nile River town south of Giza
Kush	Nubia or Sudan, south of Egypt along the Nile
Maghreb	Region of North Africa; the Barbary Coast
Libya	Libya
Iberia	Portugal and Spain
Pelasgoí	Greece
Pelepus	Fictional town in southern Greece near where Sparta would be
Palaio Faliro	The oldest named town in Greece; the port of Athens
Kaptara	Crete
Trinacria	Sicily
Melitē	Malta
Anatola	Turkey
Malakopea	Derinkuyu, Turkey
Phoenicia	Mediterranean coast of Syria and Lebanon
Jerico	North shore of the Dead Sea, Israel
Ur	Iraq, on the Euphrates River near the border with Kuwait
Halaf	Northern Mesopotamia and Syria
Sindhu	The Indus Valley, Pakistan and Western India
Kirāt	Bhutan, Himalaya Mountains
Maanu	Central and South America
Mayeb	Yucatan Peninsula of Mexico
Cachilt	Fictional village in the Yucatan
Tiwanaku	Peru on the shores of Lake Titicaca
Copper Mountains	Andes Mountains
Gugulanna	Mars
Enlil	Jupiter
Phaëton	A theorized planet that once was between Mars and Jupiter

Symbols

Certain symbols can be found all over the world, many with ancient and unknown origins. I included some of the most commonly recognized ones in my representation of Atlantean civilization. While there are many more, the following appear in the pages of my novel.

☥

Ankh—the key of life, symbolizes eternal life, a major symbol of Ancient Egypt, and is also represented in the Celtic Cross.

✡

6-point star—multiple meanings. It appeared on ancient sundials to trace the movement of the sun. The upward and downward facing points stand for the winter and summer solstices. The intersecting triangles represent the union of the spiritual and physical, divine and human, or heaven and earth. Another meaning is the union of masculine and feminine, intellect and emotion. Significantly, in my book, it corresponds to the belief, "as above, so below." This figure was around long before King David adopted it and it became the modern symbol of Judaism.

3 intersecting circles—Vesica Piscis, also the Celtic trinity knot. This represents multiple trinities: body, mind, and spirit; youth, adulthood, and old age; life, death, and rebirth; intersecting generations in the maiden, the mother, and the crone; and even strength through unity. Christianity adopted the Celtic symbol to represent the three persons of God—Father, Son, and Holy Spirit. The Vesica Pisces, or fish shapes formed at the intersections of the loops, represent the conjunction of the physical and spiritual worlds. This symbol was not unique to ancient Celts; it is also found in other cultures of the world.

Chakana—an equal-armed cross with a hole in the center represents the passage into another world. The parallel and perpendicular lines represent the physical and spiritual planes, and the hole symbolizes the passage where the divine nature/spirit could enter the physical world.

Caduceus—An ancient emblem associated with healing. The entwined serpents signify the union and balancing of the body with the soul. With a staff in the center, it is termed a Caduceus. With the wings on top, it was the symbol of Hermes or Mercury in Greek and Roman mythology.

Crescent or Sickle Moon—also waning and waxing moon. Appearing in many religions and civilizations, it is associated with feminine energy, the cycles of the earth and seasons, tides, harvest, and fertility. While some people equate it with female strength, the feminine aspect this symbol represents is the intuitive and emotional natures present in all genders.

Other important symbols tied to Atlantis include the cross, alpha and omega, broken cross (swastika), spiral (vortex), fish, bull, cow, wheel, and icosahedron (12-sided geometric figure).

Gods and Angels

In this adaptation, the citizens of Atlantis believe in one god, but give the entity different names and titles. They abide by the Law of One, recognizing the presence of a divine force within every individual and entity, which constitutes the essence of the entire universe. These words and phrases all refer to their one god: Creator, Source, Infinite Intelligence, the Universe, Compassionate One, The All, and combinations of these designations.

While not considered a separate god, Atlanteans regarded the earth herself as a living entity with the name Gaia. While she is not assigned supernatural abilities, she possesses natural powers that influence all living and elemental components that reside on and in her. They view themselves as symbiotic beings living in harmony with Gaia for the good of all.

A part of the Atlantean belief system is the existence of spiritual beings living outside their physical realm, called archangels. They are energetic forces in charge of certain powers and responsibilities that affect humans. Noah named the arks after some of the key archangels. These characters appear in many ancient texts and spiritual writings besides their mention in the Christian Bible. Various religions and nonreligious belief systems around the world recognize their names and functions.

Michael (Who is like God) protector, defender, and chief of the archangels.

Gabriel (man/woman of God or power of God) chief messenger angel, some depict as female.

Raphael (God has healed) always associated with healing, sometimes blowing a trumpet

Uriel (God is my flame) a master of knowledge and archangel of wisdom; known in sacred texts as the angel who warned Noah of the great flood. His priority is to enlighten our minds with new ideas, epiphanies, and insights.

Jegudiel (God is One—unity) or bestower of love and mercy; also angel of work and workers.

Selaphiel (I have asked God) He is known for delivering prayers to God and the spiritual realm. He aids musicians, especially those who use music for healing purposes. He also heals people from aggression.

Barachiel (God's blessings) the archangel of blessings, chief guardian angel, associated with roses.

Atlantis is also associated with several mythical gods and demigods. In this book, modern Atlanteans no longer believe in these gods, but they remain part of the culture.

Poseidon was the legendary founder of Atlantis. He was the brother of **Zeus** and **Hades** who, according to myth, were the sons of **Kronos** (king of the Titans and the chief god before his sons took over). Each was granted dominion over a part of the earth—Zeus, the land and skies; Hades, the underworld; and Poseidon, the seas and oceans. According to the stories, Poseidon fell in love with a human woman, **Clito**, married her, and together they established the Kingdom of Atlantis (which was named for their firstborn son, **Atlas**.) In my novel, the ten kingdoms of Atlantis are named for Poseidon's sons: Atlas, Gadeirus, Ampheres, Evaemon, Mneseus, Autochthon, Elasippus, Mestor, Azae,s and Diaprepes.

Terms

Some terms used in this novel may be unfamiliar to many readers. In case you are interested, I have listed some here with their definitions.

Alban Elfed—the celebration of the autumn equinox. Ancient druids and other peoples have celebrated this date since before recorded history.

Chlamys—short, oblong mantle worn around the shoulders.

Double auloi pipe—an ancient reed instrument with an unmistakable sound.

Ether—(aether) Before Plato's time, and for many centuries after, conventional science held that the spaces between objects were not empty but composed of an energetic substance called ether. The famous 1887 Michelson-Morley experiment seemed to disprove this theory, and it was abandoned until more modern quantum physics observations now support its existence. We know the earth is teeming with a field of energy waves and frequencies. Radio, telephone, TV, and satellites operate according to their principles every day.

Ham, het, hum—designations with several levels of meaning. The nine chakras can be divided into three groups of three. Ham is the head chakras (crown, 3rd eye, and throat), Het is the core chakras (heart, solar plexus, sacral), and Hum is the foundation group (root, knees, feet). They also are identified with three stages of breath: Ham for inhalation, Het for contemplation while holding the breath, and Hum for exhalation. They are sometimes spelled in all capital letters.

Hatha—In Sanskrit, Hatha translates to "force." Today, it is a form of Yoga and can also refer to the various poses.

Jjeevan Shakti—the word I coined for their concept of spirit energy, which could be pulled from the ether and used in the healing process.

Nemeš—ancient Egyptian headgear. While historians believe they were a status symbol worn only by high-ranking people, they served the practical purpose of keeping one's head cool, like a durąg or bandana today.

Protelex—the language of Atlantis

Push toss—a made-up game for Atlanteans to play. They certainly had sports; we just don't know what they were. Push toss is a team sport I envision as similar to rugby.

Ruh Mutaharika—"moving spirit". I made up this name for my Atlanteans as I can't know what they called the daily practice. It would be a type of Yoga or Tai Chi, melding spiritual and physical aspects that benefit the mind, soul, and body.

Sirius—also known as the Dog Star, the brightest star in Earth's night sky. The name means "glowing" in Greek. Sirius played important roles in ancient Greek and Egyptian astronomy and was often used to predict when the Nile River would flood.

Twenty Squares—a two-person board game of the ancient world. This was an actual game, and some fabulous sets are displayed in museums today.

Character Names

There are a lot of characters in this book, with Egyptian, Greek, Mesopotamian, Mayan, Aztec, and Inca names, some of which are still in use today and others appear quite foreign. While I couldn't find pronunciations for most, say them like you think they should sound. Any ages listed are from the beginning of the book. I debated on how to arrange them—alphabetically, in order of appearance, by the number of times they appear, categories, the city-states where they lived—and arrived at a combination approach. I hope it is easy for you to find the name you're looking for.

9 People called to the Ring of Stones and their family members
(Why 9? As part of the 3-6-9 mystery, 9 represents completion and enlightenment.)

- **Ariel**—main protagonist; 52; a farmer and powerful nature speaker; plays the flute

- Philomena—Ariel's mother; 80; a splendid cook

- Sheera—Ariel's daughter; 22; talented seamstress and clothing designer

- Mal'akhi—Ariel's son; 25; city guardian who lives in the Evamont capital

- Oma Naunet—Ariel's great-great-great-grandmother; 338; has done many things

- Aram—Ariel's brother of a similar age; farmer and family man who enjoys pottery

- Yaluk—Lysandra's cousin who married Ariel's brother; mother to

ATLANTIS LAND OF DREAMS

Aram's sons

- Hevel—Aram's older son; 18; Ariel's nephew

- Shemu'el—Aram's younger teen son; Ariel's nephew

- Menandros—Ariel's uncle

- Gamila—Menandros' second wife, who is younger than him; Ariel's aunt

- Mara—Menandros and Gamila's daughter; Ariel's much younger cousin

- **Lysandra**—second main protagonist; 54; Ariel's first and true love; a called healer and graduate of the Central Wisdom School; lives in Atala; her immediate family died in a shipwreck

- **Quetzal**—an enlightened Wisdom School Master and Lysandra's mentor; 124; looks like a red-haired Viking (According to Central American folklore, Quetzalcoatl—a large, white-skinned, bearded man—landed on their shores in a boat bringing knowledge, wisdom, and civilization to their people.)

- Demetrios—Quetzal's brother; comedy charades performer with the Pisces Players

- Malah—husband of Demetrios, also a performer with the Pisces Players

- **Noah**—Oma's shipbuilder friend; 400+ years old; descendant of Methuselah, who was born before the Great Conflagration (According to the Bible, Noah and his family conveyed two of every animal to safety in the ark, saving them from the great flood, and landed on Mount Ararat in modern-day Turkey.)

- Emzara—Noah's wife; younger than he is, possibly a 2nd or 3rd wife; sources disagree on Noah's wife's name, but this one is the most widely accepted

- Japheth—Noah's oldest son (around Ariel's age)

- Arathka—Japheth's wife (not named in the story because she had no lines of dialogue)

- Shem—Noah's middle son

- Nahalath—Shem's wife; a nature speaker who helped call and care for the animals

- Ham—Noah's youngest son

- Nabu—Ham's wife (not named in the story because she had no lines of dialogue)

- **Thoth**—the chief librarian of Atala and keeper of the Emerald Tablets; 152; de facto leader of the nine chosen to save Atlantean civilization; taught written language to the Egyptians

- Isis—Thoth's daughter; early 20s; a gifted healer

- Osiris—Isis's husband

- **Mandisa**—air speaker of Ryzen with a Nubian appearance; in her 60s; plays the drum and runs an inherited citrus orchard; is the hub of a three-way marriage

- Hashur—an athlete and citrus grower, husband to Mandisa and Agathon

- Agathon—a scholar, musician, and poet, husband to Mandisa and Hashur

- **Ziusudra**—most renowned astronomer/astrologer in Atlantis; 221 years old (According to legend, Ziusudra and his family rode out the great flood in a huge boat and saved many animals to repopulate the region of Mesopotamia.)

- Jatziri—Ziusudra's wife; also shows great promise as a healer

- Yima—Ziusudra's brother, who accompanies him on the ark (not named in the story because he had no lines of dialogue)

- **Ptah**—architect and mathematician; 80s; looks like an Egyptian stone mason; helped design and construct the Great Pyramids and Hall of Records

- **Ériu**—teacher at the Northern Wisdom School; 40s; speaks many languages and is in charge of a seed collection project; looks like an archetypal Irish woman (According to legend, three sisters who were like goddesses and their husbands arrived on Irish shores in a boat. Banba was viewed as their leader, but the island was named after Ériu, whose modern name is spelled Eire.)

- Céthur—Ériu's husband; a miner and forger

- Banba—Ériu's older sister; a former city guardian and natural leader

- Éthur—Banba's husband; a carpenter

- Fótla—Ériu's other sister; shows promise as a healer; a vintner, and dancer

- Téthur—Fótla's husband; a farmer

Rulers of the Atlantean city-states, their families, and government officials
- **Masuda**—King of Gadlan; 50s, youngest of the rulers; has a wife and two young sons

- Fáelán—King Masuda's older son, a tween-aged lad
- **Basilius**—King of Elapus
- **Kleitos**—King of Evamont; has a wife and son not named in the story
- Chanokh—a captain in the Evamont Guardians; Mal'akhi's superior officer
- **Tecuani**—King of Ampherium; older man with unnamed family members
- **Zamná**—Queen of Diaprep (where Noah lives); classically trained dancer
- **Efrayim**—King of Atala and moderator of the Council of Rulers; 60s; well-respected, capable leader; has an unnamed wife
- Korinna—Energy Minister for the Council of Rulers of Atlantis
- Raffi—chief physician of Atala; 200+; Lysandra's supervisor
- **Meresankh**—Queen of Menosus; 112; concerned with trade, tourism, and flooding
- **Ahau**—King of Autopolis
- **Izevel**—Queen of Ryzen when the story begins; 123; a royal lineage & government experience; given a vote of no confidence and removed from office
- **Temen**—primary character; 60; Ariel's "dead" husband and father of her children; moves to Ryzen and, with Lykos's help, gets elected as the new king
- Lykos—antihero; 82; a wizard, astronomer, and alchemist, with the ability to manipulate weak-minded people's thoughts and emotions;

the former headmaster of Daya's Wisdom School

- Rhoxane—beautiful heiress who inherited the bulk of Ryzen's papyrus fields; 25; becomes Queen Consort of Ryzen after marrying Temen, then acting queen

- Dareios—Minister of Trade in Ryzen; 120; bald

- Ofira—a minister of Ryzen

- Syrene—one of Ryzen's nine jurors

- Kishar—Agriculture Minister of Ryzen

- Eshkar—a servant in Ryzen's royal palace

- Sarah—Queen Rhoxane's handmaiden

- Namazu—a robust Ryzen palace guardian

- Tukumbi—an admired female palace guardian

- Ahkin—the Ryzen palace cook

- Unnamed captain of Temen's warship

- General Gershom—the commander of the Ryzen Defenders; 70s

- Captain Jabari—led the support team for Lycos; 70s; returned to Ryzen and aided Lykos

- Captain Platon—captain of a commercial trading vessel that helped try to rescue people from the flood

- **Shifra**—Queen of Mestoria; fastidious elder with a husband and daughter (unnamed)

Minor Characters

- Four immigrant farm laborers and their families who live and work on Ariel's farm

- Mahmoud—Sheera's handsome, athletic suitor from Elyrna

- Taavi—Sheera's sweet, funny suitor from Elyrna; she chooses him to marry

- Fufi—Lysandra's patient in Atala

- Helene—Lysandra's neighbor and friend in Atala

- Timoleon—Helene's husband; first mate on a ship

- Tepoz—Helene's supervisor at the tax office where she works

- Pyrrhus—townsperson of Ryzen with red hair

- Gashan—homely woman townsperson of Ryzen

- Akna—headmaster of the Northern Wisdom School

- Karpos—air speaker in Evamont

- Devorah—the top designer in Evamont; likes Sheera's designs

- Hippolytos—trader from Kaptara; Temen accepted a bribe of pearls from him before the election

- Eadric—Philomena (Ariel's mother)'s beau; she marries him before leaving Atlantis

- Bobo—runs the boat rental in Mestoria; grandmother has a restaurant

- Barak—elderly miner in Gadlan with a rickety air coach

- Kele—chief of the village of Cachitl on the Mayeb Peninsula in Maanu

- Huy—a boy in Giza who speaks three languages; acts as Ariel's guide

- Boqin—an enlightened master living in the Mountains of Kirāt to the east of Sindhu

- Nymphe—Mal'akhi's attractive, petite fiancée; early 20s

- Racheal—Nymphe's cousin

- Ocotlan—one of Lysandra's healing arts students in Evamont

- Balam—a young nature speaker who assists Ariel gathering animals; mid 20s

- Reuven—Lysandra's badly burned patient in Evamont

- Hypatia—nature speaker on Ark Barachiel

- Khafra—air speaker on Ark Michael

- Pamphilos—(Philo) Mal'akhi's associate guardian friend

- Nikanor—wisdom master who Lykos communicates with

- Erastos—Temen's prison guard

- K'an—a stonemason on the Ark Gabriel

- Tirzah—air speaker on Ark Uriel

Non-human Characters

- Ratiki (Tiki)—Ariel's pet raccoon

- Adira—a matriarch elephant friend who frequents the meadow near Ariel's farm; she has a large family, including her sisters Dalila and Shesa, and her youngest son, Barak

- Ixquic—which means Mother of Heroes; an alligator in Mestoria

- Moonshadow—a black jaguar in Mestoria

- Abrax—a camel in Giza

- Cleo—pregnant bunny on Ark Michael

- Lahun—female blue whale

- The Oldest Tree—a giant sequoia living in Immortal Glade, in the forests of Ampherium

- Albatross—tells Ariel about the melting glacier

- Blue heron—reports on disappearing frogs

- Sea turtle—informs Ariel about the dying coral reef

- Matriarch of the gopher trees—agrees to sacrifice the forest to save her species

SOURCES

B elow are some sources I consulted when researching Atlantis. While not keeping track of every website I perused (after all, it's a novel, not a doctorial dissertation) I found these particularly noteworthy.

"The Empires of Atlantis: The Origins of Ancient Civilizations and Mystery Traditions throughout the Ages" by Marco M. Vigato

"Timaeus and Critias" by Plato

"Atlantis the Antediluvian World" by Ignatius Donnelly

"Edgar Cayce on Atlantis" complied from Edgar Cayce's readings

"Visions of Atlantis: Reclaiming our Lost Ancient Legacy" by Michael Le Flem

"Ancient Civilizations" a Gaia Original Series

"Ancient Apocalypse" a TV documentary series by Graham Hancock

Various Greg Braden videos on ancient symbols and discoveries concerning Atlantis can be accessed on YouTube.com.

MORE BOOKS BY EDALE LANE

Heart of Sherwood
https://www.amazon.com/dp/B07W4M3R5L

Viking Quest
https://www.amazon.com/dp/B097NTZVPC

Sigrid and Elyn: A Tale from Norvegr
https://www.amazon.com/dp/B0B5W48342
Legacy of the Valiant: A Tale from Norvegr
https://www.amazon.com/dp/B0BZK7Y655
War and Solace: A Tale from Norvegr
https://www.amazon.com/dp/B0CGP4WVYP

Walks with Spirits
https://www.amazon.com/dp/B09VBGQF27/

The Lessons in Murder Series
Meeting over Murder

https://www.amazon.com/dp/B0B7R69R7B
Skimming around Murder
https://www.amazon.com/dp/B0B9R6FJWL
New Year in Murder
https://www.amazon.com/dp/B0BDQSPT6L
Heart of Murder
https://www.amazon.com/dp/B0BQQS57FY
Reprise in Murder
https://www.amazon.com/dp/B0C2YDKLSB
Homecoming in Murder
https://www.amazon.com/dp/B0C7M2VKSH
Queen of Murder
https://www.amazon.com/dp/B0CKRYLNSW
Cold in Murder
https://www.amazon.com/dp/B0CSXMBJLJ
Foreseen in Murder
https://www.amazon.com/dp/B0D3G5JMLP

Daring Duplicity: The Wellington Mysteries, Vol.1
https://www.amazon.com/dp/B09QDTF9YN
Perilous Passages: The Wellington Mysteries, Vol. 2
https://www.amazon.com/dp/B0B16FWN63
Daunting Dilemmas: The Wellington Mysteries, Vol. 3
https://www.amazon.com/dp/B0BMDQ8TLC

The Night Flyer Series
Merchants of Milan, book one
https://www.amazon.com/dp/B083H6WNKD
Secrets of Milan, book two
https://www.amazon.com/dp/B088HFM7Q5
Chaos in Milan, book three
https://www.amazon.com/dp/B08Q7H6DFX

Missing in Milan, book four
https://www.amazon.com/dp/B09CNXF1CX
Shadows over Milan, book five
https://www.amazon.com/dp/B09KF53VTZ

Visit My Website:
https://authoredalelane.com
Follow me on Goodreads (Don't forget to leave a quick review!)
https://www.goodreads.com/author/show/15264354.Edale_Lane
Follow me on BookBub:
https://www.bookbub.com/profile/edale-lane
Newsletter sign up link:
https://bit.ly/3qkGn95

ABOUT THE AUTHOR

Edale Lane is an Amazon Best-selling author and winner of Rainbow, Lesfic Bard, and Imaginarium Awards. Her sapphic historical fiction and mystery stories feature women leading the action and enticing readers with likable characters, engaging storytelling, and vivid world-creation.

Lane (whose legal name is Melodie Romeo) holds a bachelor's degree in music education, a master's in history, and taught school for 24 years before embarking on an adventure driving an 18-wheeler over-the-road. She is a mother of two, Grammy of three, and a doggy mom. A native of Vicksburg, MS, Lane now lives her dream of being a full-time author in beautiful Chilliwack, BC, with her long-time life partner.

Enjoy free e-books and other promotional offerings while staying up to date with what Edale Lane is writing next when you sign up for her newsletter.

Printed in Great Britain
by Amazon